T0375705

THE WIND AND THE EAGLE

Brooks Horsley

iUniverse, Inc.
Bloomington

The Wind and the Eagle

iUniverse books may be ordered through booksellers or by contacting:

iUniverse
1663 Liberty Drive
Bloomington, IN 47403
www.iuniverse.com
1-800-Authors (1-800-288-4677)

Because of the dynamic nature of the Internet, any web addresses or links contained in this book may have changed since publication and may no longer be valid. The views expressed in this work are solely those of the author and do not necessarily reflect the views of the publisher, and the publisher hereby disclaims any responsibility for them.

Any people depicted in stock imagery provided by Thinkstock are models, and such images are being used for illustrative purposes only.

Certain stock imagery © Thinkstock.

ISBN: 978-1-4620-7165-4 (sc)
ISBN: 978-1-4620-7166-1 (e)

Printed in the United States of America

iUniverse rev. date: 12/14/2011

Contents

Preface

FINISHING THIS BOOK IS a hope long deferred. Originally the story was an effort to entertain my children and several nieces and nephews. I'm not sure if the kids enjoyed it, but from the beginning I liked it and resolved it should find a home on the written page. That was many years ago.

As I began the book there was, for me, a difficult decision: emulate the old saga manner, or make the norse characters more articulate than they would be and have them tell their story in our manner and idiom. What makes this a difficult choice is my taste for Icelandic sagas; I find their spare laconic prose quite evocative. The appeal is akin to syncopated music, where one dances all around 'the beat' and in consequence becomes aware of the beat as never before. Similarly, the saga style shapes what isn't said and gives it a certain resonance. Furthermore the saga style is not lost beyond recall; a few year back, in her book <u>Greenlanders</u>, Jane Smiley told her story in the saga style and the effect was very vivid and powerful. The thing can be done.

Offering articulate Vikings, while doubtlessly a distortion and artifact, yields a huge gain in clarity; for me this was decisive.

There were several unforeseen consequences of this first decision. I found myself more focused on norse substance and reality and less on particularities of manner, though I hope I captured something of their style and manner. As the Norse came more clearly in view so did a number of our own preconceptions, and not always to our credit. The business of seeing our own verities with new eyes was not planned, but in consequence several of these seem every bit as mythical as Thor and Odin.

There is something limiting and impoverishing with narrative from a single viewpoint, so most of Miles Drake's story is told by others; there is very little direct narrative. This creates several confusing discontinuities and for this I apologize. In an effort to bridge these I have added, just below chapter numbers, parenthetical sign posts as needed.

If these parenthetical notes are ignored then confusion will follow and curses will be sent my way. Please, when you see parentheses below a chapter number read them carefully and realize a discontinuity arriveth. Then proceed carefully, alert for tigers.

My debts are many and I acknowledge them with gratitude and pleasure. These acknowledgements are also recommendations for those interested in things Norse.

The Sagas of Icelanders by Viking books. This wonderful book includes many of the best sagas and also much useful information conveniently organized. An anthology cannot include everything or it wouldn't be an anthology; omissions there must be. I liked what was offered but I would have included Njals Saga.

The Vikings by Robert Ferguson is a recent history of the Viking age. Over the years I have read several of these and Mr. Ferguson's is much the best. There is an inverse relationship between readability and authority; as the one goes up the other declines. Mr. Ferguson is a resounding exception; his book is both very readable and very authoritative.

For those with children, D'Auilire's <u>Norse Gods and Giants</u> is wonderful. It is a little embarrassing, but when it comes to this book, though I am sixty, yet I still seem to have young children.

Imagine a dinosaur Rip Van Winkle who takes a nap and upon awakening finds himself encompassed on all sides by mammals – not a saur in sight. Now, further imagine his joy upon discovering one of these strange creatures speaks saurian. I am that dinosaur: I don't type, and I'm afraid of computers.

The 'mammal' who speaks saurian, one of the lords less known mercies, is 'Pinkie', or Tracey Thornberry. As colleagues never tire of telling me, my handwriting is atrocious, and Pinkie routinely rises to Everests of intuition and brilliance. Her feats dwarf those of Champollion and his Rosetta Stone.

My wife Linda, an ornament amongst women, never complained when <u>The Wind and the Eagle</u> nibbled on our weekends. On Sunday afternoons when she saw me heading towards desk and paper she would bite the bullet and go shopping; I cannot recall a single word of complaint or recrimination.

Last weekend I offered to go shopping with her and this best of wives handed me a thoughtful list of books she feels I might enjoy writing. Her price is above rubies.

PROLOGUE
The Mall

THE BALANCE WAS SHIFTING. Several hours ago professor Eva Drake's Saturday shopping expedition had been a comfortable mix of shaping circumstance and an experienced shopper plying her art with pleasure and skill. Now it was shifting towards compelling and coercive circumstance with little pleasure in doing a familiar thing well.

Eva and Ted Drake, professors of English Literature and Biology, respectively, had recently accepted appointments at the University of Evansville in Evansville, Indiana. By good fortune they had purchased a beautiful home in the upscale peripheral community of Newburgh. This charming burb is nestled along the northern bank of the Ohio River, and the professors' home was exactly the right distance from the river; out of flood range but within easy walking distance. However, the really worthwhile things seldom come easy and the former owner, to judge by the house's color scheme and carpets, was either color-blind or had the sensibilities of a gorilla. Eva had to get the house ready for human habitation, and quickly; September was coming at a gallop.

The professor's brow might be furrowed and damp, but the real casualty of this particular Saturday afternoon was her eleven year old son Miles, who was bored stiff. To further aggravate things the professor's shopping efforts had moved to the Eastland Mall and they were practically next door to such things as sporting goods and video arcades. Miles had been remarkably long suffering, but the business of dying of thirst while side by side with cool water was too much to bear and the lad was restless and fidgeting, seriously fidgeting. Mother Eva could bear most things with equanimity, but not fidgeting, and the press of circumstance already had her a bit irritable.

"Miles, stop fidgeting; I mean it!"

But this counsel of perfection was akin to demanding of an unsupported cup it not fall. The fidgeting went on, and on.

As a rule professors are quite clever, and Eva wasted no time on useless recriminations.

"Miles, I saw a sports goods store, a McDonalds, and a video arcade. Here's ten dollars for your own shopping expedition. Is your phone charged and working?"

"Yes, Mom."

"Phone me if you have any problems. Otherwise let's meet at 3 P.M. at the benches in the mall's center. Remember those?"

"Yes, Mom."

"What time is it now, dear?"

Miles glanced at his new watch; "1:15."

"Okay, son; off you go. Have a good time and don't go anywhere with strangers."

The professor returned to her paints and Miles returned to life; this was more like it! There was momentary war when hamburgers, baseball gloves, and video games each clamored for immediate attention, but baseball was the nearest and won.

Miles wandered into the sporting goods store and over to the baseball section. He tried on various gloves. He selected two amongst the many as being unusually 'fine', and wondered if perhaps for Christmas he might come to own one of them. Footballs were then carefully reviewed, and one in particular seemed almost made for him. The baseball gloves slid into the background. He lingered lovingly near the football but eventually drifted over to the bikes. The selection was quite limited but there was an unspeakably splendid trick bike. The bike was illustrated by a video tape which fired Miles' imagination to such an incandescent heat that even the football began losing ground. At last the spell faded and Miles drifted out of the sport store. Despite a late breakfast he was starting to get hungry and at the far back of his mind the hamburger call was dimly sensed; in a vague, half resolved way he turned left and towards the food court.

As Miles strolled down the mall's central avenue he noticed a crowd of kids outside the The Pirate's Cove, a popular video arcade, usually such milling was inside the Cove a little to the right past the entrance. Curious. Miles swerved right to investigate and as he approached he noticed the kids looked frightened and seemed quieter than ordinary. There was no apparent reason for this; the milling made less and less sense. Everyone's attention was directed towards the cove – but no one entered!

As Miles neared 'the Cove' he suddenly felt cold and there was a prickly sensation along the back of his neck and scalp. It was as though he suddenly became aware there was a ghost, or tiger somewhere in the cove.

This was a most curious development in such a public place. Miles studied 'the Cove' carefully. He had been here on two earlier occasions and it seemed to him the cove was subdued and quieter than usual. He entered the Cove and the feeling immediately increased. The entrance to the Cove is situated so that only half the room is visible; the other half becomes visible beyond a corner ten feet from the entrance. Miles walked thoughtfully and carefully to this corner. The other half of the room, despite having several of the most popular games, was conspicuously empty except for a single boy about his own size and age who was playing on the old Pac-Man game at the far end. There were no ghosts or tigers, just this boy. The absence of obvious peril might seem comforting, but it was associated with a strangeness that most people would find very disturbing; in fact the room had been abandoned except for a hardy few at the near end.

Ninety-nine out of a hundred eleven year old boys standing at that corner would have either quietly turned and left, or else clothed their fear and the situation in words and then fallen into conversation with their fear. The conversation would have produced an equivalent of 'I smell big trouble. My mother hasn't raised an idiot; I'm getting my ass out of here.' Talk of this sort would give their loss of nerve a cynical, macho veneer that would leave their self respect intact; afterall, tough guys in movies are always saying things like this.

Miles was different. Without considering the matter further he brushed his fear and the strangeness to one side and focused closely on the task before him, which was to cross the room and investigate the odd kid.

Easier said than done. It was twenty feet to the Pac-Man game and within ten feet the savage, perilous tiger feeling had gone through the roof; it was as though Miles were in the presence of something else altogether. Remarkably Miles never faltered in his objective, but forward motion was glacial as he pulled fear's sticky grip finger by sticky finger from his person.

By now Miles was close enough to see the boy was handsome with black curly hair and a striking white scar above his right eye. The boy was, in a quiet way, intent on the game he was playing and did not appear to return Miles' interest. The situation was so very peculiar Miles did not specifically notice the strangeness of a new development. From where Miles was positioned he should not be able to view the Pac-Man game, yet he saw it close up and in startling detail. He began following the game and what he saw was astounding. The kid had been playing the game for awhile and there were ghosts everywhere, yet the Pac-Man nibbled his way down the trail untouched. Miles' new focus relieved his partial paralysis and he finished the journey to the Pac-Man machine and stood watching the impossible feat. After awhile the numbing fear and strangeness ebbed and Miles sensed something very different about this boy, something so different the boy barely seemed human. Miles never put the strangeness in words, but his mother, had she been there, would have said the boy wore loneliness and solitude like they were his own skin. Man is a social animal and this communicates itself in a thousand subtle ways. This boy's sense of loneliness was not an absence of sociability, rather it was the intrinsic loneliness and solitude of a soaring hawk. The stranger radiated a self-sufficiency and solitude utterly out of place in an eleven year old boy.

At length Miles realized, despite appearances, the Pac-Man was inviolable and would never be taken by the ghosts. His interest in the game gradually ebbed and he became aware the people crowded in the opposite third of the room would like to play the games in his part of the room but were unable to pass the strange kid's aura.

For the first time Miles spoke to the boy; "Do you think we might let someone else play the game for awhile?"

At first this was ignored. Then the boy said; "Do you want me to move to a new game?"

Miles thought this over. "Yes, I want us to move to a new game."

"Very well, Miles; so we shall. You choose."

This was surprising. "Do you know me?"

"Yes. Now choose."

Miles chose a secluded corner inhabited by another ancient game, Tetris.

People looked at Miles with wonder, then carefully, keeping as much distance as possible between themselves and the odd boy, moved to the other side of the large play area. Miles and his companion were now visible to people passing the Cove.

The stranger had the same success with Tetris he had enjoyed with Pac-Man, and even after prolonged play the game could never crowd or perturb him. Miles didn't quite know what to make of such consummate skill. At length he could no longer contain himself.

"You are the best game player I have ever seen. Do you play every day?"

The boy looked at him with little expression; "I have never played this game before. What is it called?"

Miles thought his leg was being pulled; "The game, as you probably know better than me, is called Tetris. Why are you pretending you've never seen the game?"

The boy, without a smile; "I have never seen or played this game before. I do not have a skill for these games, rather I am lucky."

Miles was suspicious; "If we moved to a new game how would you do?"

"Exactly as with these first two games."

"Then you are not lucky; you are very, very good."

The boy studied Miles closely; "I am not lucky as you mean lucky. I am the headwaters of all luck."

What was that supposed to mean?! The stranger saw he was puzzled.

"You do not understand, so I will show you. If you stand with me you stand in the shadow of my luck. You play this Tetris and you will begin to understand."

The boy moved to the side and Miles took his place. The game, with neither coin or urging, began again. Miles played and soon became aware Tetris, which had cornered him in the past, could not crowd him even a little. As it had been with the strange boy so it was for him. This was powerful stuff and it was only with effort he kept his focus. Soon the blocks were falling like rain; but it neither pressed nor disturbed him.

Miles was so focused he didn't notice four larger teenage boys stop outside the cove and study him. The smallest, a lad of fifteen, said; "That's the one, Tyson. He really thinks he's hot shit."

"Well; well', said the largest, 'let's educate him." The four bullies entered the Cove and approached the Tetris machine; they immediately became aware of a lurking tiger, a large, savage beast favoring human flesh. They grew quiet and thoughtful.

It was at this point Miles noticed them; he knew in his very bones they were balanced delicately on the very edge of extinction. Keeping his voice quiet and controlled he spoke with genuine urgency.

"You are in great danger. Don't think about it, just leave; right now! This may be your only chance."

Unfortunately this moment was freighted with baggage, ugly baggage. These teens were bullies and amused themselves by browbeating and terrorizing younger boys. Last week two of them were bullying a nine-year-old while Miles was playing Call of Honor II. Miles was large for his eleven years and was not cowed by the seniority and size of the bullies. He had called the nine-year-old over to play with him. The bullies had blocked the nine-year-old's passage. Miles left his game and informed them the smaller boy was with him and they should leave and amuse themselves elsewhere. One of them had come over to shove Miles around. Instead Miles had seized the larger boy by both arms and pulled him into a truly hard head butt. There was much blood. Immediately he turned towards the other boy, but this hero had backed away. Without a word Miles had led the nine-year-old to his game and placed him on the inside near the wall.

Now, a week later, the bullies were back and reinforced with Tyson, a much larger young thug. Their pride and sense of self demanded vengeance. Until this moment, it had looked extremely safe and easy. Now things were perilous and incalculable. It was as though the afternoon sky had gone ink dark and was traversed and cut with jagged lightening. They took another step and sensed three or four tornadoes approaching from the periphery; there was a low moaning in the background and a rumble of thunder.

Miles felt both urgency and frustration; "Guys, you are running out of time; get out now!"

This proved the decisive moment. Two bullies leaped back towards the entrance and two leaped towards Miles. Suddenly there were only the two deeply frightened boys at the entrance; the boys that leapt towards Miles were not there. The boys at the entrance and other spectators didn't seem aware two boys were missing; everyone acted as though two bullies had entered and two bullies had backed off.

Miles <u>had</u> noticed, and found the situation very puzzling and alarming. He decided to get his companion out of the Cove and as far from humans as possible.

Miles turned to his companion, "My name is Miles, but somehow you already know it. What is your name?"

"I have many names."

Great. "What should I call you?"

"You decide."

What?! "Well, how about Many?' Then, after a brief pause; "No; Monty."

"Monty is fine."

"Monty, I'm tired of playing games. What about getting some burgers and fries?"

"I am here to meet you, Miles. A meal together would be fine. Come."

They left the cove and walked toward McDonalds. Foot traffic began dividing a hundred feet ahead of them and didn't reform completely until one hundred fifty feet behind them. People hugged the margins of the mall's passageways and cast fearful glances in their direction. Miles felt as though he were walking with dynamite smoldering on a short fuse. There was little joy in it. He could <u>not</u> saunter into McDonalds with this guy, that was certain. As they walked past McDonalds towards a bench he glimpsed a young girl attendant's white, frightened face. Miles would rather be just about anywhere else. Paint shopping with Mom looked good.

"Monty, you sit here and I'll go get our burgers. I'll be right back. What drink do you want?"

"I will have what you are having.", replied Monty as he took a seat.

Miles joined a small queue and soon was face to face with the frightened girl he noticed when they had passed the door.

"I'll have two big macs, two large fries, and two chocolate shakes."

The girl, after she had noted the order, said; "Are you with that dark haired boy who just walked by?"

'Good question. I sure hope not', but to the girl he reluctantly said; "Yes, I am."

"Then put away your money; I won't take it. Your meals are on me."

The attendant left and returned with her purse.

"Miss, I will pay for my half of the food. Why do you want to pay for his half of the food?"

The frightened girl stammered out; "I don't know why, but there is no way I will accept money from him."

"The money is mine, miss. I'm doing him a favor."

A determined look came over her face and Miles realized things would be as she said.

"Thanks."

He took the food back to Monty and found the mall around them empty except for shop attendants. Monty ate with pleasure, while Miles chewed away conscientiously and was doubtlessly nourished. Neither boy drank their chocolate shake, but Monty seemed to approve of his fries. Miles managed half his fries.

"Monty, where are you from?"

"I am from everywhere and nowhere in particular. I am not 'from' places the way you are; for me it is different."

"Are you an alien?"

"No. An alien would be from a specific place exactly the way you are."

Talking with Monty was uphill work and Miles settled for chewing his food. Monty, as mentioned earlier, was very self-sufficient. It was like having a cat in the room; the silence did not occasion the least awkwardness. As Monty chewed Miles came to a decision. Upon finishing their meal he would take Monty for a walk in some remote corner of the Eastland Mall's vast parking lot. At three, which wasn't that far off, he'd make his apologies and join his mom. It was strange that of all the people in the mall he was the only one who could tolerate being near Monty. They finished their meal.

"Thank you, Miles. You chose well. I enjoyed the Big Mac."

"Good. I was thinking we might take a walk outside; how does that sound?"

"I have walked much, and always enjoy it. Come."

They walked towards the nearest secondary entrance. As they were passing an expensive candy shop Miles made a surprising discovery; somehow, way down deep, he liked Monty and wanted him to have some really good chocolate. Perhaps it was Monty's response to the big mac that created the bond. At any rate Miles decided to get Monty some chocolate.

"Monty, sit tight for a second. I'm going to get you a treat, a real neat treat. You stay here; I'll be right back."

Miles entered the shop and picked out a quarter pound of chocolate peanut clusters. This would be good and he could afford it. When he got out his money the attendant, yet another pale and alarmed looking young woman, broke the usual routine.

"Are you with the dark haired boy outside?"

Miles was wise beyond his years and suspected he was on the edge of some more girl foolishness.

"These chocolates are for me. If my friend wants some he can buy his own."

The lady left him standing, money in hand, and prepared a half pound of chocolate covered macadamia nuts; it would cost a prince's ransom.

"Miss, I don't want those chocolates."

"I know. These are from me to your friend. They won't cost a penny."

Miles started to remonstrate, but a glance at the woman's face stopped him.

"I will give him your chocolates, and I'm sure he will appreciate them."

"Thank you so much!" The girl beamed.

Miles left the shop and joined his friend. "Monty, the girl in the shop wants you to have these chocolates. They are the very best she has."

With dignity Monty took the chocolates. "I accept this offering with pleasure."

Monty faced the girl and bowed, then they moved on towards the exit.

They hadn't moved far when Miles spoke.

"Monty, my chocolates aren't as good as yours, but you might like them too. Try some."

Miles passed over three chocolates, which Monty quietly accepted. Then with the same quiet dignity he had assumed when accepting the girl's gift; "Miles, I give you some of my chocolates."

Monty passed over three chocolate clusters.

With a strange reluctance Miles accepted the chocolates, but rather than eating them he put the chocolates in his bag with the peanut clusters.

Monty spoke; "Try one, Miles. You will find them very good."

Again, the strange reluctance. "I'll eat them when I get home; they look great."

"Miles, please accept this token of my favor now."

Miles removed a macadamia nut cluster from the bag and took a bite; suddenly everything changed.

Signal Events That May, or May Not, Have Happened

It was night and Miles was standing behind a large pillar forming the corner of a gigantic building similar to the Parthenon. The building was surrounded by a large roofed porch. The far perimeter of the porch was supported by more of the large pillars. Without leaving the cover of his own pillar Miles glanced around. At first it seemed he was alone but gradually his attention was drawn to the pillar opposite his own on the far perimeter of the porch. The building, porch, and columns were all white marble and glimmered softly in the moonlight. There was a large shadow at the base of the column. With close study he resolved this shadow into a large man who strongly radiated menace and peril. This man had a large hat pulled low over his right eye. The man was studying the long stretch of porch to Miles' right, the part hidden from his view. Then at the distant end of this stretch he heard a boy singing; it was his friend Monty, and he was heading towards Miles and the large shadowy figure across from him. In his bones he knew the shadow man was waiting to ambush Monty.

The dark shadow was unspeakably grim and deadly; Miles could not successfully attack him. On the other hand he could not and would not stand by as Monty walked into an ambush. He must warn Monty and distract the shadow. There was no more time for thought; it was time for deeds.

Miles stepped from behind his pillar and shouted to Monty; "Monty, it's an ambush, run!"

Then turning to the shadow; "Let's see you catch me, fat ass!"

Miles took off down the adjacent stretch of porch as though his life were in the balance, which it probably was. The shadow pursued him rather than Monty. Before long he knew the shadow was gaining on him. He glanced over his shoulder to confirm this and ran, if that were possible, harder. Still the shadow gained. He glanced back a second time and what he saw confused and angered him to his very soul. One moment it was the shadow pursuing him and the next it was Monty; his pursuer flickered back and forth between the shadow and Monty.

Miles turned some deep inner corner and fear was entirely offstage; now the focus was one hundred and ten percent on death and destruction to whatever it was pursuing him. Miles suddenly turned and, with a snarl, lunged at the shadow.

The scene suddenly changed. Miles stood in a grove of large towering trees. It was high summer and the grove was cool and pleasant. Standing with him was a large man with a hat pulled down over his right eye. He knew the man was both the shadow and his friend Monty. The man's mien conveyed welcome and respect, but little or no warmth. This man was not hostile; rather there was very little warmth in his composition. He looked down at Miles and spoke in a bass voice that was quietly authoritative and regal beyond anything Miles would ever hear again.

"You may stand with me. I give you one wish. If you wish carefully and wisely I will add my blessing to your wish."

Miles thought deeply, and with care. Then, as from a great distance, he heard his mother's voice and felt a gentle shaking. "Come on, Miles; wake up."

Gradually Miles came around and found himself on the mall bench where he'd agreed to meet his mother. His mall adventures faded the way dreams fade. Five minutes later he had no specific recollection beyond spending time at the sports store, the cove, and McDonalds. His chocolates puzzled him. However that evening he greatly enjoyed his macadamia nut treat.

Had anything happened? Not so far as either Miles or his mom were concerned.

Perhaps the mall was buzzing with stories of a strange dark haired boy? No, there were no stories. No verification could have been obtained from anyone at the mall that day. There were a few strange items, but they could have meant anything. Business at the Eastland Mall, Evansville's finest and most popular mall, went into an abrupt slump and only recovered gradually over the next four months. The slump hit all merchants excepting two; McDonalds and a candy store. The candy store in particular prospered, and continues to prosper, as never before. The owner, a young woman who had recently inherited the store, pinpoints the turning point to the afternoon in question but she hasn't the foggiest as to why she harbors such a conviction.

Three days after Miles' shopping trip there were melancholy headlines concerning two missing teenage boys. They were found in a field near Evansville torn apart as though by a wolf pack. Such was the damage they were identified by tissue typing. The police are investigating, but as yet have no leads. A drug connection is being considered.

A thread more tenuous than a moon beam is Eva Drake's conviction her son's interest in poetry, in total eclipse since birth, surfaced about this time. This was a great joy to his mother, but also puzzling. Apparently Miles' interest was quite specific and did not include mid and later twentieth century poets. Particularly treasured were the great narrative poems of our language.

As it happened Miles did get the football for Christmas. He also possessed a right arm and eye that are but seldom seen. All of his father's teenage dreams of football glory came true for his son.

Chapter 1
Memoirs of Matt MacDougal

Socrates, if I remember right, said the unexamined life is not worth living. This is undeniably a sonorous phrase, but ask anybody busy with an unexamined life whether his efforts are worthwhile and you will soon realize the phrase contains more bullshit than wisdom. I suppose there is a broad division of people into those involved with living life and those involved with talking about life, and most of us have a foot in both camps, but by practice and temperament I'm a liver.

So what gives with a thirty-six year old man sitting down to write his memoirs? It has every appearance of a twenty-two carat talker, and being thirty years premature i.e. an impatient, tireless talker.

This is misleading; I really am a liver. Except on January one of a new year I'd always rather be eating chocolate than talking about chocolate. This odd situation has two components.

The first reason is I like women too much; frequently my trousers are off when they should be on. Ann is a fine wife and a good woman, and then there is my daughter Alice and son Craig. I have so very much to lose it is grotesquely stupid to put them at risk. Furthermore if I learned Ann were dropping her knickers when she shouldn't I'd be very wounded; the old double standard is alive and well with Matt MacDougal, and I'm hardly proud of it. When it comes to women more thought and talk and less immediate living is much needed. Next time, or so goes the story, I will reach for my pen and not my belt. Traditional wisdom recommends cold showers and pushups, but I know beyond certainty this won't happen; however, memorializing is just, by a skinny whisker, conceivable.

The second reason is very different. I have enough imagination to realize that beyond seventy-five, assuming this distant point be reached, when the pecker no longer rises to the occasion, when joints creak and protest, when the dyspeptic price of favorite foods overweighs immediate joys, then talking rather than living makes sense. Granting long life and health I plan and hope to examine the hell out of my life. Furthermore, I enjoy memoirs; I don't read much, but when I do as often as not it's a memoir.

These past memoirs are the root of the second reason. As these old farts sit around memorializing, their viewpoints and disposition are long since settled into concrete. There is a strong, possibly irresistible, impulse to view their history as incidents in a certain kind of story; this was not how it was lived and is long after the fact talk. The memoirist always, to some extent, makes a conspicuous effort to be fair and impartial, but too often this is transparent nonsense. Moments of frankness, speaking 'against' the earlier self, viewing earlier episodes as limited and juvenile, is still orienting and narrating against the seventy-five-year old talker. This is most certainly not how events actually evolved and were experienced.

It seems to me I am memorializing too late, not too early. Ideally one should sketch one's memoirs every ten years starting at twenty.

In summary, this halfway memoir is an effort to hedge against the old fart syndrome, and keep my trousers on. The trouser theme is not the sort of thing a wiseman commits to print, but my security measures are pretty good, and should the memoir come to Ann's attention she would notice (being both broadminded and wonderful) that her husband's heart is in the right place.

CHAPTER 2
Puerto Rico

I was born September 5, 1974 at Bella Vista hospital near Mayaguez Puerto Rico. The welcoming committee included Mom (Kim), Dad (Ken), and older brother (Craig). As best I can remember Craig was a gracious older brother and made room for me without much complaint. To this day we get on well. Two years later Bruce showed up and it was my turn to be a good sport; I believe I was. In childhood Bruce and I were quite close; in later years less so. I was five when Janice completed our family. Acceptance comes much easier at five than at two or three, so getting on with Janice was hardly the stuff of legends. However Bruce did not roll out the welcoming mat and saw Janice as supernumerary. Bruce and Janice squabbled throughout childhood, but in later teens and beyond became great buddies. This worked out nicely since in adult life both Craig and I have come to see the kid brother as pretty useless. Apart from Bruce and Janice our family got on remarkably well – much better than most other families, or so it seems to me.

There was very little supervision in our family, and this modest bit was supplied by mom, when she got around to it. We kids never sat down and explicitly worked out our policy towards the parents, but as best I can recall we picked it up from Craig. Every now and then mom would have a fit of reforming zeal and attempt to 'do the right thing by the kids.' These fits might last as long as a week, and included such things as sit down family dinners, making the beds, cleaning the house, and looking over homework. The trick was to fully and respectfully comply – it wouldn't last long and didn't really hurt anything. Mom would be quite pleased with herself, and relax back into I'm not quite sure what.

We kids had a great sense of unity and esprit de corps; we were keenly aware one didn't 'let the side down'. This, and other factors I will mention, kept us up to the mark on behavior and schoolwork. We were never truly bad and delinquent, but neither were we 'good' kids, except Janice, who has always been shiny with virtue.

We lived in Las Mesas, which is an uppercrust suburb on a hill above Mayaguez. Near us was the Seventh-Day-Adventist hospital of Bella Vista. The associated SDA community operated a grammar school for the English speaking and this is where I schooled for grades 1-5. We chummed with the Duffy kids, whose father was an internal medicine specialist. Dr. Duffy was home even less than dad. We and the Duffys had a great time together, and there was more than a little mischief in our adventures. Now and then we would get caught. Such occasions brought out huge doses of discipline and reforming zeal in mom and we would be grounded for not less than a week. What would happen to the devout SDA Duffy kids? Absolutely nothing. Dr. Duffy would question them, review their crimes, and dismiss the case with 'boys will be boys'. As far as I know none of the Duffys are in jail today; perhaps Duffy had the right idea. I can say this now, but at the time it rankled to see the fellow criminals always walk away free and clear.

The SDA grammar school was pretty good. There was good teacher control in classroom and much was learned. A steady effort at religious indoctrination was made, but evidently Craig, Bruce, and myself were not good ground for such seed and nothing took. Janice, however, soaked it up. She went on to attend an SDA university and marry an SDA clergyman. As of this writing Janice, pastor Bill, and their three kids seem happy.

The parents, to my adult eye, are something of a mystery.

Mom was a registered nurse and worked part time at Bella Vista. Dad was pretty well-off and was always generous with mom; I would guess she didn't have to work, but rather wanted to keep her hand in. Exactly what she did when she wasn't nursing or 'doing the right thing by the kids' is not clear. Whatever it was it probably included more alcohol than was advisable. Mom was a good looking woman, and were it any woman other than Mom I would suspect her of filling the empty corners of her day with a boyfriend. Doubly so as I'm pretty sure she and dad, though getting on well enough, were not very active in the bedroom. To this day I don't know if mom was monumentally discreet, heroically virtuous, or possessed of a record low libido. If I had to guess, which I don't and shouldn't, I would use the little bit I saw of her and Dr. Westphal to cobble together a view that spared her the humiliation of a life denying adamantine virtue, or the charge of no libido. I think I'm my mother's son, and I would never deny life; hence it is hard to attribute such things to Mom.

Dad is even more mysterious. Dad was a Harvard man, CPA, and lawyer. He was both bright and well met. Exactly what he did all day in Mayaguez is a little vague but to my best knowledge included forensic accounting, clever on-the-edge accounting, and tax expertise. We saw him in the evening; in the morning he was usually gone before we made the scene. In truth we saw little of dad, but what little was to be had was both pleasant and good. It is hard to come up with even a single occasion where he was mean or out of control. He loved us all in a rather vague, inattentive way, and was always generous. Good clothes, good toys, good schools, and later, good cars. Football would play a big part in my life and it was dad who gave me my first football; he would throw me passes on the weekends. To this day I love and admire dad; similarly for the rest of us, with possible exceptions for Mom and Bruce. However as I get older and have kids of my own I begin to see how absent he was; my memories are probably more attributed than real. Mom may have had a rather patchy presence, but Dad was almost an ethereal or ghostly presence. But again, the memories are strong and fond. How does this come about?

As with presidents so with dads and other authority figures; if things go well theirs is the honor and the glory. Our family was quite bright and our espit de corps kept things on track. There were no nasty scenes or active unpleasantness, and there was sufficient prosperity and generosity that all was cozy and comfortable. The upshot is that Dad was and is a warm memory. By the way, it is hardly surprising Dad is a very vague and absent Granddad. Craig confirms this.

The Puerto Rico days were golden, the happiest of my life, but all things come to an end. We left when I was two months short of my eleventh birthday. The family moved to Newburgh, Indiana, which is an upscale suburb of Evansville.

The 'why' of this move is opaque, but Craig, who is now a Harvard man, CPA, and tax lawyer, tells me it was very cleverly done and left the government of Puerto Rico holding the bag on a big tax bill. Dad is very good at what he does and is not hampered with too many scruples. Personally

I would love to screw the IRS; the only thing holding me back is a combination of fear and ignorance. Apparently dad was a knowledgeable lion. It makes me proud to be a MacDougal.

CHAPTER 3
Evansville Indiana

NEWBURGH IS A NICE little town, and Evansville is a big enough but not too big city. In fact the <u>only</u> fault with Newburgh is that it isn't Las Mesas, Puerto Rico. Back in 1805 Newburgh was a busy port on the Ohio River deeply involved with cotton. Later the town fathers said 'no' to a proposed railway line and in consequence headed their town towards small town, or suburb, status. Which is fine by me. Yes, Evansville, got the rail line, and shot ahead. Now there is very little river or railway traffic. One to two miles immediately east of Newburgh is the dam and the locks. The coal barges in the locks are our one and only spectacle, and as spectacles go it isn't bad.

Our new home was on Old Stonehouse Drive, and it was pretty nice; mom approved. Now for a minor mystery; I was enrolled at St. John elementary school. Why not Castle elementary, or Sharon? Perhaps it was an effort to balance out my Seventh-Day-Adventist indoctrination with a bit of Roman Catholic polish. In the event the school was okay, and the catholic indoctrination fared no better than the adventist effort. And Janice? She was already committed to the SDA version and was alert and on-guard to catholic wiles.

An aside concerning a huge difference between Newburgh and Las Mesas. In Las Mesas no one thought much of either walking or biking a few miles; afterall, we all have legs, and bikes are cheap and available. In Newburgh even half a mile to school was an occasion for either a school bus or a parent bus; anything to spare the little darlings actually walking anywhere.

In the MacDougal home it never crossed the parents' minds getting to school was anyone's problem but mine. I walked, and soon devised a very nifty shortcut involving other backyards and main street (the main drag in Newburgh is Jennings; 'Main' is a little back eddy parallel and north of Jennings).

The only thing standing out from my year at St. Johns' is Mary Jones; this young siren utterly and completely captured my boyish fancy. It was quintessential unrequited love, and if Mary knew of my existence she kept it to herself.

Rather than lingering over things tragic I will move on to Castle Junior High. This is far enough north and west of us that to and from school became my Mom's headache, but not much of one since she was already practiced up with Craig, who had just finished with Castle Junior High and was moving to Castle High.

Seventh grade at Castle Junior High is now hard to distinguish from grade eight. If I recall correctly I carried the torch for Amy Carothers and in the course of carrying it I passed two landmarks of youth; holding a girls' hand and, more importantly, fondling her breasts. Amy, unremarkable in so many ways, was extraordinarily precocious in the matter of breasts.

Much to my surprise I thoroughly enjoyed Mister Spittle's history of Western Civilization. Spittle was a good fellow; interesting, kept good order without recourse to a heavy hand, great sense of humor, kind, and sympathetic. I hope all goes well with him.

I remember having a pretty good fist fight with Jeremy Hanscomb. As I recall I gave him a good thrashing; I wonder if that's how he remembers it? It was closely contested and he may remember handing me my nose; he didn't.

Circa age twelve football began emerging as an important part of my life. This was entirely informal and a matter of my group; I hung out with guys who played a lot of scratch football. We picked up sides on each occasion and played a touch football requiring a two hand touch (brushing with a finger tip was far too debatable). There were two usual and customary captains and quarterbacks; Max Shelton and Miles Drake. Max, like myself, was just starting with the scratch players, or informal league. In contrast Miles, though our age and grade, was already an old stager in the scratch crowd and enjoyed a huge reputation. The reason is not far to seek. Miles was a big kid, very good, and had started playing with the scratch crowd while he was in the sixth grade; not, like most of us, the seventh grade.

Our read on our fellows is frequently more attributed than real, and this all too human failing is particularly pronounced in young teenagers. I had it in my head Miles was a conceited prig, or, in the idiom of our set, stuckup. I made it my mission to bring this puffed up creature back to earth. Later, as I came to know Miles, I learned very few people spend less time fretting over their exact position in the hall-of-fame; the 'puffed up' nonsense was in my head and nowhere else.

However, during grades seven and eight bringing Miles down a notch was a big item on my list. In picking up teams Max always chose me first while Miles chose Jerry Mercer. If I saw Miles would probably be choosing me I excused myself and claimed recollected obligations (damn, I just remembered I promised Dad…). None of this mattered; Miles, with whatever material he had, usually won. But beyond a doubt I made things hard for him by intercepting or blocking a ridiculously high percentage of his passes; it was as though I knew better than he what would be happening. Miles, then and always, had a great arm and was the consummate master of the passing game; my sixth sense of where he would be passing would have doomed him had he not also been quick and agile at running down a crowded field. When I was playing he used obvious passing situations as decoys to set up a run down the field.

I never managed to teach Miles humility, and when the ninth grade arrived I joined the Castle High football team and quit playing with the scratch crowd. I played wide receiver, and made the B team. Strangely, Miles did not join the football team that year, nor did he play with the scratch bunch. I must ask him what the hiatus was about. The ninth year of school Miles Drake dropped out of sight, and soon out of mind.

Miles reappearance was very dramatic and may, though I didn't see it at the time, have been a turning point in my life. It was early August and even though school had not started we football types were already training hard. We had a new coach, Axel Benton, and no one knew quite what to expect; it was exciting. Halfway through practice Jim Skelty, the assistant coach, came over to where we B's were toiling. He said we would be making an early day of it and practice was over, except for Matt MacDougal, Skip Mason, and Sam Alder. This was, to say the least, pretty puzzling. I turned to Max Shelton, an old friend and captain of the B team, and asked if he knew anything. He didn't, but he had a curious look about him and went on the wonder out loud if perhaps school history were about to be made. Now I was really puzzled, and I asked why he thought so. Max had observed Miles Drake and Coach Benton in earnest conversation for the past twenty minutes, and the varsity team was also dismissed, except for the captain and three other players.

The situation was clear soon enough. Miles had talked Coach Benton into organizing a game between the four best varsity players and himself and three B players of his choice. He chose me, and two other stalwarts from Junior High days. Skip and Sam made perfect sense; they had played with Miles for years. Matt MacDougal, however, was a puzzle; I had done my level best to thwart Miles.

Miles, as a kid and man, was very low key and wonderfully reassuring; everything would go well, or so you always felt. He met us as though we were good friends who had played football yesterday. Miles had always been a big kid and now he was 6'3" and in good hard training. He expected the coming game would have a lot of scoring and that unless he was way out in his calculations we'd be far ahead. He and I would see to our scoring while Sam and Skip had to slow down the opposing team; they must not score touchdown for touchdown.

He took me aside and told me I was the best end he'd ever seen and if I played even close to customary we'd be winning this game with ease and I'd be on the varsity team. He clearly meant what he said and, though I was disgusted with myself, I felt ten feet tall.

But not for long; the first third of the game put red ink under why the other guys were the varsity team and we were the B's. Gradually, under the heat of a hard game, Miles, and I began to click, to get that left hand working with right hand synergism for which we became famous. As we gained momentum Skip and Sam took heart and broke up the other team's scoring streak; those poor varsity lads felt like they were engaging with brick walls. We fell on them like wolves on lambs, and after recovering the lost ground went on to a commanding lead. The last touchdown was a honey. By now the varsity boys were double teaming me, so Miles and Skip were running the ball. Brent, the varsity captain, in a last desperate effort, made a flying tackle. Miles managed to get a shoulder under the leaping hero and carried both the captain and the football across the line.

Coach Benton had much food for thought and Miles, myself, and Skip started that year on the varsity team. Two months into the season Sam was promoted.

Miles was made captain, but beyond this Benton gave him a free hand with the team and virtually never interfered. The fruit of such relaxed coaching was Castle won state the next three years in a row.

Amidst the joy and exhilaration of these early days there was one thundercloud and pit of sorrow; Brent Chalmers, former varsity captain. In the larger scheme of things this was neither epic nor tragic since Brent has been a prick since infancy, certainly in high school, and from what I hear is currently a practicing prick. With the arrival of Miles the sun set on Brent's football career and a few months later his luscious girlfriend, Samantha Sitilski, was lured away from his banner and into my arms. Sam was a real cupcake, and her already considerable charms were rendered doubly sweet by the discomfiture of Sir Prick.

Brent and two husky friends cornered me in the locker room; blood and fractures seemed imminent. I was very intent on exactly how to play the early moments of the coming fight so as to get at least one of them out of the fight early on; two is bad enough, three is getting over into crucifixion territory. Then Miles strolled in; it was like bright dawn at darkest midnight. Two against three is altogether more sporting. But I never got to see how things would have gone; not then or later did I ever see Miles actually engaging in fisticuffs. Miles is large, he's now 6'4"and he was near that then, but in addition his invincible calm and natural authority were such that no one would ever actually raise a fist against him – it just never seemed a good idea.

In his relaxed and quiet way he assured Kirk and Ken that he had no quarrel with them, but if now or later they involved themselves in Brent's quarrel with me he would see to it they regretted it. If Brent was foolish enough to court ill will and peril over a girl that no longer enjoyed his company then so be it; neither Miles nor others should interfere. This put the ball in Brent's court, and he thoughtfully watched it go by and disappear. That was the end of the matter.

I had a blast in high school. In the MacDougal tribe I was somewhere between the manic industry of Craig and the profound idleness of Bruce. My grades, as best I recall, averaged 3.4 and I had a knack with standardized exams so my SAT scores were good. Football probably kept me on course and out of trouble, and the prestige was very useful with the girls. I chummed with Pete Difabio, who was and is a first rate guy and lots of fun. Pete's family ran a really great Italian restaurant and he and I ate there about half the time. Pete's sister Caitlin was a looker and exceptionally fun and saucy. On several occasions Caitlin and I tiptoed up to romance, but either by circumstance or innate good sense we would carefully tiptoe back to the comfortable status quo. Caitlin married Ricky Hanson and has three children; apparently all goes well for her.

Of the many football games the one I remember best was the second time we won state. We trailed the entire game and with twenty seconds left we took possession with the ball close to our own goal line; it was bleak beyond hope. Miles wanted me to head left then veer to the right. I was triple teamed so it seemed to me he planned on using me as a decoy and running to the left. However, instead of veering to the right I kept left and ran as I have never run, jackrabbit stuff. Miles threw a pass so long I'm surprised it didn't go into orbit; it was far over all heads, and a miracle I ran it down and managed to get my fingers on it. We won by a single point; sweet, sweet, sweet!

Of the many romances of high school days by far the most, what is the word, serious? Perilous? Momentous? Big? I'm not sure, but it was with Sylvia Latimer. Sylvia was an inimitable mix of wit, charm, beauty, and brains; especially brains. She was matter-of-factly focused on medical school and music and had very little attention for football heroes and studs. No indeed; I had to track her down, and it took some doing. Finally she noticed me and seemed to realize what a hell of a fellow is Matt MacDougal. The last three months of high school were a delirium of joy. The day before graduation, and ouch, this is embarrassing, I went up to Sylvia intending to offer her the post of Mrs. Matt MacDougal. With her customary acumen she spotted my serious, kneeward proclivities and put a finger on my lips. "Matt, whatever you have on your mind the answer is no. Now, help me celebrate my acceptance to Princeton!"

The college football people wanted Miles so bad they could taste it, and he wanted me. He offered us as a single deal. The coaches thought this more a suggestion than a deal breaker, but when they learned otherwise, though they didn't like it they were still keen. Miles had always planned on Purdue and, though the offer was not the best, that's where we went.

CHAPTER 4
Matt MacDougal's Memoirs Continued

BEFORE PICKING UP MY story at Purdue I want to introduce an ongoing puzzle and mystery; Miles Drake. Is he the luckiest man alive, or the smartest? To be sure both factors play a part, but where is the balance?

Start with Castle High. That glorious summer afternoon when we paddled the varsity team could never have happened during ninth grade; Coach Smith was very authoritarian and there was always only his time and way. Miles would never have gotten a hearing with Smith, and Smith would have forever been in the way. Benton, in contrast, was very open to the bold and unusual; he only required a thing work, preferably sooner than later. If an innovation worked then ego nuances and fine points could be sorted later. Benton and Drake were designed for each other.

Miles enjoyed perfect health and despite playing every and all games in high school and college never sustained significant injury; I wish I could say the same.

During both high school and college, circumstances outside our team always favored us; teams that would probably have beaten us always encountered injuries to key players and we got by them.

Look at his record; three Indiana State championships in high school and four Rose Bowls at Purdue. This is storybook stuff, it doesn't seem real – and I was there!

This sounds superstitious, and perhaps it is, but I've made money on this foolishness. We might not have won every game, but without exception we won all games when a loss would have pulled us out of contention for top honors. After three years of Castle and one year of Purdue I spotted this and got in the habit of placing bets with a Las Vegas bookie I knew; I made thousands of dollars. I never discussed this with Miles. Firstly, it might have jinxed things, and secondly Miles would have called it superstitious nonsense.

In one way I know Miles better than anyone else, and in another he's pretty much a black box. We have never, not at Castle or Purdue, chummed together. Away from football we each went our own way; me to women and parties, Miles to I'm not sure what. In high school he chummed with Joe Ling, a chink math and ping pong whiz. Also he was great friends with Wenzel Thakore, an Indian chap with an English accent, a great sense of humor, and, or so I've been told, a prodigy at chemistry. Not my crowd.

Miles and women are yet another mystery. When you are 6'4", handsome, pleasant, and a football legend, women tend to notice you. I'm sure Miles noticed them right back, but he was never much involved or linked with any one girl, and his manner was polite and courteous rather than flirtatious and interested. For all I know he may have finished university as a virgin. I have two reasons for doubting this.

The first thought would be that Miles liked boys, but from what I saw and subsequent events this is clearly not the case.

The second point; Miles didn't act like a virgin. A starving man hovering near a tidbit of food acts one way, a man who has recently had a good meal acts another. Miles always had the relaxed and pleasant manner of a man who has recently enjoyed a fine dinner.

In high school logic we learn to move comfortably from 'all men are mortal' and 'Socrates is a man' to 'Socrates is mortal'. I move with equal comfort from 'Miles acts well fed' and 'there is no gossip or news of any kind' to 'Miles is carrying on with a happily married middle aged woman'. Actually I should probably enlarge the conclusion a bit to include single middle aged college professors, or any sensible woman with a real stake in the status quo.

Once the category is before us are there any candidates? I think so, but I don't have certain knowledge. It goes without saying I needn't and shouldn't speculate, and of course I will.

For Castle High days my choice is history professor Edythe Valender, colleague and friend of his parents at The University of Evansville. Edythe was very attractive, and I have my reasons.

At Purdue Professor Charles Anderson, sixty-four-year-old chairman of the English Department, had a perky thirty-four-year-old wife with a soft spot for football heroes. It is my impression the perky one is both wily and discreet. My evidence is thin but suggestive; out of the corner of my eye I saw Andrea Anderson and Miles Drake exchanging glances.

Memoirs Continued

PURDUE WAS <u>NOT</u> CASTLE High writ large; one is older and becoming aware of the shadows of reality. Much to my surprise I found myself taking a major in history with a minor in business. This made considerable demand on my time, and football gobbled up the rest. There were fewer women and much less partying. There was no Sylvia equivalent at Purdue. I read much interesting history and learned to write, an observation I can only hope is becoming apparent.

I saw nothing of Miles except as related to football. Miles took engineering and must have been very busy; doubly so if he was entertaining Andrea Anderson.

Towards the end of university both Miles and myself were beleaguered by professional teams; we were offered the sun, moon, and stars.

One day, after practice, Miles and I were walking to the library and I asked him what his plans were. He had been offered a job with an engineering firm in Arizona, near Phoenix if I remember correctly. This firm was working on solar panels and Miles liked what they were doing. He was finished with football; it had been good, and it was time to move on.

Given the amount of money he was being offered by professional teams I found this hard to believe. He laughed when I pointed this out. He felt money was very important when scarce, but beyond moderate sums its value was greatly overrated. He would have comfortable funds, and other things were more important.

At first the professionals thought he was holding out for more, and their offers, already mind boggling, went into the stratosphere. Eventually they got the message and quit calling.

Move over St. Francis! I'm not so other worldly and played with the Vikings for one year. This yielded five million, and I picked up an extra six hundred thousand in endorsements. I would have played more but at the end of the year I tore the hell out my left rotator cuff and took this as a sign I should move on.

The year of professional ball was vaguely disappointing. There were many beautiful and delightful women, which took me back to my high school days and ways; this was bad.

I am good at what I do, but I had not realized what a specialized niche creature I was. On Miles' team and as his receiver I was extraordinary; out of this context I was just another professional receiver, probably in the lower half of the class. Miles had a calm confidence that was contagious; I was so used to having it I found its absence a slap in the face. Football without Miles wasn't the same.

It was time to leave, and I did. I didn't miss the Vikings and I doubt they missed me. I don't regret professional ball, but neither do I get all goosey when I look back.

There I stood, twenty-four, shoulder healing nicely, if slowly, and three million in the bank. I went back to school; specifically, I took an M.A. in English History at Vanderbilt. The two years devoted to History (England 1730-1900) were great. I liked Nashville, liked Vanderbilt, and liked the period I was studying. During the second year I was teaching an undergraduate course and particularly enjoyed the interest and searching questions of a very attractive coed. By good luck I bumped into her out of class at a Renaissance Fair; we got on wonderfully. By the end of the year it seemed to me a life without Ann was hardly worth living. Ann thoughtfully reviewed my case and signed on.

Did I pay much attention to football while at Vanderbilt? Hardly at all. Water under the bridge.

I toyed with taking a PhD, but eventually passed. About this time Hard Core, a football equipment company, contacted me and offered a mid level management position. The people approaching me were pleasant, the salary of one hundred twenty thousand was okay, and one needs must do something; I signed up. I was with Hard Core for two years and did well enough, though I developed bad habits with secretaries and sales reps. As I look back it seems to me there was more happy consenting than agonizing coercion going on, but then that's how it would seem; I was probably the boss mothers warn their daughters against. At any rate two years with Hard Core left me thinking I was getting into a not-so-good rut. I started looking around.

None of the women I met at Hard Core ever posed the least threat to my marriage with Ann; I was snacking and browsing as I strolled down the corporate pathway.

Recognizing bad ruts as bad rather than just wallowing them deeper smacks of insight and moral splendor; am I wise and morally splendid? Hardly; rather my daughter and all she implies arrived to both delight and sober me. I turned over a new leaf for Alice, a rare and precious little girl.

In the course of looking around I came across an opportunity with Integra Bank. They had a failing Indianapolis branch in need of tending. The base salary of sixty thousand wasn't much, but should things turn around there were wonderful rewards to be reaped. The job looked tough, and was alluringly incentivized. Ann was from Indianapolis and ached to return; I liked my in-laws, and signed up.

I rescued the wobbly branch and started up the corporate banking ladder. I enjoyed banking. There were a few lapses with secretaries, but not many.

When I turned thirty-one, Craig joined us, and from the cradle on I could barely wait to give him his first football. Once again I was mid level management and making one hundred fifty thousand. The shape of things seemed clear enough. Hah!!

September thirteenth of my thirty second year I received a phone call; it was Miles, and he offered me a job.

Since leaving Purdue I had neither seen nor heard from Miles; this call came from another life. Actually, the above statement is not quite true. One evening, while I was with the Vikings, Miles had called to congratulate me on a pass I had caught that afternoon. I was pleased and surprised; Miles didn't watch television. After this he disappeared. Gone.

While I was making my way from the ivied halls of Purdue to a wife, two kids, a mortgage, and a middle level management position in Indianapolis, Miles had been engaging in something more robust and American; forming his own company and getting filthy rich.

Back at Castle High his friend Wenzel Thakore had said something, that suggested something, and so on right up to a curious and unconventional approach to solar panel technology. Miles had held the ideas close for years, and in consequence had gone into engineering. After Purdue he had neither time nor interest in more football; his consuming interest was solar panels.

He joined Solar Inc. for three years, completed his education, and worked on his idea. His ideas not only were far ahead of existing technology but were practical and could be applied yesterday.

At this point clever lads with great ideas, no money, and no infrastructure usually cash in their chips; they sell to a large player. Not Miles. He approached the two largest solar companies and got them so excited they couldn't hold still. He sharpened one offer on the other and ultimately sold each of the big players twenty percent interest in his own company, Sun Corp.

Sun Corp. sells the new vital components to other companies, especially the big players who own stock. Everybody is winning, happy, and getting happier.

Miles never liked Arizona, or, more generally, the west coast. Once he was in the driver's seat he brought things home; Sun Corp. is based in Evansville. This is good and bad. I'm now head of sales, and air connections are like any other backwater; there are at least two, and frequently three links in every trip abroad. As head of sales I'm on the road quite a bit, which has associated perils, and I don't mean terrorists or crashes.

Indirectly being head of sales has turned me to memorializing. I'm writing these sentences in room 810 at the Weston in Seattle; be pleased to notice I'm not down at the bar scouting up adventures. Ann would be proud of me; hell, I'm proud of me!

But I'm far ahead of myself; back to age thirty-two and the thirteenth day of September. That phone call was electrifying. The first impression, after the surprise, was the very real pleasure to hear from him, and secondly I realized how much I missed him! This was really odd, since I never look over my shoulder. Remember? I'm a 'liver', deeply involved with the here and now! After much catching up,

Miles asked me how much I made at Integra. I told him and he went on to offer me twenty thousand more and he'd pay my moving expenses to Evansville. 'The dog', I thought; the call wasn't, as I'd imagined, social.

Miles had checked me out pretty carefully and was as serious as an heart attack; he was convinced Matt MacDougal was the man to take sales into the wild-blue-yonder. I was flattered and, knowing Miles I figured he knew what he was doing; the man's luck and judgment are something else. I said I'd talk it over with Ann and in the next few days get back to him.

When I hung up the phone my problem began; it had a name, 'Ann'.

Ann loved Indianapolis, she liked having her folks handy, and fledgling companies needed to be seen for what they were – tiger pits. Things were on track, they were great! Why screw it up!?

In a way I was sympathetic with Ann; she didn't have the background with Miles to see anything but foolishness.

I phoned Miles and explained the problem; I was on board, Ann wasn't. Could he give a hand?

Miles didn't waste a moment complaining, but instead drove the three and a half hours from Evansville. Miles is pleasant and sociable, but he's no personality boy, which worked well since Ann gets suspicious around 'personalities'; if something is good why all the fireworks?

Fortunately Ann and Miles liked each other, and by evening's end her fears had been calmed, and calmed with facts.

After Miles left Ann gave me to understand, in three dimensional Technicolor, that like any decent American woman she was willing to sacrifice her happiness for mine, but I needed to register the sacrifice and keep it in sight i.e. I had sold my soul to the…de…, no, angels.

Sun Corp. is on the north side of Evansville near Sixty-four so we placed the new home (the very <u>nice</u> new home) in McKutchinville. This choice was so logical, and yet so hard. I wanted the home in Newburgh, the kids in Castle High, the folks handy, and the Eastland Mall close by.

Instead I have Sun Corp. and the airport very handy; McKutchinville, neutrally considered, is the plushest suburb of Evansville. Also I164 is a comfort; it makes the Eastland Mall more convenient than first appearances suggest. I must give Ann full credit for choice of community; I argued for Newburgh, and she told me I was silly. She was right.

I love my new job as chief of sales for Sun Corp., and, while I may be flattering myself, I think I have justified Miles expectations. Things go well for Sun Corp. Miles is appreciative and generous; my salary is two hundred ten thousand per year.

Our move changed things for Miles; Ann befriended him and took his case. Soon after arriving Ann decided Miles needed a wife, and I had to agree with her; if not now, then when?!

Miles was not opposed, but hardly eager; he allowed himself to be dragged along. Ann was systematic and thorough and became an expert on internet arrangements for such as Miles. By intuition and ingenuity she divined three internet candidates and a Vanderbilt buddy of hers were all members of a hiking club in Nashville; Miles was herded into the club. On his second hike Miles met Erin and immediately and irretrievably lost his heart; it was a mercy of the good lord Erin also lost hers. Erin was <u>not</u> one of Ann's candidates, but Ann's maneuvering placed Miles to meet her so Ann gets the glory.

Erin Westcourt was originally from Chattanooga. She attended Stevens in Colombia Missouri, and after one year switched to Purdue. Her area of interest was interior design.

Erin had no interest in football, but she arrived when Miles had led Purdue to two consecutive national titles, and at that point even the mice were paying attention to football. So willy nilly Erin found herself at a football game. Much to her surprise she fell half in love with Miles Drake, and in consequence Erin didn't miss a home game from then till graduation.

Upon graduating she moved to Nashville and took a position with Interiors, a large prestigious firm. She scouted out the land and one year later she and her dad opened their own business in Franklin, an uppercrust suburb to the south of Nashville. She catered to a niche market; the upper middle class that were just a little bold. She flourished.

Why am I going on about Erin Westcourt? Well, I am a connoisseur of women, and as an expert observer Erin rather intrigues me. Remember the luck of Miles Drake? When he fell deeply in love he fell for something deeply lovely. True feminine charm, though much discussed, is but seldom seen, and, to my delight and surprise, Erin is the purest case I know. I don't refer to her curvy, slender beauty, though she _is_ a beauty, rather to a manner, a tact, that goes to her bones. I wish I were better with words. Of course she is not loud, assertive, or competitive, but neither is she a wallflower; there is an inimitable balance that escapes my pen.

She adapts wonderfully to context, but most of the time her ego is adapted and camouflaged to context. For example; is Erin smart? Hard to say, but she is <u>always</u> smart enough; there is never a context where she is not completely adequate. Is she kind? Wise? etc. Yes, but it seldom leaps beyond a specific context, wags or dominates that context. Yet, as I already said, she's no wallflower; in a quiet way she is truly fun and has a delightful sense of humor. I'm afraid I'm also under her spell.

I have a wonderful and characteristic example. When Miles showed up for the hike where they met for the first time Erin recognized him at once – and said nothing. An hour later Miles had maneuvered so they were walking together. Miles started introducing himself when, with a shy smile, Erin stopped him with 'How, Miles Drake could I not recognize Purdue's football legend?' That would have put me down for the count; we are referring to events twelve years gone by.

Miles and Erin enjoyed a wonderful courtship that included hiking in England, Norway, Maine, and New Hampshire. Once married, Erin opened a business in Evansville. For awhile she ran two businesses. When Evansville looked strong, she sold the business in Nashville, sold it profitably.

I'm at a crossroad, and I have chosen the path of least resistance. The natural progression of my story is to pass to my children, who both delight and intrigue me in equal measure, but instead I will bring Miles and Erin up to date. Why? The topic is too painful, and like a coward, I want it behind me rather than looming and darkening my path.

Erin and Miles enjoyed two of the happiest years you can imagine. They were planning children when, on a routine checkup a lump was found in Erin's left breast. This proved a high grade carcinoma. Now, one year later, with widespread metastases, Erin is dying. She is dying with the same grace and composure with which she lived, and day by day Miles seems to be more and more lost. He has lost weight and is taking the sad business far more seriously than his incomparable wife. I know Miles well, and the thing that must eat and erode him is that something so vital should lie entirely beyond his control.

Alas, the worlds luckiest has been dealt very poor cards. I don't know what will happen, and I fear for Miles.

CHAPTER 5
The Hornet's Nest

MILES DRAKE, IN THE spring of his thirty-sixth year, ran his second redlight, and was never aware there was a redlight to violate. His mind was a thousand miles from Highway 41 and redlights; one week earlier his friend and chief of sales, Matt MacDougal had died in a car crash.

Matt made it to the St. Mary's E.R., but he'd lost too much blood and an hour later, despite heroic efforts, he died. Miles had dropped everything and headed straight for the hospital, but Matt died before he arrived.

Miles was not a demonstrative man. He had never socialized much with Matt, but Miles, who had neither brothers nor sisters, had quietly and without recognizing the fact, adopted Matt as a younger brother. He had always relied on Matt, first in sports and later in business, and Matt had never let him down. Miles had also, in the manner of older brothers, always looked out for Matt. When setting up Sun Corp. Miles intended to bring Matt in, and had Matt lived to his birthday in may Miles planned to give him a fifteen percent interest in Sun Corp. Miles had never specifically noted what Matt meant to him; it wasn't his way.

When, in tears, Ann had phoned to report the car accident, and that Matt was not expected to live, everything had come into sharp, hard focus; Miles had felt sick and mildly disoriented, like he'd been kicked in the stomach; Matt could <u>not</u> die! But he had.

The hard blow of Matt's loss landed on a man who was struggling to come to grips with the imminent death of Erin, his dearly loved wife. When Miles got home he found Erin sleeping quietly, and a note from the day nurse saying they had passed a pain wracked day. With metastatic disease to the spine, such days were increasingly common.

Miles put on a warm coat and took Rusty, their bull-mastiff, out for a walk. They dutifully made the customary two mile round, being careful not to neglect any likely looking trees, posts, or hydrants. Upon returning he found Erin still sleeping, which was a blessing. The walk had resurrected his appetite, so he headed for the fridge to finish off the leftovers. But he really wasn't in the mood, and halfway to the fridge he reconsidered. He was restless, frustrated, and unhappy. Most evenings of late had been spent alone, with Erin sleeping after a day of pain. Miles' thoughts had worn deep grooves that circled endlessly and never seemed to lead anywhere. His mom and dad helped, but in truth not much. Work and associated habits seemed his one and only anchor and comfort. Tonight he would break his routine and have dinner at The Hornet's Nest. The Nest was a reminder of happier times, and he liked the prime rib.

Miles needed 'background humanity.' On his own estimate he was frayed and a bit vague; he craved the good old hard self definition of yore. Background humanity, with its buzz of human conversation and activity, would offer enough contrast and 'other' to restore his margins, might break the monotonous, eroding, cycling of his thoughts.

Miles arrived at The Nest in a better mood. While he might want and need general humanity, he had seldom felt less inclined for one on one human interaction. The table he and Erin used was free and Miles took possession. A pleasant rather plump young man arrived; "Good evening, sir. Will you have anything to drink?"

The brisk young lad cut straight to the heart of the matter, a thing Miles always liked.

"I'll have a large Guiness, thanks."

The waiter departed and Miles briefly noted a well dressed fiftyish gentleman three tables away who was thoughtfully studying him. His thoughts turned to Ann. He felt deep sympathy, and wondered whether there were anything left undone that might help and comfort her. Her mom was with her and helping with the kids; this was good. Miles was considering adding to Matt's educational fund when he was interrupted by a pleasant baritone voice with a hint of an accent; Minnesota? Wisconsin?

"Good evening. I'm Doctor Petersen. You seem busy with your thoughts and I apologize for intruding. May I have a few moments?"

Miles looked up; it was the well dressed fiftyish chap. Inclination and manners struggled briefly.

"A good evening to you, Dr. Petersen. You are quite right; my mind is elsewhere. I don't think I'll be very good company, but what is on your mind?"

"May I?", Dr. Petersen indicated the chair across form Miles.

"Please"; Miles was managing manners, but very much wished Dr. Petersen elsewhere. The waiter arrived with his beer.

"Dr. Petersen, may I offer you a beer?"

"No, thanks. I have one at my table. Now let me share an unusual story; but first, I'm curious as to who you are."

Miles was irritated and puzzled, but hid it well; "I'm Miles Drake."

"As in Sun Corp.?", Dr. Petersen was interested.

"Yes."

"My wife holds your wife Erin in the highest regard. Erin designed the interior of our new home and even a clod like me appreciates and likes it. I understand your preoccupied manner. You have my heartfelt sympathy."

Dr. Petersen paused, then; "My family came from Norway one hundred forty years ago and we've been in Minnesota ever since. The Petersen's have a very unusual tradition."

Dr. Petersen reached into his coat pocket and brought out a small very worn leather bag with a leather drawstring.

"This," and he indicated the bag, "does not belong to our family; it is held in trust for the owner. This bag has been passed from father to oldest son for at least two hundred years. I know neither the time nor the circumstances of our coming by this tradition, but they must have been strange and long ago.

"This custom might strike many as quaint, but with us it is a serious business and we believe it to be vital, of the first importance, that we get the object of our guardianship to the true owner. In some strange way everything;" Dr. Petersen looked intently into Miles' eyes, "literally everything, hangs on it. Somehow getting this little bag to the true owner is our world's life vest."

Dr. Petersen paused, as though he expected some comment from Miles, but Miles, sensing a scam of some sort, maintained a discreet silence.

Dr. Petersen sat back in his chair, tapped his fingers together and mused. At length he spoke.

"Miles, that little bag is yours, and you must take it. Unfortunately you are convinced I'm scamming you. I'm not, but how to convince you?"

Another pause, "Let me tell you of my evening."

CHAPTER 6
An Odd Tale

DR. PETERSEN SAT BACK considering how to approach what was evidently a vexed and complex evening. At length he laid aside his musings.

"Mr. Drake, I shall begin by fetching my beer over to your table, where it might do me some good. After this I will lay groundwork that begins a week ago."

Dr. Petersen pushed his chair back, recovered his mug, and returned.

"Last Monday evening I had the strangest dream. I stood on a high point of a ridge formed by low hills. On one side I faced the sea. The coast was rugged and rather like Maine, but back of the immediate shore it was more like Iceland. There were few trees, and these few were small. There was hardy grass. The sun was bright, it was on the chilly side of cool, and there was a background sigh to the wind. There was a Viking sort of boat approaching a small break in the rocky coast.

"So far, simple and ordinary. However, when you turned from the coast and looked inland things got strange. As soon as you turned you seemed to be in another world. It was much warmer, the wind was gone, and there were large deciduous trees like oaks, sycamores, and tulip trees. As you looked down the hill through the trees you could see a beautiful park. The lawn was green, there were picnic tables, and families were eating and enjoying the fine day. Children were playing with a ball. Further back there was a parking lot half filled with cars.'

"If you gazed seaward there was timeless north atlantic coast; if you looked away from the coast it was contemporary Kentucky or Indiana in the early summer.'

"I wondered at such a curious juxtaposition. When I once again looked to the coast the boat had landed and a man was walking towards me. He had at least a half mile of hill to ascend before he reached me. I felt neither menace nor much interest; the man was approaching, neither more nor less. In the curious way of dreams I half knew I was in a dream and I half expected the dream to move in new directions before the man made the ridge.

"I turned back to the Kentucky side of the tableau. As I looked down through the trees into the beautiful park, the happy children and picnickers became silent and their movements slowed. The running became 'slow motion'. The color began to bleed out of the Kentucky scene. The whole world become indistinct, more a gray mist than anything definite. Gradually the mist cleared and I got a terrific jolt; where the contemporary Kentucky scene had been was now a continuation of the north atlantic sea scape. Look where you might all was sighing wind, gulls, puffins, stunted trees, and coarse grass.'

"When I turned again towards the coast the man was much closer. He was a large man dressed in rough medieval looking clothes. He had an unusual axe slung behind him like you or I might wear a rucksack. This was not alarming; it might have been a necktie for all the impact it had. The man was in his sixties and had much gray in his beard. He approached and stood near me but did not specifically notice me. The man's attention, his entire being, was focused where the park had been. His gaze tracked where the stream had run and he conveyed the strong impression he was seeing what was now gone. His gaze was not only intent, but it also communicated longing and nostalgia. It seemed a long time, but under this man's attention the Kentucky scene gradually began reforming and took on color and life. Finally it was as it had been. The man left the ridge and began descending through the large trees towards the park. With every step he seemed to change into a younger man and his clothes were evolving into more modern garb. When he was about fifty feet down the hill he stopped and turned towards me. He was now mid thirties and dressed as we are.

"The man called back up the hill in English; 'Guard well the things held dear.'

"He then turned and walked into the park and the dream faded and I awoke.

"That was Monday night; Tuesday and Thursday I had the same dream."

Miles interrupted; "That was a powerful and exceptional dream; what did you make of it?"

"It felt very significant. As to specific clear meaning, I hadn't a clue. Please take note; I seldom dream. For me this was way, way beyond the beyond."

Dr. Petersen put his mug bottom up; "Now we come to this evening. Today is my fiftieth birthday, and my wife Lona and I planned to eat at a favorite restaurant. When I arrived home at 6:30 this evening I learned this 'date' was merely a smoke screen to get me home early for a surprise birthday party; I was greeted by Lona and close friends. Catered food and drink were at hand. In truth it was pleasant surprise, and it will be another decade before I see it's like."

Miles smiled a bit; "Excuse me Dr. Petersen, but you can't have failed to notice you are not home in your castle partying with friends."

"True, and thereon hangs a tale. An hour into festivities I became unbearably restless; this also is far from usual. To be human is to occasionally get restless, but for me such moments are few and muted. Not tonight; had I not left the house and party I think I would have gone around the bend. Just before I left I took Lona aside to tell her I was leaving to drive around a bit. I expected to be excoriated with hellfire, but my urge to be away was so strong it seemed a little thing."

Dr. Petersen paused and smiled; "Lona is a wonderful woman and wife. There have been many fine moments, but this evening is perhaps the brightest. She had noticed my restlessness and inattention, recognized them as far from usual. She also knew of my dreams. Rather than dispensing hellfire she gave me the little leather bag, saying, 'I expect you might be needing this. Be careful. The party will do better without you; don't give it a thought.'

"I gave her a kiss and hurried to the car. I was far too in the current of things to see what it might mean; the old family tradition was the last thing on my mind. That Lona! What a wife!"

Miles was impressed; "There are vanishingly few women who would extend wisdom and sympathy at such a moment. I think Erin might, but I fear I will never know. We are both wonderfully blessed in our wives."

Dr. Petersen nodded his full agreement.

"I drove to be driving, and to be away from home; I gave no particular attention to where I was going. Twenty minutes later, somewhat to my surprise, I found myself on the north side of town and far from my home in Newburgh. About this same time I felt a cold beer would go far towards settling accounts with life and the world. As this thought arrived I saw The Hornet's Nest ahead on the left; it struck me as an answer to prayer and I pulled in.

"As I entered The Hornet's Nest it was as though the peace of Eden had descended; the fidgety restlessness was gone as suddenly as it had arrived. I sat quietly with my beer, completely content. I basked in this tranquility for about ten minutes. Then you walked in and peace was gone."

Miles didn't see the connection between his arriving and peace departing; "Why? I'm generally viewed as peaceable and calming."

"You were the man in the dream. As I studied you there was something else about you that niggled at the back of my mind, something strangely familiar. Then it arrived; you are the owner of our family heirloom! This recognition was certain and clear, like the fact of the floor under our feet."

Dr. Petersen paused, and Miles spoke; "Is it possible, Dr. Petersen, you might be mistaken?"

Dr. Petersen gave him a wry smile; "I don't think so. Firstly there is the matter of family tradition. It has always been understood the owner would carry the stamp of identity in his person, that he would be recognized as deeply familiar, that no doubt would be possible. This has unquestionably been my own experience. For the owner's benefit, not ours, there is another proof; you will find a group of three small birthmarks on your posterolateral left calf. These birthmarks will form an equilateral triangle."

Miles pushed his chair back, leaned over, and pulled up his left trouser leg. He had three birthmarks on his outer back calf and they formed an equilateral triangle. Neither man said anything. Miles dropped his trouser leg and sat straighter.

After a pause Dr. Petersen took the leather bag out of his jacket pocket and placed it on the table between them. "This bag, Mr. Drake, is yours. The Petersen family has discharged its trust. The ball is now in the Drake court.

"If you leave it on the table that is your affair. For us a chapter is closed. A few things must be passed on.

"Open the bag and put the content on the table."

Miles did this and soon there was large corrugated dark brown seed on the table.

"The seed must be planted in a grove of large trees on noon of summer solstice. Preferably at the foot of the monarch of the grove. The likeliest grove would be the Joyce Kilmer grove in the Smoky Mountains, but this is only a guess and any stately grove would probably serve. I have no idea what follows from planting the seed. It is not likely to be Jack's beanstalk, or anything you could easily anticipate."

Dr. Petersen paused while Miles put the seed in the bag and the bag in his pocket.

"Miles, feel free to check me out. Stop at St. Mary's and page me. Also notice I never asked for money, or anything else; nor will I. I have no angle on this and have a reputation to lose.

"But beyond any of these points is the uncanniness of the whole business; the margins of the seed are hidden. Unless I miss my guess, Miles, you have very little to lose. You have just lost a close friend and your wife is dying; life as you know and value it is slipping away from you. Roll the dye, plant the seed. What have you to lose? Your dignity?"

Dr. Petersen stood and offered his hand, which Miles accepted.

"All the best, Miles. Now back to what is left of my party."

CHAPTER 7
Balanced on the Edge

(Norse World, Asgerd, Six years before Miles)

THE THREE MEN STUDIED the basket of eggs as though they were runes. At length their gaze turned towards the cliff. The largest, a bearded man of about thirty, spoke; "The young women who picked these belong to Odin, but perhaps we can borrow them first. Let's split up; Grim, go that way,' Whiskers indicated the north end of the cliff, 'Fridgeir, take the other end. Yell if you find anything."

The beard himself headed towards the central portion of the cliff. Out of habit he reached down for his axe.

Asgerd, in a shallow ditch on the margin of the cliff, watched these developments with dismay; she had been hoping they would stay together and start at the north end of the cliff. This made things much harder. She shrugged her shoulders philosophically; things were as they were, she'd just have to run faster. She turned to Bera.

"It is time to join the others, Bera. Keep very low, I don't want them suspecting I'm trying to draw them away. If they climb down the cliff and find you remember what needs to be done. I hope Ketil doesn't cough or fidget; after all, he's only four."

Bera was troubled; "Asgerd, they are not doing this the way we had hoped; I don't think you can make it. Maybe you should hide with us."

Asgerd assumed a confidence she didn't feel; "Bera, I'm twelve, and part rabbit; I wouldn't bet on those men if I were you. I don't think it is my fate to die today. Hurry, and keep low."

Reluctantly Bera crawled away towards the cliff's edge. Asgerd's attention came solidly back to the approaching man. Her only chance of getting an angle that might allow her to make it was to let him get very close, right on the cliff and a little north of her. She'd then run south and inland and hopefully escape between the two men. Of course the immediate risk would be an axe throw; he'd be close enough to have this tempting option. Perhaps she should run fifty to sixty feet directly south before turning sharply inland. Yes, that is what she'd do, and she'd make it!

Asgerd watched carefully and waited for her moment. The bearded man was at the cliff margin and looking at the sea one hundred feet below. Now!

Asgerd leaped to her feet and hadn't gone twenty feet before both Fridgeir and the Beard began shouting. Fridgeir responded very quickly, and in consequence she veered sharply inland sooner than she'd planned, which was just as well since an axe missed her on the left by two inches. Fear gave her the wings of a falcon and before long she was pulling away from Whiskers; unfortunately Fridgeir was very fast and was soon gaining on her. When Asgerd realized this, a spasm of cold fear galvanized her legs to a new level of activity and for awhile the race held steady; then once again Fridgeir began slowly gaining. She could not go faster, and she was beginning to tire. How long? 'We'll see', thought Asgerd grimly.

Over the next minute Fridgeir gained steadily, and when he was thirty feet back Asgerd began looking for stones. Then everything changed; several hundred yards ahead she saw Yngvar sprinting towards them. Hope leaped back into the picture; if she could last another thirty seconds it would be a new game! But, ah, she was tired. Go legs, go; go!

Fridgeir got within five feet of her before he slowed in order to prepare himself for Yngvar; however his precautions proved useless. Yngvar, without slowing, reached for his axe, and while still running threw it with deadly precision into Fridgeir's chest.

Fridgeir, surprisingly, kept his feet; the axe had missed his heart, but he was a dead man. While trying to raise his own axe Fridgeir sank to his knees. Yngvar came up to him, took the axe from his hand, and killed him.

Through gasps Asgerd spoke to an equally weary and gasping Yngvar; "There are two more, and the children are hidden under the lip of the cliff."

But no hurry was needed; Grim and Whiskers were approaching from two hundred yards distance. They now had armor, and Grim had a shield in addition to his sword.

For almost a minute Yngvar did nothing but catch his breath. Once again Asgerd began to fear. Yngvar saw this, and laughed; "Duncentyke, let me catch my breath before I send these lads to hell; please, patience."

When the enemy were fifty yards away Yngvar put his axe back on his belt and leaned over to take Fridgeir's sword. He swung it several times to get its feel. Then he spoke to the approaching men; "Is it you, Koll and Grim?! King Eirik's very own prized berserkers. You came so far to test yourselves against children?!"

Koll and Grim returned no answer but rather divided so as to approach Yngvar from different sides. With no ceremony the fight began.

Yngvar's sword dance was a thing of high music and five minutes later Koll and Grim were bleeding from several wounds and Yngvar was untouched; five minutes once again and both men were sorely wounded and dying. Yngvar remained untouched. Then, very quickly, Koll and Grim joined the dead.

Asgerd watched without a word. Her brother Kjartan had told her that in matters of sword play and war Yngvar stood far above others. It was true. But why were King Eirik's three picked warriors here? Were things moving so fast? Had they come for her father's daughter?

Chapter 8
Four Years Later

THINGS HAD GONE WELL, thought Asgerd. This had been her fourth birth by herself, and Thordis had never had children before; first times tended to be harder. Despite having been up all night Asgerd felt alert, and as she approached High Farm her thoughts turned towards what needed doing that day. She considered shearing the sheep, but that could wait another week or so. The barn needed attention, badly; but the day was quite fine and it seemed a pity to spend it ankle deep in manure. As she balanced on the edge of decision she noticed a man emerge from the long house and head towards her; he looked vaguely familiar. A minute later they were closer and she recognized him; Kjartan!

Soon she was catching her breath from a tremendous bear hug.

"Kjartan, when did you get back?"

"Thorsday evening. Frey's day was spent unloading and storing the boat. Frey's evening was spent drinking with Dad and catching up. At first light on Odin's day, despite a headache as big as a bull, I made my way to High Farm to see my sister Asgerd, who is looking more beautiful and grownup than I remember her; I hope you haven't outgrown me, Asgerd?"

Asgerd assumed a considering air; "Really, Kjartan, it's too soon to say; I'll tell you this evening."

Kjartan laughed; "I hope not. I have this very beautiful foreign dress that is about your size and I wouldn't know what to do with it if you're gone and outgrown me."

"The trip went well?"

"Very. For example, in addition to much gold and silver we now have three slaves. One of these, a husky, pleasant lad, is going to do something about that disgrace you call a barn; it's more a midden than a barn!"

'Good; scratch that headache', thought Asgerd.

"Is Yngvar back too?"

"No; Yngvar has taken to the viking life like a duck to water. When he finally makes it home he'll need two ships to hold his plunder and slaves. We wintered with Vali Gunnarson on Shapensay. In the spring all I could think of was getting home, while Yngvar could think of nothing beyond going far south along the Gar coast. Our men divided, with half coming home with me in our ship, while half joined Yngvar and Vali for the southern jaunt. They will use Vali's boat."

There was a thoughtful pause, then; "Asgerd, our foster brother Yngvar is gifted at weapons beyond anything I have ever seen, or even heard. Late last summer we raided inland, and at the town of Noth Yngvar and I managed to get separated from the rest and found ourselves trapped in a berger's home by a small army; there were at least ten fully armed men. By luck they had no bows; it was entirely axes and swords. I did not rate our chances as those of a fart in a gale, but Yngvar was even cheerful. He winked at me and said; 'Stay on your toes, brother, and we'll have a good tale for the winter fire.' In what followed I survived death by the thinnest of margins and managed to introduce two of the bergers to the Valkyrie. Yngvar killed eight, and more quickly. These men were not ploughmen; they seemed experienced. Their leader, a larger older man, died last, and Yngvar fell in love with his sword, which he now uses. The sword is wonderfully made and the steel is both lighter and stronger than any we have seen. Yngvar thinks these weapons are made farther south and this is yet another root in his desire to raid this direction. Next year only Thor knows what exotic little dress Yngvar will bring; things get richer and fancier as you sail down the Gar coast, or so it seems."

"Is Yngvar in good health; any wounds?"

"Yes, he has taken a great wound, and I fear it may plague him in days to come." Kjartan looked very solemn as he said this and Asgerd took alarm.

"Kjartan, leave the Gar coast alone and tell me of Yngvar. Where is the wound?"

"I didn't want to tell you, Asgerd, but I'm afraid it's his heart", and Kjartan put his hand over his shirt to show the exact location of the wound.

"What happened?", asked a thoroughly concerned Asgerd.

"A pretty young berger he captured has, in revenge, taken his heart from him and enslaved him right back."

"Oh, it's that kind of wound!" Asgerd was relieved; "If our foster brother has a lick of sense he'll leave the wench with Vali and not distress Astrid."

"Truer words have never been spoken, and before leaving I told him as much.

"But let's leave Yngvar's heart to its own devices and pass to something with real meat; actually, two things with real meat.

"Firstly, I greatly fear all my efforts to make a warrior of you have become a pile of rust. Have you forgotten which end of a sword is the business end?"

"Kjartan my dear", laughed Asgerd, "as you well know, one good bruise is worth a thousand words. It so happens I have two short staves conveniently near. You are no Yngvar and I only wish to instruct you with bruises rather than pack you off to the Valkyrie. Arnvid and I have trained long and hard. Come."

They located the staves and fifteen minutes later, with sweat and bruises for both, Asgerd had sustained her point. Kjartan was pleased - and bruised.

"I wouldn't want to be the poor sap who tries any rough stuff on you, Asgerd. You have progressed better than nicely."

Asgerd was pleased, and then grew thoughtful; "Kjartan, what is the other important point?"

Kjartan gave her a quizzical look; "You know what I'm about to say, don't you?"

"I do. Last night you and Dad did a little drinking and catching up. I'm necessarily a significant component of catching up, and I know how Dad feels. You, dear Kjartan, are about to share your brotherly concern over my training to be a healer and my clearing Odin's grove. At the back of your mind you wonder if I'm tiptoeing into seid. Am I right?"

Kjartan chuckled; "That's pretty much it. It is hardly an accident that Odin's grove is overgrown and neglected; as gods go he is one confusing dark bastard. Gods are there to give a hand and help, not add to our headaches and burdens. By contrast Thor is truly and without confusion in your corner. I'd enjoy sharing a beer with Thor; he's my kind of god. As it happens everyone on Westmark, with the possible exception of Asgerd Njalsdottir, is of my mind. Why, Asgerd? Do you <u>like</u> Odin?"

Asgerd grew thoughtful, too thoughtful for a sixteen year old girl. At last she organized her thoughts.

"Kjartan, I was born your sister and Dad's dottir; I had no choice, anymore than I get to choose the color of the sky. How I <u>feel</u> about you and Dad is important in its way, but at root is incidental to how things are. It's the same with Odin; he is my god the way you are my brother. It is the way it is. Now, how do I <u>feel</u> about him? Well, I like and respect him, but this liking is not a simple feeling; it is hard to explain, but real for all that."

"There's no arguing such things. I understand you, but I don't understand you." Kjartan shrugged his shoulders philosophically.

"As to being a healer, this alarms Dad more than me. Dad thinks it beneath your station as daughter to a godi. I think it rather fine. When wounds and sickness find me you'll be there to show them the door. I would encourage you to be as good a healer as ever you can be.

"You mentioned the seid, Asgerd; is this so?"

"I'm thinking this is said since I know the weather and the seasons; am I right?"

"Partly. Also you knew Gudrun had died three days before word arrived. This sounds a bit like the seid to me, Asgerd. I'm listening."

Once again Asgerd grew thoughtful and seemed far away. After a few minutes she was ready.

"Suppose, Kjartan, you live on Westmark, as you do, and a distant cousin lives on Kelsoy. There are no boats to travel between the two islands. The only way to talk to your distant cousin is with an elaborate system of large flags of many colors. Such 'talk' is complicated and subject to misunderstanding. If you and your cousin lived together on the same island you would not need the flags. Seid is like the elaborate system of flags; if you live on the same island you don't need it. Odin and I are like family living on the same island; for us seid is silly. I always know what I need to know."

"The golden question, sister, is whether you can reliably separate the voice of Odin from the inner voices of Asgerd Njalsdottir."

"It is the right question, wisest of brother, and thus far there has been no problem."

In the course of the reunion Asgerd and Kjartan has travelled from things light and familiar to a strange new country. Kjartan saw his sister with new eyes and she seemed old far beyond her sixteen years. For this reason he found himself sharing a puzzle that rather weighed on his mind.

"Asgerd, several times in the past week I have had the same dream. It seems to mean something but I'm not sure what. Perhaps you and your buddy Odin can make sense of it. After all, Asgerd, you are a healer, and putting sense to this dream would heal my peace of mind."

"Certainly, Kjartan. I will either see the meaning or I won't; if I do it is yours."

Kjartan was pleased.

"Okay, here it is. I'm standing on the edge of a large river. On my right hand is a beautiful golden ring. Asgerd, this ring is special; it is very rich and golden, it literally shines. I take off my clothes and swim across the river. When I reach the other bank I look down and my beautiful ring is now pockmarked misshapen iron. Even more distressing is that it is so heavy I can barely lift my right arm. Any thoughts?"

Asgerd smiled at her brother. "Kjartan, I don't need seid to see the meaning of this dream. The ring is Gunnhild. She is very beautiful and has many alluring little wiles. However, when you swim in the river of time with her you will learn she is an ugly, heavy burden."

Kjartan was stunned. "Are you speaking in jest?!"

"No, unfortunately I'm not. Apparently even the gods can't bear the sight of you drowning mid river. This dream is their clear warning. Don't play the fool; heed this merciful warning."

Kjartan had much food for thought and they went together to the longhouse in a companionable silence.

Upon arriving they packed their things, loaded the horses, and headed back to the main farm on the coast. Asgerd was tired but deeply happy. It was so good to have Kjartan home again.

CHAPTER 9
Life At the Main Farm

GODI NJAL BJORNSON STOOD at the door of his longhouse and contemplated the scene. Despite blue sky, gentle breezes, and flowers there was no joy. Bridy, once again, had staked those damn cows under his very nose. They could work on making next year's cheese in any of the many distant fields he owned. He momentarily trembled on the edge of righteous anger and indignation, then quietly put on his shoes and led the cows away. He just didn't have the energy, which is why Bridy usually had her way with him. Sometimes he got to wondering. Fifteen years ago when he'd captured her on the northern coast of Gar; exactly whom had enslaved whom? Look at him! A forty-eight-year old respected godi and his hopes didn't extend beyond getting back to the house unnoticed and in peace.

It was not to be. As he approached the longhouse Bridy came trotting out of the nearby barn.

"Njal, where are the cows!?"

Njal managed a puzzled look; "What cows?", and they were off on the tenth or eleventh installment of 'cow wars'.

The domestic squabble woke Hoskuld, a friend and fellow godi visiting from the other side of Westmark. Things had been convivial at the preceding evening and it was a 'morning after' sort of Hoskuld who stood at the doorway watching his old viking chum take domestic heat; Hoskuld felt not the slightest kinship with a sunbeam. Finally he boiled over.

"By Thors Thunder, Njal, silence the wench! Isn't this the girl we captured on the north coast of Gar? If Ingrid were still alive she'd beat both of you senseless!"

Njal was embarrassed and conciliatory; "Hoskuld, this is not what it looks like…"

"Horseshit! It is exactly what it looks like! Njal, if you can't bring yourself to do what is needed, then put this slave wench out on the public road and I'll take care of it."

This stopped both Bridy and Njal in their tracks; Njal suddenly grew grave and thoughtful. Then putting both hands on Bridy's shoulders he spoke calmly and with authority.

"Bridy, he's exactly right; on the public road you have no status and no safety. This is intolerable and unthinkable."

Njal turned to Hoskuld; "Thank you old friend, I should have seen this long since. As of this moment, with you as witness, I am freeing Bridy."

Slaves were seldom freed, and it was the stuff of dreams. Bridy burst into tears.

"Njal, I don't want to be free; I want to be your slave."

Both Njal and Hoskuld were nonplussed; there didn't' seem to be much to say. At length Njal gave her a hug and said; "I'm afraid you must be free, Bridy, but at home you can still be my slave."

This last with a wry smile; exactly who was the slave was more puzzling than ever. However, at least the cows were off center stage, and the three of them, in much better moods, went in the house and broke their fast.

After breakfast Njal and Hoskuld discussed the upcoming althing. The godi needed far greater unity amongst themselves. As matters stood King Eirik had far too many points at which to drive dividing wedges. Were they divided they would soon be exactly like the coastal islands. Their timber, a treasure, made them an irresistible high priority target. Even standing firmly united they were facing very trying times; divided they would be chaff in a high wind.

Unfortunately genuine unity did not seem likely. The best reasonable hope was to arrange a strict neutrality for several of the more difficult godi. Ideally this neutrality would be guaranteed with hostages. This would not happen, but there were less direct ways of getting the same effect. Hoskuld and Njal were wily old vikings with good instincts for the feasible. After several hours of sharpening their ideas on each other they had a plan, and a fallback plan.

The old friends enjoyed a parting 'snort', then Hoskuld and his retinue of five were on their way. The guests were barely gone before Asgerd and Kjartan arrived from High Farm.

Ingrid had died giving birth to Asgerd, and Bridy was the only mother she had ever known. The women were great friends , which was a blessing to Njal. Kjartan was five when his mother died and he too viewed Bridy as 'Mom'. It was the first time in a year and half they had all been together, and dinner was a jolly occasion.

The next morning Kjartan left to visit his friend Thorkel; this journey is noteworthy for being the opposite direction from Gunnhild.

Asgerd invited her father to walk with her to Odin's grove; to her surprise and pleasure he accepted. They had not walked far when he steered their conversation in an unexpected direction.

"Asgerd, this past winter I learned something I think you should know. Four years ago you narrowly escaped death.

Everything about the business was puzzling and senseless. As you know, Kjartan wintered with Vali Gunnarson. Also wintering with Vali was a Leif Assgeirson, a boyhood chum of Grim, one of the men who tried to kill you. Two years before their final adventure on Westmark both Grim and Fridgeir had been friendly with Ragnhild, who worships Odin and is extremely powerful in the dark seid. This powerful volva is the chief counselor and confidant of King Eirik. That a King of Norland should have such an ally is very surprising and shameful. King Eirik's connection with Ragnhild is probably the single largest reason many godi, your father included, refuse to deal with him. Yet Eirik, who is a bold successful warrior, refuses to break such a damaging connection. Why!?'

Njal paused, then "No one knows, and not knowing breeds deep fear and distrust.'

"Apparently Grim and Fridgeir made a pact with Ragnhild. This pact was a thing separate from King Eirik, and Leif doubts Eirik knew of it. Ragnhild gave the berserks the true shield of Odin.

Asgerd interrupted her father; "Dad, as a child on your knee I learned the steel spell is an old fable with no truth. Now, with hushed and reverent tones you talk as though it were real. Please take a side on this issue."

Njal was both puzzled and worried; "Asgerd, such talk is mostly silly. However around a powerful dark seid I'm not so sure. Leif went on a raid with Grim, and he saw what he saw; steel could not bite the flesh of this particular berserk."

"What return did Ragnhild ask for her spell?"

Njal hesitated; "The life of Asgerd Njalsdottir.'

The father fell silent to let the moment gestate.

"Asgerd, you are nearly five hundred miles from Norland and the dottir of a godi little known in Norland; why does Ragnhild fear you?'

"Even move unexpected is that Odin honors the steel spell on all occasions except one. When <u>you</u>, Asgerd, are in danger, then steel bites deep.'

Father and daughter walked in silence awhile, then; "It seems to me, Asgerd, that Ragnhild was wise to fear you. And so it is, best of daughters, that I walk to Odin's grove. I will help you restore the grove. I am honored and pleased that you stand with us in Westmark."

CHAPTER 10
Food for Thought

MILES WALKED OUT OF the Hornet's Nest deep in thought. What a curious business! He'd have to check 'Dr. Petersen' out with a fine tooth comb. But what were the possibilities? He started with scam. He had not been asked to write any checks, but that hardly excluded scam. He might leave for the Joyce Kilmer grove and return to find his home cleaned out. Knowing exactly when and how long he'd be away they could schedule a moving van. This evening might be the first step in a more elaborate scam. He might be getting off his knees from planting the seed and another stranger, equipped with dreams and family traditions, happens along for step two. Ultimately 'saving the world' might involve his checkbook; hell, it usually cost money to save anything, never mind 'the world'.

Suppose Dr. Petersen were on the up and up. Miles pondered this awhile. Any fantastic nonsense when treated seriously for long enough became an energizing and validating myth; that, in a nutshell, was the story of religion. Perhaps this was the Petersen family religion. 'How perverse we are', thought Miles. If a small group or family has an energizing myth, it's 'obvious nonsense'. If a whole society has one it is revealed, sacred religion.

Miles thought critically of his energizing myth idea. No doubt there was a component of family myth, but this didn't cover the strange dream, or why specifically he, Miles Drake, was the big kahuna. And what about those birthmarks?! Damn strange, that.

Prank? Miles pondered that awhile, and then burst out laughing. In his mind's eye he was once again getting off his knees at the base of a huge tree. He'd made it, and was dusting off some dirt when up steps a keen young journalist with a microphone asking 'What are you feeling right now, Mr. Drake?' If an enterprising journalist had set up a respected fifty-year-old Dr. Petersen for this story he'd read it with a chuckle; human interest incident revealing once again that nobody, repeat nobody, is beyond the reach of hope and superstition. Dr. Petersen had alluded to dignity in a very lighthearted and minimizing way; as Dr. Petersen was handed the microphone would he still be lighthearted and carefree?

Regardless of the exact provenance of Dr. Petersen's story Miles went to bed that night thinking of something other than his dying wife or Matt MacDougal. He'd broken out of his rut, if only for awhile.

The next day he left the plant early and drove to St. Marys. He stopped at the front desk and asked the receptionist to page Dr. Petersen and have him meet a patient in the lobby. The receptionist phoned Dr. Petersen and relayed the message.

She turned to Miles, "You're in luck. He's usually at the office this afternoon, but as it is he just finished an emergency case and will be down to see you."

Five minutes later Dr. Petersen, in scrubs, walked up to the front desk; "Where's my patient, Molly?"

Molly was confused; "Dr. Petersen, he was here a minute ago."

Dr. Petersen paused; "Was he a tall, big man with short blond hair?"

Molly brightened; "Yes, Doctor, that's him."

"Thanks, Molly, but I think he has probably left."

Miles watched this exchange from across the lobby in the gift shop. His Dr. Petersen and the St. Marys flavor were the same man.

As Miles drove home from St. Marys he reached a decision. His estimate of Dr. Petersen's story rested critically on his estimate of Dr. Petersen. Petersen struck him as reliable and real. This made the story family myth plus; the margins were, as Dr. Petersen mentioned, not defined, not clear. The situation was like a lottery ticket; very likely nothing would happen, but there was the chance it might. He'd roll the dice; besides, he'd always meant the see the Joyce Kilmer forest. He'd read some poems that were at least as lovely as a tree, but not many, and he liked Mr. Kilmer's thought.

CHAPTER 11
The Seed

MILES MAY HAVE DECIDED to 'roll the dice', but two months later the 'seed business' had descended from 'rolling the dice' to a marginal curiosity and inconvenience. It is likely nothing would have happened but for Erin.

Shortly after Miles' evening at The Hornets Nest Erin received radiation therapy to several areas of her spine, and in yet another vertebra she had a vertebroplasty. These maneuvers don't cure, but they often help with the pain, and so it proved for Erin; she felt much better. So much better, in fact, she began viewing Miles as the 'patient'.

On June 14, after a pleasant supper; "Miles, have you arranged your schedule for your trip to the Joyce Kilmer forest?"

'Uh oh'; Miles had hoped his wife had forgotten that little story. "Sweetie, I had planned to go, but it is just not convenient. August or September would be much better."

Erin looked puzzled; "How interesting! Has summer solstice been moved to August or September? If so, on who's authority? June 21 has worked very nicely for quite some time.

"I have a better idea, Miles; why don't you go in June _and_ September!? If ever a man needed a road trip, it's you.

You love walking, and the mountains are very nice in June. Besides, aren't you curious what happens when you plant that seed?; I am. Lona Petersen is eaten alive with curiosity and will never again speak to me if the seed isn't planted."

"Okay, I'll look into it", agreed Miles.

Erin knew that tone of voice; "Miles, none of that! My back is much better, but hardly equal to four hundred miles to North Carolina and four hundred miles back. If you don't go then I am taking the seed and planting it. The only choice you have is to either win the Brute of the Year Award, or have an interesting and pleasant road trip."

And so it was that June 20 found Miles Drake motoring east towards the Smokies, and, as so often happens with wise men who heed their wives, he was in a happy and relaxed mood; there is something about the open road. 'Erin was right', thought Miles, 'I needed to get away.'

Late in the day, as he entered the Smokies it began to rain. Miles found a charming bed and breakfast where he had a great dinner and a pleasant evening. The next morning, June 21, was clear, cool, and beautiful; driving in the mountains was intoxicating. Eleven A.M. Miles turned into the Joyce Kilmer parking lot and began strolling the grove. It was like being in a vast cathedral; peaceful, a touch solemn, with a subtle blend of wonder and beauty. Miles had enjoyed the redwood grove in California, but this was far more memorable.

Just before noon, at the foot of particularly grand monarch, Miles dug a small hole, planted the seed, and poured a cup of water over the newly planted seed.

Nothing happened; of course. Even so Miles was pleased; this grove was easily worth the drive, and he was glad to have seen it. He decided to have a walk before the long drive back. He returned to his car to get his day pack and then started up the trail into the mountains. Several miles after starting there was a fork in the trail with the large main trail continuing to the left while a smaller less used trail went to the right. He chose the smaller trail.

The trail ascended until it was on a gentle ridge. The trees became larger and there was very little undergrowth. It was very pleasant, very restful, but the ridge was too broad and gentle for a view. The trees shaded the trail so the light was dappled and dim.

As Miles walked further his sense of peace and wellbeing deepened to the point he nearly forgot the long drive home, but finally he realized he needed to get back. It seemed a pity to turn back without enjoying a view; afterall, he was in the mountains. Miles decided to walk to the margin of the ridge and very likely he'd find a view of the neighboring valley. He walked at right angles to the trail in search of a view. There was virtually no undergrowth and his way was easy as he followed the gentle downward slope to the margin. He walked, and then walked some more, but nothing changed. Miles was just about to give up his project and retrace his steps back up the hill when ahead through the trees he faintly made out a trail. He decided to make the trail his turnaround point.

When he reached the trail he was vaguely surprised how much it resembled the trail he had left fifteen to twenty minutes ago. He studied the trail more closely and started trying to match up specific trees and other trail features. There was a match. But there couldn't be; he'd just walked downhill for fifteen minutes. Miles decided he couldn't trust this trail to get him back to the parking lot; he'd retrace his steps and return to the earlier trail. However, he would leave a candy bar to mark this trail. It was not possible the trails were the same, but...; no, he'd leave the candy bar.

Miles headed back the way he'd come. Fifteen minutes later he dimly saw a trail; three minutes later he was holding his candy bar. Not possible. Did this have any connection to the seed? Was he trapped in Never Never Land?

Miles almost jogged back up the trail and it wasn't long till he was again on the main trail. Soon he got a distant view of the parking lot and even made out his car. He was not trapped. He wondered what to do, and idly looked at his watch. It was 1:15 P.M.! He'd been gone much longer than that! He'd left the parking lot around 12:15. Walking downhill from where he was would take at least twenty minutes to get to the car. It was another ten to fifteen minutes up the trail to reach the bifurcation. Coming up he'd meandered, strolled; the journey to the bifurcation must have taken at the very least forty minutes, probably an hour. According to his watch most of the side trail trip had been free, 'off the clock'.

Supposing the side trail was off the clock; then there was no penalty to himself or others should he take a look, see the thing through. This thought brought him up short; there was no such thing as off the clock. Exactly, and there was no such thing as that side trail. In the past there had been moments when Miles suspected our perceptions were more limited and local than we imagined; of such moments this was by far the most compelling and authoritative. There was no way in God's green earth he could turn his back on the side trail.

Miles hiked briskly back to the bifurcation and once again started down the smaller side trail. This second time he was more alert and on his toes, more like a jungle cat stalking a trail. Not for long. The peace and sense of wellbeing he had enjoyed the first time swept over him again, and his vigilance, his guard, were as a sandcastle before an incoming tide. As Miles passed the earlier turnaround point this peace became profound. This was a curious peace; it was not engendered by the ambience, rather it was intrinsic to the path, more like the grass, dirt, and trees. To be on this path was to have dirt and grass under your foot; likewise with the peace, it was not optional.

Imagine a man who carries significant responsibility and burdens, whose life is reasonably well ordered. Imagine this man has thoughtfully assigned his responsibilities to people he trusts, has turned off his phone, and is sitting in the waiting area thirty minutes before his on-time plane boards. Thoughts float by, but with little momentum or emotional connection. The background of ordinary thought, surrounded and weighted by emotional connection, is as a three dimensional Technicolor affair compared to the gentle pastels of this path. Soon Miles pace had slowed to an evening stroll and his thoughts too strolled and were enjoyed for their intrinsic features and little else. He recognized his peace as rather curious, nodded to it, and moved on.

It is hard to say how long he strolled down the side trail but gradually he noticed the gentle ridge was descending into a larger, more open country. This descent was curious; visually it was very gentle, but it felt as though he were coming down a very steep path; if it were any steeper he'd be falling. As he came into the open country this gradually faded.

Eventually his path joined a larger path and Miles faced a decision; should he turn left or right on the larger trail? In his odd state of mind there seemed no grounds for choosing one direction over the other. Ever the empiricist Miles decided to try each direction; perhaps there were subtle differences. He walked a hundred yards to the left and then walked back.

He repeated this on the right. It was very subtle but it seemed travelling to the right had a slight upward grade, while travelling to the left seemed gently descending. This grade was not apparent to the eye. Miles decided to go right.

CHAPTER 12

The Main Trail, and Where it Led

THE PEACE ASSOCIATED WITH the main trail in the open
country was of nearly narcotic intensity. On the side
trail the state of mind was compared to a man free of all
responsibilities awaiting an on-time plane due to board in
thirty minutes. To approximate the main trail we need to
add beautiful adagio background music; the waiting man
joins the music and floats free of this earth.

All true, but Miles was not so carried away by this
strong river of peace as to miss interesting trail features.
The path included a number of groves. Some of these were
grander than the Joyce Kilmer grove and others less so.
Many of these groves had totem poles. How many groves
were passed is uncertain, but there were many.

Miles passed a number of temples, some in ruins, others
in good condition. The country surrounding these temples
was sometimes cultivated and other times in a state of nature.
He particularly liked the ruined temples near rivers, where
moss and trees had partially incorporated the temples into
the background. He passed fields with Stonehenge-type

stones, deserts with pyramids, and even a ruined gothic cathedral.

The trail passed through rugged mountains with glaciers; usually these were associated with large stones arranged in various patterns, or there were once again groves of large coniferous trees such as Douglas firs. The trail always gently ascended, or rose and fell modestly; it never seemed flat in flat country such as desert, or precipitous in precipitous country. Usually a trail is contoured to the country through which it passes; here this seemed reversed, with the surrounding country adjusted to the trail. Also the trail, independently of surrounding country, was always sunny and pleasant with gentle breezes. This despite deserts and arctic conditions.

Miles began to wonder whether this country was real, or might be a hologram. He left the trail and walked to a ruined temple. The temple was very real and when he reached for a rock to pull himself up for a view an unseen venomous snake struck and bit his right forearm. There was immediate pain but by the time he made it back to the main trail the wound was completely healed; no residual swelling or mark. Good as new.

Miles passed through the temples, groves, and stone arrangements of a thousand tribes and customs, all beautiful and memorable but much muted by the trail and its intrinsic peace. At length, ahead on his right, he saw a side trail lead off onto a ridge that vanished in the distance. As he approached the side trail it seemed as though he were descending, this despite the trail appearing unchanged. At the crossroads he considered which way to go and decided to follow the smaller branch trail. To his eye the grade was gently ascending but it felt like he was ascending a very steep path. After a few minutes this eased and the grade was similar to the main trail.

As Miles walked further the landscape grew rougher and there were fewer and smaller trees. Eventually the path was quite rocky and Miles needed to pay attention where he put his feet. The gentle breezes prevailing on the main trail gave way to a strong steady wind against which Miles found himself leaning. As the wind rose Miles revery faded; his 'flight' had been announced and he was looking for his ticket and getting to his feet. He became aware it was, if not cold, a little brisk; he could have used a light jacket or sweater. Miles walked a little faster. The ridge began descending and opening into a larger country. Faintly, in the distance, he began to notice a repetitive clanging sound, and wondered what it might be. A minute later as he came over a final shoulder of the ridge the clanging noises were explained. Two hundred yards below and to his left three men with swords and shields were attacking a large man armed with a sword. The large man was maneuvering desperately to avoid being caught between them and he was moving in a way suggesting he was wounded. The large man was clearly on borrowed time.

Miles was getting ready to shout, to put an end to what was looking like murder, when he caught himself; there was a single-minded intensity to the scene and he realized his shouting would avail nothing and would destabilize things in unpredictable ways. Miles shrugged off his day pack and began running down the hill. As he ran he searched desperately for weapons. There were stones everywhere, and lots of them. Stones would do just fine.

As Miles stooped to pick several large stones, a teenage girl came galloping up on a lathered horse. She leaped off, drew a sword, and attacked the nearest assailant.

This man barely had time to turn before the girl was on him. The large man shouted something to her, and there was fear in his voice and renewed energy in his efforts. The girl made no reply; her opponent was strong and skillful and she was only managing to stay alive.

Miles came in from the side and he was noticed for the first time when a large stone hit the girl's opponent in the face. The stone was thrown very hard and accurately and dropped the man like a sack of flour. He had barely hit the ground before the girl had half cut off his head.

She turned instantly to attack the next man but Miles was ahead of her. Once again Miles threw very hard and very accurately but at the last second the man caught it on his shield. Before the man could recover Miles made a low tackle under the shield; the man went down and never had time to use his sword. Miles gained control of the man's sword arm then suddenly, with his full weight came down with an elbow to the face. The man was stunned. Miles stood up and took the sword but before he could do anything the girl had put her sword right through the fallen man's chest and pinned him to the ground.

Desperately the girl pulled her sword free and turned towards the final man. The large man to whose aid the girl had come was fallen to one knee and was feebly trying to raise his sword to fend off the next final blow. It came without ceremony and at the last moment the large man rolled to one side and the swing just missed him. There was no follow up blow. Miles tackled the last man and killed him by beating his head with a convenient rock.

As the adrenaline rush faded and Miles stood to his feet he became aware of two things; he had just killed several men, an unthinkable thing, and while he was unhurt, he seemed to have sustained a total body bruise, to the point he could hardly move. Football tackles on rocky scree without protection were the pits. Evidently in this neck of the woods they were a total novelty, and this was probably the only reason he was alive.

Miles studied his companions. The girl was crying and shaking the fallen large man who he now saw was an older gentleman closer to fifty than forty. The fellow had passed out. Miles limped over and began feeling for a carotid pulse; he found it. He had to get the bleeding stopped, and soon. He then noticed for the first time the girl had a deep nasty looking cut on her left arm near the shoulder; it was bleeding heavily. He could lose these people if he didn't act quickly.

Miles took off his shirt and tied it around the girl's arm with sufficient force to stop her bleeding. He then turned his attention to the large older man and had the young girl put direct pressure on a chest wound near the right shoulder while he compressed a long deep gash on the left thigh.

Ten minutes later he was thoroughly chilled from being shirtless and in the wind, but the major bleeding was stopped. He had passed the time visiting with the girl. He talked both to calm her and to learn what he could. The language she spoke was not English and at first they could not understand each other, but ten minutes later they were beginning to communicate. This made no sense, but, while Miles wondered at it he accepted the fact. He was getting practiced at accepting bizarre, impossible things.

The older man was the girl's father, and he was a kind of chief. The girl's name was Asgerd. The three men who attacked her father were agents of a king named Eirik. This king had designs on their island home and viewed Njal, the father, as an obstacle.

Njal had wakened early on and made an effort to get up, but he was far too weak and eventually calmed down. Njal and Asgerd were curious about Miles; who was he? Where had he come from? Miles told his story the best he could. The girl and her father had exchanged significant looks.

With the bleeding stopped Miles limped back to his day pack and brought it down to where his patients were.

He used a knife to cut his shirt into several bandages. Most importantly he insisted Njal drink a quart of water from his canteen. Asgerd drank the rest.

Miles thought it over and decided to move Njal in fifteen minutes. He glanced at his watch, which Njal and Asgerd found intriguing. Then Miles had an idea.

"Asgerd, I want to help get your father home, but we need to wait a few minutes. While we wait I need to do something. I should be back in a few minutes. Please don't leave until I return."

"I will wait, Miles, but don't be too long, night is near."

Miles limped up the ridge and back to the side trail. Five minutes later he returned. His aches, thirst, and worries were gone. The hunch, gleamed from the snake bite, was true; the odd trail restored both body and spirit. The time element was reaffirmed. He had been walking at least half an hour but to the girl only a brief time had passed.

Miles waited another five minutes then helped Njal get seated on Asgerd's horse. Asgerd led the horse while Miles walked beside the horse to make sure Njal didn't fall. They hadn't travelled more than fifty yards when Miles stopped; "Asgerd, I want to try something. If this works it is sure a tremendous improvement on what we face an hour from now. Turn up the shoulder of this hill and in the next few minutes it will be clear if my idea works.

Asgerd was puzzled; "That's not the way home, Miles."

"I know, but give me five minutes."

Asgerd shrugged her shoulders and guided the horse right, and up the hill. A hundred yards later Asgerd turned around just as Miles entered the tree. Miles found himself walking alone; the others were frozen in the exact positions of the moment he entered the tree; Asgerd was opening her mouth to speak, while the horse had one leg in the air and another leg bent. Miles walked along the trail a ways and then turned back; they were in the same positions. They couldn't enter the tree.

Miles left the tree path and once again stood by the horse; however he had not paid attention and was on the other side of the horse and facing back along the way they had come.

Whatever Asgerd had planned on saying was converted to a gasp; "Miles, what happened?! An instant ago you were facing towards me on the other side of the horse."

"I entered the tree and time stopped till I returned. You and Njal cannot enter the tree, which means we will be doing things the hard way. Let's turn around and get Njal home."

It was about three miles to the long house on the main farm and the light was failing near journey's end. As they approached the long house an alarmed woman ran to meet them.

CHAPTER 13
Of Various Wounds

SEVERAL OF THE WOUNDS bothered Miles; they were deep and involved much underlying muscle. Asgerd in particular had a long life ahead and needed a good arm. Miles was hardly a surgeon but he had paid attention during several educational television shows. One of these had involved wound care during the American civil war. Apparently boiled horsetail hair had been a good suture material. They had horses, and boiling water could be arranged. But first things first. He had both Asgerd and Njal drink more water, lots of water. While the water was getting absorbed he and Bridy arranged an operating theatre near the fire. Horse hairs and sewing needles were boiled. Finally he got Asgerd lying on the crude dinner table, cleaned her wound as best he could, and wished he had something to give her for pain. This was going to hurt like Billy O.

Asgerd amazed him. She endured the procedure with a near perfect stoicism and even paid close attention as though filing it away for future reference. He approximated the torn muscle as best he could and finally closed the superficial wound. His effort was hardly a thing of beauty, but the repair looked serviceable.

Next they got Njal on the table and repaired his wounds. This was quite an ordeal and Njal, Bridy, and himself were worn out before they finished. Long before finishing Miles was getting very practiced with his surgical knots. As a teenager he had worked one summer with a vet and had helped close animal wounds of all sizes and shapes. To his surprise and delight the basic surgical knot had stayed with him.

Neither Njal nor Asgerd complained but Miles knew they had to be in great pain. He reached into his day pack and, like a magician pulling a rabbit from his hat, produced a bottle of ibuprofen. He gave each of them three tablets and insisted they take them.

In the morning, with both father and daughter sleeping, Miles left the ibuprofen and instructions with Bridy, put on one of Njal's shirts, shouldered his pack, and headed back to the ridge from which he'd arrived.

As Miles climbed the familiar ridge he felt he was leaving wounds and trouble behind. Soon the familiar peace and floating detachment arrived and he felt contented and rested. Once again there was a feeling of steep descent as he approached the main trail. He turned left towards the Joyce Kilmer side trail and felt the grade to be a very gentle, barely detectable, downhill.

Miles' earlier journey on the main trail had been too long and varied to remember everything in detail, but he was surprised how much he did remember. He had paid particular attention to the details near the Joyce Kilmer side trial and had even piled several rocks at the origin of his trail. After a longish meditative stroll he arrived in the clearly recognizable country around his side trail, and even found his rock pile, but where the ridge had been there was now yet another grove of trees; there was no ridge or trail.

This bothered Miles as much as one can be bothered on the main trail, which wasn't much.

The root of what concern he could manage was that up until now the trail had <u>not</u> shown any variation with time; it had been thoroughly stable and objective. Miles thought the matter over and decided to continue down the main trail; there didn't seem anything else to do, and perhaps the side trails had a tendency to drift downhill.

As he walked further the trees gradually grew larger and stranger. Later, in a grove of giant trees, there were several large wooly mammoths. They seemed to be resting and were peaceable. There were no temples, nor even primitive stone arrangements; only groves. Gradually the trail and surrounding country began to visibly descend, and the subtle downhill grade became a very tangible downhill that grew steeper and steeper. Trees grew smaller and fewer and finally disappeared altogether. Soon Miles was descending through a field of large boulders with a grade of fifty to sixty degrees. The pleasant cool breezes and sunshine had long since given way to twilight and a distinct chill. The boulders insensibly shaded into a frank cliff and Miles found himself searching for handholds in the dim light.

Finally Miles stopped and peered down and to his right to see if there was an end, or a floor, to this descent. Very faintly through the deepening glow there was a suggestion of an end. He looked more intently and noticed a faint glow, as of moonlight, away from the cliff; there <u>was</u> a floor. He climbed carefully another hundred feet before finally reaching the floor and stepping away from the cliff. He looked around and again saw the faint glow of moonlight a hundred yards ahead on his left. As Miles approached this gentle glow it gradually resolved into three human shapes. Yet closer he realized they were three middle aged women who were very beautiful and taller than himself. They were busy weaving and their expressions where thoughtful and grave. If these women saw Miles they gave no notice. Near them was a well.

Miles headed towards the three women and within a few steps noticed how gray everything seemed; the change was striking, and he stopped to consider his situation. It was as though all color was being leeched from the world. He examined his own arm closely and it seemed slightly transparent. Miles took three more steps in the direction of the women and his arm was now distinctly transparent and more and more the world seemed dissolving towards a faint gray mist. Miles called out to the ladies, who were sixty to seventy feet away.

"Ladies, how is it I am unable to approach you?"

His voice was as faint as a whisper in the wind and about as intelligible; this, along with the increasing transparency, was a stark warning. The women neither heard him nor appeared to notice his approach. In a flash of insight Miles realized that should he continue he would cease to exist long before he reached the weaving woman. They weren't in the world the way he was; to be in their company was to have some different strange existence, or nonexistence. There were no words for what he sensed.

Miles turned around and retraced his steps. As he did so, in a corner of his vision he noticed the flicker of a distant fire; Miles headed towards the fire.

Upon nearing the fire Miles discovered a huge rocklike thing shaped like a man. The 'rock' stirred and there was a low bass rumble like distant thunder. Then, more within his mind as a distant echo than as ordinary speech; "Greetings, you must be a man."

In the following conversation the utterances of the rock, in addition to the physical shudder of distant thunder and the echo directly within the mind, were attended with the certainty of the ground on which a man stands, and brilliant flashes of intuition and insight. Every word was like a huge jagged lightening flash against a dark sky, or Archimedes in his tub, or Einstein and Newton rounding a corner and laying hands on their great truths. Conversing with this rock was searing and never to be forgotten.

"Yes, I am a man. My name is Miles Drake. I have never seen anything like you before. Please tell me what you are and who you are. Also, if you would be kind enough to tell me <u>where</u> we are I would appreciate it."

After saying this Miles waited and was silent. There was a longish pause before the rumbly vibrations began again.

"I am a jotun. We are a race ancient beyond your grasp of the word. My name is Mimir. You are at the roots of Yggdrasil, the World Tree. If you continue on your current course of travel you will come into jotunheim, or the domain of jotuns. You may go as you wish, Miles Drake, but I would not recommend this path."

The rock fell silent. Miles waited and said nothing. Soon; "You are the first man I have seen; how is it you stand before me? What is your story?"

Miles, deeply puzzled, was mired in mystery far beyond his depth. There was something profound about this rock, or 'jotun'; this was probably his best source of guidance; correction, his <u>only</u> source of guidance. Miles began at the beginning and told his story thoughtfully and well. Mimir listened without interruption.

After a thoughtful pause; "The rules governing this world of yours, Miles; are they fixed and firm? Many exceptions to the rules?"

"The rules are very firm and there are few if any exceptions."

Another pause. "Do the people of your world speak of fate in their lives? Do they speak of fate as a thing clearly sensed and real?"

"Seldom. If a man should speak of fate he is viewed as simpleminded."

There now a long, long pause.

"It is a sad thing, Miles Drake, but your world no longer exists."

Miles digested this and decided he and Mimir were at cross purposes.

"Mimir, the path to my world may no longer exist but my world is real and exists."

The jotun sighed, and the very ground shook; "Miles, you are confused. Yggdrasil and the paths are eternal and real, but worlds like yours come and go. To exist, to be real, is to be in the active mind of the All Father. When a world slips from his mind it has slipped out of existence. The All Fathers active interest is sensed as fate, and is always associated with some degree of variation in the rules of the world.

"The path to your world, on your own telling, is no longer there. If the world were still present the path leading to it would be exactly where it should be. It isn't there because your world no longer exists. You must put this behind you. You need to return to the world where you saved the father and daughter. Build your life there and see what comes."

One cannot truly have a sinking feeling near Yggdrasil, but if this were possible then it would resemble Miles' thoughts and feelings.

"The things you have said, Mimir, they are certain and true?"

"They are. As you return to the World Tree, Miles, do not speak with the Norns. No good can come of such talk and much harm might result."

"The Norns are the three tall ladies?"
"Yes. Walk quietly by them and climb the tree."
"Who are they?"
"They weave the destiny of all things."
Miles returned quietly to the cliff and began climbing.

CHAPTER 14
Spring in Westmark

IT WAS A CURIOUS spectacle. Immediately ahead of him was more of the usual ridge trail; cool, sunny with a gentle breeze. However over a five foot interval this changed to snow on the ground, falling rain, and a gray gusty day. Miles had dressed for summer solstice in North Carolina, not early spring in high latitudes, but even so he didn't hesitate. Miles was weary with eventless peace and ready to rejoin the current of life.

Miles walked without hesitation into the cold rain and was bracing himself for a very cold and miserable three mile hike to the main farm when on the edge of his vision he noticed a caped figure on a horse. This figure was leading a second horse. The first visit to this world made him wary; perhaps yet more killers were abroad.

Miles stopped and turned to study the approaching figure, who was small and not threatening. As the distance closed Miles realized it was the same girl he had helped last time.

"Asgerd, what are you doing here!?"

"I came to meet you.", and Asgerd passed him a large cloak.

Miles was happy to put it on. "How did you know to meet me?"

Asgerd smiled and it was the only sunshine in sight; "I always know the things I need to know. I brought a horse for you."

Miles considered; "Thanks, but I'm miserable enough as is; I'll walk.

Asgerd looked well, and a little older; perhaps it was the cape and weather.

"Asgerd, how much time has passed since we last met?"

"Fall and winter have come and gone and it is now early spring."

"You are looking good, in a cold and wet sort of way. How's the shoulder?"

"Everything healed nicely. I am ready for the next sword dance."

"How about your dad?"

"The wound in his chest healed well and quickly. The wound in his thigh did not, and is only now easing. I had to make a cut near the wound to drain blood, pus, and dead tissue. But now all goes well and he is nearly back to his old self."

Asgerd smiled; "This is a blessing from the gods; he's around the house all the time, and driving us mad."

Miles hesitated; "Asgerd, I'm new to your world and have nothing but the clothes on my back. If it's not too great an imposition I'd like to stay with you and your dad a few weeks until I see what I should do. Will this pose a problem?"

"You are the funny one! You cut the coat from your back and put your life at great risk for us; we owe our lives. What do you think, Mr. Drake; should we shove you back into the snow and rain? Our home is your home as long as you need or want it."

"Thank you, Asgerd; I hope your dad sees it that way too. Does he know I'm coming?"

"No, I'm the only one. When I left in the rain to meet you Yngvar and Kjartan, who didn't know the purpose of the trip, said I was confirming what they'd always known; Asgerd Njalsdottir is crazy! When I produce you at the farm door we must be quick if we are to catch their jaws before they hit the floor."

Asgerd looked pretty smug and Miles had to laugh.

"You can catch my jaw too while you are at it! How <u>did</u> you know I'd be coming!? When I left it never crossed my mind I'd be returning. It seems you know more about me than I do."

Asgerd went from smug to arch; "Trust me, Mr. Drake, I know many things. For example, I know when you will leave our farm and what you will be doing. I know what you will do when, in a few years, you return."

This was no longer so funny and left Miles with an odd mixture of chill, amusement, and irritation; "Perhaps, Asgerd, it would be best to keep such knowledge to yourself."

"You are right, Mr. Drake, and most of what I know is never shared. However, this is not such a time. Even a horse can see you will leave with Yngvar and Kjartan to go raiding. You own nothing and raiding will soon fix this. Besides, Yngvar and Kjartan are the best of companions; were I to go a viking they'd be my first, second, and third choice. They will be leaving in two to three weeks, and it is hard to believe you will not be with them."

The girl was right, so right there was hardly any choice in the matter; he needed a few chips in this game.

"What of my return; are my choices equally certain and clear?"

Asgerd thought this over. "Your choices in two years considered now are not likely to be as compelling as these of the next few weeks. They are clear to me, and they will become clear to you if I plant the seed. But first a question; why do you think you are here?"

"For very odd reasons I walked away from my world and onto paths between the worlds. When I tried to return to my world the path was no longer there. These paths are very wonderful and very strange, but they are only good for the occasional visit. If one stays too long they would numb the spirit. Thus, I came here."

"Yes, but why here? You didn't walk further to other worlds."

"I had a base in your world. I helped you and might reasonably expect that you would help me; and so it is proving."

"This is true and reasonable. Were there any additional circumstances?"

Asgerd evidently didn't know the answer and was curious. "Perhaps, but most likely not relevant. The main path eventually gave way to a boulder field and then a cliff. I climbed down the cliff to a land that was colder and dimmer, a sort of chilly twilight. I encountered three tall beautiful women who were knitting; they ignored me and I passed in silence.

"A little further I found a very large man-like creature who identified himself as what he called a jotun. I explained my situation to him and he assured me my world no longer existed. This jotun gentleman recommended I come here. I doubt this mattered; I probably would have come in any case. I didn't know any other place to go and I was ready to leave the paths."

Miles hesitated; "My story sounds crazy, even to me, and I was there. I will not be offended if you do not believe it."

Asgerd had been listening with shining eyes; "Oh Miles, I believe your wonderful story! Very very few are so fortunate as to walk on Yggdrasil, and no man has ever seen the Norns or talked with Mimir! You are greatly loved by Odin! Is it possible you do not know this?"

Miles didn't know which way to turn. "Asgerd, your talk of Odin is a manner of thinking and speaking, but is not real. Odin is not real the way this snow is real, or the way we are real. I do not find such talk helpful, but perhaps it is different with you."

"I think you are mistaken, Miles, but it probably doesn't matter. Things will doubtlessly go as they need to, never mind what we think or don't think. Whether you see it or not, Odin has sent you to bring King Eirik down, and to save Westmark. I am here to help you."

"You are probably right, Asgerd. When people try to kill me or my friends Odin can count on me to put a stop to it. As of right now you and yours are the only friends I have. It will be a pleasure to bring ruin on this King Eirik."

CHAPTER 15
Fifteen Years Later

(Kjartan, Fifteen years after Miles arrives)

The night had been rough, but not dangerously so and Kjartan slept well. With daybreak he took the tiller. The weather improved to fair with a favoring wind and all eyes searched the distant but approaching coast of southern Gar.

An hour later Ketil the sharp Eyed shouted, "Quarda to starboard!"

A smiling Bjorn turned and slapped Kjartan on the back; "Another perfect landfall, Kjartan! Well done!"

"Thanks, Bjorn. We're lucky to have that mountain; this coast is damn near featureless. Now all we need is Crispus. Remember that farm two miles inland near the river?"

"I do. The farmer has a delightful daughter."

This didn't suit Kjartan even a little, and he abruptly reassigned the various tasks; "Bjorn I want you to get us watered; take five men of your choice."

Ketil was walking towards them and when he arrived Kjartan said; "Ketil, your eyes are as sharp as ever; nothing can hide from you. I want you to arrange roast pork for supper. Do you know the farm two miles inland by the river?"

"No, but I can follow a river as well as the next man; especially if there's a road or path beside it."

"Good. It is the first farm on the left side of the river as you face inland. Here's ten dharma for two pigs of your choice." Kjartan handed over the money.

Then he raised a cautionary finger; "Ketil, treat this man like a neighbor, and leave his wife and daughters alone. Tell him we'll buy two pigs next year at about the same time. Ten dharma is more than the pigs are worth and he should be pleased and cooperative."

An hour later Kjartan shouted; "Give me two gentle back oars!"

Their boat slowed yet more and then gently grounded. Ketil and Thorfinn leaped into the surf and grounded the boat more firmly. As they were wallowing their way towards shore Crispus appeared on the beach.

Kjartan trusted and liked Crispus and was pleased to see him; "Crispus, old friend, your arrival is timely and you are looking well."

"Thank you, Kjartan. You too are looking well, for a savage and pagan. And, yes, before you ask; I have all you ordered and more."

Crispus was a mastersmith and armorer who made special weapons and armor for Kjartan. The design and first order were given fifteen years earlier to Crispus' father by Miles Drake. The connection was good for both parties and was carried on by Kjartan and Crispus.

Kjartan paid for the weapons with a combination of dharmas and ermine furs. After the business was concluded and the weapons were safely on the ship the two friends found a comfortable spot on the beach and caught up.

Kjartan and Unn, after having two sons, had recently had a healthy baby girl who they named Asgerd after Kjartan's sister. Crispus, who already had two girls, had just had a third little girl. This left him happy, but a trace ambivalent; girls were all well and good, but who would carry on the family business? Nothing for it but try again. Fourth tries were charmed, or so he'd heard.

Kjartan always kept an eye out for friends, and like dawn coming around he finally said; "And business, Crispus? No one bothers or interferes with you?"

The question was not merely social, and Crispus knew this and hesitated; "Musa, one of our local strong men, wants a cut of my business; for 'protection'. His thugs recently broke Mary's arm to show me how much I need his protection."

Kjartan's face hardened; "I will postpone my journey south by a day or so and fix things. Are there other strong men in the area?"

Crispus had to chuckle; "You might as well ask are there flies on the beach; I could fill your ship with thugs and strong men. Let me see; there is Mohammed, Haroun, Sandaman, . . .", but Kjartan interrupted him.

"Crispus, pick one you respect and could work with, or that you dislike the least."

"Sandaman is a fellow believer, a Christian, who went into the strongman business more to protect fellow believers than from greed and general nastiness."

Kjartan was skeptical; "Right; and Mary's arm got broken. Is Sandaman strong enough to be useful? This question is not idle, especially as the sons of that scabby prophet control all but the very top of Gar. Leave beliefs out of this; we are talking about the safety and well-being of you and your family. Whoever you pick really is going to take an interest in your well-being."

Crispus didn't hesitate; "Sandaman is as strong as any and would be my choice."

"Good. Well, Crispus, let's be up and doing; I'm going home with you. If we hurry we can have everything settled and shipshape by sundown."

Then Kjartan laughed at Crispus' alarmed and surprised expression.

"Do you find your viking chums something of an embarrassment, Crispus? Don't want to be seen with the pagans? Well, blame yourself; this is what comes of hanging out with toughs and strongmen."

Kjartan, for the third time, reassigned pig patrol so as to have Ketil along to help with toughs; Ketil had a deft way with an axe and was a very god with a bow. He picked four other men and loaded their weapons in Crispus' wagon, which he covered with an old piece of sail. On the odd whim he threw in a shirt and trousers. Then he and Crispus headed towards Crispus' hometown, Mendero. Helgi and Egil came along about a third of a mile back while Ketil, Herjolf, and Olaf brought up the rear yet another half mile back. The northmen were sufficiently spread to not be seen as a group; 'just us passing travelers, Miss.'

The journey was pleasant, and longer than Kjartan remembered; it was at least five hours before they were skirting Mendero. Musa's headquarters were the local brothel, which was run by the strongman's wife, Nubila. Kjartan thoughtfully cased the place. Then he left to meet his men and organize his raid. They were greatly favored in that four of Musa's thugs were sprawled and at ease in the front of the building. When instructions had been given and the men positioned Kjartan walked back to the brothel. Just before reaching the building he conspicuously scratched his right ear; three of the four toughs fell to arrows and the fourth fell to Kjartan's axe. The men quickly entered both front and back entrances, and with swords and axes killed four more toughs. Musa, as Kjartan had ascertained earlier, was being important and lordly in the common room. Kjartan killed Musa and Nubila. The daughter was very pretty, and Kjartan thought she would sell well as a slave so he spared her; she was sent back to the boat with Egil and Helgi.

Kjartan walked back to Crispus and the cart carrying a large leather bag and a smaller bag, which contained what jewels and money he had scrounged from the brothel. Kjartan was in a good mood; everything was going nicely and there'd been more money than he had expected.

"Okay, Crispus, let's visit this Sandaman. Which way?"

On the south side of Mendero, where the main road entered town there was a pub Sandaman favored. Kjartan enjoyed a beer, and noticed with satisfaction the nibs was 'in', sober, and in good spirits. Kjartan returned to his men and positioned his archers so they commanded a view of the front of the pub but were out of sight.

Turning to Crispus, "Crispus, Sandaman knows you. Go in the pub and invite him outside for an important business meeting. If he wonders if it is safe, which he will, assure him all is well. This happens to be true. If he is still edgy allow him all the weapons he wishes, and two friends. This meeting is a good news meeting, a real opportunity; don't let him decline."

A few minutes later Crispus emerged from the pub with a wary Sandaman, who had handy both a scimitar and a huge thug.

Sandaman was about thirty years of age and was a handsome, large man; Kjartan liked the look of him. He looked Kjartan over carefully and said; "Crispus vouches for you, stranger, which will serve. Who are you, and what is your business?"

Kjartan had a relaxed manner which thawed things, and when he spoke it was with a smile; "I am from the North and my name is Kjartan Njalson. I have two gifts for you, and news."

This was received with a noncommittal "I am waiting."

"This first gift is in this leather bag", and Kjartan handed over the larger leather bag.

Sandaman opened it and looked in. At first he was startled, but then smiled; "This is a good gift." He then pulled out the heads of Musa and Nubila. Musa was a hated rival, and Sandaman's mood improved. Not so Crispus, who looked pale and nauseous.

Kjartan resumed; "The second gift is at least as good.", and he held out Musa's largest emerald.

Sandaman took the gem and looked it over; then grew thoughtful.

"And what of Musa's daughter, Nur? Is she well?"

"She is pink with health and on the way to my ship."

"Nur is dear to me. I will trade this excellent gem for Nur."

Kjartan was surprised; "As you wish, Sandaman. But, while the girl is very pretty, the gem would buy ten like her; consider carefully."

Sandy laughed pleasantly; "You are so wrong, Northman. The emerald is not worth Nur's little finger. This will be one of those trades where each party is convinced he is cheating the other. How soon can you deliver her?"

With this question Sandy handed the emerald back to Kjartan, who looked it over carefully and put it in his pocket.

"Within three hours you should have the girl. Send two of your men with my men, and have them bring her back."

"Good. Now, Northman, let's have the news."

"As Nur evidently is to you, Sandaman, so is Crispus and his family to me. I am putting them under your protection. As you guard my friends, remember two things; I have more gifts for people who help me, and should your guard falter it might do well to remember Musa and his wife Nubila. I am holding you responsible for their safety. Please include their wellbeing and safety in your evening prayers."

"It is not necessary to threaten me, Northman; I am pleased to guard Crispus and family."

"Good, Sandaman; even so, bear in mind what I have said. Thanks for your time and enjoy your supper."

Then turning to Crispus; "Well, let's be off, Crispus."

They had barely returned to the wagon when Crispus, like a burst dam, began remonstrating; "Why did you kill Nubila!? Musa I follow, but Nubila!?"

Kjartan was genuinely surprised; "Crispus, I know nothing of Nubila, and she was dumpy and homely; who would buy her? I certainly wouldn't. These things are true, but not enough to take her life. She died so that Sandy would keep his own family in view. A man might be ready and willing to take his chances on some venture but be unwilling to put his family at risk. I am such a man, and I am supposing this consideration weighs with Sandaman."

Crispus was unconvinced; "Perhaps it changes things with Sandaman, perhaps it doesn't; it is <u>certain</u> a fellow human will never enjoy another meal or sunset."

"You are quite right, Crispus."

Kjartan mused a moment, then, "Crispus, I will lift the veil on how Northern Pagans think. When faced with a problem we think it through carefully and do everything we can towards solving it. When this is finished we put the problem behind us and shrug our shoulders; 'what comes will come.' When I leave tomorrow, I will have done everything I can towards your safety and I will shrug my shoulders. Had I left Nubila alive I would not be able to shrug my shoulders; I would have been irresponsible and negligent. My mind is on your well-being and safety; not Nubila's."

Crispus grew quiet and thoughtful; "Kjartan, if you come back next year and either myself or members of my family have died, what happens?"

"If they died of illness I would console you; if otherwise, then Sandy and whatever family he has would die. I make a point of such things. We Northmen are as strict as can be on our word. Because of this when a Northman speaks the world pays attention; especially Christians."

Kjartan looked very solemn, then burst out laughing; "Come, come, Crispus, forget Nubila. The wench is probably having a cozy little supper with your Christian God. Instead think of her daughter; this tasty little trick, a daughter of the prophet (may his name be soon forgotten), will be shacking up with a Christian. Unless I miss my guess a year from now there will be a child and many headaches; Sandy will think back on that emerald with bitter regret. Tonight the balance between the little finger of the wench outweighs the emerald. Later the entire wench is balanced against the emerald and the wench is catapulted to the moon."

Crispus, because of Nubila, which still rankled, was feeling contrary and sprang to the defense of young love. They argued it this way and that all the way to Crispus' home; nothing was resolved.

CHAPTER 16
At home with Crispus

As SUPPER FINISHED MARY absentmindedly rubbed her nearly healed right arm and studied Silas, one of her husband's apprentices. To the untutored eye Silas was the very picture of boyish charm and innocence, yet the sharp eye of Mary detected darkest villainy. The soup supplies and bread stores were declining just a little too quickly. A portion of this attrition was known and accepted. For example, Monica, a young kitchen maid, had a dying mother and two hungry younger brothers; Monica needed help, and everyday Mary sent home with her maid a quart of soup and a loaf of bread. Anthony, the senior journeyman was another known food sink; exactly how this worthy man managed to eat for three men and yet remain rail thin rather intrigued Mary, whose own person, despite modest consumption, was on the increase. These and other holes in the food supplies just weren't enough to cover the alarming way her supplies were disappearing.

How does this domestic tragedy and mystery connect with ruddy cheeked Silas? Probably through yet another kitchen maid, most likely Bridget, who was unusually sensitive to boyish charm. To Mary's eye the apprentices, while not yet actually waddling, were looking plumper and healthier than an apprentice had any right to look. But such thoughts, while interesting enough, were really more to distract Mary from a much greater worry; where was Crispus!? He should have been home hours ago. Crispus had traded with the Northmen many years and never had he been so late. The nub of the worry were those accursed Northmen; if you hung out with wasps eventually you would get stung. It only fueled her fret that she considered Crispus far too trusting; a wasp was a wasp, was a wasp, and Crispus, God love the trusting man, was a fool. A fool with a wife and three daughters who needed guarding and looking after. Mary began working up a head of steam but before actually coming to a boil the front door opened and in walked Crispus. Mary's relief was sudden and complete, but alas, momentary; just behind him were three large strangers. Could they be? No, Crispus would never bring the wasps into his home. But a moment later, when they emerged fully their height, blondness, axes, and bows left no doubt – Mary's home was invaded by savage pagans! Saint Eunice protect us!

But Crispus seemed happy and relaxed, and so did the Northmen.

"Mary, I want you to meet my friend and trading partner Kjartan Njalson."

A tall handsome man a few years older than her husband nodded pleasantly and in a gentle baritone with more than a little accent; "Mary, Crispus has talked of you for years and it is a very great pleasure to finally meet you. My friends and companions', and Kjartan turned to nod first to Ketil then Olaf, 'are Ketil the Sharp Eyed and Olaf Gunnarson."

Mary blushed very prettily and made a small curtsy; "I am honored Kjartan Njalson to extend my home and hospitality to you and your friends."

Mary then shooed the lingering and curious apprentices, including Silas, from the room and ordered the kitchen maids to bring more soup and bread, lots more soup and bread. As the men seated themselves around the table Kjartan turned to Crispus; "Old friend, we are new in Mendero and I would feel easier if several of your lads kept an eye on the street for awhile. I hate surprises, especially when I'm eating."

Crispus reached behind a nearby door and pulled out an ear, which was immediately followed by a pale and alarmed Silas; "Silas, lad, please keep watch on the street. Report anything out of the ordinary."

Silas obediently trotted off to attach his vigilance to the street, while the Northmen and Crispus, famished to a man, got earnest and busy with the bread and soup. Mary rather liked a hearty appetite, especially in men, but this was too much of a good thing, and the 'famished wolf' scene served to get her mind off the presumed sins of Silas, which now seemed venal and beneath notice.

At length the feeding frenzy ebbed and Crispus had the leisure to attend to other matters.

"Kjartan, whatever happened to that large man who got us started. Dad liked him and was impressed to the edge of awe. I hope things go well for him."

"The man you inquire after is Miles Drake, and he prospers. Your father, Crispus, is correct concerning Miles; the man is exceptional and his tale even more so."

Kjartan did not elaborate but rather cut yet another slice of bread. At length curiosity nudged Crispus.

"How is it that after designing the curious axe and shields this Miles never comes to Mendero? Dad said he seemed very interested in both our weapons shop and Mendero."

"Crispus, Miles now lives in a very distant new country. It would take Miles months to sail to Westmark, and an extra month to visit Mendero in Southern Gar. Give your hopes a rest; I'm afraid you are stuck with me. Besides I'm not so bad."

"Kjartan, you said Miles' story is most unusual; I would like to hear his tale."

"The story of Miles Drake is beyond unusual; I am not aware of a story remotely like it. The man is strange and something of a mystery, and I say this after campaigning at his side for three years."

Mary, who had been listening closely, now interrupted, interrupted with an undertone of defiance; "Mr. Drake was not as other Northmen; he is kind and gentle. Though I met him only briefly many years ago I will always remember him, and I will always wish him well."

Crispus was a little embarrassed and a great deal surprised.

"Mary, I'm sure Mr. Drake was and is a viking amongst vikings: besides, how is it you met him?"

Now Kjartan interrupted; "Crispus, Mary speaks the truth; Miles is kind and gentle, and not like other vikings. He is somewhere between a viking like me and a christian like yourself. For example, this afternoon he would have killed Musa and it would never have crossed his mind to kill Nubila as well. I find this sort of thinking foolish and misguided, but I know the man well enough to be quite certain in what I say."

The recent departures of Musa and Nubila was news to Mary. It is sad to report, but, regarding Nubila, Mary felt Kjartan, rather than Miles of revered memory, had judged things correctly. Indeed, the Musa and Nubila affair softened her towards Northmen. She poured more soup for the three vikings. A man must keep up his strength, and nothing strengthens like good soup.

Crispus returned to his question; "How is it you met Miles Drake, Mary?"

"I was twelve when Miles Drake came to Mendero seeking your father. On the particular morning he arrived I was carrying a milk jar that was too big for me. That giant of a man hurried over and took my jar and walked me home. He gave me a ribbon and was very kind."

Crispus was amazed; "The red one?!"

"Yes, I have always treasured it."

"Well, well', mused Crispus; 'Kjartan, we must have the story of this remarkable man who is balanced halfway between northmen and chrisitan ways."

Kjartan assumed a puzzled expression; "Believe me, Crispus, the story is well worth both the telling and the hearing, but there is a problem."

"Out with it, man; I am here to solve problems."

"While Miles Drake had several Christian characteristics yet he is far too much a viking to tell his story to a man who is wrapped up in a blanket. You must be attired in trousers, wear an honest shirt, and have an axe on your belt. Also there must be a jug of beer, a large jug of beer, and two man-sized mugs."

Crispus looked over at his wife, who did best when not outraged. Mary, in the interest of a good cause, believed sacrifice in order; as causes went they didn't get better than that kind and gentle giant Mr. Drake. Mary nodded slightly.

"Okay, Kjartan, but I am utterly without trousers and shirts. Also, don't you want three large mugs?"

"Two mugs, Crispus. I'm telling the story, and Mendero is neither home nor particularly friendly. Olaf and Ketil have kindly volunteered to do the drinking needed to create a northern atmosphere. As to the trousers and shirt, Olaf was just getting up to fetch them from the wagon. You can borrow my belt and axe."

Five minutes later everything was ready; Crispus was trousered, shirted, and looked very fierce with his axe, Ketil and Olaf were working on northern atmosphere, and the girls were peeking from behind a door to titter at how funny Daddy looked. Mary was a little intrigued; the axe and trousers gave her husband a little je ne sais quois.

Kjartan liked what he saw and began.

CHAPTER 17
Raiding on the Gar Coast

"Yngvar and I were seated by the fire playing a game when Miles walked into our lives; what a surprise! Several hours earlier my sister Asgerd had left the house on some vague errand, and then she was back with this great big fellow who was the same man who had rescued her and Dad in the fall. No ships were sailing yet, so where did Miles come from!? To this day I don't really know, and this creates a puzzle as to the sort of man, or being, we are dealing with. My sister Asgerd has never wavered in how she views Miles; he is from the World Tree, which we call Yggdrasil, sent by Odin, or the alfather, to keep Westmark out of the clutches of King Eirik. Time, as you will see in the course of my story, has only deepened this mystery. Unfortunately Miles himself credits neither the World Tree nor Odin. He says there is a curious system of paths between the Worlds and he happened to stumble into them. He has never talked with Odin; indeed, he considers Odin a children's story we have devised to ward against mystery and ignorance. This has never troubled my sister; she <u>knows</u> what is what.'

"For myself the ensuing weeks, months, and then years have yielded a respected colleague that has very little connection with Odin and his schemes. Evenso, there is no denying the pattern of events would suggest Asgerd is right, and that Miles is the instrument of Odin.'

"When Miles showed up he was dressed in very curious clothes, and his shoes in particular were very strange. On his wrist he had what he called a watch, which divided time into very small pieces. Back in his home everyone had these devices and it allowed them to coordinate and organize events in very exact and detailed ways. We get by nicely without such devices, but his World is far more complicated and it is strictly necessary time be treated this way. But this is not why his watch is important, and it is <u>very</u> important; with his wrist watch and a little thought Miles can tell exactly where he is in our big wide world. That, for a seafaring people, is a wonderful, magical thing. But later.'

"At first Yngvar and I could not understand Miles' speech, and his grasp of our speech was far from perfect. Yet somehow over the next few days this disappeared; he rapidly spoke our tongue as we speak it. I have never seen or heard of such a thing, and it is yet another of the many mysteries that cluster around the man. Miles himself found this very puzzling and was no help in understanding how the language situation worked.'

"When Miles awoke the first morning after arriving it was with many plans and much energy. To us this is a novel attitude. If there has been adequate preparation then winter and very early spring are quite idle; beyond basic chores there is very little to do. I'm afraid our response to winter is to drink more than we should. When Yngvar surfaced that first morning he had barely finished making water before Miles, with Asgerd to help translate, asked Yngvar to train him in our weapons. He wished to begin immediately. Why not me; why shouldn't I train him? Because we all knew that when it came to weapons Yngvar stood alone; neither before nor since have I seen, or even heard his equal. Yngvar must be seen to be believed. Miles was big, strong, and earnest – Yngvar was delighted. By the end of the day Miles had been beaten black and blue and the men were fast friends. Miles soaked up our warcraft the way an old rag attracts water.'

"I need to spend a moment on Miles and Yngvar. These two had a deep and perfected friendship that had something of the older and younger brother.'

"From Yngvar, Miles picked up that sense of rhythm and dance in battle, and involvement that clears away self awareness and fear. Miles never possessed it to the same degree as Yngvar, but he tiptoed up to its margins. Miles, ever and always, has kept the entire battle in view and under control; he could not afford to lose himself in a small corner of the battle. For Miles the battle was there to be won, and while a given battle might stray a bit, he always herded the erring thing home to victory.'

"Yngvar came to have a complete and childlike faith in Miles; he would always back Miles' luck and judgment. I was a bit slower coming to this conclusion, but it was truth; Miles was unbelievably shrewd and lucky. But I am getting far ahead of my story; these conclusions arrived in the fall, after many months of raiding along the southern coast of Gar.'

"These three weeks of early spring, while Yngvar taught bow, axe, and sword, Miles did much work with his watch and taught me how to find what he called longitude."

Kjartan paused to look over his audience; "But Mary is drooping a little and probably wants a few Christian episodes in the life of Miles Drake. I will leave longitude for later, if at all, and come to our third raid, which was far south amongst pure sons of the prophet.'

"We beached our ship amongst sand dunes and walked all night across the desert. We arrived shortly after first light and caught the desert chief with his pants down. In a short sharp fight we killed the chief, his sons, and his warriors. They fought bravely, but little good it did them.'

"Afterwards we were looting the camp and I came across a very large, fine and luxurious tent that housed the chief's wives and concubines. If I remember rightly they call it a harem. I didn't enter, but rather glanced in. This is what I saw; all but one of the chief's women were hiding in one half of the tent. They were literally out of sight, and only some movement under several blankets gave the game away. A single very bold and lovely wench stood in the far side of the opposite end of the tent. What was she doing? She was bending over with her back to me doing something with her slippers. What an utterly charming spectacle! Her slippers were either very complicated or she was playing with them, since the customary moment of getting them secured or adjusted never seemed to arrive. Me? I was in the grip of a terrific lust and quite forgot gold or just about anything else. I was just about to enter the tent and do the right thing by the wench when out of the corner of my eye I noticed a large man to my right and ahead of me. It was Miles, and he too was spellbound and transfixed, I quietly stepped back. He never saw me. At last, when it was clear to the meanest thinker that she'd had more than enough time to adjust her slippers Miles went over and started helping her out of her pants. Seemed reasonable to me. This precipitated much howling and crying, and tantrums.'

"Miles made a hasty retreat, perhaps thinking at best to stick to gold. And then, Fatima, for such was her name, once again stooped over and resumed playing with her slippers. Her spell rapidly reasserted itself. My, my, what a juicy morsel!'

"Miles studied the situation thoughtfully then reached for a silk curtain which he tore into a large piece and a smaller piece. He returned to the girl and very loosely and gently tied the smaller piece over her mouth and behind her head. The larger piece he used to 'secure' her hands; the left hand was 'tied' to the right with a four foot thread of silk. This important formality out of the way Miles once again visited her pants; there were no further problems; indeed, I saw signs of enthusiasm."

Kjartan sat back pleased with his tale; "If that isn't gentle, kind, and Christian, then I don't know what the word means!"

Ketil knew enough of the language to give a great laugh and drank a hearty toast to a wily fellow viking. Olaf didn't understand the story at all, but he'd had a bit to drink and was in a mood to laugh so he roared along with Ketil.

Mary understood the story, made out a modicum of thoughtful Christianity, but the dominant feeling was outrage at Fatima, Kjartan, Miles, and the situation generally. It struck her as an odd illustration of active Christianity.

Crispus tried hard to follow Mary's lead, to maintain his dignity and an air of gentle, Christian, censure, but he finally exploded and joined Ketil and Olaf.

When things had quieted down Kjartan resumed his tale; "Mary, I get the feeling you are not convinced of Miles' Christian virtues and tendencies; this is okay, but please suspend judgment till you hear more. I will track Fatima through her viking sojourn, and when we get her safely back to harem life then you may judge.'

"The next step is a bit bumpy, and may even be a little short on Christian virtue. Miles and his companions left the chieftains oasis in shambles and marched all night to a moderate size coastal town. At first light they attacked the town from the desert side, which proved both unexpected and successful. Evenso we lost two of our companions. The ship was brought to the town and there were was much plunder to load. While this was happening Miles and two other men once again crossed the desert and recaptured Fatima and several other girls and young men who would sell well on the slave market.'

"Gilli, a buddy of mine, was on this second expedition, and he tells me Fatima attributed Miles' return to her charm and personal qualities; she seemed pleased, doubly so in that what remained of the camp was not exactly the lap of luxury.'

"Our group now sailed back up the coast, and in the city of Almedo we sold many slaves – but not Fatima. Why not?! She didn't like any of the men who made an offer, and Miles, replete with Christianity, would not force her. This is not your average viking, who <u>never</u> mixes slave wishes with business.'

"Now, go back a bit and remember how Miles soaked up our language in two days time; well, the same thing happened with Fatima. A week after capturing her Miles and Fatima were chatting away like natives. Miles learned much concerning the customs and habits of her people, and this proved wonderfully useful; Miles could pass himself off as a desert chief.'

"We now come to the richest and best raid ever; this includes my own sixteen year experience and that of anyone I know or have heard of."

CHAPTER 18
Pyrena

"AND SO WE COME to the saga of Pyrena, on the Toltaba peninsula."

Kjartan paused, and before he could catch a breath Crispus, for the first time, interrupted.

"Kjartan, if you are about to tell us how you raided Pyrena then you will be indulging in wthat we Christians call a 'tall' tale. Pyrena has never been raided. It is true that fifteen or so years back the Northmen attacked Pyrena, but it proved both wasteful and foolish and many died. Mind you, I enjoy a 'tall' tale, but a 'tall' tale is what you are about to spin."

"Crispus, you are too trusting. My tale is of only average height, and yes, we did raid Pyrena; the mighty, the beautiful Pyrena has been despoiled. Yet at the same time it wasn't; however, it is certain every man on our expedition walked away not just wealthy, but very wealthy.

"Late in the summer we were sailing near the Toltaba peninsula and found the area swarming with long boats. Our colleagues had been lucky in a battle north of Pyrena; instead of losing and being chased away they had destroyed the only field army anywhere near Pyrena. Now, or so the

story went, Pyrena was a ripe plum waiting to be plucked..
We sailed to Pyrena to investigate.

"As we all know, Pyrena is a large fortified city on a peninsula. The southern side of the city features a large moat and a massive wall. This side is impregnable and no time on effort is ever wasted on it. The eastern side stands against cliffs and is yet another 'no go.' The city has grown rapidly both west and north and has not been stable enough to put up truly impregnable defenses. The viking colleagues had already launched an attack on the northern defenses. This had failed, yet the general feeling was it had been a near thing. Another larger attack was planned, and its success seemed certain.

Miles looked things over and decided attacking Pyrena as planned was a waste of time; we possessed no siege equipment and very little organization, and all we were likely to gain would be early deaths. Our fellow Vikings had enjoyed too much easy success and had come to see themselves as giants and gods. However, the planned attack would provide a perfect diversion for a less ambitious project.

Over rugged mountains and the cliffs near the city there were still intact trade routes; the northmen hadn't bothered closing these since they expected quick success with a direct attack.

Miles posed as a desert trader with Fatima as his chief wife. Three other Vikings posed as desert warriors and servants. This party 'borrowed' a small caravan and entered the city. Their load of dates made a handsome profit. On the night of the great and final third assault (the second had also failed) Miles and his party opened the gate and lowered the drawbridge on the 'impregnable' side. Our party quickly entered and made a very profitable and select raid on this large city. We were far too few to manage a general pillage and sac, but evenso eventually we were noticed, and not with favor.

It was challenging getting ourselves and our plunder out of the city, but Miles had learned the city lay out quite well and guided our party to a secluded portion of the wall, from which we descended by ropes to small boats. This would never have succeeded were not all attention and every able-bodied man focused on the northern defenses where a truly desperate assault nearly succeeded; it is always a 'near' thing when we northmen fail."

Kjartan paused, and smiled at Crispus; "So, friend Crispus, while Pyrena has never sustained a true sac and pillage, it has certainly been raided.

I have been very sparing of detail in the Pyrena raid, though the details are both thrilling and interesting, since Mary hungers for Christian incidents in the life of Miles Drake. The Pyrena raid has not one, but two exceptionally Christian moments, and they are coming soon, but the final moments of the raid, as we approached our ships, are very interesting and important in foreshadowing what was to come.

Unexpected archers, or ambushes with archers, is the very best way to kill many and lose few. Miles Drake has revolutionized how small battles amongst Vikings are fought. Now, if at all possible, one tries for an ambush featuring the bow. Before Miles, the bow was very much to the side in our thought.

Miles thought it overwhelmingly likely we would be approaching our boats under heavy attack by a superior force; we could lose everything, lives included, just as we thought we were home. With this in mind, though our war party was small, Miles kept twenty of our best archers back at the boats. These twenty men, ten on each side, were hidden on the flanks to the approach to our boats.

Miles fears were entirely justified; as we approached the ships we were under heavy attack by a party several times our size. The enemy beleaguering us had their attention riveted on the boats; the flanking archers destroyed them, and we got away with our lives and our plunder.

CHAPTER 19
Kalil Has a Bad Day

THE OLDER, SOUTHERN PORTION of Pyrena near the old wall was justly famous for its quaint charm. The mosque, in particular, was much appreciated by the knowledgeable and was perhaps the finest instance of the architecture of two centuries past. Older writers fell into rhapsodies when viewing the Tifero mosque by moonlight, and this particular evening featured an unusually fine full moon. So why, as he walked by the mosque, was Kalil in such a foul mood?!

Kalil's heart and soul were with his comrades at the northern defenses, where they were desperately fighting to save the city. It galled him to the very core to be sidelined to street patrol when great events were afoot; how could such a thing happen to a man generally esteemed as the finest warrior in or around Pyrena?

He suspected his commanding officer, Mustafa Aljabi, was still bitter about the girl; that was over a month ago, and Kalil was already a little vague on her name. It was some peculiar Christian name; Katrina? No, but never mind! No woman was worth such a price! Momentary indulgence of desire at the price of glory?! Fah!

Kalil stalked past the mosque and towards the old gate, his mood, if it were possible, souring even more. As he approached the gate he gradually became aware something odd was going on; there was a guard lying motionless on the ground and standing over him was a large man. Kalil looked more closely and recognized the big desert sheik he had noticed yesterday in the marketplace. Quick as thought his scimitar was out and he hurried forward.

"My brother, why is the guard down? Make haste in answering!"

The big sheik stayed quite calm; "I too, in my way, am a soldier, and I was asking that very question; I smell something very fishy. Perhaps the man behind you knows the answer."

Kalil was startled, and spun on his heel. The next thing he knew he was waking on the ground and had a most unpleasant headache. He tried to move, but found his arms and legs bound. He tried to yell, but found a gag in his mouth. What was this?!

Twenty minutes later, with badly chafed and bleeding wrists, Kalil had managed to free his hands. Soon his mouth and legs joined his busy hands. Kalil staggered out of a quiet guard room to find the drawbridge down and the gate open. He noticed several more dead guards. The city was in mortal danger! Kalil sounded the large warning gong. The crashing sound split his head; by the prophet's beard, that hurt!

An hour later, after several hair breadth escapes, Kalil had managed to get to the northern half of Pyrena. He organized a platoon of stray soldiers and citizens and headed back towards the southern gate. The Northmen were operating in a number of small bands, several of which he'd barely escaped, and their total strength was probably less than one hundred fifty. He would destroy them one by one. There were several savage skirmishes but nothing conclusive; the godless Northmen were like quicksilver.

Near the gate resistance slackened, but Kalil knew his group had inflicted hardly any casualties; where were they? Dawn was breaking so he climbed to the top of the gate to see how things were. With height and a bit of light Kalil saw an impossible thing; somehow, in the confusion the Northmen had gotten out of the city and were grouping on the main road due south. Kalil knew the southern coast well and their ship would almost certainly be at Geder's Cove. With cavalry support not one of the infidels would escape! As he was hurrying to signal for cavalry and extra troops he brushed by a large man on the stairs. The man detained him, and Kalil turned to shove him aside; as he turned he recognized the big desert sheik! The next thing he was once again on the ground and had a yet greater headache. Kalil tried to move, but found his arms and legs bound. He tried to yell, but found a gag in his mouth. Beard of the prophet!!!

By mid morning the tangle of events had resolved into a very clear and very sad tale. Kalil's ragamuffin force had been joined by a unit of regular troops, and the combined 'Punish the Infidel' team had hurried to Geder's Cove. Very few of these righteous warriors ever returned to Pyrena; they had been ambushed by archers.

And Kalil?! What luck! Hardly; Kalil was bitter for the remainder of his life, which ended in a battle two years later. The Northman, that pseudosheik, had rated him as below knife grade, not worthy of even death. The shame was more than he could bear and Kalil sought death like a friend; six northmen and two years later he met with success. Kalil's interpretative schemes had no niche for these unfortunate acts of kindness.

Kjartan finished his story and turned to Mary; "These silly acts of Christian kindness irritated me then and irritate me now. There was no time for roping the man up like a calf, and there was the chance he would free himself and trigger events that harmed us. For all I know the man may yet by my death. Stupid, dangerous bother is what it was and is. But Miles insisted, said the soldier looked like a fine man, that he needed a break. In fact he got two breaks."

Kjartan snorted. Mary was charmed and loved and admired Miles Drake more than ever.

CHAPTER 20
Summer's End

"THE PYRENA RAID WAS quite late in the summer and left us wealthy; many of the men wished to go home. Our party had one hundred eighteen men distributed between three boats, which offered us a bit of latitude. The plunder was divided and two boats and eighty-three men went home. The returning party ran into a terrible storm and one boat and thirty-eight men were lost.

Yngvar, myself, Miles, and thirty-two remained on the Gar coast. Our boat, the Sea Serpent, was not roomy but was very fast. We no longer had the men to mount big raids, but we knocked off two small towns and picked up six more slaves. At this point the Serpent was bursting at the seams and was no longer safe in a gale. We headed for a southern slave market. We sold eight slaves at good prices. Fatima, after hearing about long houses and the winters in Westmark, decided the far north was not for her; evenso she remained fussy and refused three offers. Fatima began to pose a problem; she wouldn't settle down in anyone's harem, but she refused to come with us. Of course the problem was only as real as Miles allowed.

Then, the day before we planned to leave Mylon, we got a break; in the marketplace Fatima caught sight of

Abdul Alibaba. This skeiklet didn't strike me as much of a catch, but what do I know? Abdul had been a buddy of her recently departed husband and apparently he and Fatima had cuckolded the old boy and enjoyed a rare old time; Abdul, I was given to understand, was an artiste and had great style and energy. Unfortunately Abdul wasn't looking for more wives or slaves; he was in Mylon to sell his dates. This didn't daunt Fatima even a little. She organized a little charade that worked like a charm.

THE MORNING WAS WEARING towards noon and sweat was trickling down his back. The heat and bother were beginning to get on his nerves; exactly how much longer would this son of a camel haggle with him? It didn't' help that he needed to take a leak. Abdul heard shouting and running coming his way. Now what?! Two of those northern savages were chasing an attractive but bedraggled young woman. The young girl's clothes had been half torn off and Abdul liked what he saw. Then, with a despairing cry the unfortunate creature turned her tear stained face towards him and, …..sweet prophet! It's Fatima!

Fatima, exhausted, collapsed at his feet and embraced his knees.

"Shield of the helpless and Scourge of the wicked, help me!"

"Fatima, it's me, Abdul!"

Fatima burst into tears, and said very simply; "Then I am safe at last."

Abdul toyed with turning his five husky warriors loose on the Northmen, but there was at least one other Northman in the vicinity, and he was a big one. These savages could be very dangerous; perhaps it were best to see what dharmas could do.

The big Northman raised his hand and spoke in an authoritative tone with the young Northman. The young Northman seemed to recognize his authority and answered him respectfully. The big Northman then turned to the kneeling Fatima.

"Woman, this man says he owns you, that you were captured south of here; is this true?"

Balls of the prophet! The savage could speak like a human?!

Having an interpreter handy was a gift from Alah. After much dickering and many, many dharmas 'The Shield of the Helpless' took Fatima home with him. He never regretted it.

KJARTAN PAUSED TO CHUCKLE at the memory; "That Fatima was something! We all missed her and the boat seemed kind of empty after she left. I remember the last scene very well since myself and Rory played the part of the pursuing young Northmen. Miles had always been on the generous side of fair and he shared with us the prince's ransom he exacted form Lover Boy.

Kjartan turned to Mary.

"By the way, Mary, there's yet more Christianity in Miles' first summer. Before that last charade Miles sewed a large emerald into Fatima's clothes. One of the 'tears', the one over her upper thigh, was sewn back to contain the emerald."

"Now, let's see; where did we go next?"

Crispus knew posturing when he saw it; "Try Mendero. You headed further south."

"Ah, yes; so we did. Throughout the second half of the summer Miles had been asking knowledgeable people who the best weapons smith might be; seven out of ten pointed to your father.

After the first few fights Miles had decided that our weapons were not very good. What hid this from us was our training and the hidden conventions governing how we use our weapons."

Kjartan paused; "Mary, this probably won't interest you but your husband might like to hear why the weapons he makes are as they are. With your blessing may I make this brief excursion into shop talk?"

Mary laughed; "Kjartan, don't take this the wrong way and get offended, but though you don't see it, you too are a little more Christian than your average Northman; that foolish, that silly Miles Drake has rubbed off on you."

Kjartan smiled and feigned outrage; "Never! Those are fighting words!"

"Sorry, Kjartan, but the average Northman doesn't clear it with the wife to talk shop with the husband. But consider yourself cleared; and I'm going to bed."

Kjartan protested; "Mary, there is another instance of Christianity; Miles Drake makes like a Christian one more time."

Mary, getting to her feet, said; "I know; I already told it to you. A little while ago you had no idea Miles Drake had carried my milk jug and given me a red ribbon."

Kjartan laughed; "You're too smart; well, off to bed with you."

Chapter 21
Mendero At Night

After Mary left, Kjartan got to his feet and moved the beer jug.

"We are far from our own hall and I half expect some strongman buddy of Musa's to drop in; it's what I would do were I in their shoes. Our staying with Crispus is a rare opportunity for a strongman to assert his authority and exact vengeance; all at low risk due to presumed surprise. I may be wrong on this, but I wouldn't bet on it."

Ketil and Olaf looked longingly at the distant beer jug.

"Cheer up, lads; we'll make merry some other night. Besides, you should stay awake for my story; what's coming is good."

These remarks had been in norse and Crispus was left in blissful ignorance. Kjartan now turned back to Crispus and the tongue of southern Gar.

"Imagine two men coming at each other with sword and shield. They stand back at a distance where a sword swing is comfortable and effective. They then proceed to deliver and block these blows. A rhythm develops and the dance ends when someone makes a mistake or guesses wrong. Now suppose we take some husky lad, arm him with your small rounded shield and your small modified axe. Further suppose this man refuses to dance in the time honored manner but rather rushes forward to stand against his opponent's shield. Once he moves in closer than the conventional distance the enemy's shield protects our man; he's no longer in effective range. The enemy holds the shield on his forearm, which puts him in perfect range for a small axe blow."

Crispus chuckled; "The small hook on my shield catches the upper edge of his shield, and our man pulls the opponent's shield lower and kills him."

"You're a natural, Crispus. Now, let's suppose the enemy is very adroit and somehow manages to parry the blow, which at such a short distance is a very difficult and awkward thing to do. Then, when the blocking sword meets the downward swing of the axe our man supplies a sharp forward thrust to the axe and the short spearlike blade on the front of the axe does its work. This blow may not be mortal, but if not then what follows will be very unequal."

Kjartan paused; "Not only are Miles' weapons effective, but notice how quickly it is effective; no time is wasted on the conventional dance. Also notice the large round handguard on the axe; not only does it protect the hand but under desperate circumstances it doubles as a small shield to parry a sword blow. You should have seen Miles use it as a second shield! Your shield is small, rounded so as not to shatter or buckle under heavy blows, and has a small spikelike blade at its center, just above the hook. Miles frequently would parry with his axe and strike with his shield. This maneuver is greatly helped by your shield being held in the hand rather than secured to the forearm. When a man is familiar with these weapons both hands may serve as combined shield and weapon.

Against conventional weapons the new weapons are very effective; it is almost like reaping wheat. When new weapons meet new weapons the contest is much faster than conventional fights, largely due to the sudden conversions of a downward swing to a thrust. The use of the shield as a thrusting weapon also speeds and complicates the fight. Conclusions tend to come much faster than with conventional weapons.

Your weapons are the lightest, strongest, and the best. We probably should charge more than the already exorbitant price we ask. Raiding is exciting and lucrative; there is no better way for a young man to pass the summer. However, as middle age creeps up the life of an arms merchant looks better and better; the profits are nearly as great, the peril of the occasional Musa is pretty minimal, and it is a fine thing to meet old friends."

Kjartan paused; "Now, to get back to our story; the Sea Serpent was one of the last boats to leave the southern Gar area, but, with fall advancing even we were sailing north and west for home.

"The weather was fine with a favoring wind, and the mood on the Sea Serpent could not have been better; all going well we would be arriving home in health and wealth. I, Kjartan Njalson, in particular, was looking forward to the winter months with plans of learning more of Miles' world, and especially navigation. In truth the evening fire would be a better place with Miles there. So it came as a rather rude bump to learn Miles did not plan on returning with us; Miles intended to winter in Norland."

Kjartan was about to proceed with his story when there was the rapidly approaching sound of running feet, then a breathless Silas burst through the door and in an excited gasp announced the imminent arrival of bad men with swords.

Silas' arrival had told the tale and Kjartan, quick as thought, retrieved his axe from Crispus' belt. In two strides he reached the door. A burly man was pushing the door open as Kjartan pulled the door open. This unbalanced the intruder and before the man knew what was happening Kjartan had brained him. As the man was falling Kjartan placed his right foot on the thug's chest and gave a powerful push; the body was flung back through the door and tripped a closely following second intruder. Kjartan slammed the door and held it closed.

He turned urgently to Crispus; "Quickly secure the rear door; they may already be there, so be careful."

Then to Ketil; "Ketil, have your bow ready when I open this door! Olaf, attend the rear door with Crispus!"

Kjartan was a powerful man and after a brief effort to pull the door open the invaders resorted to axes. By the third blow the door was in bad shape and on borrowed time, but Ketil had strung his bow and had an arrow notched. Kjartan flung the door open and stepped aside as Ketil put an arrow through the axe wielder. As heavy blows started on the rear door Kjartan lunged through the door and came within a whisker of being skewered by a sword thrust. Kjartan parried the thrust with the large circular hand guard and without drawing back for an axe swing thrust home with the blade in front of the axe. As this third intruder went down Kjartan leaped to the side of the door and Ketil put a second arrow through a fourth man.

Ketil put down his bow and grabbed his axe. He and Kjartan advanced on the three remaining thugs, who lost their nerve and turned to flee. These men hadn't run five strides before four armed men emerged from the shadows and killed them.

Kjartan and Ketil missed this last bit of drama since they were running as hard as they could towards sounds of violent activity at Crispus' back door. They ran up behind four armed men and had drawn back their axes for battle when Olaf shouted; "No! These men are with us!"

Sandaman, like Kjartan, had sensed trouble; he too would have made a vengeance raid had Musa been a friend. It was the Sandaman's firm conviction there were too many strongmen around so he set a trap hoping to eliminate yet another strongman, most likely Yousef, a good friend of Musa's. Yousef had taken Ketil's second arrow.

Sandaman's plan had worked, after a fashion. Yousef and eleven of his thugs were gone. Evenso, Kjartan and his party would have died but for Kjartan's quick response. The complication was Silas. Had this alert lad been in bed sleeping, Yousef and his thugs would have quietly approached the front and back doors – and been ambushed by Sandaman's men. As it was Silas spotted the bad guys and then most conspicuously went to alert his friends. Yousef was forced to run after him if there was to be any hope of surprise. Sandaman had arrived a little late, but had killed the three departing front door thugs; at the back door his men had borne the brunt of the battle and killed four thugs.

The Christian strongman had a fine evening of it. Flushed with success Sandaman went from Crispus home to eliminate yet another rival; this was wonderfully successful and he didn't lose a single man. He had picked up Kjartan's breezy, offhand way with strongmen. As he went to bed with his rescued lady fair Sandaman had forged a strong and important viking link and rubbed out three rivals. Sandaman knew then and always that God was a Christian.

CHAPTER 22
The Rise of Sandaman and Mendero

OVER THE NEXT TEN years Sandaman came to be the only strongman in the Mendero area. In the past 'strength' in strongmen was a measure of scope for extortion and coercion, whereas with Sandaman it was a measure of control, a control bolstering and affirming law and custom.

Kjartan proved wrong regarding Sandaman and Nur. Theirs was a union of mutual affection and respect, and five years and two children later they were married – actually, married twice; there was both a Christian ceremony and a Moslem ceremony.

Unlike most dominions in Gar there was a single law applying to both Moslems and Christians and all were treated equally. The rule of law promotes commerce and trade, which independently strengthens religious toleration. In consequence Mendero did well and grew in strength and influence.

There was a further factor favoring growth and tolerance – the connection with the Norse. The Norse promoted growth by raiding surrounding Moslem towns and communities till these unfortunate people, desperate to escape viking rapine, begged Sandaman to take them in and protect them.

Sandaman would incorporate them into a greater Mendero, and the predatory vikings would move their operations more peripherally.

Northmen more and more treated Mendero as a friendly base of operations. Rather than passing winter in a frozen stupor up North, the vikings began wintering in Mendero, and some settled in Mendero and farmed Sandaman's new 'protecorates.' The Norse, especially wintering vikings, ultimately relaxed Moslem laws against liquor, and both Christian and Moslem leaders came to turn a blind eye on 'professional' women. The Vikings brought much wealth to Mendero.

Saldana was a large Moslem coastal kingdom north and west of Mendero. This caliphate was ruled by Kahlid al Batuta, a man of peace and reason, but a man who stood squarely in the way of Sandaman's ambitions.

The norse had been raiding the coastal regions of Saldana for some time, but the past two years these raids were more frequent and penetrated deeper; they were well past mere irritation and demanded a strong response. Kahlid made his preparations and the next year when an unusually large viking war party raided deep into Saldana he made a sudden attack. Kahlid did not succeed in destroying the norse, but, while maintaining good order, the norse withdrew as fast as they could towards their ships. As the northmen approached their ships they seemed on the edge of disintegration; Kahlid ordered a final all-out assault. This 'coup de grace' proved an ambush and the Kahlid's army was placed in a lethal crossfire of archers; this was followed by an overwhelming Mendero cavalry charge, which destroyed the Saldana army and left the wily Sandaman in control of Saldana.

Kjartan planned the whole business and organized and led the viking component of the operation while Sandaman organized and led the Mendero component.

Vikings do nothing for free and Kjartan's war band had been both large and select, cream of the cream. Kjartan had been paid half the agreed sum before the raid and was now back in Mendero to collect the remainder. He had spent the night with his old friend Crispus, and a jolly evening it had been. There was a light rain as Kjartan and five sturdy lads set out to walk to Sandaman's palace; despite the rain Kjartan was in a good mood. In the recent battle it had been a close thing and the norse had walked the very margin of disaster. Kjartan's sons Eyvind and Hall had both been with him, both had survived without significant injury, and, best of all, both had distinguished themselves. Eyvind, the second son, had performed a stunt more often sung over than actually seen; he had caught a javelin flung at him, spun on his heel, then flung the javelin so as to kill its source. Eyvind had been on the beleaguered left flank, the hardest pressed point of the battle; the Norse had held, but one man in two had either died or been badly injured.

Hall had been an archer on the right flank. After using every arrow, and some twice, Hall and his fellows had grabbed up their axes and attacked Kahlid's left flank. This attack was sufficiently energetic to take pressure from the viking's hard pressed left flank, and the Norse had managed to survive till Sandaman's cavalry arrived.

So it was that Kjartan was pleased with his norse colleagues and with his sons in particular.

Two years back Sandaman had began living in a palace, a pretty grand one at that, and when meeting the public Sandaman had taken to putting on quite a show; much ceremony and hoopla. The norse in general and Kjartan in particular were impatient with this sort of thing, and as

Kjartan approached the center of government i.e. Sandaman, his good mood began eroding. Fortunately Sandaman saw him from afar and, knowing well the Norse's view of Moslem court etiquette, he quickly laid his dignity to one side and hurried to meet his old friend. The greeting was genuinely cordial and Kjartan rapidly thawed back to his good mood. The five sturdy lads, which included a trusted steward, were dispatched to count and load silver that was owing.

Sandaman and Kjartan were left to themselves, and welcomed it.

"I heard about Hall and Eyvind, Kjartan. You must be very proud."

"They did well enough; and both are alive. On the left flank we lost one man in two.'

'Did your agents pick up any of Kahlid's sons or brothers fleeing the capitol?"

" I received word early this morning; we have picked up two sons and a brother. These were heading north. As of yet no word from the east. Being ready to collect brothers and sons before the battle was fought was excellent advice, Kjartan. I sincerely hope the well of your wisdom has not run dry. My neighbors will now view me as a dangerous menace and may ally against me."

Kjartan was surprised; "Has anything changed? We've been over this, and your situation is pretty good."

Sandaman smiled; "No, things are about the same. The problem is I can see how things could unravel, and if I can so can others. If Rota organized a coalition with Balba and Satago they could crush us. There are many reasons they might proceed with this.

None of this disturbed Kjartan; "As of this moment you are probably right, Sandaman. However, in the next month norse raids on their coastal towns and lower river towns will capture their attention and military resources. Their plates will be full. Also I can't help but think your embassy to Latcha will be successful. Latcha and Balba have an enmity going back centuries; Latcha will welcome an alliance against Balba. If and when Balba moves against you they will have Latcha at their flank. Ultimately you and Latcha will divide Balba, leaving a small central strip as buffer state. Latcha will find the alliance and plan irresistible."

Kjartan paused, and smiled; "However, suppose our raids on the coast are not as distracting as we hope, suppose Latcha, for reasons of its own, doesn't ally with us, and suppose a coalition army is on our northern frontier."

Kjartan grew thoughtful; "And that is supposing a lot, since long before a combined army arrived on your border you would have attacked single forming armies. Waiting and watching while a coalition army was developing would be stupid, and you, Sandaman, are a clever man.'

'But back to it; if a combined army were on your northern frontier we would fight and win.'

'Sandaman, old friend, you'd better know this is true right down to your bones. Knowledge and conviction of this sort percolate into those around you and shape events. Doubt and fear also percolate and shape, but we won't like what shapes."

"This is all true, Kjartan, but it is balanced, perhaps overbalanced, by the perils of wishful thinking."

"Such thinking is for very late events, when the shape of things has hard edges; at the moment the shape of things is like a young child, and your convictions are part of the shaping."

"You are a remarkable man, Sandaman, and you need to hear the story of another remarkable man; I will tell you the story of godi Miles Drake. All you will need is hidden in his story. Yours is the task of building a larger and stronger Mendero, while his was the task of taking kingship from a very strongman and giving it to another more suitable man. The strongman was Eirik, former king of Norland, which is the center and home of we northmen. The more suitable man is Bodvar Einarson, the current king of Norland. Miles Drake arrived in Westmark, my home, with the shirt on his back and the decision to bring down Eirik. This decision had its roots in Eirik's recent effort to kill my sister and father. Eirik wanted my father removed as a step towards controlling Westmark.

CHAPTER 23
Gretil the Fat

"Miles Drake arrived in Westmark in early spring and went raiding with me and Yngvar, my foster brother."

Sandaman interrupted; "This is the first I have heard of a foster brother; was this Yngvar a good sort?"

"Sandaman, they don't come better; Yngvar was the greatest warrior and finest viking of us all. I have never seen his equal."

"Where is he?"

"The Valkyrie collected him twenty years back. His death was even greater than his life."

"Your people send their sons to be raised by a respected friend; how does this work?"

"It usually works well; the foster brother and son frequently come to <u>be</u> brothers and sons. The path to manhood is straighter and truer when the indulgences of childhood are removed at age seven or eight. Foster sons are treated well and fairly, but not as their mother's or aunt's darling; this might happen in their own homes. It is a good custom, and works well. It also ties families more closely to each other.

"Your interest is flattering, Sandaman, but it is well to the side of my story."

"You are right, carry on."

"During the long summer of raiding Miles Drake spoke with many men from Norland and he always directed the talk to the godi and leading men of Norland; how they viewed each other, and how they viewed King Eirik.

"Miles was quick, and before long realized the key to events was Gretil the Fat.

"Gretil is in north-central Norland and is very wealthy, very successful, very shrewd, and most importantly for Miles Drake, is revered by his peers for his shrewdness and judgment. In Norland when a thing of consequence is being considered the first order of business is to see how Gretil the Fat views matters."

Sandaman chuckled; "In Gar we never refer to an oracle as so and so the fat; only you norse tag all and sundry, great and small, with frank descriptive and evaluative tags. I have met Thorkel All Thumbs, Gudrun the Chatterbox, and Gilli the Undecided; now I meet godi Gretil the Fat. Is the man truly fat?"

"There is enough of Gretil to make three ordinary men. It was not always so; in youth Gretil was an energetic and very respected viking. Everyone, even grandmothers, wanted to go raiding with him. Whatever Gretil turned his hand to succeeded brilliantly. Gretil, every ounce of him, is successful; and my people worship success."

Kjartan paused, considering how to proceed, when an odd thought came to him; "Sandaman, I just now, for the first time in years remembered an odd occurrence. Miles Drake arrived in Norland late in the fall. The spring of that same year Eirik had traveled to Gretil the Fat's farm to seek Gretil's advice on whether to go after Westmark and neighboring islands.

Gretil advised him to leave Westmark alone. In fact, Gretil advised Eirik leave well enough alone, and should he proceed bad things would follow.

"No one else in Norland would have spoken so bluntly to this particular King. Eirik hadn't really wanted his advice; he wanted Gretil's agreement, the prestige this would give his project. Eirik left quickly, and in anger. Gretil shrugged his shoulders and turned his attention to other things; he stood in awe of neither man nor god, and certainly not Eirik."

Sandaman was intrigued, and interrupted; "I wonder why Gretil advised against the project? From what I have heard the timber of Westmark is very rich and her strength and unity are but small. Does Gretil have friends or kinsman in Westmark?"

"No, he doesn't; his advice to Eirik was frank and disinterested.

"Sandaman, you should hear the story of Miles Drake; it will educate and encourage you. With this in mind you need to stop leading us off on sidepaths. Unfortunately your question is a very revealing one; if I explain it well enough it will prove a window into how we norse think. So, I will answer, but then, put your attention on my story.

"A man with a habit of success is said to be lucky. You and fellow Christians view luck very differently; your luck is a particular configuration of events that by chance favors a man. We turn this around and view luck as an intrinsic trait of some men; a man with luck will find events shaping so as to favor him."

Sandaman began to interrupt, but Kjartan anticipated this; "Now, now, I know as well as you it is not a question of either one of us being wrong or right; we are both right, and we are both wrong. There are many instances of both kinds of luck; the trick is to know in a given instance which kind of luck is playing. Gretil the Fat had an excellent nose for judging whether an event was entirely chance, straw in variable breezes, or whether the event was straw revealing a steady current."

Once again Sandaman was about to cut in, and yet again Kjartan anticipated him; "Yes, yes; what were the events requiring such nice judgment?!"

"Gretil kept his ear to the ground and had many friends; what a young viking told another young viking had a way of coming to Gretil's notice. Six years earlier three veteran berserkers had been dispatched by Ragnhild to kill my sister. Ragnhild is Eirik's volva, or, as you would say, witch. This should have succeeded; instead all three men were killed by my foster brother Yngvar. These men had been under Odin's shield; steel could not bite them.'

"Then five years later Eirik sent three trusted berserkers to kill my father. This too should have worked, and didn't; all three men, once again under Odin's shield, died. My father and sister were wounded, but survived.

Gretil smelled Viking luck at work and warned Eirik away. Eirik's luck was either ebbing or overmatched, and in either event he was well advised to keep away from events where the luck of others was strongly involved; especially in Westmark.

"And Gretil the Fat, as ever, judged the situation correctly; Eirik didn't begin to have enough luck to contend with Miles Drake. Comparing the luck of Miles Drake with the luck of other men is like comparing mountains with a bump in the road.

"This man is so very lucky?!"; Sandaman was politely skeptical.

Kjartan laughed at Sandaman's simplicity; "Events shape around Miles Drake the way your clothes shape to your body. The luck of Miles Drake is almost more than luck, it is as though Odin walked beside him. Your Christian God walked with his son the white Christ and gave him visions and the odd miracle. The Allfather walks with Miles and gives him luck."

Kjartan gave Sandaman a quizzical look; "If you could have either visions and the stray miracle, or luck; which would you take?

Sandaman hesitated, and Kjartan continued; "I'll give you a hint; visions seldom do a man any good. But not to worry. Sandaman; I think you have more luck than you know.'

"Now back to my story. As it happened Miles' ship included Gretil the Fat's favorite nephew and foster son, Bolli Halldorson. Bolli was a good viking, and a pleasant companion; he is held in high regard by all who know him. Miles liked Bolli from the first and the two men got on very well.'

"That fall Miles wintered in Norland, which disappointed me since both Yngvar and I had expected he would winter with my father in Westmark. But of course Miles had his reasons; he went with Bolli and spent several weeks at Gretil the Fat's hall. Bolli liked and admired Miles and was quick to share these thoughts with his uncle and foster father. But independently of this Gretil liked Miles and from the start smelled exceptional confidence, know-how, and luck.

Gretil held a greater share of the trade with the Saami in the far arctic north than any other Norseman; more whale bone, walrus tusk, fox and seal skins came through his hands than the rest combined. This trade was the single biggest source of his wealth, and Eirik knew this, as did all others. Eirik coveted this far northern trade and Gretil would need to be very sleepy indeed if he didn't realize Eirik meant to have it, and in the not too distant future. Why bother being King if you can't have the lion's share of a lucrative trade pattern? This would be true of any king, and doubly so for Eirik. Gretil was far from sleepy.

Miles knew how things were, and knew how to approach Gretil. Three weeks after arriving, and two days before moving on to Steinthor's Hall and farm Miles went out to the barn with Gretil where they would not be overheard. He explained to Gretil he would be pulling Eirik down. He needed two things from Gretil. First, he wanted two or three men who would be good replacements for Eirik. These should be men who were strong enough and wise enough to be king and serve Norland well; they also should be the sort of men who would leave the northern trade alone. Gretil recommended Bodvar and Knut; especially Knut.'

"The second point was vital; for the next two summers and falls Gretil needed to manufacture some peril to his arctic trade so as tie up as many of his men, and those of close friends, as possible. In the early stages of his war with Eirik Miles needed these men on the sidelines. Later, when Gretil could see clearly how the wind was blowing, he might wish to lend a hand; Miles neither expected nor wanted the help of a man who had much to lose; not until that man had things clearly in view.'

Kjartan chuckled; "Miles knows us well. He might seek help and want early support, but he would not get it; much better to be conspicuously confident and reasonable. Were help to arrive it would arrive earlier on this approach than being needy and demanding when this made no sense.'

"Now back to the barn. Gretil smiled and said it was curious Miles should mention it, but there had been recent incursions into his Saami's hunting and trapping patterns by a rival tribe situated yet further north and east. He had been planning an excursion into the far north. Miles and Gretil understood each other.

CHAPTER 24
The Fall of King Eirik

MILES, AFTER LEAVING GRETIL, visited many jarls and halls. As a rule he spoke little and listened much. Occasionally, when he deemed it safe and useful, he ventured to suggest that should trouble arise the wise man would stay out of it as long as possible. He visited the halls of Knut and Bodvar. Both were sensible, decent men, but Bodvar impressed him more.

Kjartan paused and chuckled; "You will like this, Sandaman. When Miles finally got Bodvar out for the chat in the barn he discovered Bodvar had lured him to the barn! Bodvar had sized Miles up and decided Miles was the man to bring Eirik down! He suggested Miles become king and promised to support him; he put his life and fortune on the line right up front – most foolish, but wonderfully encouraging. After hearing him out a surprised Miles assured Bodvar that yes, he would be bringing Eirik down, and could use the help, but no, he had no interest in being king. They were going to need a king, and he, Miles, had picked Bodvar for that role. Bodvar was both surprised and delighted.'

"Bodvar's unexpected support settled another question; where to land in Norland. Miles decided to land so as to join

Bodvar and then quickly crush several jarls loyal to Eirik before they could unite. Evenso the southern jarls would have time to gather against him.

"Miles took steps to weaken Eirik's forces before battle. The single largest factor was timing; Miles landed in Norland after the various Viking crews had left for summer raiding. Bodvar, Knut, and Gretil kept their men in the area. In fact all three men offered their ships to the sons of southern jarls who had no ships of their own. These energetic young men jumped at the chance to go raiding and easily filled these ships with young warriors keen for wealth and adventure; these men were not available for Eirik's muster."

Kjartan smiled; "By the way, Sandaman, these raids were very successful, and Gretil, Knut, and Bodvar received twenty percent of the take."

"Miles left a final point with both Bodvar and Knut; manufacture extra bows and many arrows, also, get the boys practicing. All of these men were skilled with the bow, but Miles wanted them trained to increase their rate of fire.'

"This matters, Sandaman, since up to that point we seldom used the bow in war. The bow was handy for hunting, and retiring a troublesome bear.

Early the following spring Miles and Bolli joined Yngvar and my party at a small island we had agreed on.

Our raiding that year was very successful. At the end of the season we swung by Mendero and picked up twenty of the special axes and shields.'

"Weapons are treasured amongst us and Miles made personal gifts of these weapons to close friends and associates. For example Yngvar, myself, and Bolli all received the new weapons. Miles explained how he saw us using them and there was much enthusiasm and practicing. On the way home we travelled north along the coast of Gar and made a final raid on an unusually hardy and belligerent tribe loyal to the prophet. They fought with the scimitar and conventional shield, we with the new weapons. It was an eye opening encounter; the Valkyrie had quite a harvest. These people had little wealth, but Miles liked their bows and thought them superior to ours; we took many bows and many, many arrows, also slaves. One of the captives was a master fletcher and bowmaker.'

"That winter Miles stayed with us in Westmark, but we saw very little of him since Miles spent the winter visiting the important jarls. That winter Miles organized his expeditionary force, and jarls refusing to support him had their oars and sails quietly removed; these ships would not be alerting Eirik.'

"Late the following spring the expeditionary force sailed for Norland, and it wasn't much; three hundred men in seven ships.'

"Eighty men and two ships went to the northeast corner of Norland; I led this force. We were to begin on summer solstice and crush jarls loyal to Eirik before they could unite. On no account was I to risk a major battle; setbacks would end things. I must do all that could be successfully done; Knut would be watching and if all went well he would join me. I was to work with speed and accomplish much before Eirik's retainers were sufficiently organized to make success doubtful.'

Sandaman had been quiet for sometime but now curiosity got the better of him; "Kjartan, this was quite some time back; how old were you?"

"I was twenty, which strikes you as a bit early for great responsibility. This was what I thought too, and I asked Miles to give the command to my father, who was shrewd and experienced.'

Kjartan paused significantly; "Instead he put his seal on me, and it is a source of pride and comfort to me right up to this moment. Miles said I was perfectly free to take my father with me and counsel with him, but the final decisions were mine and the responsibility was mine. He told me my judgment was sound and I needed to trust myself, to never act on counsel that went against my instincts and innate sense. I have borne this in mind, always.'

"And, as I review Mendero's situation I am very comfortable with what I find; the situation only seems perilous. For a thousand little reasons your neighbors will not unite against you, and if they do we will bring them down earlier rather than later. Relax, steady she goes, and get on with your project.'

"But back to Norland, and our war. My part went better than I could have hoped. We landed by night and moved very quickly so that we managed to destroy the forces of two jarls. At this point we were hardly a secret, but now comes the surprise; many of the 'loyal' jarls distrusted and disliked Eirik, and rather than 'back to the wall' resistance several volunteered oaths of neutrality, and one actually joined us. Knut felt the time was ripe to come on board, and as a result our forces were about equal to the combined forces of the kings' men who finally opposed us.'

"My father and Knut suggested a forced march and night attack. This was a bold plan, and probably would have surprised our enemies and succeeded. However, I went against their counsel. I doubled my scouts, since I didn't want any forced marches surprising me, and then proceeded forward at half day marches. Both Knut and my father were disgusted, but I was firm and Miles couldn't have been plainer concerning who was in charge.'

Sandaman was intrigued; "This story has the young man and the older men switching roles. You are hardly timid, Kjartan; what were you thinking?"

"I was thinking of the big picture rather than the local one. Miles had landed on the other side of Norland on the Northwest coast. He had begun operations at least two weeks earlier than me. His was the major operation and I was a side show. Knowing Miles I suspected decisive events had already happened and news hadn't had time to reach us. If Miles had lost there probably wasn't much hope of our success and no point in risking life and limb. Had Miles won then my fight probably wasn't necessary; wait for the news to arrive and let the opposing jarls adjust to the new political reality.'

"The tricky part would be where the western war was active and undecided. In this case, should I fight and lose, the forces opposing us would then reinforce Eirik; the best thing was to keep them here and away from Miles. I thought of thinning my forces and sending eighty to a hundred men to Miles, but as it was we were slightly outnumbered and it was risky; remember, we were in no position to suffer setbacks. So that was my choice; keep the southern jarls out of the fight and avoid setbacks. It proved the right decision; just about the time battle could no longer be avoided the news arrived; Eirik's forces had been destroyed and he had fled to the far north with a few men and his volva, Ragnhild. The opposing jarls quietly parted and went to their various farms. Had I fought that battle a lot of good men would have died to very little purpose.'

"That's my side of the Norland war; Miles western theatre is where great things happened. Bodvar was even better than his word; he promptly, right on schedule joined Miles and he brought more men than he promised. They briefly divided in order to smash more jarls, but reunited before Eirik arrived on the scene. And arrive Eirik did, with almost a two to one superiority in force.'

Kjartan paused briefly to consider how best to proceed; "Sandaman, if you are to sufficiently appreciate this I must tell you how we wage war. First, we all, every last mother's son of us, like early decisive battles. We are fatalistic and feel our deaths were assigned before we were born. We, as a rule, are ready to back our luck and see what comes; so, bring on the battle, and what comes will come. Secondly, we love hard marches and unexpected attacks. More generally, we love ruses. These things would seem to head in different directions, but that is how we are.

Miles' first ambush was, from a Viking standpoint, irresistible. He made camp in a meadow surrounded by woods. In the meadow there were many fires and tents; it sure enough looked as though Miles' men were home and at their ease. But they weren't; only a few, a noisy few, were really there. Most of the men were hidden in the surrounding trees with bows at the ready.'

"The evening in question Eirik's army was three miles away. When news was leaked as to Miles' whereabouts it was inevitable that Eirik make a fast march and night attack.'

"Eirik's first clue should have been the fires; they were far too big for a late night camp, but our archers needed light, and we risked the fires. In the event this was not noticed and Eirik attacked in full force, which resulted in many deaths. Our men shot as long as they had targets and then slipped away to agreed on muster points. We never locked horns with Eirik; that was for later.

"After the ambush Miles withdrew by night to a prepared battlefield about five miles distance. In the morning Eirik, angry and panting for vengeance, chased hard after Miles. He found Miles' forces drawn up at one end of the field, and there weren't many of them. When Eirik got closer Miles' army, with a great shout, charged. Eirik saw an easy victory, and began forming a forward shield wall. Unfortunately for

Eirik the charging warriors were a ruse and distraction, to keep all attention fixed on them; yelling berserkers catch your attention every time. Along the flanks of the field Miles had dug long trenches where he concealed his archers. These men threw off the straw and grass over their heads and began pouring accurate arrows into the unprotected flanks of an army which had placed its shield wall facing forward. When all arrows had been used these men grabbed their axes, swords and spears and sprang to the attack.'

"The ambush with the archers helped even things up, but evenso the fight that ensued was close and desperate. The critical factor was Yngvar and the twenty men in the center using the new weapons. The shield wall, rather than being an invincible barrier and protections was a death trap. Yngvar and his men parried the spear thrusts and stood against the shield wall. They were too close for effective sword and large axe swings and they were protected by the enemies' shields. They then hooked the leading shields with their own shields, pulled the shields down and brained the unfortunate men behind.'

"I wasn't there, Sandaman, but every report centers on Yngvar, who was like a wolf turned loose on sheep. Nothing could touch him, and death followed closely at his heels. Ultimately the day was a complete disaster for Eirik, yet somehow, and this is hard to understand, he, and twenty or so men escaped our encircling forces. No one seems to have seen him leaving.

For my own part I doubt he was there to begin with, but several reliable men claim to have seen him; I don't know what to think.'

Kjartan paused, and drew a deep breath; "Well, however the man came to be outside our circle we tracked him far, far north and killed both him and his volva. They were burned, and that's not easy to do so far north as we were."

"Was the final hunt in the far north without event?", asked a surprised Sandaman.

A strange look came over Kjartan, and he hesitated, hesitated yet more, and finally, reluctantly; "No, there was event, and too many of us died. Our trek into the far north shadows me to this day and I never have sorted things into any kind of sense. This part of my tale is painful to me and absolutely without any use or lessons for you. Instead of hashing over long done craziness I will circle back to where I began and conclude with a very important lesson.'

"We have already taken the necessary steps to preserve Mendero against her enemies. The thing you must take from my old mentor is the invincible calm and confidence that is more infectious than plague. When Miles took first Knut, and then Bodvar back to the barn and told each he would be bringing down Eirik it was as certain and uncontestable as dawn in the morning. Both men, even as they stood amazed, believed him; there <u>would</u> be a new dawn in the morning, a good dawn. <u>You</u> believe it, like the air you breathe, and others will believe it, and soon it will be so.'

Kjartan fixed Sandaman with his eye; "I'll let you in on a little secret, Sandaman. Odin stood with Miles, and Odin's luck was with him. Miles stood with me, and his luck is with me. I stand with you, and my luck is with you. Going all the way back to Odin events will shape to favor us and bring us where we would be.'

Then, with a smile and twinkle in his eye; "I'll even let you in on a deeper secret, Sandaman, but only if you promise not to tell any of my norse colleagues; Odin doesn't care a rat's fart that you are a Christian. Both your Christian god and Odin are pulling for you."

Sandaman laughed; "Allah and his warriors don't have a chance; the problem being that as of yet they don't know it. I suppose we must teach them."

CHAPTER 25
A Surprise for Kjartan

THE SILVER WAS LOADED, the weapons from Crispus' smithy were aboard, and the ship was victualed and watered. The weather had cleared.

The steward poked his nose in briefly and by sign indicated things were ready for departure. Kjartan turned to Sandaman; "Old friend, it is that time; will you walk with me to the ship?"

"I will, but there are a few items left, and one of them is important to me. First, I have two gifts for you; a token of my gratitude for Saldana."

Sandaman reached into his pocket produced a very rich golden necklace. "This goes to Unn.

Sandaman then crossed the room and opened a drawer. He removed an axe of the type favored by Kjartan, and it was incandescent with beauty and merit. Beyond its perfection as a weapon there was a sapphire embedded in its handle. For Kjartan it was love at first sight. He took the axe from Sandaman almost reverently.

"Sandaman, this is a wonderful gift; I accept it with deep pleasure. I only wish I had as good a gift for you."

"Actually, Kjartan, you have in your gift a thing I would prize above all others."

Kjartan was both wary and curious; "What is this thing you so prize?"

"Come, Kjartan, let's stroll around Mendero and give you a last chance to stretch your legs. Have you seen the new cathedral we Christians are building?"

"I have; it should be very grand when finished. Now, what is this thing of mine you covet?!"

Sandaman laughed; "Very soon I may be able to share it with you; let's get walking."

As they strolled through Mendero the particular circumstances brought into the foreground a conflict which has long simmered on the margins of Kjartan's awareness.

Westmark, and norse islands like it, have no towns or villages; there are only isolated and self sufficient farms. The only villagelike experience a native of Westmark knew was the two weeks of the yearly althing, or general council. During these two weeks the various godi and retainers set up booths, or tents, and briefly lived as a community.

For many years now Kjartan had raided and traded around towns, and of these towns he liked Mendero best. He especially liked the taverns, or pubs, associated with towns. There were no pubs, not even the idea of a pub, in Westmark. The usual Viking pattern was to raid for six to seven years in one's twenties and then settle down on one's farm, and perhaps become a godi. This rustic idyll was punctuated and spiced with the odd feud.

Kjartan broke this pattern; at forty-six Kjartan was away from the farm more than at thirty-six.

Town and farm gave each other spice and contrast, and gradually, all unawares, the pattern had gone from town life as a spicy break from farm life to the opposite, where farm life is a refreshing break from town life.

So it was, as Kjartan strolled Mendero preparatory to sailing home to Westmark, he became aware it was duty and custom, rather than inclination which called him north and home. This was a sobering thought; Kjartan was a northman's northman, and he'd <u>rather</u> be in Mendero!

Sandaman and Kjartan for some time had been walking towards the new cathedral. Ten yards agead of them three boys, ages eight to eleven, were moving cautiously forward, constantly checking for unseen perils. The lads were armed with wooden shields and wooden scimitars, and they clearly anticipated trouble.

The boys care and caution communicated itself to the two men, who slowed to see that all went well for the young warriors. This also broke Kjartan's rather bitter train of thought.

Suddenly from a six foot building rock awaiting its place in the temple a fourth boy dropped amongst the three boys. This fourth boy also had wooden weapons, but they consisted of a smaller shield with a hook, and a small axe with a small wooden spur at right angles to the wooden blade. This fourth lad was dressed like a Viking.

As the fourth boy was landing he knocked one lad down, quick as thought he turned and immediately crowded and hooked the shield of a second boy. He whirled the second boy around so as to block the third boy. He then, with savage and irresistible force, pulled the shield down and struck the boy behind. Now it was boy to boy with the third lad who promptly grounded his shield and fled.

The young Viking was starting in pursuit when he noticed Sandaman and Kjartan; "Aw, Dad, it's not fun when you're here." But the boy gave up the pursuit and layed down his weapons, and walked towards his father.

"Kjartan, this young Viking is my son Michael."

Then turning to his son, "Michael Sandámanson, this is my friend godi Kjartan Njalson.

Mike's eyes became big as saucers, "Dad, is he the one who got you started, the one who brought mother to us?!"

Sandaman laughed; "This is the one; and he is a real godi too!

"Wow; godi Kjartan Njalson, I am so happy and honored to meet you!"

Kjartan smiled, his former angst gone as though it had never been; "Michael, it is a great pleasure to meet you. Your attack on your enemies was carried out in the finest traditions of my people; it is not only a pleasure , it is an honor to meet you."

Sandaman interrupted; "Mike, hurry home; I'll be along shortly."

The two men continued their walk.

"Kjartan, it is my deepest wish and desire that you take Michael as a foster son. Since infancy he has admired you norse, and I think he has it in him to be a better norseman than any of you. I both need and want a strong alliance with the north, with Westmark, and with you."

Sandaman paused; "<u>But</u> there is more. Andrew, my oldest son, is a good and deserving lad, but I judge him unsuitable to lead Mendero. My hopes are strongly with Michael. Furthermore either a Christian or Islamic successor would raise fear and cause trouble. Nur and I have been lucky, and evenso we walk a knife's edge.'

"By contrast you norse are broadminded on such matters and, more importantly, both Christian and Mohammedan judge you differently than they judge each other. Neither Christian nor Mohammedan are fond of pagans, but you are not so objectionable as each to the other. You represent the least of the available evils, and you would treat all equally and well.'

"Kjartan you are free to introduce Michael to Odin. For my own part I am a Christian, and will always be

Christian, but above everything else I am a ruler, and I am practical. God understands; and if he doesn't he can keep it to himself.'

"That last sentiment is thoroughly norse, Sandaman; you are groping towards the light. Of course I will foster Michael, it is an honor, a pleasure, and an opportunity. However you should keep a few thing in mind.'

Regarding the succession, a thing of the utmost importance; it is too early to judge. Your third and fourth sons may prove more suitable, or Andrew may yet surprise you. You must do what is best for Mendero rather than play a favorite. Also you need to remember that while life is uncertain for all men it is yet more uncertain for us. The flukes of weather now matter; Michael and I may drown in a storm as we sail north to Westmark. Face and honor count for much with us and, as you know, these things tend to put your life on the line. War is prominent in our lives, which introduces further uncertainties.'

"Long may Michael carry your hopes, but keep your mind open and have other bulls in the pen."

CHAPTER 26
Ljotabani

MICHAEL HAD PASSED TEN years with Kjartan. In the course of this formative decade Michael, like a sponge, had soaked up norse skills, customs, and attitudes. In the course of sharing what he knew and loved Kjartan had regained his grip on all things norse; urban life and pubs were still treasured, but as spice to norse life on Westmark.

Michael was particularly gifted at arms, and in the skills of war he had few peers. In many ways he resembled Yngvar in that while both fit and powerful he was neither so large nor powerful as many men, but his size was more than compensated by his quickness. Michael and Hall were two weeks back from a successful raid.

Eyvind was no doubt with them in spirit, but his life had taken a different direction. Sandaman had settled him on an estate and he had become a central figure in Mendero's military operations. Eyvind had recently married a charming Christian who was from a wealthy and important family. Eyvind, unusually daring and reckless in youth, had become quintessential Mendero establishment.

Kjartan awoke early, and in an odd, ambivalent mood. On the one hand the novelty and pleasure of having Michael and Hall home lingered, on the other, Bjorn, son of an old friend and fellow godi, would very likely be killed today. Something needed to be done about Ljot, and best it were done before the bastard killed Bjorn.

Ljot was a huge, powerful berserker from Norland who, in the course of the summer, had killed three good men of substance. He had done this by trumping of quarrels, which led to duels not easily or honorably ducked. Ljot was large, very powerful, skillful, and added to this, really was something of a berserker. This particular hound of Odin was a death machine. He had seized the land and property of two of his victims as a right of conquest, and no one had organized against him or protested.

Bjorn was a quiet, responsible man of small build who had more of the steward than warrior about him. Bjorn's wife, Olga, was very beautiful and his farm valuable; these were the real reasons behind Ljot's quarrel with him.

Hall and Michael were away visiting friends and probably wouldn't be home for a few days. This was a blessing, since neither man would like the course of things and might intervene; intervention carried a very real chance of death.

Kjartan was fifty-five and his right knee was gimpy from an old wound, evenso he was still both able and effective. He strapped on his favorite axe, the gift from Sandaman, and hid a short powerful bow under his cloak; Kjartan had nothing specific in mind but wanted to be ready for all eventualities.

Kjartan arrived at the dueling grounds and considered it thoughtfully. He stood near a tree. He had just decided to ambush Ljot before the man arrived at the very public dueling grounds. This decision was reached too late; both Lyot and Bjorn approached the dueling grounds from opposite sides and both had a number of supporters.

Kjartan notched an arrow and held both the bow and arrow under this cloak. He walked over to join the dueling officials and kept the tree at his back; he did not want anyone between himself and the tree. He decided to kill Ljot at the first good opportunity and deal with the consequences as they arrived. As he planned it Bjorn would spend this evening with Olga, and he doubted anyone would be other than relieved. Should some difficult sort wish to make something of it he had a few extra arrows.

Kjartan noticed a knot of men clustered around Bjorn and he walked towards this. As he got nearer he noticed black hair in the thicket of brown and blond locks; an uneasy feeling niggled at him. As he hurried forward the uneasy feeling gave way to grim certainty; Michael was in the center of the cluster.

"Michael, what is this!?"

"I have taken on Bjorn's quarrel with Ljot. Bjorn will certainly be killed if he fights, whereas I have a good chance with the bastard. I have a hunch the dark sands of Ljot's life are about to run out; it is past due."

Kjartan was silent, but it was the silence of fast incisive thinking.

Michael was about to speak, but he knew the concentrated expression on his foster father's face and held his peace.

At length Kjartan spoke; "This will not be easy, but it can be done. First, take my axe; yours will not penetrate the man's chain mail, mine will."

Kjartan's axe, unlike the flatter and rounder blade of Michael, came to a sharp point on the outside edge of the blade then curved sharply as it proceeded to the inside edge. This was designed with chain mail in mind.

"Secondly, take Bjorn's shield."

Michael interrupted him; "It is a very poor shield."

"I know, it will be perfect. Being very careful so as to avoid injuring your arm see that Ljot beats it shapeless. I want the shield visibly useless within one to two minutes of starting. With the shield destroyed I will insist both you and Ljot put away your shields. At this point it will be your axe and his sword. When the fight starts again within the first several blows I want you to do the quickest and best heel spin of your life; Ljot should receive a significant flank wound. Please stick to the flank; don't risk a head blow. The flank wound should even things up; if you can stay out of harms' way for the following five minutes you should be able to kill him at will."

Michael had been listening carefully, he now spoke; "Are you sure you can get shields out of the fight?"

Kjartan smiled; "It is my sincerest wish Ljot ignores my request and goes for you; if so, he dies right then", Kjartan patted his cloak.

Kjartan paused; "Michael, that man wields one hell of a blade. Few men could use such a large and heavy blade but he handles it as though it were a twig. In blocking his blows be extremely careful to deflect rather stop the swing. Direct blocking will destroy your weapons and break your arm. You have no margins; your fight must be a thing of the highest art. Yngvar used to dance and weave his way through harm like he was responding to hidden music; you have some of this too; use it! Stay with our plan, stay focused, tightly focused, and we will enjoy our beer tonight; your honor will be great!"

Shortly the dueling ground was cleared and two men went at it. The power of Ljot's blows was numbing and Kjartan could tell Michael's shield arm had been sprained. However as the fight progressed Kjartan, who had an expert's eye for such things, was delighted with how skillfully Michael was getting his shield destroyed; there were no more jarring sprains, and the shield was going fast.

Kjartan quietly worked his way behind Ljot and waited, and not for long; Michael's shield was trash. Smoothly and quickly Kjartan pulled his bow and notched arrow from under his cloak and drew it fully. In a loud, clear voice; "Stop, now! Ljot, if you move even a little you die."

The fight stopped and silence fell; "This fight is no longer fair; the smaller man's shield is destroyed. Both of you drop your shields when I reach three. One, two, three…"

The shields were thrown to the side, and Kjartan was truly disappointed; had Ljot so much as quivered or hesitated his problem would have been solved. As it was Michael wore no mail and had only a small axe; Ljot saw no harm in shields gone, to him things looked better.

With a savage yell Ljot sprang at Michael and delivered a very fast two handed sword swing that would have beheaded an ox. Michael smoothly deflected the blow down and left, and spun to the right and around on his heel to sink his axe in Ljot's right flank. The maneuver had been almost too fast to follow; Ljot's chain mail had not held and he had sustained a serious wound. Kjartan gave Michael a grim and satisfied nod.

The next five minutes were truly amazing and numbing. Ljot revealed true berserker powers and it was as though the flank wound had never happened; Michael parried or ducked an impossibly fast flurry of stunningly hard blows. As things proceeded it became clear Michael moved as though charmed, that Ljot could not touch him. Kjartan was very, very proud and not for the first time thought of Yngvar; it seemed as though Michael was his heir.

Gradually blood loss and fatigue took their toll and Ljot slowed down and became a little awkward and clumsy. A little later he took a deep wound to his left thigh. A few minutes later, the Valkyrie took him. All eyes were dry; he was mourned by neither man nor beast.

Michael's honor was truly great, and the evening beer was never before nor since quite so good, so refreshing.

In future years Michael would be known as Michael, son of Sandaman, prince of Mendero. On Westmark he was known as Ljotabani, the slayer of Ljot.

CHAPTER 27
Wykl

(Norse World, Miles, First year)

"So the husband walks in...", but Miles thoughts were on the approaching town of Wykl, and Hoskuld's acknowledged art as a raconteur was wasted on him. Hoskuld gave an unexpected grunt and exhaled; this broke the flow of the friendly tale and Miles stopped midstride and looked over just in time to see Hoskuld hit the ground with an arrow through his chest. It brought Miles out of his revery like an electric shock.

"Shields up!!", he barked, as he looked around. There was only a hint of dawn and it was hard to make out more than an outline of things. Several other men were down, and about half the men standing already had their shields up. The men instinctively came together in something of an oval shape so the shields faced all points of the compass. There was no panic. Good.

Then, with a great shout, they were attacked on all sides. Again, no panic: back to back with their fellows, with the Valkyrie hovering on the margins, these men were almost happy. They fought heart and soul, as though possessed, and over the next ten, fifteen, twenty minutes the pressure eased. The enemy were fewer, and, while earlier they had seemed a mighty host, it became clear their numbers were now equivalent. As the fight turned against them the strangers showed no sign of quitting, rather they died where they stood, scimitars swinging. Then it was over.

The sun rose on a scene too familiar in coastal Gar; the road and surrounding fields were littered with dead men. The attackers included sixty men, and all were dead. There had been forty-two northmen, but the arrows claimed seven while the scimitar and spear claimed another five. Four vikings were seriously wounded; two would die later that day.

Miles was numb and puzzled. They had been less than a mile from Wykl and were poised for a dawn raid. Then the men planning a surprise had been surprised. How?! And why hadn't the attackers withdrawn when things went against them? It made no sense.

Miles looked over at Kjartan, who also was pondering the strange turn of events. Then Kjartan made up his mind.

"As a young viking dad saw something like this. Based on what he told me here is what probably happened. The leading men of Wykl got word of our raid on Mustk and, reasonably enough, assumed they were next. I'm guessing they took their wives and children inland well out of harms way. But, with their thoughts on their property they did more; they took with them the wives and children of every able bodied serf and poor man and held them hostage. The deal was crystal clear: no property damage and you get back your families. Property damage and the families are either killed or sold as slaves. The will of Allah for these men has been revealed, and my guess would be these families will be sold into slavery; it is the will of Allah."

'It's tough being a poor man around here', thought Miles; 'if we don't get them, then their own people do them dirty.', but Miles said nothing and was soon busy doing what could be done for their wounded. This was early in his viking career and only his second raid. The first raid had been a cake walk, while this one left him numb; he would miss dear old cheerful Hoskuld, and he wished he'd paid more attention to the comic tale, though with the certainty of gravity he knew it would feature a half-witted cuckold. The cuckold was a bottomless source of amusement for the norse while he'd reached the floor long since. As Miles cleaned, closed, and bound wounds a plan began shaping. When he finished he huddled up with Kjartan and Yngvar.

"Kjartan, if things are as you suspect, our raid on Wykl will yield some sport with the women and a few slaves; nice, but not much. For now let's forego the pleasures of raping and pillaging, and let me scout the situation. If the rich men have left town I will find out where they went; when they return we can pick them up and make a real profit. Besides, the men who fought us died well, and I think we should see their families get back home. We can start a tradition of professional courtesy, what is due one warrior to another."

Kjartan and Yngvar thought 'professional courtesy' the funniest thing yet, but they agreed to lie low while Miles scouted. Miles walked amongst the dead until he found a man close to his size, whereupon he donned the man's robes and scimitar. On the Mostk raid Miles had acquired enough of the local language to pass himself off as an itinerant warrior.

He walked to Wykl and made polite inquiries as to who might be in the market for an hardy and skillful scimitar. Sure enough, there was a ready market for such as he, but the men who might want him had all left several days gone by; left for the larger town of Kletl, which was four days travel north and west. They'd be back in four days. Why? Northmen in the area. Had many left for Kletl? Oh yes – with bitterness – they had everyone's wives and children. Miles found parchment and ink and returned to his friends.

CHAPTER 28
The Education of Kjartan

MILES HAD FOUND KJARTAN remarkably, almost preternaturally gifted at mathematics. Educating Kjartan had become a major consolation and comfort in a thoroughly strange and savage world. Late in the afternoon, after returning from Wykl, Miles and Kjartan were back to discussing the elegant, the strange, the wonderful association of time and longitude.

"Miles, I'm with you; you were crystal clear the first time. The world is a round ball rotating on its axis, which is oriented top to bottom. The midpoint between top and bottom is the equator; this is a circle that goes around the ball at its waist.'

"Think of this equator as a large clock lying on its side with the motion of the watch being the rotation of our earth. Each point on the equator may be thought of as the center of a slightly different day, a day that arrives earlier and departs earlier if it lies east of us, and arrives later and departs later if it is west of us. You think our equator to be smaller than your equator and estimate it to be 22,000 of your miles. Our rotation time for one day is twenty-three hours."

Kjartan paused, and Miles nodded approvingly.

"Now, if I have sailed a few days and want to know how far east or west I have travelled I wait till exactly midday and note the time difference from midday of my starting point. Suppose it is five minutes and twenty seconds different. There are 60x60x23 seconds in a day, which on the large clock formed by the equator represents a journey of 22,000 miles, so five minutes twenty seconds would be three hundred twenty seconds. This would give…"

Kjartan paused a moment; "Something close to ninety miles. If the new midday time is earlier than the original time then we are ninety miles east, if later, then ninety miles west."

"Nicely summarized, Kjartan."

But Kjartan stopped the compliment almost mid sentence; "However, teacher, we are <u>not</u> on the equator; we are well above it. Our circle around the ball is considerably smaller, so the three hundred twenty seconds is considerably smaller than ninety miles. Our circle would have a radius of the cosine of our latitude multiplied by the radius of the earth. This number doubled gives a diameter, so our actual circle length is π multiplied by this diameter."

Kjartan was silent and thoughtful for a moment; "Teacher, our voyagers have travelled about forty-five miles; they must have suffered serious headwinds to take so long!"

Miles viewed Kjartan as a norse prodigy, a cousin to the precocious Indian mathematician Ramanujan he had read about in school. Kjartan's instant, intuitive grasp of mathematical ideas astounded a delighted Miles in equal measure; for awhile he was able to forget his own lost world, a world that now seemed so very lost and so very desirable.

"Kjartan, you have this longitude business down as well as I do; want to hear more about my world?"

Kjartan was ambivalent; technology utterly charmed him, it almost seemed magical; but of late the business about human rights sounded like the silliest sort of make-believe. Miles assured him it was a useful and good make-believe, a fairy tale at least as worthy as Odin and Thor. Miles explained some benefits of more or less equal opportunity. For example, an able poor man might get a chance, but Kjartan looked around and everywhere he saw very different abilities, circumstances, and personalities. Pretending things were other than they were seldom worked, and Kjartan distrusted the idea and wished Miles would give it a rest.

"Miles, I would love to hear more about airplanes, but not if you plan to chat up the rights-of-man."

This frustrated Miles, since 'airplanes' carried absolutely no practical sequel, whereas a bit more rights-of-man might actually plant useful seeds. As he reviewed this predicament Yngvar strolled over.

Sharing is fun and gratifying. Miles saw Kjartan as the perfect, made to order, repository for what he had to share: that's exactly how Yngvar saw Miles. Yngvar was charmed at how Miles had taken to norse weapons and techniques, and he had Miles on a heavy schedule of improvement.

"Miles, your quarter staff technique would shame my grandmother; there's another hour before sundown so let's get busy." Whereupon Yngvar threw a large quarterstaff Miles's direction. Miles caught it and they left camp to pursue his education. In his way, Yngvar, like Kjartan, was also a prodigy. Miles knew Yngvar for a consummate master of weapons and both admired and appreciated him. These two men, Yngvar and Miles, formed a friendship that came to be legendary amongst the norse.

Around the evening fire Yngvar, Kjartan, and Miles discussed what to do about the wealthy men of Wykl. Miles, possessed of both great natural authority and good sense, carried the day in counsel; this prefigured the future, where Miles's preeminence would be unquestioned.

The next day the norse conspicuously returned to their ships and left the area. Two days later, by night, they quietly returned to a hidden cove. The next evening, unobserved, they walked three miles north and west of Wykl. They selected a quiet wooded section of the road into town, hid, and waited. Their timing was perfect and a little after noon the next day the fat cats of Wykl walked into their hands. The fat cats and their wealth were separated, sometimes painfully, and a large number of valuable slaves were obtained. Miles's star was rising.

CHAPTER 29
A Toss of the Axe

KJARTAN SAT QUIETLY WATCHING the lemming. It was reddish brown in color and sat on its hindquarters giving Kjartan a careful look over. This thoughtful rodent had an air of dignity and solemnity that tickled Kjartan and reminded him of several greybeards back home. Around a winter fire these men looked grave and profound; yet when they opened their mouths out trotted the rankest nonsense. The lemming would not have found the comparison very flattering, but might have been mollified to learn its ears saved the day; for cuteness lemming ears are right up there with an infant's toes and fingers. Kjartan was in a whimsical mood and mentally put lemming ears on the greybeards… it seemed to help.

At length Kjartan stretched luxuriously and put the whimsy aside; "Come off it, Yngvar; quit sneaking up on me and put your bow away. I don't look like Eirik, and he's many miles north of this cozy spot."

Yngvar laughed; "I was just beginning to wonder if it might not be you; but of course it couldn't be since you are leading a war band many, many miles south and east of here. You were ever the sly boots!"

Yngvar reached down a hand and pulled Kjartan to his feet; "Kjartan, it is good to see you! I have heard the best reports of your conduct of the eastern war, and Miles is very pleased and proud."

Kjartan chuckled; "You mean he is pleased with the things I very carefully left undone."

"Those, too, brother. Now, what are you doing here!"

"First of all, Yngvar, well and wonderfully done!! You and Miles have fought and won a legendary battle, of which you are the acknowledged centerpiece and shining star: may I kiss your toes?"

"Absolutely not! I never take off my boots at this time of day; besides, out of pique and jealousy you might bite them."

They both laughed. "Thanks Kjartan; at the end of the battle I was happy to be alive. To be uninjured was beyond the reach of hope, yet I am entirely free of wounds. But you dodge me; what are you doing here?"

"That brings us to the second point. Eirik's army may have been destroyed, but he and a handful escaped. As a greybeard by the fire I don't want to explain to my grandchildren how, amidst stirring and titanic events, I held the cloaks of the warriors while accounts were settled. These are huge times; a very powerful and evil king has been brought down by a handful of men; I want a piece of the glory. Hunting down King Eirik and a remnant few may not be much, but I want to be there at the end."

Yngvar grew thoughtful; "Miles is on the other side of the main trail; let's join him and decide what is best. This would have been the logical point for an ambush so we stayed off the trail and are travelling well to the sides, hoping to ambush those who would ambush."

Yngvar stopped, gave Kjartan a quizzical look, then smiled; "but of course you know all this; you knew we would go around such a perfect ambush spot, and here you are waiting for us!"

"Of course; now let's find Miles."

They walked off the low hill on its north side; Yngvar, after a bit of recent event shop talk grew more serious.

"Something about Eirik and his chosen few smells. To begin with, he has Ragnhild, which always suggests a devious, dangerous, and dark side to things. More immediately, though, is that repeatedly, when there is hard untraceable ground on which to lose us he leaves unmistakable traces of which way he went. He is heading into open tundra, which offers little or no hiding place. We have thirty-five men, and we are certain he can't have more than twenty, perhaps eighteen men. It would seem he is leading us into a trap, but how?! Everything suggests he has taken leave of his senses and is himself walking to certain destruction. What are we missing? The man can't be both King of Norland and a fool!'

"How many men do you have, Kjartan?"

"I have fifteen, and all are stout good fellows. We have food for three weeks."

"Good. We have, as I mentioned, thirty-five. We have strength to spare."

At length, up ahead they saw a large powerful man who could only be Miles. Miles was surprised and delighted.

"This is better than I could have hoped! We now have more than enough to finish Eirik. I want either you, Kjartan, or Yngvar, to get south as quickly as possible and make good my claim on the mid-sized ship of the three ships of Eirik. I have spoken with Bodvar and this ship and five cows are my share of the spoils of war. The cows should include four cows and one bull, and I want the best of them. Leave the cows with your father, then victual and water the ship and get raiding. At the end of the summer be sure and pick up the weapons in Mendero. If all goes well we will winter with your father in Westmark. If this doesn't work then we meet early in the raiding season at Vali Gunnarson's on Shapensay."

Miles looked at Yngvar; "Yngvar, yours has been the lion's share of this war; it seems to me you and ten of our men should hurry south; let Kjartan and his fifteen remain."

Yngvar was silent; "Miles, you are correct in all you say, but I have deep misgivings. The eighteen or so men with Eirik will all be under Odin's shield and very dangerous; the numbers may be misleading. I <u>know</u> my axe cuts through Ragnhild's steel spell and I should be there. I would urge that Kjartan and I finish Eirik and you head south."

Miles considered this; "No, Yngvar; I started this and I must see it through. Kjartan, any thoughts?"

Kjartan did not raise his voice, but there was steel in it; "I will be at the finish; there is nothing to discuss."

There was a long silence. Finally Miles spoke; "Will you both agree to abide by an axe toss?"

Yngvar and Kjartan looked at each other and nodded. Yngvar handed his axe to Miles; "There is a large ding on one side; I want ding up."

Kjartan agreed Miles threw the axe in a high spinning arc and it landed with the ding facing down.

Kjartan had just won the darkest chapter of his life.

CHAPTER 30
Miles Third Winter

MILES HAD FOLDED HIS cloak into the shape of a pillow and placed it behind him against the wall of timber and sod. The bench, as always, was hard, but he'd found a good spot and was warm and comfortable; in fact, considering it was twenty below and dropping, he felt snug. The dark, the cold, and the wind made creature comforts dear, and the wind possessed a soughing quality that set off the music.

The music was elusive, beautiful, and soothing. The singer, captured this past summer in southern Gar, had a rich contralto voice that bordered on mellow, and filled the longhouse without dominating it. She accompanied herself with a stringed instrument a little smaller than a guitar and with a brighter tone. The woman's voice held tones a long time, while the accompaniment formed a rippling background that moved in and out of a subtle dissonance with the sustained vocal tones. It reminded Miles of flamenco music, though it was slower. Miles joined the music; his thoughts lost cohesion and purpose and he was content and at peace for the first time since killing Eirik up on the tundra.

The events around Eirik's death were intractably strange and unsettling and nothing came of pondering them; Miles wished very much to put them behind, to let them float away unresolved, yet they lingered, and lingered. But not tonight.

The singer, Nylla, was a large woman with dark eyes and dark hair. Her nose was a shade too large and she had a birthmark on the left side of her neck that would not have been missed. Nylla was not beautiful, but her figure was good and she was attractive in a rough and ready way. Unfortunately Nylla's life had been hard and she wore sorrow like a second skin. Only of a winter's evening when she sang or played would her features soften and her face grow expressive. The young vikings who leased Bodvar's ship had captured her at a coastal oasis where she was a slave to a wealthy son of the prophet. Her owner had been killed in the process, which pleased rather than troubled Nylla since this man, before her six year old eyes, had killed her family. She had the musical gift, and by twelve had become valued as a musician. She was now twenty.

Nylla was untouched by man; in her world this was unexpected to the point of miraculous. Yet there was no miracle: Nylla kept a very sharp dagger on her person at all times; if a man's attentions grew too pointed she took her dagger and, in a manner leaving no doubt as to her intentions, proceeded to kill herself. Her singing was a treasured magic, and in her former situation any man approaching her received twenty lashes. A young viking, six weeks at sea and aching to share himself, had passed instantaneously from lust to alarm and barely had time to avert tragedy.

Miles' revery made a gentle and comfortable counterpoint with Nylla's music and we shall leave him warm by the fire and a well earned peace and quiet.

This, Miles' third winter amongst the norse, was in many ways the hardest of his life. He had entered the norse world a homeless man bereft of all that was dear. The hero of a picaresque novel takes life as it arrives and seldom looks back or peers far ahead: Miles would flunk picaresque 101. Miles needed anchor points and purpose, and reached for them much as he reached for air and drew a breath. Many of his anchor points were rooted in his own world, which was now gone. Yet his basic viewpoint and approach to things had survived intact; now strange events out on the tundra had challenged and eroded even this very basic root. The first two winters had been strongly anchored by Eirik, and learning new skills. Now the basic skills were in place and Eirik was dead. Miles remaining anchor was badly frayed, he sorely missed his wife and old world friends, and he, a man who needed a plan, had no plan. More immediately he needed privacy, a thing not to be found in a winter longhouse, and he needed something to read – anything at all would do! Educating Kjartan would have helped, but food is scarce in the winter, so to spare Bodvar an unduly heavy burden Kjartan and nine of their men (half of the party returning from the tundra) were wintering with Gretil the Fat.

Miles had hoped to acquire skill at trapping animals, but the sun made a very brief appearance at noon and then was seen no more. Though he was bursting with prestige and social standing Miles insisted on chopping wood and bringing it in near the fire. He also, against heavy protests, put out hay for the livestock and kept barn manure levels reasonable. His peers' approach to winter was to drink more mead and beer than was advisable. Miles liked a drink, but couldn't stand the fog attendant to drinking long and deep. So it was that Miles was restless and unhappy. His only peace and quiet was working on the wood pile and in the barn, also in the evening when Nylla sang.

Yet the third winter, which started with every indication of proving a dark night of the soul, in the event was an occasion of healing and balm. This miraculous reversal had two components. The first and most immediate component was Nylla: six weeks after his arriving, in the wee hours of the morning, she crawled into his bed. Given her history this doesn't seem possible. Nylla's move into the world of men, and Miles in particular, may not be so strange when considered carefully. First and foremost is that our basic mammalian nature is very much on the side of such a move; it should happen unless specifically blocked. Secondly Miles was showed tremendous respect and deference by one and all; this never hurts. Thirdly, Miles, like herself, had lost his home and everything dear; in some deep way she may have sensed a kindred spirit. Lastly, Miles was thoughtful and kind towards women. Two nights before joining him in his bed the quantity of meat for the evening meal had been underestimated. Miles, who was always served first, had his usual generous portion, while Nylla, who was served last, received gristle and fat, and not much of that. Miles noticed such things and motioned for her to come over. When no one was looking he cut her a reasonable piece from his own portion. He would have done this for anyone and thought nothing of it; that was probably not how it was received.

Time heals most wounds, but when aided and abetted by loving and cuddling the cure is much quicker and completer. Present woes and problems move downstream at a gallop. The following spring found both Miles and Nylla better adjusted and comfortable with existence, and as an unexpected bonus Nylla was three months pregnant.

The second factor in Miles third winter recovery occurred around the evening fire somewhere midway between supper and general drunkenness: he became acquainted with the legend-rumor of a rich and strange land far to the west. No one had actually seen it, but the stories were quite persistent and consistent. Miles remembered from his school days how the norse had discovered North America nearly five hundred years before Colombus's westward jaunt in 1492. With this in mind he paid close attention to specifics of the various stories, such things as weather conditions and sailing times. This proved a little discouraging in that the distance from the westernmost isles and the conjectured North America equivalent was probably quite a bit farther than the distance from southwestern Greenland to the coast of Labrador or Newfoundland. His voyage would probably be longer and more perilous than the earlier voyages of the norse navigators in his own world. Nonetheless, gradually conviction was born; he would be making this voyage. He began planning towards it.

That spring, as Miles and his new comrades prepared to leave, he took Bodvar aside.

"Bodvar, your hospitality this past winter was princely and much appreciated. I have a last favor to ask, and it is a great one. If you should choose to decline helping it would in no way damage my esteem for you, or our friendship.'

"Nylla is several month pregnant with my child; Nylla is a fine woman and I accept the responsibility, accept it with pleasure. However, I will be sailing west in search of the elusive far western lands, and I will not put Nylla and our unborn child at risk. If and when I return I will be able to assume their care. Until then they will stay either with you or Njal Bjornson."

Bodvar laughed; "Considering as she is my slave she will be staying with me; besides, I like her and would miss her music more than I can say. The child will be raised as my own; I consider myself as the foster father. But a thing needs clarifying; do you wish her for yourself, or do you wish her happy and well cared for?"

"I wish her happy and well. If two years from now I am settled and she wishes then she may join me. If she should have no such wish then that too would be fine."

Miles hesitated, then; "Bodvar, I have an odd sense Nylla carries a son, and that he will be the finest sort. Should this prove true then he is free, at anytime, to seek me and inherit as my son. If and when he comes let him bring this with him."

Whereupon Miles handed Bodvar his axe, which had killed Eirik and was the first of the new weapons.

"I know this weapon well and will recognize it. He will always be welcome."

Then; "With you as his foster father he will have strong good roots. If Nylla carries a girl she too will I recognize if she brings the axe."

CHAPTER 31
The Courting of Herdis

BRYNJOLF KVIGSON WAS A hersir of considerable wealth and importance. He owned a large and successful farm in upper Reykir. Of his many possessions by far the richest and most coveted was his oldest daughter, Herdis.

Herdis's mother, Thora, had died when she was thirteen years of age and she had taken over managing the household and her younger brother and sister. Herdis was more than equal to her station as the managing daughter of an important hersir: not only were the cheese, hay, meat, and clothes ready for winter, not only was she loved by her family and subordinates, but she was generally regarded as the wittiest and most beautiful woman in all of Westmark, and many would have extended this to include Norland. The men of Westmark between twelve and seventy years of age dreamed of Herdis, and this includes twenty-two year old Michael Sandámanson, who stood in the front ranks of her worshippers.

Bjorn Ovirson (rescued by Michael from Ljot) was cousin to Herdis, and this might seem to work in Michael's favor; if so Herdis hid it remarkably well – until four months ago, when Michael had been promoted to active favor. It turned out she <u>had</u> appreciated the rescue, but Michael was <u>not</u> to presume!

It was against this background that Michael paid his foster father a visit.

"Uncle, I am thinking of getting married and need your help and counsel."

"Who?"; this was more proforma than actually seeking information since Kjartan had a pretty shrewd idea who was under discussion.

"Herdis Brynjolfdottir."

"Does Herdis know she is included in these plans?"

Michael smiled; "She does, and seems willing and pleased."

"Come, Michael, walk out to the barn with me."

This barnward inclination surprised Michael but he strolled along willingly enough. They walked a few minutes in silence with Kjartan deep in thought. Then Kjartan stopped and faced Michael.

"A few moments back I was getting ready to dissuade you from the marriage. Of course as a rule such efforts are a thankless waste of time: doubly so with a shining star like Herdis. However, as I thought it through the marriage has come to seem a good thing. Have you thought it through?"

"I think so, but I could be mistaken. I'm listening."

"Your plan would be to have me sound Brynjolf on the idea so as to avoid the risk of a flat refusal, which would involve a huge loss of face and is not acceptable. However, I know the Brynjolfs of the world very well - afterall, I am one – and with a high degree of certainty I assure you Brynjolf will nix the idea."

"If you were in Brynjolf's boots why would you nix the marriage?"

"You do not have a good farm, Michael. If Herdis is to shine and flourish as your partner she will need a place in which to shine. She will need to clothe, feed, keep warm, and nurse to health you and your children. You must have a farm, a good farm, and you have none. Your prospects in southern Gar count less with Brynjolf than you might imagine: he knows what you seem to have forgotten; that centers of power are constantly shifting, that what was true twelve years back is not necessarily true today. There is no way he will place his daughter's well-being and happiness on a perhaps, a possibility. The bird in the hand is the only bird there is."

Michael grew thoughtful; "I know you well, Kjartan; what is the situation in Mendero?"

"Very much changed, and thoroughly murky; no one can see the future clearly. Your younger brother Siddiq is poised to push your father from power. Siddiq and your mother are strong and pure in their Islamic faith and are strongly backed by believers in Mendero and adjoining moslem states, especially Balba. The christians of Mendero support your father, but don't care for his breadth of mind, tolerance, and the presence of moslems in his government. Our people, the norse, are the only ones unequivocally with him, and hence he is still in power; but civil war and bloodshed are feared, and smart money is on Siddiq backed by outside power. Your father's work is unraveling; a deeply divided country is teetering on the edge of a fight to the knife. The only real winners will be neighboring moslem states."

Michael, who had gone norse to the point of only occasionally remembering Mendero, was deeply concerned and embarrassed.

"Is there anything to be done, Uncle?"

"There usually is. Your father, Michael, is extremely able and would have taken care of things long since had the problem not originated in your mother and Siddiq: he is paralyzed and needs help. It is clear what needs doing, and he simply can't do it. I can and will."

Kjartan paused; "Your father has seen very little of you in recent years, but as best I can tell he's still backing you. I will secure your kingdom, Michael, but your days of viking up and down the coast of Gar are coming to an end. This should be your last cruise, Michael."

"Wrong, Uncle. Last year was my final cruise; I'm coming with you."

Kjartan was pleased; "I'd love to have you, but not this time. This will be an ugly business, and you, as future ruler, must have no part in it."

Michael was not stupid; "I understand you, Uncle, but is there nothing I can do?"

"There is; we need to trick Balba into a vulnerable position and crush them. They have connived with Siddiq, and all rulers in our part of Gar must know in their very bones what this means and what comes of it. Mendero has deep divisions and it must be very clear to our neighbors what happens when they intrigue with one of our factions. I need you at the end of the summer with as many hardy men as you can muster. The lure would be Balba itself, which has much to plunder. Arrive two months past summer solstice."

"I'll be there, and I can probably muster a few boats besides ours."

"Good."

"You sound very confident, Uncle, but if things are truly desperate perhaps I will be rescuing you at the end of the summer."

"Things are not so bad, Michael; not really. Your father has been very discreet, and Siddiq and Nur are not aware he is on to them; appearances are preserved. This is vital. The second helpful thing is your father not being aware Eyvind and I know the score; he will not get in the way. Lastly, Latcha, a long time and bitter enemy of Balba, does not want a larger and stronger Balba."

Kjartan paused; "Michael, listen closely, this is important. Latcha has the best and most elaborate system of spies, and they were the first to hear of Siddiq's plot. Did they go to your father? No; they went to Eyvind. Why? They like your father, but he's a Christian and they'd rather deal with a northman. Remember this when you come to power: you need to stick to Odin."

"What comes next makes me proud of Eyvind; he takes after his father. Eyvind thought things over and did two things: he sent a message to me, and he used an indirect route to inform your father; with the happy result your father is unaware of Eyvind's knowledge.'

"Your father repositioned Siddiq's corp so that it is far from the Balba frontier, and he placed a trusted man amongst Siddiq's officers."

Michael was surprised; "Does Siddiq have a corp?"

"Certainly he does, and this underlines how out of touch you've become. Siddiq, like yourself, is an energetic and gifted man of action; by all accounts he is an excellent leader and very much deserves a corp: until recently why would your father not give him a corp?"

"Now, Michael, you sit on that stool and I'll hold down this one; let's get back to the business at hand: you want to marry Herdis. I'm entirely in agreement. It is clear your success as a ruler in Mendero is deeply connected with your being norse, and no one can keep your toes norse and pointing the right direction quite like Herdis. You may occasionally get confused on such matters; Herdis will not. Brynjolf is a friend and I know well what a charming and exceptional woman she is; you literally cannot do better."

Michael interrupted; "I am pleased to hear your good opinion of her, and there is no other woman for me, but in light of events in Mendero perhaps it were best to wait a year."

"All true, foster son, but we must take steps now if you are to wed Herdis early next summer. You must have a farm, and Brynjolf must believe in your farm; also the bride-price must be in hand, and it should be handsome."

"My raiding has been successful and the bride-price is in hand; the farm is another matter: there is no farm, and all land in Westmark is long since claimed. My only hope, Uncle, is that you will give me the shieling and some adjoining land; perhaps we can work up a third farm."

"It's a thought,' agreed Kjartan, 'but what would I use for a shieling?"

There was a thoughtful silence.

"If our land were a little larger this would work nicely. The High farm began as a shieling and gradually grew into the High farm. Five years back I gave Hall the lower farm on the coast and moved to the hills. Now there is nowhere to go."

Michael waited; from his foster father's manner he knew a reasonable solutions would soon be unveiled.

Kjartan gave him a quizzical look; "I must be an open meadow; you don't even look worried! Do you think farms grow on trees!!"

Michael waited.

"By Thor's hammer, you're not much fun, Michael!"

Kjartan paused and sighed, "What I am going to suggest is so christian it embarrasses me."

"Be careful, Uncle; christianity is like measles – it starts as a few blotches and then grows on you."

Kjartan laughed, "I can see I am to get neither concern nor sympathy; so be it. I will give you the High farm. However, we must understand this gift: the farm is truly given, but if things go as I expect in Mendero then you will never actually take possession, rather you and Herdis will load your ship with your worldly possessions and move to Mendero. There is a lovely bit of land near Eyvind that is just right for a crown prince. Five years of being a prince and, unless I miss my guess, your father will step aside for you. Your rule will bring good and great things to Mendero; and your father, your foster father, and your brother, Eyvind, will be solidly with you."

There was a pause, a moment of quiet reflection; Michael broke the silence.

"And if things do not prosper in Mendero and we survive the change of fortune?"

"The High farm is yours, and you would take possession. You and Herdis should have a good life; perhaps better than ruling over christian and moslems in Mendero: certainly your life on Westmark would be more peaceful."

"And you, Uncle, have you thought so far ahead as to consider what you would do? For example, you could stay with me."

Kjartan chuckled; "I could, but Unn and Herdis, both strong willed queen bees, would soon be quarrelling and we, very much against our will and inclination, would be dragged in. No, thanks; I, regard you far too well for that.'

"Eyvind and I would move to Miles Drake's New World. Miles is now gone and my sister Asgerd, his wife, is alone on an excellent farm with nearby sons and daughters. She would gladly take us in, and Eyvind could have his pick of wonderful land. Before leaving, and after bitter, bitter war with the skraeling, Miles finally crushed them. Today the New World enjoys as much peace as it is in the nature of our people to allow themselves. It is a good place, and my sister, Asgerd, is very dear to me. Whether or not things prosper in Mendero I am of half a mind to join Asgerd."

Michael remained thoughtful; "Perhaps Herdis and I would join you in going to the New World."

Kjartan shrugged his shoulders; "That would be for you to decide. Herdis would not wish to move, and things are good on Westmark. Besides Hall will want you as a neighbor."

Michael let it go.

"Do you think Brynjolf will smell a rat when you 'give' me the High farm?"

"There will be a tendency that way; we will need to outsmart him."

Michael was interested; "How?"

"We will use good old Unn. I will tell Unn we are giving you the farm and not explain the qualifications. Unn will be outraged, outraged to the bone. She will share her outrage with her friends, who will share it with theirs, soon the news will come to Brynjolf, and it will come in a manner suggesting it is true."

Michael and Unn got on well, and Michael didn't care for this trick.

"Is there no other way?"

"None as certain of conveying our message of a genuine gift. But not to worry; four or five days of Unn thundering from a tower of outrage is all we will need: we will then clue her in and ask her to keep the secret. She is a good sort, she'll be discreet."

Michael looked very grave and thoughtful.

"Uncle, you are signing us on for several days of headache and genuine sorrow; perhaps we should visit Hall."

Kjartan laughed; "Suit yourself, Michael. My plan is to break the news and head for the lower farm."

CHAPTER 32
An Unexpected Visitor

(Norse World, Miles, Ninth year)

IT WAS MIDMORNING, AND a fine one, with just the right degree of sun and breeze. Kjartan, was back from a month of fishing and had spent the preceding evening with his old friend Veleif Aevarsson. He had not drunk too much and was in fine fettle. As he rode his horse towards the low or coastal farm, he reviewed his fishing trip with real satisfaction. His family had used this camp for decades, but of late he had spent his time raiding and trading, to the extent he had not been fishing in four years. Fish was an important item of diet and he needed to keep people in mind of custom and his rights, to not be viewed as an outsider and intruder. He had been well received by the other families and caught and dried many cod, saithe, and halibut. It had been hard work and they had nearly been caught by a storm; the fishing had been good in every way.

Kjartan also planned to reestablish his place amongst seal and whale hunters, and while he was thinking through the details he noticed a large bundle of furs moving along the road several hundred yards ahead. There were two legs beneath the bundle, so the spectacle was a thing of nature, but the bundle was so very large and the legs so relatively small it approached the preternatural. Clearly the idiot had never heard of horses.

Kjartan was curious as to the identity of the horse equivalent and nudged his horse to a trot. As he got closer he realized the leg weren't so diminutive; in fact, they were pretty long and large. Finally he pulled ahead and looked back: the legs were attached to his old friend Miles Drake! How?! The man had been years gone and thousands of miles away!

After a warm greeting Kjartan got off his horse and walked with Miles while the Bundle took his place on the horse, which was where it belonged in the first place.

"You're being here pretending you are a horse must be connected to the tree; is there another branch to our world near where you live?"

Miles smiled; Kjartan was as quick as ever. "There is; about twenty mile from the eastern margin of my land. By accident I bumped into it a year ago. This prompted me to investigate more carefully. The large limb to our world has five smaller branches; the other three come out in strange remote corners of the world and are not useful."

"Is Asgerd well?"

"She is pink with health. We have a fine young son we named after you, and Gyda, a delightful little girl. Asgerd is several months pregnant with our third child. We prosper and are very happy together."

After a pause. "Do you remember how I didn't want to take her with me and she insisted? Well, now I look back and bless her for overriding me."

"Miles, I stood with you in Odin's grove that day: how could I ever forget?!"

"How are Biddie and your father?"

"Both do well, though Dad is slowing down quite a bit. I've been managing the farm for several years now."

Kjartan caught himself and smiled; "Actually that isn't true; Unn manages the farm, and does a good job. Most of the time I'm away either raiding or trading. Remember those weapons you designed and had made in Mendero? I now trade them; they are much in demand and make a very tidy profit. That has proven a wonderfully fortunate stroke."

"Good, and I need to talk to you about that, but first, any kids?"

"Until a few months back Unn and I have sown much seed to very little purpose; our first child is on the way. This is fortunate since Unn was at the point of trading me in for a new bull; this kid had better look like me!"

Kjartan's tone belied the words and clearly he lost little sleep over the matter.

"Didn't my old boyhood chum Thorleif go out with the first wave of settlement? How are Thorleif and Fridgeir?"

A cloud passed over Miles's hitherto sunny face.

"Kjartan, both Thorleif and Fridgeir are dead; and they are not alone, there are many others. Which brings up the purpose of my visit and this ridiculously large bundle of furs: the skraeling."

"So I have heard', agreed Kjartan; 'according to Thorstein Ashjarnarson they are sufficiently evil to keep a wiseman from moving to Newland; are your numbers holding steady?"

"Just; we are not increasing, and there is much good unsettled land. The skraeling are a serious and hard to solve problem. They hunt and fish as a way of life and have no settled land or herd animals. We, however, are settled and have herd animals. They know exactly where we are and we have no idea where they are; and they think our cows, pigs, goats and sheep tasty. They delight in ambushing and killing us; it is something of a prestigious sport, with our blond scalps as prized trophies. We love a decisive fight, and in the few we've forced on them we won handily. They have no metal, so our weapons are better, but as they ambush us one by one we are more and more facing our own weapons, which they take from their victims. They strike at will and only under favorable circumstance, while we strike only by lucky chance.'

"They are like wolves, only with intelligence, axes, and bows."

Kjartan had heard all this from others; "Miles, your only hope is to move the fight from your homes and fields to their forests; have you figured out how to do this? Can you get your own wolves hunting them in the forest?"

"In a general way you are exactly right, Kjartan, but this is much easier said than done: we need skillful, resourceful men prowling for them day and night; how do we motivate and pay for this?"

Kjartan had a thought, "Miles, have you tried talking with their chiefs and war lords? If this does not prove useful you might at least decoy and kill central leaders."

"Talking was the obvious first step, but it has proven very frustrating and eventually I realized it is futile. The problem is there are a number of tribes, and their customs and authority patterns are such that no leader can guarantee anything worth having. Very soon the peace established by treaty is fractured, and when we retaliate the skraeling leader swears his innocence and is aggrieved, he feels betrayed. In our society every jarl is a law unto himself, but most abide by decisions at the althing; also, so far I have enjoyed great respect and authority. We can talk to some purpose; the skraeling, unfortunately, cannot. Given the differences in our way of life and political patterns I'm afraid it is a war to the knife; we will exterminate them, or they will exterminate us."

Kjartan was thoughtful; "These are hard words, Miles, especially coming from you."

"They are', agreed Mile, 'but don't take them too literally. In our case should our number go into significant decline we will leave for some smaller skraeling - free island. Their boats are not so good as ours, but in northwest Newland there is a fifteen mile strait between the island and the mother continent where a hard pressed skraeling could leave to seek a new life. Neither we nor the skraeling will be facing literal extermination."

Kjartan was relieved to hear this. "How does Asgerd see things?"

"She says we will inherit Newland, that the skraeling will prove a relatively brief headache. Hold firm, fear nothing."

"That's Asgerd!', laughed Kjartan; 'I suppose Odin whispered it in her ear?"

"No doubt; but, Kjartan, your sister has deep wells of wisdom in her. In the beginning I would have chosen a very nice spot further south on the mainland. Asgerd, usually easy and agreeable, was inflexibly opposed; inflexibly. She said we must start on an island. Had we settled on the mainland there couldn't have been a solution to the skraeling problem anymore than there is a solution to the tide. After much sorrow and loss we would have needed to leave. As it is, while the problem is large it is finite."

Soon they were arriving at the low farm, where they joined a delighted and very surprised Unn, Njal, and Biddy.

CHAPTER 33
A Summer Evening
At the Low Farm

WHILE IT IS TRUE The Bundle had ridden the horse home to the low farm, this point of privilege had been shared with several large fresh haddock, and in consequence the supper was a real treat: doubly so in that Kjartan had picked up from Miles the habit of using pepper and several other spices; southern Gar was not without its uses. Norse culinary artistes, of which Unn was an accomplished specimen, vie with each other in an effort to achieve the blandest dishes; the fish that evening represented the fruit of several years of Kjartan wheedling and coaxing, and was living proof even the largest glaciers can melt.

After supper – this particular supper would be more aptly called a dinner – Biddy and Unn fell under the spell of postprandial fetal activity. Unn felt several kicks, which she pronounced manly, and Biddy, after placing an inquisitive ear on Unn's mildly distended belly identified baby heartbeats. This was a first, and created no little stir. Biddy had spoken with vast authority, but notwithstanding Kjartan was required to corroborate. After listening very carefully for some time he delivered the opinion Biddy had an overactive imagination. This tie and roadblock to truth mobilized the great hersir and godi himself and soon Miles was on his knees with bead bent and an abstracted and attentive look on his face.

"Get the wax out of your ears Kjartan; it's like the galloping of a large horse!"

Miles left them to a scene of great rejoicing and went outside. He emerged at the back side of the house and was treated to a great surprise, which, as with the spices, also had roots in southern Gar; a patio!

There was an awning, and like the sail on a ship this could be taken down. The awning was attached to the side of the house and covered an eight by ten foot patio of closely fitted reddish sandstones. The individual stones were quite large and flat and could be taken up for winter. This was miraculous enough, but the wonders were not over: rather than the customary plank benches there were three comfortable fairly light chairs! As he sank into the most comfortable looking of the three an odd thought crossed his mind; he sat agog and charmed by this avante garde cutting edge patio, but, Erin, his dearly loved wife from the old lost life, would have dismissed it as the last word in tacky, the sort of thing in which 'trailer trash' delighted. Perhaps, but damn it was nice!: he'd obviously 'gone a long way back, baby!'

Miles chuckled at his reversal of the old Virginia Slims line and then fell to musing where to put his own patio when he got back home; Asgerd was going to love it! Getting the stones would not be easy.

From his patio revery Miles fell to musing on Erin, an activity much indulged in early years of his Norse era but neglected of late. Erin was a soft magical gold, and his throat tightened while his heart gently ached.

Not for long; Kjartan came up with two mugs of beer and sat in an adjoining chair.

"What do you think, brother?"

"I love it! I'm already planning how to make one for myself. You borrowed the idea from southern Gar?"

"I did. Be pleased to note the idea had a home, which is more than can be said for that 'thunder of hoofs' you went on about; that originated from thin air"

Miles laughed. "You are quite right, and brace yourself for more. This is a long awaited first born, and women can't help themselves; every little thing the cute scamp does, or thinks about doing will be exceptional and wonderful. The poor girls find themselves saying with conviction things they know are not true, and which they find laughable on the lips of another woman. As the later children arrive there is less of this. I kind of like it; I rather hope my mother went in for it. It is the only time most of us have to be exceptional."

Miles paused; "Any names in mind?"

"If the child is a girl the name will be 'Asgerd'; if a boy then, 'Hall'."

"Miles would make an excellent moniker.", suggested Miles.

"There are two problems with 'Miles': the first being it is not 'Hall', a favorite uncle of Unn's and a friend of mine; the second being the name 'Miles' might predispose the lad to half-baked, foolish ideas."

"You are on to something, Kjartan; I wince when I remember some of the things I have told you. Fortunately you had enough innate sense to ignore me."

Kjartan was surprised and charmed; Miles had never critically reviewed his own ideas. "Which particular silliness did you have in mind?"

"This is embarrassing, Kjartan; you are the only person in this world with whom I discuss my own world; you seem, at least to me, to have a foothold in my world, though admittedly it is a peculiar foothold."

"Thanks Miles; what particular foolishness are we considering?"

"Unconditional human rights."

"Ah', comprehension dawned; 'I would imagine the skraeling have helped clear your head."

"They have, but there is also regret and embarrassment. My ancestors, unlike ourselves who are beginning on an island, landed on the continent, a continent teeming with every sort of skraeling. The skraeling, as might be imagined, were every sort of headache, but my ancestors were hardy and more numerous than ourselves; over several hundred years the skraeling were strictly confined to chosen small areas and the continent was settled and placed under a reasonable law.'

"So far so good. A generation after this hard task was completed my people, with 'human rights' in mind, looked at the inoffensive domesticated skraeling in cages, forgot the wolves who had ambushed and scalped their ancestors, and judged themselves evil and perfidious. There was much wailing and beating of breasts over our many sins."

Miles paused; "This view was so pervasive, so saturated with 'human rights', that I myself halfway bought it. Now, having met genuine skraeling I look back on my ancestors with respect and understanding; the amazing thing is not that skraeling were hunted and pushed onto reservations, but that they weren't hunted and pushed harder. Had I been directing operations the reservations would be small indeed and the resident skraeling few."

Miles paused and took a pull at his mug; "However, Kjartan, were I back in my own world I would never tell another what I have told you; it would be like telling Asgerd Odin farts."

"That bad?', laughed Kjartan; 'so, Miles, why do you pine for this silly world!? For pine you do, my friend."

"Less and less as time passes; I'm turning norse. Besides a lot of good pining will do me around Asgerd and skraeling!'

"Furthermore, 'human rights', as people get closer in culture and situation, really is a wonderful and useful idea; unfortunately when this qualification is not understood it is a beguiling abstraction, high minded nonsense – a bear trap!"

"Believe me', chuckled Kjartan, 'it was an obvious bear trap from the very start.'

"You have been telling on your world, Miles, but I have had a stray thought that rather tells on ours. In your tale of difficulty in Newland substitute 'sea' for 'forest' and 'norse' for 'skraeling' and you have a nice approximation of how responsible leaders in Gar see ourselves."

"To be sure you are losing sleep over this stray thought?"

Kjartan laughed; "You know I am not – this is only the stray thought on a pleasant summer evening. For me 'rights' are things you carve out for yourself; when the people of Gar force me to respect their 'rights' then I will; until then they are not my problem and I will deal with them as it suits me."

"It seems', interjected Miles, 'that though there are similarities between ourselves and the skraeling, yet there is a crucial point of difference. There are parts of Gar where hard-pressed princes have ceded land to our people in return for peace and quiet. Have you noticed what happens?"

"We settle down, farm the land, and keep the law."

"Exactly. All of us, the various people of Gar, Norland, Westmark, and the other islands farm and have domestic animals – it is quite a bond. We can share laws, and even 'rights' with such people. If the skraeling would settle and farm their own land and keep the law I would love them as brothers. This is not possible, and things must come to a finish where either they or ourselves possess Newland. At the moment it is hard to see us standing at the end, but Asgerd is quite certain we shall inherit Newland – and in the near future."

"Which reminds me: tell me of Newland; in what ways is it like and in what ways different from Westmark?"

"Newland is half again as large as Westmark and not quite so far north. Winters, despite the lower latitude, are a little colder and summers a little warmer. Westmark has more forest than an island so far north has any right to expect, so this is not meant to diminish Westmark, but Newland is better wooded. Birds and their eggs are comparable, or perhaps not quite as good as Westmark. Seals, whales and walrus are comparable. However, fishing, while good in Westmark, is astounding around Newland. Pasture is comparable.'

"A thing I like, which, as you were raised in Westmark, would mean less to you, is a genuine day and night in high summer and deep winter. Right now in Westmark 'night' is a twilight between midnight and two in the morning while 'day' in midwinter is a hint of dawn seen between noon and 2 P.M.'

"Newland has some mountains, but none so big as those of central Gar. Our home is on a hill looking down on a quiet bay."

Miles paused; "Newland is both a good and a fair land; the only problem is the skraeling – and the isolation. It is so far away trading is hard; though perhaps there are more developed non-skraeling peoples farther south; if so these would be potential trading partners. Time will tell."

Kjartan leaned back in his chair and stretched; "I can see for myself you have many and rich furs; I have seldom seen better fox, mink, or ermine pelts than those you were carrying – all one hundred eighty pound of them! You, Miles, are more ox than man."

"It was quite a burden; thanks for coming along."

"There is one other thing needful; we hope to find iron deposits. Do you know any men knowledgeable in such things who could come out, survey the land, and get us started?"

"I suppose we could trade for metal products, but we are so distant it would be better to have a degree of independence in metals."

"Our Mendero connection may help us, Miles; they have a good supply of incoming metal and we can beg, borrow, or steal one of their experts. I'll look into it next year when I trade your skins for weapons."

The men sipped their beer in a companiable silence. At length Kjartan spoke; "In your world do they have anything like my paving stones and awning? Surely so."

"Very much so. We pretty much all had either a patio, a porch, or a deck. This is a patio, and a deck is an open wooden platform situated alongside the house; some decks completely encircle the house. On the deck and patio there are several comfortable light chairs that are not harmed by a bit of rain. Usually there is a low table for drinks, or perhaps your feet."

"The porch, Kjartan, is something of a hybrid, and involves screens, which you have never seen. The porch is 'outside', but not completely."

Miles thought a moment; "Imagine walls of chain mail along the margin of your patio. These walls extend from the ground to the awning. Now start removing metal from the walls till the components of the mesh are finer than the finest thread of silk or cotton. This would no longer blunt a spear or sword thrust, but it keeps out bugs and animals. Such screens let light through and, believe it or not, you can see things through it – cows, enemies, clouds, trees; everything."

Chain mail that fine and with such properties boggled Kjartan's mind; "that's the trouble with what you tell me, Miles - I never know how or when to believe. I accept your airplanes, afterall, there are birds, but this magical mesh is a bit much.'

Kjartan paused; "Miles, is this mesh for real?"

"Like your long house and the chairs in which we sit."

"If, if this is on the up and up, then what does such a miraculous mesh cost?!"

"Very little. Everyone has much of it; even the poorest. It is very handy stuff Kjartan."

Kjartan was baffled and hardly knew what to think. He changed the subject.

"Did you notice how quiet the long house is?"

"I did, and it was wonderful; almost like home, but not quite – there were a few servants. I had meant to ask: what is going on?!"

Kjartan was pleased; "I am very seldom home in the summer and two thirds of my lads are out raiding with friends. Those left are at the high farm putting new roofs on both the long house and barn. A few are still fishing; but they will be along soon. It is the odd chance things are so quiet; apparently Odin, who knows how you hate our crowded long houses, has yet again favored you. The cup of your luck, Miles, has no bottom.'

"Now, how long can you stay?"

"I'm leaving after breakfast, and don't pretend you aren't relieved; you <u>are</u> the man who needed to get off whaling and sealing? You certainly look like him!"

"I am that man, but even so I will travel with you to the tree; I have always wanted to see you enter the tree. According to Asgerd it is most alarming and unusual. It is three miles to the tree and if we walk rather than ride we can work out the details of your project for Newland. I'm not sure you have thought it through completely."

"Sounds good to me; if you are consistently so hospitable I will have to visit more often."

CHAPTER 34
Miles Shelves His Plan

IT IS NOT POSSIBLE to beat the sun out of bed during high summer in Westmark; Kjartan and Miles were up before 5 A.M. and were greeted by the broadest sort of daylight.

The first order of business was to clarify a blunder Mile had made last night while on the patio with Kjartan. Miles had told Kjartan he would be leaving immediately after breakfast; Miles meant by this he'd be leaving early after minimal social amenities; the day would be cleared of him; all original plans were untouched. Norse customs, however, were different from ours. There were two meals a day, breakfast at 9 A.M. and the evening meal, or supper, at 9 P.M. The norse rise early and usually are working shortly after 6 A.M. Three hours later they take a break for the morning meal.

Miles had been living amongst the norse for the past nine years and knew this very well; the problem was Kjartan, who was the only northmen with whom Miles had shared his world in other than the most perfunctory way. Around Kjartan and the patio the old associations had momentarily returned, and 'breakfast' had ambushed him.

Miles and Kjartan headed for the tree carrying a bit of bread and leftover fish for a trail-side breakfast at the tree entrance. Evenings on a patio tend to promote broad views with a touch of the speculative; mornings are inherently narrower and more practical. This truth surfaced early.

"Kjartan, I said many things last night, and much of it was thinking aloud with a close friend. I <u>do</u> want you to trade the furs for weapons, and if possible get two mail shirts. I do need an expert on iron mining. However I do <u>not</u> want you recruiting young vikings for Newland; the idea has merit, but after sleeping on it perhaps it is premature. I plan to review a modified form of the scheme in two years."

Kjartan was surprised; "Why Miles? Your scheme of trading skraeling scalps for farms has much to be said for it. You must be aware our bright young men of high mettle raid in the south in order to win a farm, animals, and wife when they are in their thirties. Providing these things in exchange for skraeling scalps would unquestionably divert some lads to Newland. This would be a double blessing: it increases norse numbers in Newland, and diminishes skraeling numbers. So, again, why delay this?"

"I agree with all you say, Kjartan, and I've even gone into some detail on exactly how to count scalps; for example, a male scalp between ages sixteen and fifty will count as two scalps, while old men, women, and males ten to fifteen count as one scalp. The very young are half a scalp. Sixteen scalps get you a farm, which include a hall, an animal shed, two cows, three sheep, and rights at common fishing and hunting camps. You are launched.'

"I hesitate for several reasons: the skraeling have much woodcraft and know the land well; our sending small bands of green young men onto their homeground may be supplying them with scalps and metal weapons. This would prove very demoralizing for us."

"The details of exactly who goes, how they are organized, how they are armed, probably matters much. For example, our mail shirts and helmets are extremely good protection against their stone tipped wooden weapons. Should parties of fewer than seven be allowed? Greater parties of more than twenty-five would probably pose considerable danger to ourselves; why should they take little farms here and there as we choose when they might just as well take the whole area of large farms? These and many other questions need careful thought before we loose these dangerous young men.'

"There is very little public spirit and even less authoritative government amongst our people. Supplying the labor and animals to set up the farms will tax our resources, goodwill, and customs past their breaking point. A farmer who is on the coast and surrounded with good neighbors won't be seeing much of a skraeling problem and will find little inclination to send his share of animals and workers. We will inevitably fall to quarrelling amongst ourselves, and we tend to quarrel with axes and spears."

Kjartan had grown thoughtful. "Sadly, Miles, I must agree. Westmark was largely settled by people leaving Norland rather than cooperate with and submit to the early kings of Norland. As a people we are very independent and don't tolerate interference in our affairs."

"Just so', agreed Miles, 'and if you play the story out it would bring about the very outcome it was devised to avoid."

"Explain", was Kjartan's laconic reply.

"Take our farmer who won't pay his share on the 'scalps for land' projects; if the project is not to collapse he will need to be killed, but this would inevitably flag me an overbearing would-be king type and ultimately many would load their ships and move to nearby smaller islands that have no skraeling. The skraeling would inherit Newland, which is what the project was seeking to avoid.'

"This possibility is quite real, and in consequence I don't want to take the risk unless I have little to lose."

"When would that be?", asked a curious Kjartan.

"Well, certainly not now. At the moment things are stable; we are neither growing nor losing ground. For now we play for time. However suppose the skraeling burn three or four farms and people begin to leave: we know exactly where things are tending and we no longer have anything to lose by loosing hungry war bands on them."

Miles fell silent and began smiling; "We know something most people miss, Kjartan; 'playing for time' in our case is a loaded die."

"I'm pleased to learn this, old friend, but you are the only one who knows the die is loaded; I have seldom seen a die that seems so neutral and fair."

"Asgerd says the skraeling will soon be gone; she has a well established record of being right with her pronouncements; I rather expect what I need is patience rather than war bands."

At this Kjartan couldn't help laughing; "Miles you are too much! Despite our late summer experience with Erik out on the tundra, despite our day in Odin's grove, despite Yngvar's death, you think of Odin and the Aesir the way I think of 'human rights' – both are fairy tales for children. Now you treat Asgerd as the word of god and hold back our war bands; I don't get it!"

"Kjartan, ability is one thing, understanding exactly how the ability works is another. Asgerd is the real article – I have eyes in my head – but Asgerd's own understanding of her ability is confused and misplaced."

Kjartan found Mile's childlike faith in Asgerd a little disconcerting and out of character; "Miles, do you have the slightest idea how this will come about? If you don't then surely this must bother you."

"Of course I have my ideas. The overwhelming likely event will be some routine norse virus with which we have lived for centuries will cause a ghastly epidemic amongst the skraeling, basically wipe them out."

"What is a virus?'

Miles looked at him helplessly, shrugged his shoulders; "It is a way of describing illness; an illness we routinely survive may destroy the skraeling."

They walked on with great good cheer until at arriving at the tree portal. Kjartan had never been around when Miles had entered the tree and this offered Miles a bit of sport. As they approached the portal area he walked well to Kjartan's left and conversed and gestured so as to capture Kjartan's attention. Once on the tree trail he turned around and looked back; Kjartan was 'frozen' with one foot in the air and looking left. Miles walked off the trail on Kjartan's right side and tapped him on the shoulder.

Kjartan was so startled he had to sit down.

CHAPTER 35
Thorkel

(Kjartan, age 58)

Thorkel Eyjolfsson was in good mood as he walked through the early morning drizzle towards the palace. There were a number of reasons why he might not be in an upbeat mood: firstly, rain at any point of the day shields a man from a good mood, but rain is particularly detumescing first thing in the morning; secondly, Thorkel's plans for the morning might easily get him killed – this also tends to put cold water on one's mood. The second point didn't much bother Thorkel; death would come when it came, and there was nothing for it but to shrug the shoulders and make sure to arrange as much company as possible. Thorkel was six feet two inches and was lean, quick and very strong; his appearance suggested tanned rawhide. He was about to turn forty and had enough experience and knowhow for three men. Thorkel was calmly certain there would be much company when he signed off.

The roots of Thorkel's sunny mood reached back to last night's pub chat with Hrafnkell, and long time buddy and former shipmate. But first some background.

At eighteen Thorkel had become Kjartan's man. For the next ten years he had raided and traded with Kjartan. He came to be much valued by Kjartan and was Kjartan's chief lieutenant. During this decade Kjartan saw to it Thorkel did well; so well he could easily have settled down.

When Eyvind allied himself with Sandaman and became chief of military operations Kjartan was much concerned his son have a capable and loyal group of men with him. Kjartan was slowing down and he sent his best men with Eyvind; inevitably this included Thorkel.

Twelve years later Thorkel, approaching forty, was ready to settle down on his own farm. Eyvind had a lovely spot for him and also slaves and animals to spare. Of course there must be a wife, and this is where complications set in. Two years earlier during a lull in military operations Thorkel and several other norse made a visit back home to Westmark. Thorkel had wintered with Kjartan, who was delighted to have his old friend back. A pretty servant girl, Hildirid, had done a superb job warming his bed and entertaining him. Thorkel was in a settling down frame of mind and so charmed was he by Hildirid he had half promised to transplant her to Mendero to preside over his hall.

Upon returning to Mendero Thorkel had become involved with Dorothy, a pretty young chrisitan widow with two small children. Dorothy had baggage, no doubt possible, but such was her sweetness the luggage seemed more like handbags than trunks. Dorothy's christianity? Thorkel didn't much care – once you've seen one god you've pretty much seen them all. If he had to pick he preferred Thor, but as long as Dorothy kept a low profile with her religion Thorkel hardly noticed. Thorkel liked the kids and took to bringing them toys and treats.

And Hildirid? Thorkel's conscience was a little turbid on that point – until last night; on their third beer his old shipmate Hrafnkell had confided he was retiring to Westmark to take over the family farm and marry Kjartan's servant girl Hildirid. Establishing one's own hall is serious stuff and Hildirid, smart girl that she was, had long since decided it best to put out more than a single line.

So it was that as Thorkel walked through the light rain to meet Kjartan and Jon he was in a good, a very good mood.

CHAPTER 36

Council of War

THERE WAS A LULL in traffic and for the moment Kjartan, Thorkel, and Jon had the steps to themselves. Kjartan looked around to confirm this then turned to Thorkel; "Thorkel, be tolerant of an old man and carefully tell me your part and responsibilities in our mission."

Thorkel thought this excessive and revealing a bit of the anxious mother hen, but Kjartan was the shrewdest of men and perhaps it was for the best; "If we disarm when we enter the hall then alongside your axe you will leave a small bundle containing a map. If we are not disarmed you will ask one of the soldiers near the door to keep an eye on the bundle, and then place it outside the door. Once in the hall you will go to the table and discuss the upcoming operation. You will take careful note of who is present. If Siddiq and most of his officers are present then things will proceed as planned. If Siddiq is not there then the plan is aborted. While you discuss plans, Jon and I will quietly get the weapons we have hidden in the fireplace. If we are watched too closely I will create the distraction we discussed and Jon will quietly get our weapons."

Kjartan interrupted; "Thorkel, if you need to use the distraction remember to act with dignity; you aren't much of a talker so when you speak people notice, especially if you speak deliberately and with care. Your point about the river ford is going to capture all the attention the hall has to give."

"Not to worry', chuckled Thorkel, 'I will be a lion at the council.'

"After creating the distraction I will step back near the door and a few moments later you will call over to ask if there is anything else you have forgotten. If we have our weapons I will reply there is nothing else. If Jon is not yet successful I will say there is a further point that occurs to me and return to the table for a second distraction.'

"When we are ready you will excuse yourself to get the other map which is outside the door. If you leave the bundle where it was, then after you reenter the hall our archers strike. If you move the bundle further from the door the mission is aborted."

"Good, Thorkel; I am satisfied. Jon, tell me your part."

Jon, like Thorkel, had suffered more than enough, but like Thorkel he remained attentive and respectful.

"I will stand near the fireplace and if necessary move the bench in front of the fireplace. When I get the chance I will lower our weapons from where we hid them in the chimney. Once lowered they will be just behind me; ready to hand. I have practiced this maneuver and can lower the rope behind my back without moving my arms.'

"When we go into action my responsibility is the rear door, which must be open for our men or we will find ourselves outnumbered in a nest of hornets; to be sure the hornets will die, but it would be best they die quickly and by themselves."

Kjartan was pleased; "Sorry for worrying this thing to death, but much hangs on it.'

"Well, let's go and get the thing done."

The rain had stopped and their walk to the Prophets Hall even included a few moments of sunshine. As they approached the courtyard a squad of ten or twelve men came in on either side of them and all three men were grabbed, one man on each arm. The northmen were large and had passed at least half their lives rowing long boats. Jon and Thorkel shook off the smaller men and reached for their axes. Kjartan, who was approaching sixty, managed to free his right arm and trip the man on his right, then, as by magic, there was a long thin knife in his right hand, and in an eye blink he thrust it up and under the breast bone and to the left. The soldier whose hands were engaged holding Kjartan's left arm died almost immediately.

There was a stunned and momentary silence during which Kjartan stooped and wiped his bloody blade on the dead man's tunic before thoughtfully putting it in his belt.

Kjartan spoke with quiet authority; "Who commands!?"

"I do", spoke a grizzled old thug with a turban and a hideously deformed left ear.

"Is it possible, you get of a pig, to be unaware we are here as friends and commanding officers of Prince Sandaman for a council of war!? Do you place so little value on the lives of your wives and children!?"

The thuglike officer managed a surprising degree of dignity; "The lives of our families are in the hands of Allah, not yours, rudest of infidels. We know who you are and your business. Our measures are drastic since we fear there is a plot against the life of Sandaman. It is said to arise from those close to him."

Kjartan looked at him with incredulity; what impudence!

Kjartan burst out laughing; "Prince Siddiq's concern for the safety of his father is most touching, and becomes him.

I too want Sandaman safe, so I will cooperate – to a degree. You may walk around us in the manner of a prison detail, but we will keep our weapons and you will keep your hands off us. Is this clear?"

"My orders, infidel….", but Kjartan interrupted; "There is nothing to discuss. We have allowed Prince Siddiq to name the time and place of our war council; this is more than a gesture of good faith. If you persist, our plans for the upcoming operations will not include your corp, or we will be meeting in council at a time and place of our choosing. You are not acting as a corp commander in Sandaman's army should act; do you work for another?"

There was a pause; "We will either be leaving to make different arrangements, going with you in the manner I described, or finding out right now who the Valkyrie will take."

Kjartan clearly meant what he said, and after a thoughtful pause the officer gave his orders and his men formed up around the three northmen, who were left armed and alone.

Thorkel was pleased, indeed, delighted, with his old leader. With his own eyes Thorkel had never seen a knife hidden in a sleeve be anything other than a nuisance. Kjartan had shown him how to secure the blade with a delicate thread that broke when you shook your arm in a certain manner, a manner that propelled the blade into one's hand. So, that bit of silliness actually had some point! The thrust itself was a beauty – fast and accurate. The old chief might have a gimpy leg, might be a bit grizzled and weather beaten, but he was still the real article.

They were being escorted to a new destination; this was exactly what Kjartan had expected, and Thorkel was curious how well his old chief had guessed. As they walked down La Vida Avenue their prison formation attracted, as moths to a candle, the attention of every stray norseman. Soon there was much company, angry company, company trembling on the edge of control. A friend of Thorkel's, Thorstein, approached Thorkel, clearly seeking clarification. An arab soldier began to push Thorstein back and instantaneously received a savage head butt that knocked him senseless. (Thorstein was wearing a light helmet). Thorstein looked around the neighboring soldiers as though to say, 'who's next'; there were no takers and he turned to Thorkel; "What is going on? Do you need help?"

"No, all is well', then he chuckled, 'if it weren't, my axe would be in my hand and these men long since feeding crows."

"So why the prisoner formation? We are norse in a public place: I don't care whether this is acceptable to you or not, Thorkel; the formation changes immediately or these soldiers are dead men. You know I mean this, so get things changed quickly."

Kjartan had overheard this, and had even expected it. He turned to the commanding officer.

"These men are angry at our public disgrace. You must disperse the formation and keep your authority and lives, or do nothing and lose both. This must happen right now, seconds count.

The officer looked around; he had eyes in his head and things were exactly as Kjartan presented.

"We will break formation; tell these stray northmen what is coming so there is peace and understanding."

Kjartan spoke to the group; "This officer is about to break formation; as a favor to me I want a quiet, peaceful transition."

Kjartan nodded to the officer, who gave the order, and soon there was only a large body of unorganized men moving down La Vida. Gradually the norse dispersed and went about their business. At length they arrived at Medina Hall. Thorkel was impressed, once again the chief had been right.

But events were still in play; a new squad of twelve soldiers took them to yet another destination. Five minutes later they arrived at The Oasis, an informal Islamic meeting place, and one not staked out by the wily Kjartan. This caused great concern amongst the three northmen, but not for long; a third squad now marched them towards a new location. Fifteen minutes later they were once again approaching the Prophets Hall; they had come full circle, and Kjartan, as ever, stood revealed as the cleverest of men. Thorkel looked over at Kjartan and gave him a appreciative nod – touché.

At the hall entrance everyone was requested to disarm. Kjartan placed his axe, dagger, and a small bag up against the wall near the door; Jon and Thorkel followed suit and placed their weapons by Kjartan's. Then they entered the hall.

As they entered the hall Thorkel noticed there were too many men, and they were more heavily armed than was appropriate; instantly he came to a fine point of alert attention. Thorkel was like a drawn bow for what happened next; there was an alarmed shout and a man with two arrows protruding from his chest staggered through the door.

Quick as thought Thorkel pulled a dagger from the belt of the soldier ahead of him and thrust it home; as the soldier fell Thorkel managed to grab his scimitar. With almost superhuman quickness Thorkel blocked a sword thrust aimed at Kjartan. Before the owner of the sword thrust could recover Thorkel ran his dagger through the man's neck. Kjartan had been slower off the mark, but he was now up to speed and caught the dying man's sword as he fell. Kjartan and Thorkel were now armed, but in a desperate position.

Jon had not adjusted as quickly and was on the floor dying from multiple knife wounds.

All but one of the outside guards, both front and back, had died from arrows, and now the northmen were at the doors with axes. There were men at the doors ready to fight and die, but when the heavy doors were smashed the incoming vikings would have shields and could effectively rush the soldiers; things would be over soon, but would it be soon enough? There was, however, a major consolation, Siddiq and most of his officers were in the room – and utterly intent on selling their lives dearly.

Thorkel and Kjartan fought desperately and tried to work their way to a corner of the room where they could limit the approach of the enemy and survive till the doors were down. Unfortunately the room was large and the nearest corner was fifteen feet away. It is hard to parry ten sword thrusts at the same time, and Kjartan's age soon showed; he was just not quick enough, and Thorkel quick and strong though he was, could not parry his share and half of Kjartan's. The men they fought were experienced, desperate, and had nothing to lose; the pressure on Thorkel was impossible and finally, as Thorkel lunged to parry for Kjartan his own side was exposed and he took a deep sword thrust to his left flank. Things were such that he hardly noticed the wound in the sense of being overcome and helpless with pain, but, experienced man that he was, he knew with calm certainty the wound was mortal and his time limited – the Valkyrie were in the room with him and it was time, not to live, but to take many with him.

The rage of Odin enveloped Thorkel and he began moving with overdrive strength and speed; he brushed risk and cost to the side, he went berserk, and men began dying on all sides. Thorkel received many wounds, with the last wound being a deep right groin thrust that severed both the femoral artery and nerve; Thorkel could no longer move his right lower extremity, so he hopped on his left leg amidst the few men standing, and split Siddiq's head down to mid neck. After this Thorkel collapsed and could no longer lift a weapon.

Kjartan, in his uninspired workman like way, had killed two men, and as the doors finally gave way he killed the last soldier, who had been intent on beheading the collapsed Thorkel. Kjartan had received a nasty but survivable cut above his gimpy right knee – why was it always this leg? – but he completely ignored this and knelt beside Thorkel. "Thorkel, I saw how it was; you took my death wound on yourself; thank you; I will strive to be worthy of it. Is there anything I can do for you?"

Thorkel grasped Kjartan's hand weakly and tried to smile; then, in a weak whisper, "Guard and care for my girl Dorothy and her children."

Kjartan squeezed his hand and said; "She is my daughter; sleep well." Thorkel died with a faint smile on his lips.

CHAPTER 37
Loose Ends

NUR STUDIED HER MIRROR thoughtfully. There had been a time when she was an acknowledged beauty and envied by other women; perhaps there were echoes of that time, but in truth they were growing faint. It didn't help that she favored her mother and was a little, well, perhaps more than a little, overweight. Where was the maid who was to do her hair?

Nur turned from the fat middle-aged face in the mirror and looked out the window, hoping for a more cheerful scene; alas, the weather was gray and rainy, no birds chirped or sang in the garden.

Neither the mirror nor the window had much cheer to them, so her thoughts turned in a direction ever interesting and encouraging: Siddiq.

Nur knew this was an important morning, knew the infidel commanders were to die, knew this was just, necessary, and to the greater glory of Allah; and Siddiq had looked so handsome and lordly in his new uniform!

There was a knock at the door. The maid; late again, the hussy! Still, having her hair done was always pleasant and Nur was looking forward to it.

"Come in."

It was not the usual maid; this girl was larger and had blue eyes; probably one of those northern infidels she had specifically requested not be allowed in her service. Nur was vexed; heads would roll!

"Who are you, girl, and who hired you?!"

"Shareen is sick and I was sent in her place." The accent matched the blue eyes; this was sure enough one of those savage northern infidels both she and Siddiq so detested.

"Who sent you?"

"I do not know his name, princess, but he was short and fat. Shall I begin?"

"Do you know anything of hair, girl?"

"I am from north of here, but where I come from I am considered very good."

This was spoken with a becoming modesty, and a new hair style would be curious, interesting.

"Just this once; I don't want to see you tomorrow."

As the girl came over she glanced above Nur's left shoulder. Nur turned to see what had caught her interest and never saw the flashing knife blade.

Later the girl went to the window and signaled someone in the garden. Ten minutes later the new carpet Nur 'had requested' was delivered; Nur left in the old carpet.

SIDDIQ HAD NEVER BEEN interested in Kjartan's campaign plans; the 'war council' was entirely an occasion to kill important commanders, especially Kjartan, who was generally recognized as a wily and dangerous enemy.

Both Kjartan and Siddiq were intent on their own treacherous use of the council and neither had considered the other might have the same intent. Given the overall pattern, all commanders, both norse and moslem, should have died: how was it Kjartan got away only slightly scathed?

Certainly Thorkel played a critical part; subtract his quickness off the mark, skill, strength, and selflessness and Kjartan would have died. Yet Thorkel, while necessary to Kjartan's survival, was not sufficient. Siddiq's original plan had been to have his victims around the table in the center of the room. While unarmed and studying a map he would have struck them down from behind; this would infallibly have worked. Siddiq's timing was ruined by the premature viking attack.

This attack should not have happened till much later, when one of the three norse leaders had come outside and moved Kjartan's bag. The missing ingredient in Kjartan's survival was Stein's colon.

At 2 A.M. of the morning in question the Vikings had staked out three likely sites for the council; the Prophet's Hall was the agreed on meeting site but Kjartan anticipated Siddiq would change the meeting place – he knew he would had he been Siddiq. The buildings near these halls had been emptied and their owners temporarily moved to Eyvind's estate. The viking archers were positioned to kill all men around these halls at one stroke.

Stein, a phlegmatic, competent man was in charge at the Prophet's Hall. Stein was very clear on the plan and arranged signals; his subordinate Thormod was not. Stein had the front of the hall under thoughtful scrutiny when Kjartan first arrived. However the men never entered the hall. Stein half expected this and was not alarmed. An hour later it began looking like the show would be elsewhere and Stein at last gave in to the importunities of nature and went to answer nature's call. When Kjartan's party returned Thormod was on-duty, and in consequence the norse archers struck immediately after Kjartan entered the hall. Kjartan had luck.

LATCHA FEARED AND DISTRUSTED Balba far more than she feared and distrusted Mendero.

Latcha was fabled throughout Gar for her secret service. A few months earlier an envoy from Latcha approached officials in Balba and with the news Latcha expected to be attacked by Mendero. Latcha had received the news and the plan of attack from reliable sources. Latcha presented to Balba that while there was little love or trust between them yet Mendero was the greater threat; Balba could fight alongside Latcha now, or alone later. Balba was already planning to invade Mendero and establish Siddiq, so this afforded yet greater security for their plans: Latcha, Balba, and Siddiq's corp would now enjoy not only surprise but vastly superior force. As Balba saw it, Mendero was going down, and the fatheads in Latcha would wake up at the end of the day to find themselves isolated and on borrowed time.

Kjartan's battle plan had Mendero invading through a little known pass. Having this information in advance Latcha could ambush Mendero as they entered Latcha. Latcha wanted Balba to cut through a very convenient and remote pass on the Mendero – Balba frontier and attack the Mendero army from behind. This should allow the complete destruction of Mendero's army. In the future it would be business as usual without interfering norse and christians.

Kjartan intended to march his army as per public plan towards the Latcha pass and then, by night double back to the Balba pass and destroy Balba's army within the pass.

To strengthen Balba's confidence Kjartan leaked his battle plan via an entirely separate route, and this arrived in Balba the day of the assassinations.

Latcha was in a position to double cross either Mendero or Balba so both Mendero and Latcha decided their spirit of cooperation and trust would be strengthened by exchanging hostages; these would be returned at the end of operations. Eyvind's son Miles, and Haroun, crown prince of Latcha, were exchanged. This established a strong working trust.

Two of Siddiq's officers were absent from the war council and these men were picked up as they and their families made their way to Balba. This was not blind good luck; Kjartan had posted squads on major roads to Balba starting two days before the assassination and included men in the patrols who could identify all of the officers.

KJARTAN WINCED AT YET another sharp jab, and sighed: sewing up wounds never got better; not with age, not with experience, not with anything. He was fortunate Thorfinn had been in the cleanup detail; the man had a way with wounds. Not that at the moment – ouch! – he was feeling especially fortunate.

But all things come to an end and twenty minutes later, after declining a horse, Kjartan was painfully making his way down La Vida towards his favorite pub. With a hundred yards to go he heard a horse approach behind. The horse slowed and shortly Kjartan was facing what he'd hoped to put off for a few hours; the horseman was his old friend Sandaman.

"Kjartan, you are not looking very spry; want to ride the horse?"

Horses were the last thing Kjartan wanted; "Thanks Sandaman, but the thought of getting on and off a horse, or my leg pressing against a horse, is daunting; right now I'm best afoot. I'm on my way to the pub and if you'll join me I'll answer the questions you are about to ask me."

Sandaman was both surprised and not surprised; "Of course I'll come, and I'm afraid of what you may tell me; should I be?"

"No, Sandaman, my news is good, but hard. Let's leave it for now.'

"Can you disguise yourself so as not to ruin pub life?; these men are here to relax and put their feet up, and they can't do that if the prince is present."

"I've long since solved that problem, Kjartan; the publican is an old friend and I have a quiet side room I use."

A little later they had their quiet room and beer; Kjartan had his injured extremity elevated on a stool.

"So, Kjartan, what is it I want to know?"

"Three months ago, Sandaman, you learned Siddiq and Nur were plotting a coup to remove you from power; the reasons for this treachery were based on much high-minded nonsense concerning their religion. Of course your own difficult path was and is where the true welfare of Mendero lies."

"How do you know this?" This was the part Kjartan feared; Eyvind not informing his prince of his own knowledge.

"Eyvind was informed of the plot by Latcha. Eyvind saw to it you received the information but in such a way as not to suspect he knew. His thinking being that you could inform him if you wished, but should the plot paralyze you he would be free to act.'

"You, old friend, were paralyzed; so Eyvind and I have done on your behalf what clearly needed to be done: as we sit here Siddiq, his officers, and Nur are out of the picture. If it is any consolation, Siddiq and his officers died well; they were fine men, and it is sad indeed they chose a path making such hard measures necessary."

There was along pregnant pause; Sandaman was a very conflicted man, but there was more sorrow than anger in his mien.

"You have the kingdom you built and deserve, Sandaman, and your son and my foster son has not been robbed of his inheritance. Michael is going to rule long and well. Your early instincts about Michael were truer than you could have hoped; posterity will refer to him as Michael the Just, or Michael the Great."

Kjartan was intent Sandaman's attention be fixed on what he had, not what was lost; "We are lucky Sandaman, we have Mendero and Michael; let's drink to them – come on; bottoms up!"

The friends quaffed a mighty quaff. When their mugs were tabled Sandaman spoke; "This has not been easy for either of us, Kjartan, but thanks."

"Good; I had hoped you would understand. Now down to business; we are only half done: we must deal with Balba."

The friends discussed the campaign against Balba and before long Sandaman was deeply involved and looking forward to the arrival of Michael and the reinforcements.

THE PUB WAS ALSO an inn and Kjartan, courtesy of his wound, passed a restless night.

In the morning he set about settling a last loose thread; Dorothy. Kjartan was fortunate in his daughter-in-law, Rebecca, who was both a christian and his buddy; seldom has a father gotten on so well with his daughter-in-law. This happy state of affairs was tangibly strengthened by Unn having never set foot in Mendero.

The christian community in Mendero, while a substantial minority, was small enough that Rebecca and Dorothy knew each other well and were friends.

Indeed, it was Rebecca's happy marriage with Eyvind that had encouraged Dorothy to overlook Thorkels' heathenism.

Early in the afternoon Dorothy was outside her humble home washing clothes. As Rebecca and Kjartan approached, Dorothy laid the clothes back in the water and slowly dried her hands. When she finished she modestly greeted them, but there were tears in her eyes; Kjartan being at her home without Thorkel could only mean one thing.

When she heard the story Dorothy tried hard to be brave, but before long she was crying in Rebecca's arms.

Eventually she composed herself and was deeply happy to learn she was to be Kjartan's daughter and sister to Rebecca and Eyvind. There was a good dowry being held for her, and more immediately Rebecca had come with extra food and clothes.

Dorothy decided to stay in Mendero rather than live with Eyvind and Rebecca. Her home was much improved and Rebecca sent regular gifts of food and clothes. The neighbors became very respectful and none dared trifle with her.

The dowry put her marriage prospects on an entirely different footing and two years later she married Seth, son to Mary and Crispus. Son?! Yes, on the fifth try Crispus had finally had a son, who was a fine fellow and was now running the forge. The marriage proved strong and happy.

CHAPTER 38
The Skraeling and the Tree

(Miles, Eleventh year)

IT WAS EARLY AUTUMN as Miles Drake walked towards the Low Farm. He was only five minutes off the tree and its peace and sense of well-being lingered, working in concert with a gentle breeze, a surprisingly warm sun on his back, and the near prospect of seeing Kjartan and Unn; his mood was excellent.

The first two miles of the three mile walk were almost a continuation of the tree, only with a little more edge and definition to the good mood; then it ended, abruptly.

Some distant niggling thing from the far back nether regions of his mind suddenly came into sharp hard focus, and it arrived with conviction and authority. Miles swinging pace slowed for several hundred yards while he digested his sudden insight; then, though the thought had a certain darkness and saddened him, he resolutely put it to the side and his thoughts returned to the dear friends he had not seen for over two years.

The eternal day of high summer in high latitudes was gone and Westmark was approaching the autumn Equinox with its well demarcated and beautiful sunrises and sunsets; as Miles arrived at the Low Farm there was an unusually fine sunset settling on the land.

Kjartan was not only home but was sitting on his patio. In the gloaming he saw a man approaching and wondered who it might be. He got to his feet and went out to meet the stranger. The walk of the stranger seemed familiar and full recognition followed quickly; "Miles, is that you?!"

"It is", arrived by return shout.

When the general joy was a little abated they entered the long house and met master Hall, who was only recently become master of his own legs. Unn was looking good, as was Biddy, but Njal, though of good cheer, was visibly aging. The big news was very recent; Eyvind was on board! Apparently Hall had broken the log jam.

Later, while the women finished the cooking, the men returned to the patio. Njal had practically moved out to the patio and had his own very fine chair lined with a woolen fleece; indeed, things were getting decadent out on the patio – there was even a small low table that could double as a foot rest.

"You're axes, chain mail, and bucklers are in the barn gathering rust. For being such an urgent item, Miles, you seem very relaxed about getting them to working hands."

"Thanks, Kjartan; I'll take them, but the skraeling business is pretty much finished. It must seem odd, but I hardly need them. Still, they are fine weapons and may come in handy, though not for braining skraeling."

This was news, news bordering the miraculous. Following a stunned silence Kjartan spoke.

"Was it, as you suspected, some plague?"

"No; it worked out in a way I could never have foreseen."

"Did we lose many people?", asked Njal.

"None. Not even a sprained ankle."

Kjartan interrupted; "So, coming together in council with the skraeling chiefs worked better than hithertofore?"

"No; there was no council or talk. We could never have gotten so far as agreeing on the weather."

The artful Miles allowed a prolonged silence to build the moment; "Well?", nudged Kjartan.

"There was a single triggering event that began the skraeling migration to the mainland. This migration is in full flood and is not yet finished."

"Well?", nudged Njal.

Miles was enjoying his moment; "It happened several weeks after returning from visiting you, Kjartan.'

"Late in the afternoon I was out looking for several straying cows. I had a rough idea of where they should be and wasn't paying much attention; in fact, my mind was on the skraeling problem. Then it was like I had received several heavy thumps on my back; I noticed several arrows sticking out beyond my chest and I felt very weak. While I had been musing on the skraeling problem they had been busy with what they do best – ambushing fatheads."

Miles paused thoughtfully; "I was much as Yngvar was the day he died; how he managed to kill eight skraeling in that condition seemed amazing at the time, but since I've been there myself it looks flat out impossible: it took everything in me and then some just to stay on my feet and stagger forward. The tree was forty yards from me and I staggered towards it – it seemed impossibly distant. I was hit with a third arrow in my lower back. The skraeling drew their knives and raced each other for the honor of my big blond-grey scalp. I managed a curious staggering run and my race with the skraeling was a tie – I reached the portal as a skraeling knife reached my scalp. I fell forward into tree country and just lay there a great while. Later I got up and walked until I felt twenty-five and in perfect health and spirits.'

"When I returned I studied the skraeling tableau before me: one large skraeling, running fast with one foot just touching the ground had his knife where my head had been. Others converging from left and right just behind him were also running fast. There were fifteen in the tableau but there were others behind them. Thus far I had not touched my axe; I drew it now and planned by moves.'

"I left the tree well to the side of where I had entered it and when I came back four skraeling had died.'

"I left at another spot and before I returned three more died. There were no more skraeling within ten yards of the tree. If I persisted I would become vulnerable to arrows.'

"I walked to the Westmark portal and waited five minutes in Westmark. When I returned there were fresh skraeling close to the tree tending their dead and dying fellows; five more died.'

"I walked to Westmark for another hiatus. When I returned the skraeling stood in a loose circle well back from the scene of carnage; they looked frightened and awestruck. One large skraeling stood amongst the dead and seemed to be urging them to be men and not women. He I killed. Then once again I went to Westmark. When I returned the skraeling were gone, the dead were untouched, and the area was circled with large stones and their best and more ornate weapons. The site had been marked as holy, mysterious, and very, very scary."

Miles paused, then; "A few weeks later they began leaving Newland. Wherever I went the skraeling would come up to me with great reverence, bow, and with both hands offer me their weapons of war. At first I took them but soon I began returning their bows and tokens of respect and I would close their hands on their weapon and gently decline them.'

"The crossing to the mainland is all of fifteen miles and in a heavily loaded small open boat, what they call a canoe, the peril is great. At first, during unexpected heavy weather, we rescued several heavily loaded canoes that were sinking. Later I had two of our boats start picking them up on the beach and taking them to the mainland. The skraeling are now mostly departed, and they have departed as friends.'

"Soon I hope to trade with them, but on the mainland, and only at designated trading centers. They are a dangerous and treacherous race and we must never forget it."

The skraeling's reaction to their adventure with Miles, seemed, at least to Njal, a little excessive; "Miles, I'm the first man to see you as Thor's own hammer, but I can't help thinking we are missing something; the skraeling are not adding up."

Kjartan interrupted; "Dad, I would agree with you had I not seen the tree portal for myself. It allows a kind of discontinuity that is profoundly disturbing. Add to this the skraeling saw Miles covered with arrows and, though still standing, essentially dead; then suddenly he's not only not dead and arrow covered, he's four yards elsewhere in perfect health and killing your best. You organize to kill him and suddenly he's five yards and behind you, still killing and quickly. Everyone is deeply frightened and stops to digest events and consider things. Finally your toughest and most respected man stands and says exactly what you just said; 'You are overreacting; what is it to be – skraeling tough guys or little girls and old women?!'

"Suddenly, from thin air, out pops the uncanny enemy and kills the voice of manliness and good sense. Then the uncanny one is gone; the skraelings look around their circle – anyone else for manliness and good sense? Who's next?

Would you step forward to be the mouthpiece of manliness and sense? I emphatically would not – 'manliness' can look after itself. I would mark the spot as utterly perilous, and as I walked away I would realize my happy forest home harbored something I had thought I knew but now I realized was uncanny, unknown and perhaps unknowable, and utterly dangerous. A few weeks of this shadow and I would pack my canoe and set out for a new life on the mainland. The skraeling were spooked to the tips of their little red toes, and I for one think the sentiment reasonable."

Kjartan was entertaining and persuasive and Miles couldn't help chuckling – Kjartan should have been a preacher or lawyer; it seemed he could convert the world or sue the world as he wished. Still it was evident, though chuckling good naturedly, Njal was not convinced. Miles was curious.

"What did you have in mind, Njal?"

Njal looked at the sunset and thought a moment; "In truth I hardly know what I mean. Did the area of the portal have any place in skraeling lore? We think the tree quite real and perhaps there have been odd things associated with it that crept into their stories. If this were so it would have primed and given a certain turn to their adventure. It might have triggered a larger reaction than would be found in its absence."

Njal shrugged his shoulders as though to say 'but what do I know?'

Kjartan stepped into the conversational lull; "How do our people understand the skraeling mainland migration?"

"Have you told them what you told us?"

"I have not shared my story with my fellow norse, and they are mystified; but the mystery is a friendly one and no one wants to rock the boat by looking too deeply – they hold their breath and pray it should continue.'

"I would appreciate it if you would keep the tale to yourselves; for example, sharing with Biddy or Unn would not be helpful.'

"You and Asgerd are the only people who realize how anomalous I am; let's keep it that way.'

"But I am monopolizing the hour; any developments in Westmark?"

Njal and Kjartan thought a moment, then both began to speak, then both deferred to the other; Njal nodded to Kjartan.

"Thanks, Dad. My friend Sandaman has developed real power in and around Mendero and he favors a strong norse link. Mendero is becoming an effective middleman in our fur and walrus tusk trade and more and more of our young men are joining the army in Mendero and then settling in Mendero. We are importing things from Mendero, such as my patio and the chairs in which we sit.'

"I was born with ambivalence in my marrow, so instinctively I see both sunshine and dark clouds in the link. I'm hoping there's more sunshine; but certain it is we are shaping Mendero and they are shaping us. Now doubt this has been working for some time, but it is coming out now in such a way as not to be missed.'

"Dad has spotted a trend about which he is ambivalent, after all, he is my father, but he suspects more dark clouds than sunshine."

Kjartan nodded to his father; "The christians and their religion are getting a toe hold amongst the norse, and it scares me; I sense it will grow and divert us from our old ways, ways I know and love.'

"The muslims, though much more powerful, do not pose the same threat; they conquer a people and then establish conditions tending to convert the native population."

"What conditions are these?", queried Miles.

"Unbelievers have additional taxes, and education, state office, and other good things are only open to believers. If we were conquered and these conditions imposed soon we would bid farewell to Thor and welcome Allah.'

"But of course conquering us is not likely; we control the seaways and they are far too busy putting out fires on their own shores.'

"The Christians, however, are different; they come in peace with open hands and are treated, as our customs demands, as guests; unfortunately they are what they call missionaries, and their poison is hidden away in their heads.'

"It passes me by why they should trouble themselves over what I believe or do not believe; as it is the state of my beliefs seems to burn a hole in their souls. I believe what I believe in a very different way than they believe: what I believe adapts to changing circumstances, while what they believe changes the circumstances around them. For this reason I fear greatly; they will gradually effect change and we will gradually adapt to it, and in the end there will no longer be norse as we know them. We will have ceased to be ourselves."

This was a sobering thought and a reflective solemnity settled on the friends. Knowing what he knew Miles had no comfort to give, and he kept his counsel.

"Everything Dad has said seems true to me, and I have already observed change is coming. Yet circumstances in Gar are such as to maintain us as recognizably norse. Jehova and Allah are seen by one and all as very real, and as being so utterly opposed as to be unable to speak to each other. Odin, by contrast, is not nearly so huge and momentous; he has about him something vicious, no doubt, but also childlike and negligible. No one likes Odin, Thor, Frey and company, but they at least can be approached and one can talk with them, if only to convert the foolish. Neither Christian nor Muslim can trust or talk to each other, but both talk to us. If there were no norse Gar would need to invent us. Lucky for them here we are, and it is vital we become neither too Muslim nor too Christian. I see us as neutral power brokers, and Mendero will be the cradle of the new order."

Newland was isolated from the main currents of life, and while Miles had many friends in Newland, they were neither so close nor so bright and informed as Kjartan and Njal. Getting back to main currents with friends like these was wonderfully invigorating; one took a fresh grip on life. Awash in this sense of well-being and noting the chill in the autumn evening and the fading light Miles was about to suggest they join the women and have supper when Kjartan spoke.

"Miles, the departure of the skraeling is a large event, so large it rather sidetracked me; are there other events?"

Miles thought a moment; "For Miles Drake the norse leader there is not much to add. For Miles Drake the man, father, and farmer there is much to tell, and it is easily summarized; I have come to love and value your sister more than I can tell. She is a warming fire on a cold winter evening, the play of sunshine on water, and much, much more. Never has a woman been so well loved; but you lads, the fortunate father and brother, already know this. You are greatly blessed to have had her for twenty years."

The father and brother loved Asgerd greatly and it was music to their ears to hear she was properly appreciated. They entered the hall and sat down to a meal featuring a more liberal use of spices than two years earlier; things were truly looking up.

IN THE MORNING MILES left to visit old friends. He travelled much and visited many. Two weeks later, with autumn well advanced, he was back at the Low Farm. There was a wonderful lamb feast featuring generous use of garlic, and early in the morning Miles and Kjartan loaded a horse with what weapons and armor Miles could use and carry while the remainder was gifted to Kjartan. Kjartan was surprised; why not make another trip and get it all?

"Kjartan, what remains is yours. I have my reasons and, since I tell you pretty much everything, I'll share my reasons; but let it spice our journey."

Later, a mile into their three mile journey, Kjartan out of nowhere recollected a question he had meant to ask Miles.

"Two weeks ago on the patio with Dad you shared a striking and wonderful tribute to Asgerd. Dad and I loved it, but it raised a question; was the tribute general, or founded on something specific to the past two years?"

"Very specific, and near last winter solstice; for me this event towers over the skraeling exodus. But I doubt it would seem so extraordinary to you since the roots of the incident are in my old world."

"Miles, given the sort of man you are I wonder at the incident; you do not impress easily. Suppose me to have a little imagination, and then tell what happened."

"I don't mind telling my tale, but it may come to puzzle more than enlighten.'

"In Westmark, Newland, Norland, and Gar our children frequently die of illness. This saddens us, but like the weather, we can only shrug our shoulders and move on. In my old world things are otherwise. The various illnesses have been clearly identified and can either be prevented entirely or treated quickly and effectively. One of these illnesses is appendicitis, which causes great pain in the right lower abdomen. The treatment is surgery, where the appendix is removed. This surgery is safe, routine, and due to anesthesia, painless."

"Anesthesia?", queried Kjartan.

"A special medicine that stops all pain; not, like mead, merely some of the pain.'

"The surgery features much special equipment and a special room and table. Everything is very, very clean and there is a powerful bright light that shines right on what is being done. All is safe, painless, routine. If the appendix is not removed and ruptures the patient usually dies.'

"Now, Kjartan, since you are just starting down the path of fatherhood I will tell you what it will be like: when your eight year old son looks at you with perfect confidence and trust, but with great fear in his eyes, and asks if everything will be okay a man comes face to face with darkest despair. He sees you as the complete and perfect shield, and over time you have come to see yourself as such a shield, to identify yourself as such a shield. If the shield fails, you not only lose your son, but something deep in yourself is also shattered. I would much, much rather face my own death than such moments. This past winter I faced just such a moment, and then, by magic, Asgerd lifted it from me – I floated, floated! My gratitude and appreciation are not easily expressed."

Kjartan was thoughtful; "I take it your eight year old son Kjartan had appendicitis?"

"He did indeed, with fever and terrible pain in his right lower abdomen. What to do – watch him die? Operate? But operating without training or needful equipment, with only torchlight and a sharp knife. I would not have anesthesia, so my son would need to be held down, and even then there would be unexpected movements. Such operating conditions carry a very high mortality with them.'

"There it is, Kjartan; operate and he probably dies, don't operate and he probably dies. Operate and he dies, and then always wonder what would have happened had you not operated; don't operate and he dies and you will be left wondering how things would have fared had you operated.'

"For you Kjartan there is nothing to do but wait and see what the weather brings; for me there is an agonizing decision."

Miles studied Kjartan's face to see if he was connecting, and saw that he was; Kjartan <u>did</u> have a bit of imagination.

"Good; you are ready for Asgerd.'

"I sweat blood over what to do, and as you know, this is hardly like myself. It didn't seem to me the abdomen was so rigid and boardlike as I had heard it would be with general peritonitis; but if I waited till it was boardlike it would probably be too late to save him no matter what I did. I was tilting towards not operating but was far from arrived when Asgerd took me aside, gave me a hug, and said; "Kjartan will live; whatever you decide is going to work."

This was spoken calmly and very matter-of-factly.

"How can you know, Asgerd?!"

"Last night I saw my own death. I was very old and Kjartan was at my side. He was about as old as you are now, quite gray, and not so big as you; but it was him."

"I did not operate; instead I floated. Kjartan, sturdy lad, did indeed survive."

Miles walked awhile in silence, then; "There was an odd twist to the affair. For no reason I could think of I asked Asgerd if I were present at her death. I was not – which, given the difference in our ages, is hardly surprising. It seemed I was long off the scene. Was anybody else there?'

"Yes, Kjartan held one hand and the other was held by a man larger than me and a little older than Kjartan. She felt towards him much as she felt towards Kjartan. Apparently it was a very good death.'

"Neither Asgerd nor myself has any idea who the large man might be. Whoever he is I'm happy he's there."

A mile later and they arrived at the tree portal. They unloaded the horse and arranged things so Miles could carry the weapons and mail as a single large bundle strapped to a wooden frame. When they finished Miles paused.

"Kjartan, do you know why I visited my old friends?"

"You didn't visit them last time, Miles, and I wondered at it; why the impulse to spend two weeks visiting?"

"In my way I was saying goodbye; I doubt I will see Westmark again. You I will miss the most, and I will explain myself. For the past several years it has been growing on me the tree is more than my tool of convenience. It is on loan for awhile, and for its own purposes – I sense I have few if any journeys left and must save what remains for truly dire circumstances. Should no dire circumstance intervene then as I near death I want a last journey. So, much as I love seeing you and old friends this is likely goodbye. If I get that last journey I will stop in Westmark to bid you farewell, but with any luck it will be many years from now. It is truly the pity Newland is so distant and the journey by sea so arduous and perilous."

This was unexpected and Kjartan was shocked and a little numb; just what Miles meant to him came into sharp focus. Miles was a second father and brother rolled into a single man.

"Miles, why do you think this?; could you be wrong?"

"Yes, I could be wrong, but as I left the tree this journey my vague misgivings came into focus like a lightening flash and this was attended with conviction: I suspect my fears are true.'

"In my early journeys the tree country was always at high summer. Of late the leaves are turning and autumn is on the land, and this autumn advances. A little with each journey. I have been put on notice.'

"In the early days the portals were as fixed and stable as lakes and mountains. Of late the portals are moving back. On my last journey where we now stand would be have been tree country; now I can only walk further along this crest and hope the portal is there."

Kjartan could only look at him in silence. Then he stepped forward and gave him a hug; "Then until we meet again."

CHAPTER 39
Abdul Alibaba

MICHAEL HAD GAMBLED, HAD won, and had lost. He had managed to scrounge up one hundred seventy men, which was far better than he had hoped, but this caused delays, and upon arriving in Mendero he learned the army had left two days earlier. Kjartan's plans typically involved tight schedules and Michael imagined the norse had delayed as long as they could; ah well, he'd learn what he could and adapt. With this in mind he and Kvig, a smart and experienced older friend of thirty who acted as his lieutenant, headed towards army headquarters which was a little west of Mendero proper.

The friends had not gone far when they were approached by a litter borne by six husky men. The procession stopped in front of them, a small curtain was drawn back, and out stepped not an exotic hanoum but rather a slight older gentleman adorned with a turban half as large as his person. The turban enjoyed a splendor that rather dwarfed the man, but it in turn was a mere sideshow to the gentleman's nose, which was hooked and splendid almost beyond the powers of speech. The gentleman's age was indeterminate; he could have been fifty or he might have been seventy five. Michael thought there was something vaguely familiar about him.

The gentleman approached them on foot, made a grave and dignified bow in which the nose, such was its immensity, approached the ground.

"Young masters, I, Abdul Alibaba, greet you on behalf of lord Sandaman. His lordship is occupied out of town and has asked me to guide you to him."

Michael gravely returned the bow, then; "Most excellent Abdul, we thank you. Have you any token left me by Lord Sandaman?"

Abdul reached under his robe and produced Sandaman's seal, which he handed Michael.

Michael turned the seal over thoughtfully; it was real enough, but this odd duck was a most unexpected guide. Surely some norse colleague would have been more suitable, and infinitely more engendering of trust. Michael handed back the seal.

"Abdul, there is something familiar about you; have we met?"

Abdul relaxed his dignity; "Master Michael many is the story I told you when you were a young boy; you called me Baba."

That was it! Michael too relaxed decorum and took the old man's hand warmly; "I remember you well! The stories were always good.' Then, turning to his friend; "Kvig, it is a pleasure to introduce you to Baba; and Baba, meet Kvig, a good friend, and acting lieutenant."

After the men had bowed to each other Baba went on to explain how supplies for two weeks were being organized, as well as horses and wagons to carry them. When he finished Michael spoke.

"Baba, we are a little short on arrows; have you any extra?"

"Yes, there are more arrows than you can carry. The fletchers have been working around the clock."

Michael curbed his impatience to be off; "When can we leave?"

"Tomorrow morning."

It was early afternoon and Michel had hoped to leave in an hour or so.

"It shall be as you say, Baba, but I want to leave with first light. Let's meet at the fountain on the north side of town. Also, no oxen; we plan to travel hard and fast."

"As you wish, young master. Choose some strong men to bear my litter."

Kvig and Michael looked at each other and burst out laughing; "You dream too much, Baba; we are northmen and Thor himself would have to walk. Your litter stays in Mendero; however, for your many stories and our early friendship I will arrange a comfortable spot in a wagon. You will not suffer."

Michael could see much thought going on behind the nose, but Baba kept his peace. The men soon parted.

Kvig went to set up camp while Michael supervised the victualing and examined arrows. While doing this he learned how Siddiq and his officers had recently died and that his mother had not been seen for several days. His foster father had escaped death by a whisker. Michael was relieved to learn his father was in reasonably good spirits and was with the army; Kjartan evidently had things well in hand.

He also learned his guide, the grandfatherly Baba, was much closer to seventy-five than fifty, and had been a close friend of Siddiq. To his surprise he learned Sandaman and Baba saw little of each other. He would need to keep an eye on their guide.

Next morning, with first light, the norse were off. True to promise Baba was comfortably ensconced in a supply cart. The trip was initially on the main north road, but ten miles along they turned west on a less traveled road, a road so pristine as to make the recent passage of seven thousand men nigh unto miraculous; Michael was skeptical of miracles. Five miles later, midway through the afternoon they approached a narrow valley with steep sides; the valley was heavily wooded.

Michael called a halt to his column and walked back to join Kvig.

"Kvig, what are your thoughts on our road and the upcoming valley?"

"They stink of ambush; I think we need to have a heart to heart with grandfather."

These were Michael's thought too; "Certain it is we will not be traveling down the main path of yonder valley; let's hear what Baba has to say for himself."

They were half way down the column heading for Baba's cart when lo, as by magic, there was the man himself – on foot, fresh as a daisy, and as ever, nosed like a god.

"Young masters, I do not like the looks of the approaching valley. As a boy I used to herd goats in these hills and, with your permission, I'd like to recommend a goat path along the western flank of the valley. If an enemy lies in wait this would put us above and behind them."

This was an unexpected development; a moment past it looked as though Baba were running with the fox, now he was back chasing with the hounds.

"Baba, there is much wisdom in what you say. What lies above and behind the goat path?"

"An overhanging rock wall; if there is an enemy he has no possibility of surprising our surprise."

Michael considered; "Is there a path bypassing the valley altogether?"

"There are such paths, but the carts cannot use them, and even the horses would need at least some goat ancestry.

If there is an enemy, we need to surprise and remove them prepatory to taking our supplies through to Balba.'

"Prince Michael, surprising and removing enemies is an activity at which you northmen excel; we have at least three hours till evening, which I expect would be more than enough time. Come, I will lead you."

Michael ignored Baba's importunities and thoughtfully studied the steep western wall of the valley. At length he turned once again to Baba.

"Do you see that large rock', and he indicated a point of eminence along the western wall of the valley that was just past the entrance to the valley; 'Does your goat path pass near that rock?"

Baba looked pleased; "Yes; it passes immediately below the rock."

"Good. Kvig, I will take one hundred thirty of our men and leave you forty. When I stand under that rock and wave my arms two of your thirty need to conspicuously but very carelessly scout the valley via the main trail. They need to chatter away and appear to be scouting in gesture only – if they do this correctly they will return with their lives, and they will fix the attention of the enemy on themselves rather than on the men moving into position behind them.'

"Kvig, you must wait for the signal. If no signal arrives you will see us walking out of the valley and it will signify no enemy. If you hear a clash of arms it means we need help – which you would give in whatever manner seems best.'

"Let's go; there's only a few hours of daylight."

Their force was rapidly divided and the men with Michael took many arrows. Forty minutes later the larger force had arrived at the rock.

Baba, despite his years and penchant for litters, proved nimble and surefooted. A few men scouted further along the path and soon were back with report of an enemy hidden along the west side of the main path. Michael stood under the rock and waved his arms. Kvig waved back. When the scouts entered the valley Michael's force quietly deployed; this was not noticed.

When the scouts and their careless chatter were safely out of the valley Michael attacked.

The enemy were a larger force than Michael's but with surprise the norse archers rapidly evened the fight. When things were fiercest Kvig attacked the enemy from the main road. This demoralized the foe and soon they lost cohesion and were become a motley crowd of escaping individuals; it was every man for himself. Very few escaped. Thus ended the remnant of Siddiq's corp.

As the sun set Michael had half the men retrieve arrows and half prepare camp at the mouth of the valley; he and an assistant busied themselves with the wounded. Nine men had been killed, while twelve had significant wounds; of the wounded one died just before daybreak and another died midmorning.

Though the day had been long and hard, after the camp and wounded were settled, Michael met with Kvig and Baba around a small fire.

"Young master, it is most unusual and a little unseemly for you to tend the wounded yourself; have you no surgeon?"

"It is a little unusual in our ranks, but unheard of amongst the sons of the prophet. My foster father Kjartan tends the wounded and I picked up the custom from him; I find I am quite good at it, and things one does well give pleasure."

Baba was still curious; "How did your foster father come by the custom?"

"He picked it up form a very famous godi, Miles Drake. This custom of ours has a most excellent pedigree, but let's leave this for another day; we need to consider our plans."

"Baba, how many days travel on our road to the plains of Balba?"

"Two days hard travel; it is two and half days of reasonable travel."

"How many days travel on the plains to the path of Balba's invasion?"

"Three or four days, and this would be hard travel."

Michael sat quietly thinking, then; "Baba, we need a quicker way; any more goat paths?"

Baba in his turn grew thoughtful; "Young master, there is a way, but the mountains are high and the paths are truly hard and dangerous. Horses and wagons are out of the question."

"How long?"

"With Allah's blessing two days, but probably closer to three."

"Does this bring us near the route of Balba's army?"

"Yes, it will be very close."

"There is a final question, Baba, a question I hate to ask a man of your years and dignity; we cannot go without you, but can you keep up? Can you make it?"

There was a wry smile; "We shall see, young master; as a rule I am able to do what I must. As recently as ten years ago I could have walked your legs off; now, perhaps you northmen can keep up. But, and I say this before we begin, I will not carry you."

Kvig and Michael laughed at the old man's sauciness, and both men, from that moment, began to like Baba, liked him even as they were unable to decide if he was fox or hound.

Thus far Kvig had remained silent; now he spoke; "I suppose I will be taking our wagons and supplies around the long way?"

"Yes, Kvig, I'm afraid so. However if today is a typical sample of the 'easy route' then yours may prove the harder task', he turned to Baba, 'Is the ambush today likely to be repeated further down the road?"

"No. Today we faced the remnant of Siddiq's corp; it is most embarrassing to have been his tool in leading you here. Siddiq suggested the route."

"The standard bandits will make it a point to stay clear of you; it should be quite safe."

Michael thought this likely, but even so he left Kvig thirty men. His medical assistant and two men were given two of the wagons with instructions to get the wounded back to Mendero.

Michael left and Baba remained to give Kvig detailed instructions on the longer journey. The way was quite simple but Baba directions anticipated the few possible points of confusion.

Shortly after first light Michael, Baba, and one hundred seventeen men headed straight into the mountains. Each man carried seven spare arrows and food for four days; water was abundant and posed no problem. Michael, despite protests, divided Baba's burdens between himself and several other men.

CHAPTER 40
The Vettler Mountains and Beyond

BABA WAS STRONG AND Baba knew the mountain paths - forty years ago. The general shape of his knowledge was remarkably preserved but the details of specific paths were, as might be expected, greatly changed, and several former trails were no longer in use and new alternate routes served. Baba walked well and was surprisingly durable for a man of seventy-three years, but it was not in the nature of things he should walk with men in their third decade who were in hard condition. So progress was slow and both Michael and Baba were sorely tested. Michael was a reasonably patient man and instinctively knew a show of impatience would only slow things further. Baba, with all his imperfections, was all the direction they had.

As he tired Baba became less focused on the greatly altered trails, and they would stray from the desired direction; this caused backtracking and further loss of time. Yet both men held firmly to their purpose, so while progress was slower than planned it was steady.

The country was, in a sharp and hard edged way, very striking and beautiful; especially the furious mountain streams and associated cataracts. In later years Michael revisited the Vettler Mountains several times and always came away refreshed and blessed. But this was much later. Michael's first night in the Vettler Mountains passed in a light, cold rain sharing his cloak with the exhausted Baba. The second and third days were hard but the weather held fair and in the late afternoon of the fourth day they were looking down on the Vettler plain and could faintly make out the road to central Balba and the capital city of Kagah; Baba had brought them through. Very faintly in the distance they made out a troop of cavalry approaching.

Two hours later, with the sun setting, they were much lower and closer to the margin of the Vettler plain. The cavalry troop set up camp approximately two miles north and west of where the norse emerged on the Vettler plain.

That night, despite grumbling from the weariest, Michael led a night attack on the cavalry troop. This proved completely unexpected and was successful; with light losses they destroyed the troop and came into possession of both food and horses.

They returned to their own camp with a prisoner whose tongue was duly loosened. What they learned was electrifying.

The commander of Balba's army, Amer the Astute, when halfway into the pass to Mendero had smelled a rat and managed to get half of his army out of the trap. The forward half of the army was destroyed. Half the army escaping was remarkable and due to a clever ruse. The vanguard of the army had continued moving forward very slowly and with much blowing of trumpets – this had lulled and confused Kjartan long enough for the rear half to get back to the Vettler plain. But Kjartan was not the man to be fooled for long and he woke up in time to destroy the forward portion of army still in the pass.

Currently Amer the Astute was retreating pell mell towards Kagah, and Kjartan, still hoping to destroy Balba's army, was in hot pursuit. The cavalry troop they had destroyed was rushing to cover Amer's retreat. Both armies were steaming north and west on the very road by which Michael was camped; they were athwart Amer's line of retreat.

During the prisoner interrogation Baba said little, but when they finished and were on the very edge of killing the prisoner he interrupted.

"Young Master, there is something familiar about this man. Please let me speak with him."

Michael was surprised. The prisoner had seemed pretty standard issue before a very thorough, hard beating and now there was precious little to set him apart from other men.

"Sure, Baba, but don't make a night of it."

Baba spoke briefly with the prisoner, then; "This man is the grandson of my sister Yasmin. In return for his life I will share something important; is this agreeable?"

Michael was a little vexed; "Baba you should be sharing what you know whether or not this man has need of you. We cannot take him with us and I don't want him alerting others to our presence; what am I to do with him?"

"None of this matters young master; only time matters. If we tie him up well away from the road this will be enough."

'So, time is everything. Okay, godi Baba; I will agree to anything and do as I must after you have spoken.' So thought Michael.

"Okay, Baba; it shall be as you wish."

"We are eight miles from the only bridge across the Ligeri River. If you control this bridge Balba's army is trapped and your foster father will surely destroy it. If the army crosses the river who knows what will happen? The question of the hour is who will reach this river first: you or Amer the Astute? Don't worry about this poor man. Take the horses Allah has provided and hurry to the bridge."

Michael's mind raced. Baba was right as to the importance of the bridge. However if Amer was even a fraction as clever as his name suggested the bridge would be heavily guarded. Was he strong enough to seize and hold the bridge? There was only one way to find out.

And the prisoner? Truly he hardly mattered one way or the other.

"Thank you Baba. The prisoner is yours."

Baba was pleased and shared the news with the prisoner. There was no 'Yasmin', and certainly no grandson, but Baba was not the man to stand around and see a fellow believer pointlessly killed. In later years the young prisoner had many fine sons; the eldest would bear the name Abdul and was known as Baba to friends.

There were forty horses and this gave an irresistible shape to events. Their war party was already small but in the interests of speed Michael divided it. Forty men, including himself, took the horses and hurried to the bridge. Bolli the Sarcastic assumed command of the larger group following on foot.

Bolli's sarcasm, a breathtaking thing of agility and edge, became with fatigue a burden too heavy to bear. No sooner had Michael galloped away towards the bridge but Bolli announced a two hour nap with Baba holding the 'clock' – when a certain constellation passed a specified tree they were to be up and moving. This may sound a bit relaxed, but the men had been going since first light, walked long and hard all day, then walked yet another two miles, fought a hard but short skirmish, and then walked two miles back to their camp. It was well past midnight and Bolli, both by judgment and inclination, opted to let slumber knit up the raveled sleeve of care. The men slept where they sat. Baba dozed a bit but evenso three hours later they were back on the road and heading towards the bridge.

CHAPTER 41
Ոofni Salamah

HOFNI LAY AWAKE THINKING; what was he missing? He had not one but two levels of sentries and at all times, day and night, scouts reported in every two hours. His men were outstanding in morale and training; Balba had no finer troops.

He should be sleeping rather than thinking the same thoughts over and over. But Amer's manner and closing words haunted him; there would be no rest till the army was safe across the bridge. What were they exactly? Ah yes; 'Hofni the survival of the army depends on the Ligeri bridge; but much beyond that, the survival of Balba is tied to the bridge. So very much comes down to a thing so small. You must hold the bridge come what may.'

Those words were numbing in the responsibility they placed on him. His heart would be light as thistle down once the army was across. Then the fun: his men would be as a stonewall stopping those godless northmen; they would not be crossing the bridge. The army could retreat at its leisure.

At last, knowing it was idle to think he could sleep Hofni got up. There was the bridge, a reassuring sight and quite beautiful in the bright moonlight. He turned to walk the perimeter of his camp. All was quiet and orderly. Hofni felt like a father as he walked amongst his sleeping men; their slumber was safe and secure; he, Hofni, had them under his eye. There were a hundred sixty men and they were spread over two acres. It was too large an area and tomorrow he would bring them into a smaller and more easily patrolled camp.

Hofni had started on the western perimeter and had already passed an alert sentry. He was now halfway around the eastern perimeter and had not yet seen the sentry; why? Hofni began to worry. Then, eighty feet away, in the corner of his eye he noticed several shadows move. He continued walking slowly, as though all was well, but when he came to a sleeping man he quietly stirred him with his right foot. No response. Then he looked more closely; the man was dead – his throat had been cut. He checked the next man; also dead. The third man, however, awoke quickly and grabbed his scimitar. Good!

Hofni spoke very quietly; "Soldier, without making a great noise let's wake a few of the others."

This was soon done. Hofni and his squad of six walked towards where there had been moving shadows. The 'shadows' saw them coming and, dispensing with caution, stood up and quickly headed towards the bridge, killing the convenient sleeping man as they went.

At this Hofni gave a great shout and the camp lurched into wakefulness. Soon there was a clash of weapons and shouting. Hofni hurried forward towards the bridge, strengthening as he went. Around the entrance of the bridge there was a fierce fight in progress.

Slowly the northmen were forced back on the bridge. The bridged narrowed his approach to the enemy and he could not bring his greater force to bear. He was losing men to no purpose. Hofni pulled his men back and waited for the approaching dawn when his archers could clear the bridge. He stayed focused on what he was doing rather than the bone crushing responsibility of the bridge.

Hofni reviewed things by the light of dawn. The enemy numbered thirty-six and held the bridge quite securely. They had taken many of his shields with them on the bridge and were clearly expecting his archers. He had lost twelve sleeping men and ten in the fight around the bridge. His force was down to a hundred thirty-eight, which was vastly superior to thirty-six.

An hour later and his archers had exhausted their arrows and three more northmen were down.

So it would be hand to hand and he would push them off the bridge by main force. Thus began a very bloody and bitter fight. Only when Hofni had committed half his troops did Bolli the Sarcastic's archers strike. All attention had been on the bridge and Bolli had positioned his archers without being noticed. This surprise attack was very effective and when the arrows were exhausted the sides were about equal. The ensuing fight was harrowing and gruesome; no quarter was sought or given and neither side yielded so much as an inch. Finally Bolli's left wing began to falter and Hofni's men surged forward, irresistible. This took pressure off the bridge and Michael's men also began surging forward in an irresistible manner. When Bolli's right wing joined Michael the previous irresistible surge of Hofni's right wing picked up speed and the son's of the prophet found themselves running like hares away from the bridge. Not Hofni; he and ten others did not run, but fought and died by the bridge. Hofni's death was very bitter; he died knowing he had lost the bridge and failed his responsibility.

LATE IN THE AFTERNOON the army of Balba limped to the bridge and found it strongly held by the enemy. That night

Amer quietly disbanded his army into small groups of four or five men which slipped away as best they could. Early the next morning Amer and a remnant few fought a desperate last stand. They meant to die scimitars swinging but instead were captured.

Michael and his few were the heroes of the day and Kjartan's surprise and delight knew no bounds. Bolli became yet more sarcastic.

CHAPTER 42
On the Road to Kagah

MICHAEL PAUSED TO BRING his full attention to guiding his horse around what was a veritable gully in the highway – these damn Balban's couldn't even keep their roads in good repair – then he continued.

"Dad, I've been in many a hard fight but the fight for the Ligeri bridge was the toughest. Those soldiers were good men and the fight could have gone either way."

"There's really not much more to tell…; actually there is: I wish you could have seen Kjartan's face when he discovered who was holding the bridge! I think he suspected witchcraft, or as we northerners would say, <u>seid</u>."

Sandaman smiled at Kjartan's confusion. Wizard though he doubtless was, Kjartan's plans had gone all ahoo until Michael got things back on track. As it was they were enroute to Kagah to institute the new order.

"The wild card in events is my old nemesis Abdul Alibaba; and how on earth did he get his mitts on my seal?!"

Nemesis? "Dad, Baba has served us like a hero; how is it you call him 'nemesis'?"

"Our walk through the Vettler Mountains was hard on me, never mind a seventy-three year old man. He pointed us to the bridge and urged speed."

Sandaman gave his son a quizzical look; "Abdul may be 'Baba' in a young lad's recollections, but to the rest of Mendero he is an important moslem holy man who feels entitled to meddle in things not his concern. He was a great friend of your late mother and brother and he hates Christians, of which I am chief. You may take it as given that he was involved in the plot against me."

Sandaman paused a moment; "All I just said is indisputably true, but for all that he was unquestionably fond of you as a child.'

"In fact, son, you saved his life."

"I don't remember saving his life, but if I did then it has worked out rather well; it seems he has repaid the favor."

"Don't kid yourself, Michael. The man is a survivor who saw the coming order of your mother and brother collapse; he then made moves to secure a place in the new order. I hate to admit it but this was almost certainly done so as to be in a position to help fellow believers; in his way he is not self seeking."

"Every word of what you say is doubtlessly true, Dad, but evenso Baba has made a friend of me. And as for his moslem chums, so long as they keep the laws of Mendero and pay their taxes I'm on their side too.'

"Now, exactly how did I save Baba's hyde?"

"You really did, son; but first a bit of background.'

"I kept your mother and her religion far from your older brother. He was not allowed in a mosque and father John was his tutor. This didn't work out so well and your mother never tired of sharing her thoughts on this. When you made the scene she felt it was her turn. In a qualified way I agreed. You would attend both church and mosque, but your mother could pick your tutor.'

"Of course she picked Baba – and a lot of good it did them! From infancy on you were all for soldiers and war; there was never the slightest tendency towards peace and religion. Evenso you always liked poor old frustrated Baba.'

"As you grew older it became clear you would not be buying into any one's religion; early on this was far from clear and I came to bitterly regret my agreement. Finally I went back on the agreement, but not to your mother's face. Instead I took Baba aside and in the clearest manner you can imagine made him understand two things: first, there were to be no more Moslem stories or religious instruction. Secondly, no word to your mother concerning the new operating instructions. Violation of these instructions would be a sudden unexpected accident that ended his life. He understood.

A few weeks later I came in unexpectedly and received the unmistakable impression Baba had been telling you moslem stories. Understandably he denied the charges, so I turned to you and asked if Baba had been telling a story about Mohommed. You lied stoutly on his behalf and I still remember the surprised and relieved look on his milk white face – even his nose looked meek and shrunken!"

Both men laughed at the reference to the magnificent appendage, whereupon they moved on to what should be done with Balba.

KJARTAN AND SANDAMAN WERE very shrewd and the ensuing four months were for Michael an education in statecraft. The 'road' to Kagah was not so direct as Michael had thought. There were five cities in Balba significant for trade and population; the smallest of these was Carr. The armies of Latcha and Mendero invested Carr and demanded the towns surrender. Carr, like all cities in Balba, was walled and fortified; Carr was not interested in surrender.

Kjartan, who habitually thought ahead three or four steps, had planted friends in Carr to seize a gate. This gate was opened and Carr got the full Viking treatment: the men were killed, the women raped and sold into slavery, all the moveable wealth taken, and the town burned.

In consequence when surrender was demanded at the other four cities, Kagah included, there was compliance and no loss of life. The children and wives of the wealthy were captured and sold at a slave auction. Usually the wealthy man ransomed his family. If such a man hesitated an enemy or competitor, who knew his worth would buy his family and return them at a handsome profit. This raised enough money to pay the soldiers.

In Kagah the caliph was deposed and the head of a rival family was placed in power. This guaranteed the rich and powerful would focus on local political squabbles.

Both Latcha and Mendero annexed select portions of Balba that adjoined them. If there was so much as a hint of future plotting or interference the two countries would act together to take more of Balba – much more. The attitude conveyed was 'go ahead, make my day; please plot against me.'

What Sandaman did not do was significant: the conventional approach would be to convert Balba to a vassal state; but a vassal to who – Mendero or Latcha? This would tend to divide the allies, which was already going to be a prime mission of future Balban diplomacy; it is seldom wise to make things easier for your enemy.

A truly independent Balba, by its very existence, would tend to work to keep Latcha and Mendero united in common cause and interest. Indeed, this was clearly recognized and Latcha and Mendero exchanged permanent ambassadors.

Seeing all these things worked out was politically a coming of age for Michael. The Michael who returned to Westmark in the fall was quite a bit older and cannier than the Michael who arrived in Mendero midsummer.

Sandaman would never completely get over the loss of Nur and Siddiq, but having Michael back at his side and deep involvement with affairs of state worked wonders towards restoring him.

Kjartan? He and Eyvind had always been great pals, and Eyvind working side by side with pubs and town life nearly pulled Kjartan off the path – again! He returned to Westmark with Michael, and not a moment too soon.

The next summer Michael and Herdis married. Ten years later the occasion was still considered the bench mark against which such things are judged.

Late in the summer the young couple moved to Mendero. Herdis was ambivalent; being a queen sounded interesting, but home is home. Home for Michael was and always would be where Herdis happened to be – and she knew this. So she got busy and soon her home was the much loved center of norse life in Mendero. This worked to glue Michael into his norse status, which kept him neutral and reasonably unobjectionable to his Christian and Mohommedan subjects.

Five years later Sandaman stepped aside for his son; behind the scene he remained Michael's chief counselor.

Baba lived another ten years and was instrumental in getting the Moslem community in Mendero and Michael off to a strong start. Baba would drop by once a month for a chat. Initially Michael found this something of a nuisance, to be born with patience and fortitude; in time he came to look forward to these visits, which streamlined and smoothed political life in Mendero. Baba was a true friend both to his people and to Michael. A year before he died Baba took to bringing a successor, who in the event succeeded him well.

During Michael's watch Mendero, and for that matter, Latcha as well, doubled its size. This did not reflect Napoleonic ambition, but rather the malice and stupidity of Balba.

Before Siddiq's attempted coup Balba was larger than Latcha and Mendero combined. Later it was a pygmy state between its larger neighbors.

The leadership in Balba could not leave things alone; despite attempting a byzantine subtlety, they were always the underlying source of trouble on the borders of Latcha and Mendero. Balba attempted to use their neighboring states as cat's paws, but these other states, after losing wars and land, caught on and took to minding their own business. Eventually even Balba got the idea; unfortunately they caught on too late - and Latcha and Mendero were too prosperous and reasonable in their governments. Most of the land acquired by Mendero and Latcha truly did not originate in Balban duplicity, rather the provinces of Balba bordering Latcha and Mendero compared their own crippling taxes and corrupt government with what they saw across the frontier, and then created an incident putting them under better management and lower taxes. Latcha learned religious tolerance from thoughtfully studying Mendero, and both countries supported trade and established good roads.

Michael ruled Mendero long and well. Before he was doddering and senile Michael stepped aside for the ablest of his sons, Kjartan. This son carefully preserved norse customs and tolerance. During Kjartan's reign Latcha entered a time of weak government and terrible strife between Christians and Mohommedans. At last, in desperation and exhaustion,

Mendero was asked to rule them. Law and order were reestablished and prosperity and peace soon followed.

Mendero ultimately became one of the larger and more prosperous countries in Gar. Evenso, the largest instrument of norse impact on Gar was not Michael, it was Eyvind.

This summary of Michael and Mendero omits a crucial moment fourteen years into Michael's reign, a moment of great danger hinging on the charismatic Christian missionary Poppo. His foster father once again saved the day.

CHAPTER 43
A Grim Problem Resolved

(Miles, age 64)

MILES, AS WAS HIS custom was up at daybreak. He splashed cold water on his face and enjoyed a fine and luxurious stretch. He might be sixty-four but on this particular early fall morning he felt like a lad of forty-five.

Asgerd had sensed he would try to leave early and was already up and busy reestablishing the fire. Coffee was not available, but many years past while raiding in Gar, Michael had discovered the equivalent of tea and somehow kept it in supply; Asgerd treated early morning tea as a sacred ritual.

On Miles second cup Asgerd broke the companionable silence; "Miles, sometime this morning Kjartan will be along looking for his father; what should I tell him?"

Miles swallowed his tea and thought a moment; "Tell him his father is out searching for stray cows."

"And if he counts the cows and finds them all here?"

"He won't."

"Which way are you searching? You know he will ask."

"I haven't decided yet."

Miles finished his tea and a thoughtful silence enveloped them.

"Asgerd, I know you don't like this business any more than I do, but surely you see I have no choice?"

"I'm avoiding him since the last time he utterly wore me out with his remonstrances. He is a wonderful son and I'm the man I am; he needs to shrug his shoulders and leave it alone."

Asgerd, with sadness and resignation; "Duncen, he knows all this better than you; the thought of losing you under these circumstances is just too bitter, he can't face it."

"Well he must, and the sooner the better; I'm planning on having supper with my favorite wife day after tomorrow."

Asgerd smiled; "I'm glad to hear it, but from what I hear Grim is a strong wall between now and supper with me tomorrow evening – far more so than Kvelduf last time."

"No doubt, good wife, but though I'm sixty-four I still have a handy way with scaling high walls.'

"But I'm off to find those cows and duck hours of lecturing. I'm looking forward to roast lamb this evening: things like Grim are almost the only way to get a bit of lamb."

Miles hurried out the door; he hardly ever got the last word and he didn't want to spoil it.

It was a beautiful autumn morning and Miles thoroughly enjoyed the walk to his shieling. Tomorrow morning he faced a duel with Grim, a large, powerful, and experienced berserk of thirty who had been imported from Norland by a godi who resented Kjartan's growing influence and prestige amongst the other godi. Kjartan was slight of build, so-so at the arts of war, and very shrewd. Grim had managed to quarrel publicly with Kjartan in a way that could not be ignored and a duel was arranged. Upon hearing this

Miles had publicly insulted Grim and this resulted in a more immediate duel; Miles rated his own chances against Grim as much better than those of Kjartan – this despite his being sixty-four as opposed to Kjartan's twenty-five. This was the second time Miles had intervened on behalf of his son; Kjartan had felt shamed the first time and had not appreciated Miles efforts on his behalf. Now there was Grim.

Grim was beyond doubt a lethal man; Miles was uncertain about tomorrow, but stepping aside would get his son killed.

Many men would have given the cool beautiful fall morning an elegiac or valedictory spin; not so with Miles: Grim merely brought the lovely day into sharp, hard focus; Miles felt very alive and judged the day unusually fine.

Upon arriving at the shieling Miles located the pathetic norse excuse for a shovel and began clearing away the cow dung. The day warmed and before long Miles stripped off his shirt; soon there was real progress. It feels good to be getting through a long deferred project and Miles was so absorbed in his rhythm he only gradually became aware Kjartan was standing near watching him – how long?

As Kjartan scouted up a second shovel and took off his own shirt he said; "Dad, you are more and less norse than any of us; this slave work has always called to you and at the same time you are the most respected godi in Newland. You are the only man on record who is constantly freeing his slaves – and they won't go!"

Kjartan did not mention the imminent duel and they worked well and steadily in a companionable silence. An hour later the shieling was cleared and the men put away the shovels. Kjartan had brought food and they had a tasty lunch.

During the meal Miles gave way to curiosity; "How did you find me?"

"Mom said you'd be here. She also forbid me to mention duels, so I won't; but Thor only knows this is a kindness you don't deserve."

Kjartan's eyes were twinkling and there was a smile on his lips: both men burst out laughing.

After lunch they made a few repairs and then enjoyed a leisurely walk home that passed along the rocky coast. The fall equinox was just around the corner and once again the days seemed finite; and so as they arrived home the sun was setting. It had been a good day.

Nothing puts the benediction on a day quite like roast lamb, so it was a little jarring and off key when the usual fare of boiled pork was brought to the table.

Kjartan spoke for both of them; "Mom, on the eve of a duel don't you usually let us have lamb?"

"What duel is that?"; Asgerd affected a gentle surprise.

Kjartan was a little shocked, and certainly surprised; this was most unlike his mother.

"Tomorrow morning, Mom, as well you know!"

Asgerd feigned open incredulity; "Kjartan, it takes two to duel and this afternoon Grim was killed; he won't be able to keep his appointment. Sorry; no lamb."

Kjartan looked at his father and his father looked at Kjartan; "What?!"

Asgerd enjoyed their stupefaction.

"This afternoon Grim was killed; apparently it was done smoothly and quickly by a yet bigger and more savage brute from Norland. The insult Grim received was so public and offensive it came to immediate blows."

"What happened?!", asked Miles.

"Grim as you know is staying with Hogni Ingolfsson. The stranger walks up to Hogni's Hall by himself and asks to see Grim. After some delay Grim comes out to speak with him. The stranger says; 'Are you the man who fights Miles Drake in the morning?'

"Grim looks him over; 'Why do you ask?'

The stranger says, 'I ask that I may avoid killing the wrong man. If you are not the man, then we have no quarrel; if you are, then your father is a troll and your mother is a goat. Which is it?' Five minutes later Grim was very dead and the stranger left."

Miles and Kjartan were deeply puzzled. The puzzle had two parts: Why would a stranger shoulder his quarrel? And how did the stranger leave Hogni's Hall alive? Hospitality is sacred amongst the norse and Grim enjoyed the formal status of guest; Hogni had ten or twelve retainers and he was duty bound to avenge this insult to his hospitality. The shame to Hogni was huge; how could such a thing happen? How could the stranger go on such a task alone? Why? Why?

Asgerd understood the predicament well.

"Hrefna was there and ran to tell me what happened. Apparently the stranger is very large and powerful and very self-assured. He made killing Grim look like child's play, and when Hogni's retainers came out armed and angry he neither ran nor showed alarm. His manner suggested he would kill the lot of them if that's the way they wanted it. Somehow it never came to blows."

A thoughtful silence ensued, which at length Kjartan broke; "This whole business was instigated by Hogni and has landed a huge shame and disgrace on him."

"Where is the stranger staying?" asked Miles.

"He is the guest of Ari Thorkelsson. Ingibjorg is a good friend and in the morning I will visit and learn more."

WHEN ASGERD CAME HOME the next evening she was radiant.

"Miles, the stranger is the other man holding my hand when I die!'

He sends you this', and she handed over a much used old axe, 'and he will visit us tomorrow. His name is Gunnar Milesson."

CHAPTER 44
Eyvind

Eyvind's story is a large one, but marginal to the story of Miles Drake. While beyond the horizon of the story told yet it shapes and completes that horizon.

Eyvind stood by Sandaman through thick and thin, and was greatly honored and rewarded. He was an exceptional soldier and general who enjoyed a perfect success in putting down revolts and quelling the enemies of Mendero and Sandaman. However, by neither temperament nor ability was Eyvind the man to play second fiddle in Mendero, so as Michael came of age he began looking around to see where opportunity and destiny might lead. The opportunities were so large as to crush a man.

East of Gar were a hardy race of mounted steppe warriors who were united by a brilliant charismatic leader and then went on to begin conquering the world. The instruments of their conquests were a remarkably strong and effective bow, small superbly hardy horses, and consummate skill as horsemen and mounted archers. Their tactics were perfectly adapted to their strengths. They never committed to decisive head-on battles but rather circled and killed their enemies at a distance till they fragment and could be destroyed piecemeal. The mobility of these mounted archers was legendary; they could ride forty miles in a night and attack at dawn.

Ghengis Khan and the mongols are a useful analogy. Imagine Gar corresponds to a Europe where Charles Martel did not stop the Islamic invasion; all but Denmark and Saxony, or Northern Germany, fell. Now imagine the mongol epicenter to be west of where it was in our world and the mongol thrust more west than towards China, India, and the middle east; in Eyvind's world the mongol invasion did not stop at Hungary, but rather all of eastern Europe was under attack. Our timing of events is very different from Eyvind's world. For us the Mongols arrived in 1240, for Gar they arrived in 980. Gar was beleaguered on the west by the Vikings and in the east by the mongols.

The Islamic rulers decided to stick to the devil they knew best, and to fight fire with fire; Viking war leaders were ceded already half conquered eastern provinces and promised more if they would agree to rule as vassals of Islamic overlords and, above all, stop the mongol advance. Eyvind was one of the earliest of such viking leaders and he developed the tactics that stemmed the mongol advance, saved Gar, and brought viking culture and leadersip to eastern Gar. This war was long enough and hard enough to forge a strongly felt 'us' that included both Christians and moslems as against a feared and hated mongol 'them.' The viking leadership greased this development by an impartial neutrality vis a vis Christian and moslem.

In many ways the norse were not suited to the role they played; more than most they sought decisive engagements settling issues quickly and completely. In our own world the norse in Russia fared poorly against the mongols. They would seem exactly the people most suited to be victimized by the mongols. Fortunately Eyvind instinctively understood this and began steering towards a very different mindset. 'A good day at the office' no longer meant a decisive battle won but rather success was judged by how many horses and mongols had been killed, against how many men you lost. Success and consequent rewards were distributed by scalps and horse tails. An heroic death was still highly esteemed, but killing many enemy whilst staying alive was even better. When absolutely unavoidable by all means die well, but be sure there were at least three mongols killed for every viking death.

The basic military field formation was radically changed. The new unit comprised seventy men all trained in both bow and the now customary Drake axe and buckler. In addition to the light hand bucklers they carried large reinforced shields where one such shield could quickly be slotted into the upper end of another to make a narrow wall a little higher than a man's head. When attacked they could quickly form a circle of these doubled shields and in effect 'circle the wagons' and play settlers and Indians with the mongols. No decision was sought, merely to keep their archers protected and busy. Occasionally the mongols, in frustration, would try a direct assault and go hand to hand with the vikings; this was viking home ground and seldom prospered. There were many of these units of seventy on the field and they usually stayed eighty to one hundred yards apart, which was important since enemy horseman were always under enfilade fire. This was most important when the mongols strove to overrun a unit by main force, since they were then necessarily clustered, and the cross fire from adjacent units was devastating. The units communicated by flags raised on a long pole.

Initially Eyvind had spears on tripods placed before the shields to discourage direct cavalry assault; in the event this was hardly ever encountered and soon the spears and associated braces were replaced with a greater supply of arrows.

The mongol bow was studied and improved. Eventually all of eastern Gar trained extensively on the bow and every month or so there would be an archery competition with a substantial associated prize. Fletchers and bow makers became numerous, busy, and prosperous. In many ways eastern Gar came to resemble fourteenth century England, where during the one hundred year war yeoman archers carried the gentry on their backs.

Fortifications, always important, became, against the mongols, vital. With elevation and protecting walls the 'shoot out' between mounted archers and defending archers intrinsically favored the defenders, doubly so since horses are a relatively large target and the bounty on a horse was almost as high as a mongol warrior. This war was hard on horses.

Wooden walls are susceptible to fire arrows and early in the war many wooden fortifications were burned. Countermeasures were soon developed, and eventually large rugs were draped over the walls and soaked with water; every few hours additional water would be thrown down on the rugs.

The Elyva (Eyvind's 'mongols'), as would be expected of steppe warriors, possessed neither techniques nor siege equipment for dealing with stone fortresses; Gar had an abundance of both. Inevitably when the Elyva needed to take a fortress they forced captured Garians to produce and operate siege equipment. This only happened once; a month later Eyvind completely destroyed the town from which the siege equipment and talent was taken. 'Destroyed' meant men, women, children, and animals were all killed and the town burned to the ground.

This horrible lesson was not lost on the eastern towns and cities of Gar; across eastern Gar siege equipment was destroyed and one and all carefully 'forgot' there was ever such a thing as siege technique. The first major fortress to fall was also the last.

Eyvind adapted Eastern Gar and ultimately saved it, but all the measures described took time, and the initial attacks were massive and crushing. During these early and very dark hours there was an incalculable factor that played a small but pivotal role; another warrior came off the tree, a woman, who stood with Eyvind. But this is another story.

In the fullness of time the countermeasures were well developed and operating smoothly. Eventually the Elyva were dying in large numbers to little purpose; they withdrew and looked elsewhere for greener pastures.

The Elyva invasion gave rise to a greater unity and cohesion amongst moslems and christians, but the subsequent peace saw the gradual reemergence of the old strife; fortunately it was milder than earlier and there was a tradition and habit of norse arbitration, which kept sectarian nastiness within bounds. In the centuries to come many, perhaps a majority, of the norse converted to Christianity or Islam, but it was vital the northern paganism remain intact to control and arbitrate between the two mighty giants; the spectre of holy war is a terrible thing, and one and all knew the importance of the norse 'convention.'

In our own world the trappings and conventions of royalty linger on in modern times; England being an example. In a similar way the trappings of norse royal power are occasionally preserved into their modern age, but with a difference; such 'kings' also wield power to arbitrate on matters religious, though only under very specific circumstances.

CHAPTER 45
Ulf the Fearless

IT WAS AN OVERCAST, cold fall day as Miles made his way home. He had been visiting Osvif Helgason, a friend and fellow godi, and was now hurrying home to meet his son Gunnar, who was to visit in the afternoon; he should have plenty of time to arrive before Gunnar, but even so he was stepping right along.

As he crested a small hill he spied a man a hundred yards ahead. He had left Osvif's farm quite early and none had left before him. The man ahead must be from Thorgrim Kjallaksson's, and he must have started near daybreak and walked fast; Miles wondered at his destination. Logically it should be his place, but his son Gunnar was coming from another direction entirely, and was the only scheduled visitor. Ah, well – that's life, never a dull moment. Miles stepped up his already brisk pace, but the fellow seemed more horse than human and Miles gained so slowly he at length shouted for the stranger to mend his pace so they might travel together.

The stranger found this agreeable and stopped while Miles caught up. As Miles neared, the stranger's face broke into a broad smile of recognition and pleasure; Miles could not place him, yet there was something vaguely familiar about him. The man was lean, closer to fifty than forty, and sported a flat, deformed nose that had clearly seen the world. His eyes were lively and blue. He had a small axe at his belt and looked as though he knew its uses.

As Miles approached, the stranger extended his right hand.

"Miles Drake, what a pleasure! – what's it been; twenty-seven or twenty-eight years!?"

Ulf? Ulf the fearless? That's it! Ulf had been twenty when he fought at Miles's side during the war in Norland. Ulf was one of the few men who had been in at the kill and lived to not talk about it. All song and story clustered around Yngvar and the battle that destroyed Eirik's army. The deaths of Eirik and Ragnhild were a fine print post script, triggering an unusually comprehensive reticence in all but one of the survivors. Galti the talkative was willing, even eager, to share, but the tale came off as a children's tall tale and was received with a good-natured chuckle; Galti was understood to be adorning what was most likely a prosaic, even dull tale. All the survivors, excepting Galti, found the events profoundly disturbing and puzzling; they instinctively knew their story could only discredit them – besides, they didn't know what to make of their own tale.

The men shook hands warmly; "Ulf, what brings you so far from home?"

"I'm with your son Gunnar."

'What a lucky break!', thought Miles.

"I'm heading home, Ulf, to meet him. Tell me about Gunnar; start from the beginning."

Ulf too was pleased; "Gladly; your son is a pleasant topic of conversation. I'm on my way to your hall to make sure all gets said that needs saying, and now is a good time to start.'

"Gunnar is not particularly forthcoming, or talkative?"

"He is not. He's much as I remember you; both of you enjoy sociability and the winter fire, but more as an appreciative spectator than as a participant. As my foster father used to say of a man, 'he likes a warm fire, but without any urge to be one of the flames.' For example, Gunnar will not bother telling that he's the acknowledged Yngvar of his generation; for him, in the arts of war, there are no peers.'

"You will not be hearing of his life or plans, yet his circumstances are unusual and it is important you get the picture in mind."

"So, Miles, we are of a like mind; I want to inform, and you wish to be informed."

"About six months after Gunnar was born, Bodvar moved him and his mother Nylla to another farm he owns. This move is hardly mysterious; Bodvar's wife Helga was irritated with and jealous of Nylla. I like Nylla, but can't help sympathizing with Helga. Nylla is poorly organized and useless when it comes to practical affairs of running a farm; Helga is effective, well organized, and was bound to find Nylla vexing and in-the-way. That Bodvar found Nylla charming did not help matters. So the move ten miles farther east worked well. Nylla was a loving mother to Gunnar, but as is her way, was a little negligent. Nylla and Bodvar had and have quite a story together, a story that includes two children, a boy and a girl.'

Ulf paused, and chuckled; "If a sensible farm were trying to run smoothly Nylla would trip it. Bodvar is no fool and he has an excellent steward who is responsible for the farm."

Miles interrupted; "Does Nylla still make the wonderful music?"

"My, yes! She's only gotten better. Indeed, she has modified and developed her art so there's many a winter evening I thought I sat in Asgard. No one appreciates her more than Bodvar.'

"Now a word on the sons of Bodvar. An was eight years older than Gunnar and a fine man – alas, he died six years ago in one of Bodvar's many wars. An liked Gunnar and was old enough to not feel competitive towards him. Gunnar greatly admired and liked An.

"Valgard, the second son, was one year older than Gunnar, and was a nasty, spiteful boy consumed with jealousy of Gunnar. There is much to be said on Valgard's behalf. Gunnar, since crawling has excelled all others at swimming, sports, and weapons; Balder himself would have struggled with jealous impulses. Three years back, in another of Bodvar's many wars with the jarls, Valgard was killed. Later I will return to Valgard's death; unless I greatly miss my guess it scarred Gunnar more than he would admit.'

"Now we come to Bardi, the youngest son, who is two years younger than Gunnar, and now rules in Norland. From the beginning Bardi loved and admired Gunnar, who loved him greatly in return and was his careful and exacting teacher in all the skills of war. Bardi learned well, and is a fine soldier, but beyond this he is shrewd and wise far beyond his years. He is ruling Norland far better than his father Bodvar ever managed.'

'Now back to Gunnar. When arrived at eight years Gunnar and Valgard left home to be fostered in norse skills and ways with the fine old viking Thormod Refsson.'

"Two years later, when Gunnar was ten, Thormod took Bodvar aside and told him bluntly it was a miracle Gunnar had no yet killed Valgard, and furthermore, if things continued as they were, he, Thormod, would be killing Valgard."

Ulf paused in his narrative.

"That's quite the dilemma; what did Bodvar do?"

"Refsson is as good as it gets, and Bodvar left Valgard with him – hoping a few Viking virtues might rub off. As Bodvar originally promised, he fostered Gunnar himself. Bodvar's story is very uneven and does not sit well on my tongue, but he proved a strong friend to Gunnar and was an excellent foster father. In return Bodvar received unswerving loyalty. It is this loyalty that shapes our current difficulties, but this is for later.'

"When he turned eighteen Gunnar went raiding, at which he proved very successful. A year later, when nineteen, he organized and led his own raid. He was considered lucky and had more volunteers than he could use. This second raid was even more successful. At twenty Gunnar was already wealthy.'

"You, Miles, are something of a legend, and Bodvar himself loves to tell his portion of your tale, especially how he took you out to the barn for earnest talk only to find you had lured him out for solemn discourse. Your consummate generalship and Yngvar's hard to believe luck and skill have been Gunnar's daily fare. Had things had gone differently I think Gunnar would have visited you after the second raid. Alas, it was not to be.'

"Instead Gunnar spent the next eight years in a very bloody series of wars in southwest Norland.'

"Were these wars necessary? Hardly; Bardi would have easily steered around them. Bodvar is a worthy and good man, but he hasn't even a pinch of political savoir faire. It is easily true that but for Gunnar his foster father would long since have been thrown from power and killed. Gunnar has come to enjoy such prestige that his enemies are beat in their own minds before the battle is joined."

Miles interrupted; "Ulf, I understand such details are not in step with your intent, but in a rough way what are the causes of these southwestern wars?"

Ulf thought a moment before answering; "There are a thousand particulars, but it seems to me the underlying causes are few and come to high handedness, breeches of custom and prerogatives, and of course, excessive tribute, or taxes."

"It came to an end when the northern earls got involved. Gunnar and the army, once again, were sent south, and one week after they left the northern earls seized Bodvar and deposed him in favor of his son Bardi. I don't know it for certain but have always wondered if the whole thing were organized by Bardi. At any rate a new age of peace was ushered in; which brings us to our problem.'

"There is not a single southern earl who has not lost a son or relative to Gunnar; your son, Miles, is a much hated symbol of Bodvar's regime. It was only a matter of time till he gets a knife in his back. Bardi and I agreed he needed to be gotten out of Norland. Gunnar has always wanted to meet you, Miles, so when peace arrived I suggested we pay a visit; he was delighted. He feels as though he is leaving Bardi vulnerable, but the truth is he's an embarrassment and liability to Bardi. Of course Bardi knows this, but I think Bardi's primary concern is for Gunnar's safety. That is <u>my</u> only concern; it is certain Gunnar will be killed, and sooner than later, if he stays in Norland."

Ulf paused; "So we come to it: Miles, you must persuade Gunnar to stay in Newland; if he returns with me to Norland I very much doubt you will ever see him again."

This suited Miles very well indeed and he couldn't help thinking of Asgerd's dream, which strongly suggests Gunnar would be staying.

"If need be I'll tie him down, Ulf; we won't let him go back. Not only is Gunnar my son and a fine man, but my second son Kjartan needs a strong friend – I'm getting too old to play the part. I even know where Gunnar's farm and hall will be – there will be no finer hall and farm in Newland!" Ulf was visibly relieved and pleased.

"Now, Ulf, clear up a loose thread; earlier you mentioned Valgard's death troubled Gunnar. What happened? Did Gunnar kill him?"

"He did, and he didn't; Gunnar could never bring himself to kill Bodvar's son, but Valgard acted in a way that must inevitably get himself killed. I was there when it happened and I know Gunnar as well as any man alive.'

"Gunnar, Valgard, myself and four other men were ambushed by a force of twenty men. Everyone had their hands more than full and Valgard and three of our men died. However, under the same circumstances had Bardi been with us instead of Valgard he would have survived – Gunnar would have made a point of it. Gunnar saw exactly who killed Valgard and before the enemy withdrew he killed the two men.'

"So, the enemy killed Valgard and Gunnar saw to it he was avenged; only I'm pretty sure Gunnar let it happen. I think it bothers him now and then. Were I Gunnar I wouldn't give the matter a second thought – best riddance ever!"

CHAPTER 46
Ulf the Fearless (Continued)

MILES AND ULF, AFTER realizing they were of one mind concerning Gunnar's future, talked general life and politics in Norland and Newland. They reminisced over old friends long gone, and especially lingered over Yngvar, who was dear to both of them.

"I heard Yngvar's death was magnificent and fully in keeping with the man; weren't you there?"

"Very much so! Had Yngvar's death been even a shade less magnificent I wouldn't be here talking.'

"Yngvar was with me on the first expedition to the far west. We landed on the north end of Newland and in an effort to see the country and find water we climbed a coastal mountain. There were four of us; myself, Yngvar, and two others. Returning we were within a mile of the ship and had just entered a small meadow when a skraeling war party ambushed us. The first thing I noticed was a grunt from Yngvar, who suddenly had two arrows in his chest and one in his abdomen; one of the other men looked like a porcupine and was probably dead before he hit the ground. There was no time to do anything but grab your axe and parry the first blow. Vali Retilsson and I fought back to back and when the enemy withdrew there were seven dead skraeling in our portion of the field.'

Miles paused; "The wonder was what we found behind us – Yngvar was lying on the ground surrounded with six dead skraeling. Had he not managed to cover our back we would all have died. But how does a man dead on his feet kill six other men?!"

Ulf considered; "It must happen very quickly or not at all; every motion must count and end in a death. Never since the world began was there a man who could kill so many so quickly.'

There was a moment of silence, then; "Miles, is it true Asgerd warned Yngvar against sailing west with you? Unlike most men, where death is assigned and sealed, Yngvar had choice – sail west and die, or stay off the ship and live many years till a different death finds you."

"Too true, Ulf. Asgerd loved Yngvar greatly and pleaded with him to stay. Her direct approach could only fail. She should have come to me with the problem. I would have diverted Yngvar with a projected raid or war and promised to meet back on Westmark in two years. Instead, staying off the ship was seen as fleeing death, a totally unacceptable course. Unfortunately for Asgerd, once stated there was no recourse, no going back. Her efforts to save him guaranteed the very thing she sought to avoid."

Miles shook his head sadly; "Ulf, to this day Asgerd mourns Yngvar and regrets her well intended efforts to spare him. Asgerd has very few things to regret, but not even her cupboard is completely clean."

There was a silence which at length Miles broke; "Ulf, just before heading into the far north to kill Eirik Yngvar and Kjartan disagreed over which of them should come north with me. Finally, in order to settle the question, I threw an axe and Kjartan won the toss.'

"Later, when fewer than half of us came back Yngvar was curious as to what happened – especially since he had sensed a dangerous trap.'

"In answering him I admitted there had been a trap, but our greater strength tilted the balance our way. I never ventured details, never told him what happened. Did you tell him?"

Ulf was thoughtful; "He asked, and like yourself I evaded him. Our tale just doesn't bear repeating; it is not the sort of thing one grown man tells another grown man. Galti, as you probably heard, tried to tell our story and only managed to push it out of sight. Are such events frequent? Do they always disappear from view?"

This was an imponderable and the men traveled a while in a companionable silence. At length Miles spoke; "Ulf, over the years what part of our northern adventure do you suppose has stayed with me?"

Ulf considered; "I would imagine you have developed a strong sense of the fated quality of the whole business."

Miles laughed; "Far from it, Ulf; I remember how very focused and on-my-toes I was that morning. The ironic, the crazy thing being that 'on your toes' was, in our strange circumstances, necessarily a kind of madness; any deviation whatsoever from usual and expected had to be viewed as lethal, and one needed to be tuned to even subtle deviations from expected.'

"When I ordered our archers to shoot those unlikely rocks no one smiled, they just did it – and probably saved our lives."

Ulf came to a full stop and looked directly at Miles; "Twenty-eight years later what you remember is being on your toes?!"

Ulf was about to go on but suddenly a look of understanding dawned on his face; "I see; Kjartan never told you what happened, did he?"

"Over the years Kjartan has told me many things; what do you have in mind?"

"At the height of the fight, when events were balanced on a knife edge, you were locked in a closely contested fight and completely missed a large berserk immediately behind you who was well into his downswing aimed at your head. Kjartan and I were about seventy feet away and both happened to look over at the same moment; you were within a small part of a second of being killed – there was no time to cock an arm for a throw.'

"This is hard to explain, but I'll try: Kjartan's axe was suddenly moving at a blinding speed, yet he never cocked his arm and never released the axe; it was as though the axe were taken from him.'

"Kjartan's attention was more on his axe than the berserk and he missed the truly strange part; the berserker crumpled and died before the axe arrived. From where I stood the axe did not arrive till the man was halfway down. When he hit the ground the axe was protruding from the other side of his chest – the force was incredible!

Kjartan may not have cocked his arm or released the axe, but the force for that blindingly fast journey came from him and he was suddenly weakened to the point he fell to his knees.'

"Fortunately I saw what happened and rushed to his defense; after a hard fight I managed to extricate him. By the time I got him sidelined things were winding down.'

"Later Kjartan and I examined the berserk and discovered the axe had entered his back blunt end first and was sticking out through his breast plate in front. I told Kjartan of the odd reversal of events; instead of the axe arriving and the man dying the man had died, then the axe arrived. I'm sure there is a connection between the axe and the death, but it is not the usual one.'

"Kjartan and I felt you were fated to win against Eirik and Ragnhild; that any of us survived links to this.'

Miles had a thoughtful moment; "No, Ulf, Kjartan never told me this story."

"There is another curious side to our northern adventure. But before you disagree remember my experience is truly large; I have seen more of war and death than any two other men. Odin's steel spell is more talked over and presumed than real. Not, however, with Ragnhild; hers steel spells were the real thing. The only time they didn't work was around you, and according to Yngvar, around your wife. During our morning with Eirik the steel spell didn't hold, but neither did it altogether fail. When you struck Ragnhild's berserkers they died on the usual schedule; for the rest of us those berserkers took three times the usual amount of killing. This created desperation and fear amongst us that was barely kept in check – only your matter-of-fact manner kept us up to the mark. Had you not been there we all would have died. This was Kjartan's impression at the time and I agreed with him and have not changed my mind.'

Miles and Ulf had broken a twenty-eight year silence and it felt good: they were not alone, and they were not crazy. The conversation had unexpected fruit that surfaced near the end of the journey.

"Over the last twenty years we in Norland have heard a thousand tales of your skraeling. They sound as though they are thoroughly nasty customers. Now I am here and they have departed. This developed suddenly for no apparent reason. As they left they showed a marked respect and deference to Miles Drake."

Ulf paused; "Any ideas concerning their mysterious departure?"

Miles chuckled; "Of course Ulf; I always have ideas. This strikes me as yet another of those children's story scheduled to be forgotten; a tale hard for one grown man to tell another. Eirik's tale had Galti, while the skraeling have only me, and I'm not particularly talkative.'

Fifteen minutes later they walked into Miles Hall and found Asgerd, Kjartan, and Gunnar all cozy-cozy by the fire. Gunnar had arrived an hour earlier, and by the time Miles arrived the others had not only made introductions but become friends.

Miles Drake was a tall man, but in his son Gunnar he at last found a man he could look up to: Gunnar was six foot six inches and physically was a larger edition of his father, except for his black hair. His dark blue eyes and black hair made an unexpected and striking contrast; Gunnar might not be remarkably handsome, but his manner, presence, and appearance were memorable. Miles could easily believe what he had heard from Ulf.

CHAPTER 47
Poppo

MICHAEL HAD MUCH ON his mind, and as he hurried out the front door of the government building he entirely forgot Poppo.

But, alas, Poppo had not forgotten him, not for a moment. Poppo was seated, much as usual, in the dust near the front door, only, after a week of nothing but water, he <u>did</u> look a little thinner. Poppo was five foot eight inches, light brown hair and round head with average features, except for thick, thick eyebrows. What set Poppo apart from other men were his eyes, which were very much the man's point of focus and latched to other men the way a barnacle attaches to a pier. Poppo didn't look at other men, rather he branded and seared them.

Poppo was dressed in standard monk garb and after a week of living in the dust in front of Michael's government building he should be an object of pity; he was not. Despite his circumstances it was no more possible to pity the man than to pity a falcon or an eagle.

There was something about Poppo, an air of unshakeable purpose and power, that Michael sensed and respected, but he wanted no part of the man's Christianity. Hence the deadlock: Poppo was resolved on speaking with Michael and Michael was equally resolved he should not.

The late afternoon Michael forgot to leave by the backdoor Poppo was in the eighth day of starving himself before the front door of this same building.

It was as though Poppo had expected him.

"Lord Michael, will you speak with me here, or should I walk with you?"

Damn! Michael considered walking back into the building – but his dignity would not allow it. Days ago he should have quietly had Poppo killed; but he did not need a Christian martyr, and Poppo struck him as too fine a man to end up in a ditch – he didn't want to kill him. Then Michael had what seemed at the time to be pure inspiration.

"Poppo, your vigil and fasting are most impressive. I have come in person to invite you to a public hearing five days from now. Clean up, strengthen yourself with food, and an hour past noon five days from now, in this very building, we shall talk. Will you submit to testing?"

"I will submit to any testing you wish so long as it does not involve harm to others."

"Good. Now, go have a good meal and bath."

Michael hurried home to Herdis and his children.

FIVE DAYS LATER POPPO arrived at court. Michael had arranged to have an iron bar brought to white heat. The test was that Poppo should hold the bar in his right hand until Michael permitted him to put it down. This was a modification, a nasty modification, of a trial by ordeal where suspected criminals briefly held a hot iron bar and three days later a panel of judges reviewed the burned hand to judge if the blisters and third degree burns were healing ahead or behind expected and usual. This involved much judgment and allowed judges to herd events where they thought they should go.

Michael had his bar so hot men could not stand near it; he expected, and sincerely hoped Poppo would decline the ordeal. Poppo did not decline.

Showing neither fear nor hesitation Poppo picked up the bar and walked around the room discussing his god, the god's great power, and the even greater love he bore his creatures. After a few minutes Michael indicated he could put down the bar. The bar was still too hot to be near and by all rights Poppo's hand should have been utterly destroyed: it wasn't; indeed, Michael could not find so much as a small blister.

Talk is only talk, but this was utterly real and not to be ducked. Michael was profoundly disturbed. Important decisions, however, should not be made on the spur of the moment, and, while there was a part of Michael wishing the Christian god in his camp – and the sooner the better – he strangled the impulse. Instead he thanked Poppo and asked him to return in five days, when he would announce his decision.

After Poppo left, Michael sent a messenger to his foster father, asking Kjartan to meet him that evening at their favorite pub.

CHAPTER 48
Gunnar

MILES DRAKE ALWAYS, EVEN in bitter weather, enjoyed walking his trapline. Spring was near, but there was still much snow. The days were lengthening and this particular morning featured real sunshine and blue skies – a very much appreciated break from the twilight that in winter passed for morning.

Beyond these pleasing particulars was the deep pleasure Miles took in having Gunnar along. Miles was a student, an artist, of trapping animals; never a day passed but he didn't learn some new and interesting habit or characteristic of the animals he hunted. Kjartan had never been very interested, but Gunnar felt as Miles did and drank in Miles' tips and craft-lore. It had been a wonderful winter, and as it drew to a close Gunnar had become an expert trapper. Asgerd, Gunnar, and Miles were now good, companionable friends. Kjartan had his own wife and home but had visited frequently. Both Miles and Gunnar were quiet, and Kjartan, in his bright quick way, brought them out. Kjartan was the yeast that leavened their sociability.

Spring was close, and the ships would soon be leaving. Miles now felt he could counsel and advise his son, and this was scheduled to happen at the third fox trap, his 'lucky' spot.

The third trap sported an unusually fine silver fox. As the men approached, Miles turned to face his son; "What are your plans for the spring, Gunnar?"

"I have seen you in the corners whispering with Ulf so you probably realize it would not be wise for me to return to Norland. I might make a home on Newland, or I might seek my fortune with Eyvind in eastern Gar. It probably sounds odd in a man not quite thirty, but I have seen enough war for two lives; I was hoping you might help me settle in Newland."

"With all my heart, son! I have already picked a lovely spot for a farm and Asgerd has picked the perfect wife. Of course these ideas are subject to your approval."

Gunnar smiled; "The farm I have met – and love. I expect it is the land by the river, which you have now pointed out three times. As for wives, it is true I will be needing one, but a thought intrudes: did Asgerd have anything to do with choosing that, ah, 'spirited' wife of Kjartan's?"

Vigdis, rib to Kjartan, was 'spirited' shading into shrewishness. Gunnar's question was hardly idle.

"Absolutely not; Kjartan, as young men will, married in the teeth of his mother's opposition. Your stepmother, Gunnar, is as smart as they come and I would think three times before crossing her counsel."

"Who does she have in mind?"

"Gyda Thorisdottir."

Gunnar looked relieved and pleased; "Good. I have already halfway lost my heart to her; I kept back half since my plans were not clear. If things go as seems likely sometime in late spring or early summer I will be asking you to approach Thorir on my behalf.'

"But first we must establish Gyda's kingdom."

It was too fine a day and the news far, far too good to kill the silver fox, which was duly released with life attached. The whole business left the fox in a thoughtful and rather puzzled mood.

As Miles and Gunnar neared home their mood was closer to baseline and Gunnar said; "I have much treasure and can pay well for labor and animals. My settling will not cost yourself or others anything. As you help me organize events please keep this in mind. The early raiding was extremely profitable."

After a pause; "Father, you probably see this, but sometime this spring or early summer, Hogni Ingolfsson will organize and ambush me for shaming him. If they use the bow then events are on the knees of the gods; however, if, as I think more likely, they come at me with axes and swords then I will live and they will die. In either event I doubt you can help me, but you could certainly lose your life. Perhaps you and Kjartan should not walk or travel with me till this is over."

"Thanks for mentioning it, Gunnar. Kjartan has two wonderful hunting dogs that will almost certainly spoil the party for Hogni. Kjartan, myself, or both of us will try to be with you when you travel. The only thing better than to die fighting at your son's side is to live at his side. Gunnar, with these hounds we will either ambush them or there will be a stand-up fight."

IN THE EVENT THE ambush came while Kjartan and Gunnar, under some pretext or other, were walking to Thorir's farm to see Gyda. The dogs came to full alert and the suspicious brothers sneaked up behind a clump of bushes on a hill near the trail. There were seven men, five with nocked arrows. When the brothers struck each killed a man. After this

Kjartan distracted one man while managing to stay alive and Gunnar killed the other four.

The seventh man, the one entertaining Kjartan, had his right hand cut off but was not killed. He bore a message to Hogni Ingolfsson explaining the account was currently even, but if anything whatsoever happened in the future then, certain as sunrise, Hogni and his sons would die. Gunnar meant what he said and Hogni knew it. The business was finished, and faded away.

IN THE EARLY FALL Gunnar married Gyda Thorisdottir. The marriage proved very happy. The couple was blessed with four children, three boys and a girl.

CHAPTER 49
Kjartan

DAMN! IT SEEMED AS though everything he did these days hurt and wearied him; now he was planning out a one mile trip to the pub as though it were a journey to cross Gar!

Kjartan had to laugh at himself, but it was a wry laugh shadowed by the awareness that when he no longer had the detachment to laugh at himself, then he was swallowed entire by his pains and peevishness. He would be yet another of those useless old farts that bothered everyone and had worn him out in younger days.

Why couldn't he have died in a good stand up fight in his sixties? Had he been 'lucky' for this!? Being seventy-five with his right knee was to be cursed by the gods.

But not tonight; he could be a pain-in-the-ass seventy-five year old curmudgeon on his own time, but tonight Michael needed him.

As Vali Ketilsson drove their mule and cart Kjartan thought over what the messenger had told him of Poppo and the white-hot iron bar. It had been a mistake to give Poppo a public forum: had Poppo ducked the test and been shamed, or had he been maimed for life there would have been anger and embarrassment amongst the Christians; this would have been bad. As it was Poppo had delivered the goods but

Michael never had been in a position to respond – he needed Michael crystal clear on that point – so Michael looked a mite foolish. No good could come of giving a Muslim or Christian a public forum with the government. Kjartan knew exactly how the evening must go, but he was not clear on the smoothest and best way to bring them into harbor.

ON THE OTHER END of town Michael (and four norse who served as his guard) were strolling towards the pub. Michael's thoughts turned to his foster father and then passed, as they so often did when he considered the Kjartan of the last several years, to his wife Herdis. No man had ever been so blessed in the matter of wives. Five years ago Unn had died of pneumonia, afterwhich she came to be appreciated as she never was in life. Kjartan was so crippled with his knee he went to live with Hall. That lasted an everlasting six months. Then he transferred to his daughter Asgerd, which lasted, impossibly, an entire year.

At this point the peevish Kjartan shook the dust off his feet and left for Mendero, 'where they knew how to treat an old viking.'

Herdis rapidly took his measure and also took him in hand. She had a small long house built near, but not too near, her own home, and Vali Ketilsson, a cheerful, patient man, was assigned to befriend and help Kjartan. Herdis and grandkids were frequent visitors – and could leave when it suited Herdis. In conversation Herdis gave her father-in-law at least as much guff and sass as she received, and the old man seemed to love her the more for it. 'Yes', thought the grateful and besotted husband, 'There was no one like Herdis! Maybe tonight he really would kiss her toes.' This 'threat' had hung over Herdis's head for more than a decade and her toes had yet to be kissed.

Kjartan might be difficult, but since the death of Sandaman five years back his position with Michael was unique; Michael honored and respected him above all others. This particular night Michael knew exactly what Kjartan would tell him, and why; and he knew Kjartan would be right, but at the same time Kjartan would make his path smoother and more reasonable than it seemed at the moment.

THE FRIENDS MET AND were duly settled in a private room of the pub. Michael left instructions with the publican for his men, who were to have two beers each, neither more nor less.

"Michael, imagine you are Muslim with a family and a small business. Your norse ruler, hitherto a fairly reasonable man, has just converted to Christianity; will you sleep better at night? For this man and others your conversion would open the door to fear and uncertainty. If any sort of chance offers, such men will try to change things, and their religion, far from discouraging them will urge them on. If they are not sleeping well then it is to be hoped you are not so much the fool as to be sleeping well yourself."

"All true, but if the Christian god really is the high and powerful one then in the long run it might be best to align with this reality."

Kjartan chuckled; "We know the Christian god is so powerful because Christians serve and are secondary in their own homeland of Gar?! I certainly need such a god!"

"I have heard Christians explain this and I must admit it was most unconvincing. This, uncle, is a simple and weighty point."

Kjartan sat thoughtfully for a full minute, "Michael, all water is wet, and all gods, Christian, norse, Muslim, and any other god, occasionally breaks the ordinary rules of life. This is in the nature of things and proves nothing; it hardly exempts you from being reasonable and responsible. That the Christian god protected Poppo from harm today has very little to do with what is wisest and best for you and Mendero."

"This is very likely true, respected elder, but I have never seen with my own eyes anything remotely similar amongst we norse. Have you?"

"I have seen things Michael, that loom beyond Poppo's hot iron bar as whales loom above minnows."

"This is the first I have heard of it, uncle; why?"

"The 'why' is most simple; If my friend Vali took you aside and told of his conversations with trolls and elves would you respect him and seek his opinion on matters of importance? Probably not. If in fact Vali is a sensible man, and if in fact he talks with elves, then he will keep the conversation to himself."

"Fifty-five years ago I was with Miles Drake when King Eirik was killed. No one ever mentions this expedition and it is quite forgotten. Of the fifteen survivors I am the only one left. No one talked, and the truth will die with me. In this case there is no harm, since the truth is hardly very useful."

Michael found this unexpected and surprising; "You have never, uncle, told this story to anyone?!"

"I have not."

"Then let's not allow it to slip into darkness; tell me the story. And don't fret over Poppo – if your story is any sort of story I will send him packing."

Chapter 50
The Tundra

As he cast his mind back over the years Kjartan momentarily seemed distant and preoccupied; Michael waited patiently.

Kjartan remembered the cool breezy weather and scudding clouds as they approached the tree line and passed amongst the last few stunted spruce and birches before emerging on open tundra. He had been pleased and hopeful – more fool he!

He thought of his fifteen lads, eight of whom were Westmark men he knew personally – then the old ache returned. 'Well', thought Kjartan, 'into the tale!'

"We had chased Eirik and eighteen men into the far north. Against these nineteen, including Eirik himself, we had forty good men. We had supplies for two, in a pinch three weeks, while Eirik had few if any supplies. There is nowhere to hide on the tundra and at the time it seemed to me Eirik was our meat, the only question being would it be sooner or later. There was, however, a consideration clouding the shape of events: Eirik had with him Ragnhild, a volva extremely powerful in the dark seid. But against this we had Miles Drake, who possessed enough luck for the world itself.'

"Early noon we came out on the tundra and the afternoon and the evening were uneventful."

Michael interrupted; "Uncle, how much of an evening was there?"

"We were two months past summer solstice and there was true night.'; Kjartan paused, "Michael, I said the early hours on the tundra were uneventful, but as I look back there were several unusual things about the tundra that were present from the beginning. Usually the tundra is boggy, while this tundra was firm and we traveled well and quickly. In high summer the insects are unbelievable, but two months past summer solstice they are much diminished – we had none. I don't remember a single insect. For that matter I never saw a fox, wolf, lemming, or caribou either. We were they only life on this particular bit of tundra. The next point is subtle and certainty is not possible, but it seemed to me there was a glittering, sparkling quality on the edge of vision; if you turned to view a thing directly it would look normal, but this same object, when on the margins seemed to sparkle – like the sun on water."

"Did others mention this?", asked Michael.

"Only one man mentioned it specifically, but I saw other men constantly turning to put things in central vision."

Kjartan paused; "Actually, Michael I have this backward. Ulf the Fearless asked me about the sparkling on the edges and only then did I specifically notice and become aware."

"The last point was not subtle; in the evenings the northern dawn was a fiery curtain along nearly the entire horizon. I have never seen anything like it, neither before nor since.'

"It was the end of the second day when things went very sour. But I must belabor a few very obvious things to make this clear. Our first camp on the tundra included several fires since we had carried the few small pieces of wood we found at Timberline. In the morning we walked due north and the rising sun was on our right. The sun was straight ahead at noon and was on our left all afternoon. Towards evening, with the sun low on our left we walked into our old camp! There were the fires, the cooking stones, the favored spots where we had slept. We had traveled unerringly north and were back where we started! Shortly after walking into our old camp a second jolt arrived; Vefrod Aevarrson, a Westmark man, was gone. Verfrod had made no mention of leaving and no one had seen him leave. Our war party was now thirty-nine men. That night two more men disappeared.'

"As we left camp early the next morning Ulf took me aside. 'Kjartan, conviction can take many shapes; watch this.', and he placed a valued knife near an old fire and under a flap of loose lichen. I saw his direction; 'We'll be back this evening being your point?'

'It is, and though once again we are heading north I suspect it wouldn't matter which direction we take – all paths will lead back to this accursed camp. I am certain more men will walk out this morning than will walk back in the evening. Kjartan, we are up against some very powerful and very dark seid.'

'Have you shared these thoughts with Miles?'

'I have, and he's not ready to take seid seriously. When he is perhaps something can be done – I hope there will be a few of us left to benefit from his efforts. But this is for later; today we make another circle and a few more will die.'

"That evening Ulf recovered his knife and there were two men missing.'

"Thirty-five men sat down to the evening meal and a very odd situation prevailed; everyone, with the possible exception of Miles Drake, knew what was happening to the missing men, but no one spoke of it; not me, not Ulf – no one spoke or even considered speaking. We only hoped we'd last the night and be there to greet the morning light."

Michael found the situation literally inconceivable; "How is such a thing possible?! And how could you know what the other fellow thought if he didn't tell you?!"

"You could see what the other man thought by his manner; you could see it in his eye."

'How to explain', thought Kjartan. A thoughtful silence ensued; Kjartan had never explained to an 'outsider', and anyone who had been there didn't need explanation.

"Michael, it was like a strong call of nature, like a full bladder or bowel, like being ninety percent down the path with a woman – the tension is terrific and the promise of release is irresistible. No man can argue any length of time with a full bladder. Peace, or release, 'emptying your bladder', was to be found by leaving the others and walking toward the horizon, which in the evenings was the northern dawn. The problem was that as you ached to walk to the horizon you knew it was a walk to oblivion; you would not return."

Kjartan paused, and there were tears in his eyes; "Michael it was chilling, awful: you were balanced on the edge, and it seemed irresistible, only a matter of time till you broke and walked.'

"Miles didn't feel this call. Ulf did, but for some reason not so strongly as the rest of us.'

"I was quite desperate, and upon arriving at our camp I took Miles aside and told him what Ulf had said that morning. Furthermore I tried to explain the call and the conviction it was terminal.'

"Miles listened intently and asked about the call, when was it strong, when was it weaker. It seemed to me it was weaker round other men and strengthened as you separated from others. He wanted specifics; for example, how was it with two men? With three? The most telling difference was going from two men to three; with two men the call was still strong but with three it was manageable and weak.'

"Eventually the questions ended and you could see the man focus, and then resolve on a plan; it was as though he had put a death grip on our dilemma. For the first time since last night I felt certain we would persevere and succeed."

Kjartan paused. "Miles Drake had many fine moments in his most unusual life, but the finest were those from his conversation with me that evening till the deaths of Eirik and Ragnhild the next afternoon.'

"Miles, called the men together. He began by walking two hundred yards away from us and towards the Northern Dawn, then he walked back. Miles explained that since infancy we had been trained to hold death in contempt. This contempt, learned on our mothers' knees, had no exceptions; for example, death by seid is as contemptible as death by axe or illness. We were norse and our nerves were not like a cluster of butterflies scattering in the wind because there was a bit of seid in the neighborhood.

He allowed the last few days were enough to make you think you were in a children's story; at this point if a troll strolled up it wouldn't surprise him.

In a way it was true – we were in a children's tale. The rules in this sort of story had to be followed strictly, or the volva would eat you. This got him a laugh, but it was weak. The rules were then layed out, and ignoring them would probably get you killed.

Firstly, the loose formation of days past was finished. Tonight we sleep close together, side by side, and tomorrow we walk in close formation. When any man separates from the others, for scouting or making water, there must be at least two other men with him. No party of less than three should separate from the larger party; no exceptions.

Secondly, choosing direction from clues within the story was not working – they had made large circles the past two days. In the morning they would choose their direction differently; they would choose by their rules, not by story rules. They would create a strong world of their own, a world created by song, and this would keep out story influences. In the morning he would show them.

Third point. They were the good guys in the children's story and they would win; that's how it goes in the children's story. You would think Ragnhild would know this and stay away from children's stories! She'd made a big mistake, and it would kill her, certain as dawn.'

"Men, stay by the rules and this will soon be over!"

Miles then got them singing a well-known and popular marching song. This had a wonderfully positive impact on our mood. Afterwards there was the usual banter and conversation – the silence and whispering were gone.

CHAPTER 51
The Old Saami

KJARTAN, AT THE ZENITH of his tale, now grew silent and sipped his beer in a meditative way. At length Michael nudged him forward.

"So, respected elder, in the morning you all awoke refreshed and full of piss and vinegar? How exactly did Miles Drake steer your course?"

"No, Michael, our evening was most strange; alas, I only vaguely remember. Miles seemed entirely free of the tundra and its enchantments, and to a large extent Ulf too. Not your foster father, Michael; I was smack dab in the middle of the children's story with the others. What I know of this evening is mostly taken from Ulf, though I do have a vague recollection of an old Saami herder.'

"When Miles finished his pep talk and plan it was still forty or so minutes till true darkness arrived. We had walked long and hard all day. Many found a comfortable spot and went to sleep; this was much more grouped than before. There was a little wood left for the return trip so there were two small fires around which those not ready for sleep gathered. I was around a fire with twelve others. Eventually Ulf joined our fire. Before this Ulf spent quite some time with Miles.'

"I will tell you how it looked to me and then share what Ulf told me later. As we talked around the fire it emerged the tundra we travelled was, according to ancient Saami lore, under terrible curse and interdiction by the old gods; no one who entered ever walked out. I have no idea where this originated, it just came about in our talk. I also have a vague memory of an old Saami herder, nothing clear or specific such as a large nose or black eyes.

When I first talked to Miles I shared the impression Ulf seemed more resistant to the call than the rest of us. After Miles talked to us he took Ulf aside and shared with Ulf his resolve that from now till the death of Eirik they would not lose another man to a 'fucking witch's call'. If necessary Miles would pace our camp all night every night. If possible he would like to share this responsibility with Ulf, at least for a few hours. Miles then studied the call as it worked on Ulf. It seemed to come alive when Ulf moved thirty to forty yards from Miles. The call could be broken by singing the marching song, especially if Ulf became completely involved with the song. The song needn't be sung aloud, it could be sung silently in the mind, but the involvement was vital. That marching song was our tower of strength. Miles decided Ulf could share his burden, with the understanding Ulf keep within thirty yards of our perimeter and sing the marching song should the lust to head towards the northern dawn grow strong.

This finished they approached my fire and found an old Saami herder holding us spell-bound with tales of hexes and cursed ground. We had shared our food with the Saami and this conferred guest status and duties of hospitality.

Miles took the Saami aside – we never noticed the Saami left – and clear hard words followed. The Saami could sit quietly by the fire but if he spoke again of Saami lore, hexes, or curses he would lose two fingers from his right hand

and be put out of camp. He was free to stay or leave, but if he stayed those were the conditions. Miles opined that a wiseman would leave, but that was the Saami's affair.

The Saami chose the second fire and sat down quietly. Miles returned to our fire and managed to share the view that Saami lore was nonsense and fit only for children, old women, and perhaps lemmings. This got a laugh. Miles then discovered we had only the vaguest idea an old Saami herder was in our camp.

Alarmed, Miles went quickly to the other fire, where the old Saami was yet again holding the men spell-bound with tales of hexes and curses.

Miles motioned for the Saami to slip away from the fire; he could see the old man was startled and amazed to be noticed.

Without ceremony Miles put a knife to his throat. This occasioned yet greater surprise. When the Saami tried to get free Miles pricked his neck and drew blood – the Saami was stunned, astounded. Miles told Ulf to cut off the fourth and fifth fingers of his right hand. When the Saami struggled Miles drew more blood and promised a quick death if there was further struggle. The Saami grew quiet but when Ulf tried to cut the fingers the knife twisted in his hand and he cut himself, fortunately the wound was not serious. At this point Miles looked thoughtfully at the Saami.

'You are a very unusual Saami and probably should be killed. You are going to lose those fingers and you would be wise to keep in mind I am looking for any opportunity to kill you. Put out your hand.'

The Saami stood in the shadow of death and knew it. He put his hand out and Miles cut off the fourth and fifth fingers. Then Miles and Ulf walked the Saami away from our camp. Two hundred yards distance from camp they found they were walking by themselves, the Saami was gone. Miles knew then he should have killed the 'old man'. It was a mistake that cost us dearly.

CHAPTER 52
The Bard

ASGERD AND KJARTAN WALKED along side by side leading their heavily laden horses. The thing, or assembly, had been full of surprises for Asgerd and she was studying her son Kjartan with new eyes.

"Two years ago when your father stepped aside for you I had my doubts: you are the youngest Godi on record and your father's boots are larger than those of most trolls. Miles has never been visited by doubt. He probably was, but his trick was to point the doubt in my direction. Doubt and I would talk things over and never seemed to come to any conclusion – until now. Yesterday, after your judgment on Valgerd, Einar, and Bjalfi, I gave Doubt a good paddling and sent him back to his own hall. I was very proud of you, Kjartan; you will be an exceptional godi. But also I am mystified. The first mystery is why, on such a confused and important matter, should they accept judgment by the youngest and least experienced of the godi? The second mystery is the judgment itself; it seemed pretty hard on Einar, and to a lesser extent Valgerd. Of course Bjalfi would find the judgment as comfortable as a warm bath on a winter day. Yet all three accepted the judgment well, and when all is settled it seems Einar will have his own farm – a pretty good one at that!'

"I would have proceeded differently. The bride price and dowery should have been the central issue, and its division would hinge on choices of Valgerd. But no, let's not be sensible! Instead you come on with a high and mighty hand – and everyone is charmed!'

"Clearly I am missing something; perhaps a thoughtful godi and son can lend a hand and gratify his mother's curiosity."

Kjartan chuckled; "Ever the shrewd one mother-o-mine. Valgerd, Bjalfi, and myself arranged a legal charade for the benefit of Einar. Valgerd wanted Bjalfi back but didn't want to tell Einar herself – too painful and embarrassing. So it was that I, godi Milesson, got to break the bad news; poor little Valgerd, though bowed with grief, must submit to the judgment, must leave Einar and return to Bjalfi."

Now Asgerd was really confused; "You are not helping.'

"Here's what I see. Six years go Bjalfi married Valgerd and they settle on a farm contributed by Bjalfi's father Thorkel. Things go well enough and the couple seems reasonably happy; hardly on epic passion but not bad.'

"Now Bjalfi decides to go raiding. Four years go by and there is no word of him. Along comes Einar visiting from Norland. At the end of the fourth year he moves in with Valgerd. Einar, as to character, is more capable and industrious than Bjalfi ever thought of being. Moreover of the two men Einar is the handsomer and kinder man. The farm prospers as never before. Thorkel, who could have thrown the couple out, likes Einar and there is no problem. The new couple seems quite happy. Then, two years later, and six since leaving, Bjalfi comes home with a story of hardship and shipwreck. For my part I don't believe his tale, but that is neither here nor there. So, problems, problems, problems. The problem is laid at the feet of a wise godi and all parties agree to abide by his judgment. This judgment is that Einar must leave in favor of Bjalfi and Valgerd must accept him. However the godi sympathizes with Einar and his sympathy takes the form of a slave, two pigs, and a cow. The godi invites others to give a hand and keep this good man in the community. Bjalfi himself contributes a bull – since his household only needs one bull and he has two! Others have offered animals and labor. These promises were publicly given and must be kept. Einar will soon have a prosperous farm above Gunnar's place, and he will be an unusually loyal thingman of yours."

Kjartan smiled; "Of course he will, and will be treasured as such."

"This is all wonderful, Kjartan, but my problem is that were I Valgerd I would be moving with Einar and I would expect my dowery to go with me and perhaps half of the bride price. And so I ask again; what are the missing pieces?"

Kjartan gave his mother a quizzical look and chuckled; "The reasons are so very ordinary, so of this world, that a high-minded norse woman like yourself would find them negligible, beneath notice. Perhaps it is time to shift to a more elevated and interesting topic – Dad; of all things in middle earth he has the most surprises!"

"I am sure you are right, Kjartan. Doubtlessly your tale is all you say; exceptionally ordinary and negligible. However, while I <u>am</u> a high-minded norse woman, yet I have always loved middle earth and its details."

"Okay, best of mothers. But this tale is for your ears only, and upon hearing the tale you are not under even the slightest obligation to share your impressions with your son, who already has a shrewd notion of what shape they will take.'

Asgerd smiled; "My, my! This sounds ripe."

"The world at large looks at Bjalfi and sees a man of average physique with features that are closer to homely than many would find comfortable. But this glance misses much: below the belt the man is more stallion than man. Many, but certainly not all, women, once they have galloped with stallions, find the average mortal as exciting as old ashes. Valgerd is one of these.'

"There is a second thread to my tale. Rachel, her Christian slave, is both spirited and pretty; Valgerd, whether rightly or wrongly, suspects this wench of luring Einar off the path.'

"Against this background Bjalfi hides in the barn on a day Einar is away. In the course of the morning Valgerd comes out to the barn; one thing leads to another and they find themselves in the hay."

"This adventure in the hay, in combination with her suspicions, get Valgerd reoriented towards Bjalfi. Yet she remains kind towards Einar and has even given him her slave Rachel."

Asgerd laughed; "That isn't kindness, Kjartan; Valgerd wishes to preserve Bjalfi from temptation and peril."

"No doubt, mom, but enough of Einar, Bjalfi, and Valgerd – what are we to make of Miles Drake, our most respected and revered godi and hersir, playing at being a bard?! This is truly an arrow from the deep sea! Has Dad lost all shame!?'

I half think Dad went in search of Gunnar to avoid riding home with me and discovering what I think of Miles Drake the bard."

Asgerd interrupted; "Yes and no, Kjartan. Both Dad and myself are worried for Gunnar; he has been gone nearly a month and both Orn and Arni are strong and dangerous. Gunnar is the last man to hunt down outlawed men who leave others alone, but those murders in the southwest were brutal and unnecessary and the situation cannot decently be ignored.'

"The southwest is not our assembly area, Mom; this is the concern of Vebjorn.'

"It is, and his loss of nerve is a shame to him and will bring him down. Meanwhile the job needs doing and Gunnar stepped into the gap.'

"I know Gunnar survives this, but his survival may hinge on some part we play. At any rate your father is the man he is and it is impossible he should not search for Gunnar; both your brother and your father are exactly in character.'

"Having said this, your father would unquestionably travel many miles out of his path to avoid your thoughts on elderly godi bards."

Kjartan was frustrated; "I know, Mom, but the thing is so absurd, so, so…; what does one say?! The man is a legend amongst our people – and now he is the entertainment for the odd corner of the evening or winter fire! I don't know what to do; what to think. Both Dad and Gunnar usually go along with whatever I decide, but this one occasion I really miss Gunnar – let him decide and I'll follow.'

"And where in middle earth does he get his stories!"

"These stories are from his world, son. You forget he is not really one of us.'

"What did you think of the war between George Washington and King Georgie the Second, or was it Third? My favorite part is where the great hersir crosses the river on a fat, flatulent old sea lemming."

"Exactly, Mom. Great hersirs, when crossing even mud puddles, use sea stallions! Dad utterly trampled our favorite kenning! And his lines are without order; I'm not sure there was even a single line of the correct length or beats.'

Asgerd interrupted; "Son, give your outrage a rest; what did you think of the game?"

"The team from a place called Purdue?", asked Kjartan.

"Yes, that one."

Kjartan hesitated a while, then, reluctantly; "I liked it. I think Dad was their leader; he told the story as if he were there."

"He was. In a country many times larger than Norland, Westmark, and Newland combined, where a large number of such teams compete, your father stood out as Gunnar stands out amongst norse warriors. He was a legend in his own country, much as he is in ours."

Kjartan, inspite of himself, was intrigued; "How is it I have heard nothing of this?"

"There is no way back to his own country and he has put it behind him – until now. Besides, when it comes to your father there is quite enough to tell of his life amongst us."

Asgerd paused; "you know what I particularly liked in his story of the game?"

"That last throw, when all was lost, when the warrior Matt flew like a falcon and caught the ball?"

"No; when that mountain of a man came bearing down on him 'like a heavily loaded knorr in a strong wind!' That, Kjartan, is an irresistible, a perilous approach."

"Later, as I thought about it, I began to understand; your father is reversing the direction of travel we have created with our kennings. All the kennings liken things at sea to vivid things from land; a long ship becomes a 'sea stallion'. Now things of the sea are used to make things of land more vivid – a charging warrior is likened to a heavily loaded knorr in a strong wind. I liked it; it is <u>very</u> vivid.'

A thoughtful son nodded; "I see what you mean, mother, but so what?! Wouldn't it be best for all parties if he put barding to the side?"

Asgerd smiled; "Let me ask you a question; the bard invited for our althing is from Norland and is quite famous. He faced unfavorable winds and arrived two days late, so your father filled in for him; of the two bards, Miles Drake and Narfi Eidsson, who did people enjoy more?"

Kjartan grew thoughtful and quiet.

"Let me help you. The first evening people were an odd mixture of being both shocked and intrigued. The second night there was no room anywhere near the fire and people drank it up. The third night Narfi took over and it seemed to me people would rather it was your father."

Asgerd was reporting accurately, and Kjartan knew it. At length Asgerd spoke.

"A wise godi picks his battles so as to win things of value and importance and to risk little. People seem to love Miles Drake as bard and your father is at a point in life where he will suit himself. In his home world the sense of honor is very different from ours; he has much of what we call honor and is much respected, but for himself he values it only because we value it. In our society he could not act effectively without the respect of our people. Now, however, he is sixty-eight and you are a respected godi; a godi supported and backed by Gunnar. Your father has nothing further to prove or do – he will please himself. He doesn't particularly care for our bards and kennings and now feels free to go his own way."

"I imagine you are about right, mother."

"Count on it. No one, least of all your father, wants your opinions and interference. There is nothing to win and much to lose – a smart godi would steer his ship some other direction."

THE ALTHING LASTS TWO weeks. Miles concern for Gunnar was great, and he left after one week, which for him was a first. He returned home with Gunnar three weeks after leaving the althing.

Gunnar had taken three other men when he left to hunt Orn and Arni, but when Miles found him he was the only one left alive, and only barely. Sigurd Eysteinsson, one of Gunnar's men, was, unbeknownst to Gunnar, cousin on his mother's side to Orn. Sigurd arranged an ambush with Orn and Arni, and in the wake of this there was only a badly wounded Gunnar; all the others, including both Orn and Arni, were dead. Gunnar would have died but for his father's arrival, and even so it was touch and go. Only in the spring was Gunnar more or less restored; by midsummer he was back to full strength. It had been an harrowing ordeal.

THERE ARE LOOSE ENDS to round and complete.

Kjartan was, as his mother both hoped and suggested, a smart godi. He did not remark or make an issue of the bard side of his father. And, if the truth be told, Kjartan came to prefer his father's flavor of story, which steered away from Homeric heroes and grandeur towards the Garrison Keillor and <u>The Prairie Home Companion</u> end of the spectrum.. Kennings were preserved – but only for drollery; there were far more flatulent lemmings and many less prancing stallions.

Kjartan's judgment at the althing worked out well. Bjalfi, after six years of adventure abroad, settled down and worked hard; things went well for he and Valgerd.

Einar freed Rachel, and then, canny fellow, approached Kjartan with a bride price for Rachel. Kjartan rose to the occasion and managed a modest dowery on her behalf. Bride price and dowery are controlled by the husband but are property of the wife – this anchors many a stormy marriage since if the wife leaves, as occasionally they do, the bride price and dowery go with the wife. In norse marriages you never hear of a husband leaving a marriage, and only occasionally do the wives pack up and leave.

In the event Einar and Rachel had a happy and strong marriage. Einar, as predicted by Asgerd, did very well and ten years later was wealthy man. He was a good neighbor to Gunnar and a strong supporter of Kjartan.

Chapter 53
The Death of Eirik

THE RIGHT KNEE WAS back at him, and Kjartan winced and then shifted position; better. He completed his therapeutic maneuvers with a good pull at his mug. He was about to resume his tale when Michael interrupted.

"Your story, uncle, is very good, but doesn't seem quite as strong and certain as picking up an iron bar brought to white heat. The minds of you and your men were altered and it is uncertain what really happened, as opposed to what seemed, or appeared, to happen. This seems a cousin to the tales that come from a night of heavy drinking. The tale is subtly tainted at its source."

"All true, Michael; notice how carefully I have tried to keep track of my own state of mind. Miles Drake, and, to a lesser extent, Ulf, seemed untouched, and both are thoroughly reliable men. When I am not reliable I will not pretend otherwise; sit back and suspend judgment till I finish. I see you now fully understand why I have kept this tale to myself.'

"Sleeping close together, and having either Miles or Ulf circling our camp and humming our song brought peace, and a good night's sleep. In the morning we were all present and in good spirits.'

"Ragnhild, explained Miles, was subtly twisting our minds so we could not steer a straight course. Now we were to fill our minds with our song; if we held our song fast we would march a straight line. The line would be drawn from ourselves as we sang our song. He formed four groups of three men in each group. One man in the group would be buried past his ankles in a standing position. These three would take turns singing. The rest of us would walk just under a mile due north, then a second group of three would stay behind with one man buried just past his ankles; these three stayed together singing. The third group was placed in a line with the other two groups and Miles himself made the judgment. Then the whole group marched carefully along this line for about half a mile, and this was judged by repeatedly looking back and double checking our position. Then Miles would wave both arms, a gesture relayed back to the rear most group which then walked forward to the main group.'

"This is a slow and tiresome way to travel but we kept strictly to the plan. By midafternoon we had gone more or less five miles. Then about a mile ahead we saw a group of ten people. They were too distant to clearly identify, but they seemed to be Saami. This was the first decision point; should we continue our careful and slow method of travel, or steer directly to the distant Saami?'

"We proceeded slowly, and with constant reference to our line. Then, when we were within two hundred yards of what was clearly a group of Saami, a second decision point was reached: should we leave some portion of our line in place and reconnoiter the Saami, or should we let our line go and mass our strength. Miles chose strength, and all our men were brought forward. As they came Miles studied the Saami thoughtfully. Three things bothered him. The Saami and the caribou are like left and right arms – they are always found together. This group had a single bull; no cows, no calves. Secondly, the group stood within a circle of nine large stones. The stones didn't fit; thus far we had not seen a single stone. Thirdly, the group didn't seem to be doing anything; Sami don't loiter. It is impossible to both loiter and stay alive on the tundra. These 'Saami' seemed to be waiting.

When our group was back together Miles posted a sentry and the rest of us gathered round. In a manner leaving no doubt in our minds be told us the 'Saami' were no more real than the lines of travel we'd been using our first two days on the tundra. Two hundred yards ahead was the quarry we came to kill. The 'stones' must be assumed men until we knew otherwise. In retrospect Miles including the stones as enemies was both brilliant and critical; had we not done this I doubt we would have survived.'

"The plan was very simple and foolproof. The 'Saami' would still be hoping they had fooled us, or that at least we were uncertain. They wanted us within the 'stone' circle.'

"As we neared the stone perimeter we would spread out to form two lines, with the men in the second line having bows with nocked arrows under their cloaks. At the last second the first line would spread out to allow our archers room to work. Every 'Saami', 'stone', and 'the bull' was to receive at least two arrows. Miles didn't want it to come to axes while there was a single arrow in our quivers. He then said something that needed saying. These enemies were probably going to need a little more than the usual amount of killing. Our situation was very simple – we could either kill or be killed. Any running would bring you to the deathwalk to the horizon. Having pointed out the obvious Miles assured us that if we held the course we would live and they would die.

This was sobering, but one and all needed to understand no running or retreating was possible.'

"Our delays and grouping up must have unsettled our enemy and left them uncertain as to what we knew or suspected. But they wanted us in the stone circle, so they waited.'

"Our front line came forward with open and outstretched hands; this reassured Ragnhild and kept her hopeful. The first line also did an excellent job of screening our archers; the 'Saami's' first clue was the thud of arriving arrows.

Michael interrupted; "You, uncle, have a steady hand and good eye; I would imagine you were one of the archers.'

"Aye, so I was; and strange it was to shoot those stones. The arrow should have shattered or deflected; instead, with a good 'thunk', the arrow nearly disappeared in the stone. These 'stones' quickly shook off all 'stoniness', grew arms, legs and heads, and grabbed swords and axes. It was alarming how little our arrows stopped or slowed down our enemies; yet slow they did – only it took three or more mortal wounds to stop Eirik's berserks. We drove through their circle and divided them, yet outnumbered and divided it was a near thing and we lost many men. I lost track of the larger picture and was soon lost in killing the man in front of me while managing to stay alive.'

Kjartan paused; "In one way, Michael, the coming to blows cleared the air; balancing precariously on the thin edge of a deathwalk to the horizon is deeply unsettling and scary – this was gone. But now a new and deeply disturbing problem took its place.'

"Remember that fight for the Ligeri Bridge? You fought crack troops and there was no room for either you or the enemy to yield an inch – win or die, no middle ground. It was the same with us, but with a difference.'

"After a desperate and quite equal fight <u>you</u> managed to land a lethal blow and the enemy went down – but, suppose he didn't?! Suppose he fought on as though nothing had happened? That is what we faced, and it was <u>very</u> alarming; it crosses your mind that perhaps the only end is when <u>you</u> receive the lethal blow. But there is nothing for it, and you fight on, but with increasing desperation and fatigue!'

"At the end those of us still alive were barely able to stand. I somehow wasn't wounded, but I was off my feet and on the ground before the end, and it was sheer fatigue – but fatigue from a single throw of my axe!

This particular axe throw is still, fifty some years later, a puzzle to me; Ulf saw both the circumstances and the throw and he, in a quiet and assured manner, tells me what I think happened did not happen.'

"I was at a momentary interlude and happened to glance over to my right where I saw a large berserk coming up behind Miles, who was busy with the enemy in front of him. The berserk was raising his axe prepatory to killing the unsuspecting Miles Drake. The next thing I remember is waking up on the ground with Ulf in front of me hard at it with another berserk. Later I found my axe in the chest of the large berserk who had been on the verge of killing Miles. The berserk was some distance from where I must have thrown the axe, and the axe had gone clean through his chest and was half way out the other side. A throw like that would require a full swing from a fully cocked shoulder, and there had been little, very little, time available. I must have twisted at the waist and moved an extended arm back and under so the axe travelled, not before me, but rather in the reverse direction from that which I was initially facing. This would not require time to cock the shoulder and would still bring great force to bear. At any rate the effort must have been terrific since I lost consciousness and afterward was too weak to stand. It <u>was</u> an amazing throw – much better by far than any before or since."

Michael was as expert with an axe as any man alive and he was unable to see exactly how such a throw could go right through a large man's chest.

"What does Ulf say happened?"

"He says there was no time for any of what I describe. On his telling we both saw Miles danger late in the berserk's swing – no time whatsoever. He says it was as though the axe was taken from my hand by a sudden irresistible force and the berserk crumpled like a man suddenly dead as the axe left my hand; the axe caught up with the falling man halfway to the ground."

Michael didn't find Kjartan's version of events credible, but Ulf's was even more incredible.

"Uncle, are you positive certain the axe in the deadman's chest was yours?"

"It was my axe."

Michael puzzled on; "Is your friend Ulf of a playful turn?"

"No more nor less than most. Why do you ask?"

"You were unconscious, uncle. Someone might have put your axe in the berserk's chest after the event."

Kjartan laughed at this 'clever' notion; "Michael, our mood and circumstances were impossibly distant from those of light hearted pranks; whatever happened; it wasn't that. There was no time; I was down only briefly, and had Ulf not hurried to stand over me I most certainly would have died.'

"How does Ulf understand the event?"

"It was fated Miles should both survive, and kill his enemies. That many of us also survived was tied to this central outcome."

Michael chewed on this awhile, then; "How did Miles see events?"

"It sounds odd, but I never discussed it with him. Yet I know what he would have said; events fell a certain way and there are no gods with which to connect them. We like to make such connections, but this in no way assures us they are real."

The men sat in a thoughtful silence, then Kjartan gave a wry laugh; "I hold back my story for fifty years. When I finally share my tale it is under circumstances that give it an odd twist."

"How so?"

"Poppo, because of the firm conviction he stands in his god's hands, picked up fire, and was not harmed.'

"Miles, with no convictions, walks in fire, and is not burned. Ragnhild, a lifetime servant of Odin, has enough conviction for both herself and Miles, and she is burned.'

"Ragnhild's convictions brought her to ruin; that Odin is one complex dark bastard!"

"So, is that the end of the story; Eirik, Ragnhild, and their berserks dead on the tundra?!"

"Almost. A young norse lad, about twelve years of age, was alive at the end and I assumed him to be a hostage Eirik had taken during his retreat. Miles got to this boy first, looked him over carefully, then, without ceremony, cut his throat.'

"I was shocked; this was out of character for Miles Drake. When I demanded an explanation Miles suggested I wait. I had only moments to wait before the lad bled out and died, whereupon there was only a very dead Ragnhild lying before me. Miles had noticed the 'lad' was missing the right fourth and fifth fingers; recently missing them."

The men once again sipped their beer in a companionable silence.

"That was quite a tale, uncle, and, given the twist the dark seid put on your minds I understand your reluctance to share the tale. As mentioned earlier the tale is tainted at source. Evenso, I need to politely decline Poppo and his god."

"For me, Michael, the tale is incontrovertible and compelling. When Poppo picked up fire you were there in both person and an ordinary state of mind; for you this is compelling and not lightly put aside.'

"I too have a tale of great power which I witnessed in a very ordinary state of mind. Perhaps this is the story I should have told; many neutral parties were present and, unlike the story above tree line, this tale is well known in Westmark. Perhaps you have heard of the day Odin's grove was destroyed?"

"Indeed I have, uncle; were you there?!"

"You can't get closer – I stood between Asgerd Njalsdottir and Miles Drake. Perhaps you would like to hear the story?"

"Very much indeed, especially as the story is fading fast. I have only heard second or third hand accounts. First hand from a reliable man is bedrock."

Kjartan chuckled; "Michael, it will be sunshine and gentle breezes in hell before the Christian god can field a stronger and better show than Odin!"

CHAPTER 54
Halcyon Days

IT WAS LARRY AGAIN! Damn but that fox was exasperating!

Miles carefully released Larry, the beautiful silver fox he and Gunnar had freed several years ago. The lazy beast had taken to plundering his number three fox trap, the 'lucky' one, then napping till Miles arrived to release him. This foxy line of conduct had put Miles in mind of an ultra-minimal effort artiste he recalled from Castle High, Larry Whitfield.

To show just how irritating a lazy fox is Miles patted Larry's head and rubbed behind his ears before releasing the 'minimalist'.

Miles had two daughters, Gyda and Thora, and they and their children were visiting. Miles liked grandkids, and as he snowshoed to the next trap he planned out his evening stories. 'Brer fox' was a given; the grandkids loved it when he talked and acted like brer fox, and so did he! He planned on unveiling a modified Tom Sawyer and Huck Finn series.

The thing was approaching, so when Miles finished with stories for the kids he started on stories for grownups. The life of Hannibal was rich in the things vikings love, and, even better, Miles always found Hannibal an engaging and rich topic. They were going to love how Hannibal repeatedly eluded the romans when they hunted him after the war!

Before he quite knew how, Miles had completed his trap circuit and was home with several fine pelts.

THE WINTER DAY JUST reviewed is a very fair sample of Miles Drake's closing decade amongst the norse; apart from the very last year, this decade was truly Halcyon. His joints were in good shape, back okay, blood vessels wide open, wits and memory present and accounted for – the real gold in 'golden years'.

Evenso life is never quite a storybook. Kjartan's wife Vigdis died in childbirth. Such things are desperate and wearing. After thirty-two hours of hard labor with the infant stuck in breech position and not descending Vigdis was utterly exhausted and sliding towards the grave. Miles broke rank, gently put an exhausted Asgerd on the bench, and performed a crude caesarean section. The baby, a beautiful little girl, lived and did well, the mother did not.

The other shadow was also quite large. Gunnar, in many ways so like his father, picked up from his mother a tendency to depression. In this last decade there were two episodes of depression that each lasted the better part of winter. Miles insisted Gunnar help him with farm chores and walk the trap circuit; this proved something of an anchor and life line. Asgerd and Gyda were patient and kind, Kjartan was exasperated, but Gunnar's children were the real magic that finally pulled him back into the strong river of life.

Miles stories and the art of telling them well consumed him, and in the course of the decade our own world was brought to vivid life. Miles the Bard was greatly prized and his stories gathered the largest crowds yet seen. Other Bards came to study and learn the new art, and soon Miles's stories spread to Westmark and Norland, where they were enthusiastically received. Miles success as a bard was a deep satisfaction to him.

Kjartan's career as godi was another satisfaction. In time Kjartan came to be not only the most highly regarded and influential of the godi, but Lawspeaker.

Kjartan's rapid and smooth rise in the norse community was greased by Gunnar's support. Those who would have made trouble quietly shelved their nastiness and ambition – it would only get them killed.

And so we come to Miles's seventy-eighth year, a year starting with slight shade gradually deepening into impenetrable shadow.

The first hint was during vorping, or the spring assembly. Miles had just finished telling stories when Asgerd urgently pulled him aside. Her manner was a curious mix of fear, excitement, and wonder.

"Duncen, the alfather was here tonight!"

Then she clouded over; "I wonder why? What does it mean?"

What it meant was the beginning of the end for Miles Drake. This first night Odin came to hear Miles's stories only Asgerd sensed his presence, but in subsequent entertainments his presence tangibly strengthened towards a sense of ghosts and large man-eating tigers in the area, towards pitch black skies fractured with jagged lightening, towards a background moan and roar of tornadoes approaching. Finally it was all the above, only much, much stronger. By autumn you could offer a poor man two cows and a pig to go hear Miles Drake tell stories, and, with tears of frustrated avarice in his eyes he would decline.

Miles's dearly loved and richly deserved career as a bard turned to ashes. Yet, while the whole world desperately tried to escape Odin's presence yet to Miles Drake it was vaguely familiar, and in an even vaguer sense was somehow friendly. Companionable? Perhaps, but such an uneasy companion!

Then it invaded his home. The first casualty was story hour with the grandkids, but finally, out of consideration for others Miles took to sleeping in the barn – which put the animals in a frenzy. Cows and pigs don't sleep well if they sense a lurking tiger.

As winter arrived Miles was living alone in a small building well away from the main house. Remarkably he was neither particularly lonely nor embittered, but he was unquestionably somber and thoughtful. As winter solstice approached Miles understood the path he must walk and gathered his family. His farewell was taken with Asgerd, Kjartan, Gunnar, Gyda, and Thora standing together fifty feet from where he stood.

"Never has a man been so blessed in his wife and children as I have been. I am leaving to seek Mimirs Well at the roots of Yggdrasil. If I am successful in this I will follow his counsel. I am not sure how this will end, so this is goodbye. My thoughts and love are always with you. Please subtract these last months from my record; remember me as I was."

Miles shouldered his pack and turned to go, but at the last moment Asgerd, with a cry, broke free and ran to embrace him – it was an act of unspeakable love and courage and there were tears in Miles's eyes as he hugged her.

Then he walked to the tree entrance.

CHAPTER 55
The Destruction of Odin's Grove

KJARTAN, AS IS THE way with old gentlemen, was called by nature both urgently and frequently. Michael, professing a similar inclination but in truth along to see that no one took a tumble, again noticed the same confused and agitated cockroach he had seen on the way out; the foolish thing hurried every which way and seemed fully aware it was living dangerously, but was unable to organize a coherent response. It is a very basic human inclination, even obligation, to step on cockroaches; Michael felt this more than most and itched to put a foot on the perplexed and troubled insect. As it happened the cockroach was eight to ten feet away; exactly the point at which bother overbalanced inclination.

The two men once again were sitting down in their quiet room when the relative peace was fractured by harsh, angry, norse words, a sudden jarring movement of benches, the sounds of a hard blow, and the louder sound of a large body hitting the wooden floor. It sounded like Bjorn, and Michael was halfway to his feet when a silence ensued; evenso he decided it best to look.

As he left his own room he noticed, in an absentminded way, the silly roach was still trying to get someone to step on it. Upon entering the main room of the pub what Michael found was a medium sized man only recently back on his feet and barely able to stand. The Tottering One was near the door Michael had entered, and just across the room was an angry Bjorn. Bjorn was angry, but in a mood to leave things alone if nothing further occurred.

Unfortunately it did; the Tottering One caught his balance well enough to turn his head sharply to the right and thrust out his left cheek. To Bjorn this said clear as the spoken word: 'Have I been hit? Did a fly fart?! Do you call that a blow?!'

Bjorn went white with anger at this very public insult and there was murder in his eye. Behind the man, in a flash of insight based on a memory from two years ago, Michael realized the unfortunate man was a christian who was practicing what christians called 'turning the other cheek.' No insult was intended.

Michael acted quickly; stepping from behind the christian so Bjorn could see him but the christian could not, Michael raised his left hand in a gesture of 'halt!', then pointed to his own head with his index finger and made a vague circling motion. Comprehension dawned on Bjorn's face, he grew calm, then turned his back on the 'cheek' and resumed pub life with his friend and colleague.

This small pub incident contained the seed of both a pseudomiracle and a real miracle. First the pseudomiracle; till his dying day the christian never tired of telling fellow believers of the tremendous power of the true christian witness – even the savage northmen were quelled and rebuked.

Humbler, but far more miraculous is that on the way back to his own room Michael went over to the anxious cockroach, stooped, scrapped the roach onto his left hand, walked the beast outside and way from harm, and released him. This had never happened before, and it never happened again; it was far indeed from the course of nature. The incident also killed all inclination to adopt Poppo and his God.

It was a quiet and philosophic Michel who resumed his seat opposite his foster father.

"So, father, you were about to tell me the story of how Odin's grove was destroyed. Damn, but <u>was</u> it destroyed! To this day it is grass and a few residual splinters."

Kjartan chuckled; "You should have been there, Michael; it was so very, very destroyed I'm surprised you can find splinters and grass.'

"When we came back from killing Eirik, Miles got it in his head to sail far west and find the elusive land that was occasionally talked about but never seen. He thought there probably was land, but he was far from sure. For various reasons, however, he figured if there really was land it was far, far away. This view of things would judge the venture as truly perilous, and perilous in a very nasty way; if you have sailed far enough west to find land, and it's not there, then there is no water or food for the return trip. We like to die with axes swinging; there is no glory, nor anything but misery, in dying of hunger or thirst.'

"Miles called for volunteers, but he was very clear about the risk and its nature. In the event he had more volunteers than places on his ship.'

"How was that?', inquired a puzzled Michael; 'did he promise some extravagant reward?"

"No, on the contrary; Miles felt immediate reward unlikely, and he said so. Men joined because they knew he was lucky – it drew them like bees to honey."

"But it didn't draw you, foster father, and you never tire of telling me of the man's luck. How is that?"

"Ah, Michael, that was a miserable tussle! Two strong and compelling reasons appear immediately. Firstly, I am my father's only son and in consequence my future is anchored both practically and by honor to our land on Westmark; furthermore Westmark is home and I love it!'

"Secondly, the ripe conditions for raiding Gar were too good to last; the wise man seizes opportunity when it offers. Opportunity cannot be stored in a warehouse – use it or lose it!'

"Beyond this, I didn't expect anything would be discovered but undeveloped land; no wealth to pillage, no opportunity for trade. In this estimate I proved right; but I missed the skraeling, who were a terrific problem that darkened our lives for years.'

"Evenso, despite everything, I would have gone."

"What settled the balance towards staying?"

Without hesitation; "Yngvar. I overheard my sister Asgerd plead with him not to go, that if he went he would surely die. I knew Asgerd well, and as she spoke so it would be.'

"I joined Asgerd's entreaties, joined with my whole heart and then some, but to no avail. I wanted no part in an expedition that would kill Yngvar and I backed out; I just could not be there when it happened, knowing it to be avoidable."

"Ever wish you had gone?"; Michel was curious.

"No, not even once. My life has been good and I have played a larger part in life by staying; being your friend and foster father not being the least of it. Eyvind may play the largest part of many of us, and this probably would never have happened had I gone with Miles. No regrets."

"But this is all background to the tale, which is how Odin's grove came to be destroyed.'

"Miles liked and respected Asgerd; he felt towards her as a younger sister. She was exactly the sort of person you did <u>not</u> take on such a voyage. Later, under different circumstances, when the route and destination were known, there would be time to take the Asgerds of our world on this long and difficult voyage. So it came as a surprise when Asgerd asked to come. Miles thanked her for the interest and assured her the boat was complete; perhaps some other time.'

Kjartan chuckled; "You have never met your aunt, Michael; intelligent, very loyal – and unbelievably stubborn. The third time she asked to go, Miles came down with a 'no' that had a bit of ice and winter wind in it. The natural response to ice and winter is to hand back a larger chunk of ice; Asgerd didn't, instead she grew very calm and moved her request to a new playing field. As I recall her words; 'Miles, you don't understand; it is fated and very important that I go. There is nothing to fear on my behalf; there <u>is</u> land, you <u>will</u> find it, and you <u>will</u> return, as will I. You know me well enough to realize I see and report as things are. You are favored, as a son, by the Alfather, and if you want a sign you will be given a sign, but do not request this sign lightly since it comes with a price."

"Her words left Miles thoughtful. It was good to hear from a reliable source there was land in the far west; he was still not sure, but his confidence increased. He still wanted to spare Asgerd hardship and risk. He was sure Asgerd had real powers, but her understanding of her own gifts as proceeding from Odin seemed at best a quarter truth. At length he spoke more or less as follows:

'Asgerd, if your sign fails to arrive will you quietly and with a good grace stay home?'

'I will.'

Another thoughtful pause; 'You mentioned a price; what is the price?'

'I don't know, and this worries me. Nothing is free with the Alfather; a price there will be, and very likely heavy.'

Miles considered the matter closely for a bit, then put it aside; "Asgerd, I will give an answer to your request at noon tomorrow. Your words are always heavy with significance and it is fair neither to you nor our expedition to leap lightly, so, tomorrow.'

"MEN WERE GATHERED FOR the expedition, and where men are gathered there is beer, mead, and talk; the evening was large and filled with good cheer. So first light found me distinctly less than my usual alert self. That first light found me at all was owing to Yngvar tripping over me on his way to make water; and he was fully dressed, wideawake, and armed! Whoa!, says I to myself, what is going on?"

Michael laughed; "What was going on, father-o-mine, was Miles, Asgerd, and Yngvar slipping away to see Odin's sign."

Kjartan nodded; "Just so, foster son; I see I haven't raised a fool. However, the particular morning in question found me slow off the mark and they were nearly gone before I put two and two together. I quickly huddled into my clothes and shoes and hurried outside. I was not wanted; actually, Asgerd didn't want me. She hadn't wanted Yngvar either, but he'd out-lawyered her and wangled a berth on the sign mission."

"How did he do that?"; Michael was curious: this aunt sounded formidable and he was wondering how a man might circumvent her; as the husband of Herdis he liked comparing notes with other experts.

Kjartan chuckled; "Even the nastiest weather brings something useful; Yngvar was scheduled to die thousands of miles away in as of yet unfound lands; Odin might want his price, but it couldn't be himself Yngvar. So Yngvar voted himself on the mission.'

"That left me, and I flat out let them know I'd be coming; nothing to discuss.'

"Evenso Asgerd extracted a promise; I would stay between her and Miles. I intended to be there, so I agreed.'

"Asgerd felt certain we should walk, and it was a good hour's walk from our hall.'

Michael was yet again curious; "Why? I would imagine horses would be quicker and easier."

"Asgerd said the horses would die, and, in the event, she was clearly correct in this.'

"We were a hundred yards on our journey when Rory came running up."

Kjartan could see Michael was puzzled, so he paused; "As a lad of ten Rory had been captured by Dad during a raid on the island of Tel. Dad liked him and had brought him home rather than selling at the slave market. Rory was about my age and we were soon friends. Rory was apt at the skills of war and had been with us on early raids and during the war against Eirik. He had long since been freed. Rory was a close and trusted friend; not one of us wanted him put at pointless risk. We remonstrated with him, warned him away, and generally firmed up his resolve to come. At length, since we were getting nowhere and others would soon be up and wanting to come, we left with Rory.'

Kjartan paused for a thoughtful moment; "Earlier I said the walk to Odin's grove was about an hour; this estimate was probably optimistic. It was early morning when we arrived on that little hill overlooking the grove; dawn was all finished and our walk was probably closer to two hours."

Michael chuckled; "I kept quiet when you shared 'the hour walk' notion. As I remember, it is every bit of two hours from the low farm to Odin's grove. I remember only the ruins of the grove; was the grove attractive? Memorable?"

"Yes, very. There were several very large fir trees, a number of pines of good but hardly startling size, and, believe it or not, given how far north it is, there were several oaks; the oaks were good sized but not so grand as those farther south. The trees were strong and lovely – and but for Asgerd would long since have been converted to barns, halls, and long ships. Sad to say, it doesn't take too many blots before a grove is given a certain darkness; as a lad of ten I still remember the stench of a rotting ram hung from the oak. For me, the grove never again 'skipped in the sunshine.'

"But that particular morning, as we stood on the overlooking fell the grove was bright and charming. As we came off the fell and approached the grove things started changing, and Michael, these changes were vast and dark; from horizon to horizon the sky began going black, dark as night, and there were long streaks of jagged lightening and a very low rumble of thunder that shook the earth. It was most impressive and frightening.'

"Asgerd turned to us and, I remember her words yet; 'If any of us gets more than five feet from Miles that person dies; Miles is our place of refuge and safety. Please, please, please stay close together; our lives depend on it.'

"She spoke with terrific concern and urgency, for she knew the peril to be very real, and she loved all of us. I was, without ceremony, shoved between herself and Miles and she put a strong arm around my waist; I was going nowhere. Nor, at that moment, did I have any impulse to stray.'

"Over the next five minutes the surrounding blackness increased, the lightening diminished, then stopped, and the thunder increased and gradually became continuous, with the earth developing a low shudder that never stopped. Then the blackness began organizing into black, thick encircling cords or bands; it was as though we were surrounded by a nest of midgard serpents, each biting his own tail and closing the circle. A high whining or keening noise developed and individual 'serpents' could be separated from each other by flickering light that was intermittently golden and blue.'

Kjartan paused, and was puzzled over how to speak of what came next; "Michael, those black bands, or midgard serpents, conveyed two strong impressions: first, somehow they seemed to be moving at a terrific speed, so fast you hardly sensed there was motion; they seemed to pulse with it. Secondly, they were utterly destructive – if they touched a tree all that remained was the finest sawdust with a hint of green color.'

"Now for the amazing part; there was a cone of sunshine and fairest blue sky that centered on our group; we were surrounded with high outward sloping walls of black destruction with a roof of a misty blue sky, and there was even an unusually large and vivid overarching rainbow, as though bifrost touched midgard where we stood.'

"When all the changes were fully developed Asgerd shouted across me to Miles; 'Walk! Anywhere you please! This beauty and destruction will follow you like a hound.'

"So Miles walked slowly towards where the other end of the grove used to be; the cone of light and beauty stay focused on him and moved with him.'

"Where the black serpents passed nothing remained; Odin's grove was no more."

Kjartan grew quiet, and both sad and thoughtful. Michael knew in his bones they were arrived at the price of the sign. At length Kjartan spoke once more.

"Michael, you never knew Rory, but all you need know of Rory is that he was dearly loved and treasured by all of us; from early days of boyhood Rory had been with us every step of the way. Rory fought back to back with me above the tree line when we killed Eirik, he stood with me in eastern Norland during the war, he raided with me; he was always there, always reliable, always cheerful and good fun. I never realized how much he meant till he was gone. Rory was Odin's price for the sign; and may it bring him little joy, the bastard!"

Over fifty years later the resentment and anger were still in place, alive, playing a part.

Michael was touched and curious; "What happened?"

"For Miles, Yngvar, Asgerd, and myself the dark walls and serpents were incredible, but they were the contrast, the background that enhanced the cone of light and the rainbow. With Rory the fascination went the other way; the blue sky and rainbow were the contrast and background that made the serpents yet more deadly and fascinating. I warned him away several times, but in a moment of inattention he tried to touch a serpent; he must have figured he was risking and bit of skin, or perhaps, at the unimaginable worst, a finger. However, in the event the lightest touch of the finger proved more like getting your whole hand caught in a river of resin moving much, much faster than a galloping horse; one moment Rory and his curiosity were with us, the next they were gone."

"How did it end?", asked Michael.

"After ten minutes of strolling the destroyed grove Asgerd asked Miles if the sign was sufficient, was it acceptable; he nodded his head that it was. From that moment the serpents began expanding, became greyer, and moved towards the horizon; over the next minute the whole vortex dissipated and soon it was just an ordinary morning. Rory and Odin's grove were spread out over the encircling ten miles of Westmark countryside.'

When Kjartan finished the men sat in a friendly silence for awhile; then, "Kjartan, that story does rather surpass

Poppo's hot iron bar; I will need to extricate myself as gracefully as possible from my predicament with the man. When I do, rest assured it won't happen again.'

"A thought occurs to me, foster father; I know you have a respect verging on awe for Miles Drake, but was requesting the sign one of his smarter moves? Asgerd specifically warned him there would be a price, that with Odin nothing comes free. He already knew Asgerd to be reliable; she wasn't merely being creative to indulge a girlish whim. As it was you lost a beautiful grove and a rock solid friend. Where's the wisdom?"

"Believe me, Michael, I raised the question in anger as we walked back to the low farm. Here is Miles's side of things; he felt it likely that nothing would happen, in which event Asgerd would not come and not face the considerable risk and hardship of the voyage. Should a sign arrive he wanted only himself, Asgerd, and a single horse present. He knew blood figured in the ceremonies of Odin and the horse should cover the costs. The sign would set Asgerd apart and spare her unwanted male ardor on the voyage, make her something of priestess of Odin and not to be touched. In the event he and Asgerd fell deeply in love during the voyage and 'the little sister' was touched a lot.'

"Nobody was invited. Yngvar overheard them unseen and had an airtight argument to be included. Yngvar tripped on me, and I came; Rory carried a full bladder out-of-doors and I personally think Odin timed the moment. Asgerd loved the horses and wouldn't hear of them coming to the party.'

"Miles would seem clear of overt folly, but he himself felt deeply responsible and deeply the fool. Around men, and we norse in particular, nothing ever goes as planned, and Miles knew this better than most. The deeper wisdom is not to accept risk if it can be avoided, and then only for substantial gain. You are right, Michael; Miles was foolish, and his own harshest judge."

CHAPTER 56
The Tree and
Norse Farewells

MILES WALKED TOWARDS THE tree entrance with nothing but a few bare necessities on his back. His heart was heavy; he would never return to hearth, home, and loved ones unless he could do so freed from the dark presence that never left him. If by chance he could no longer enter the tree he planned to die by his own hand. However, his luck was still with him, and though the tree entrance had receded to within ten feet of a cliff yet he entered without event.

It had been years since he last set foot on the tree, and the balm and peace had become a distant item of knowledge; now it descended quickly and strongly. One moment his thoughts were dark and accompanied by a profound sense of loss and sorrow, then, quickly, his burdens were passing items of casual reflection, of no more moment than an oddly shaped piece of wood floating by on a pleasant stream. In an absentminded way Miles wondered why he had not sought the tree sooner; there was nothing like it.

On the tree it was high autumn just past zenith; the colors of the maples and birches were wonderful but many leaves were down. The oaks sported quite a bit of brown. As

Miles walked by the branch trail to Westmark he idly toyed with taking it and having a last visit with Kjartan and other friends, but in his bones he knew the presence would join him and he'd probably not be able to reenter the tree. He kept on; his destination was the well of Mimir amongst the roots of Yggdrasil.

After walking quite a while he came to where his limb joined the main trunk. Again there was the descent that felt so very much steeper than it looked; at the bottom he turned left and started toward the distant cliff above the well. Miles had worried a little over that cliff, but not much – he would, as usual, be sufficient to any and all occasions. But none of his residual toughness and resolution would be needed; he was no longer seventy-eight, he was thirty and in perfect health and condition.

Miles walked on and on through impossibly beautiful country and amongst wonderful ruins, but he never arrived at the cliff, rather he arrived at the limb to our world, complete with the marking stones he had placed forty-two years earlier.

Miles, after the briefest hesitation, took the trail to his home world. This may seem ordinary and expected, but it is not; it needs examination. The world he left forty-two years past was hardly there for Miles. Erin's face had long since gone misty and he would no longer remember how she looked. His past life and his corporation were also long since blurred and gone. He seldom recalled Matt or his parents. His sincerest wish, despite the seventy-eight years entailed, was to be free of the presence and once again in Newland with Asgerd and his family. Had he travelled on to Mimir he would have gained insight and knowledge, which might, or might not, have revealed a path back to home and loved ones. Perhaps just being on the tree scrubbed away the presence, perhaps there was a shrine or grove on the tree where, with appropriate ceremony and sacrifice, the presence would be lifted. Perhaps not.

So why, with only minimal hesitation, did Miles strike out for a world no longer his own? Our world was an alien world, a world free of the Alfather; a world where the presence would be gone, where it made no sense. This was all below the level of conscious thought, but it infallibly guided Miles. Miles turned to our world the way an oxygen starved seal turns to a hole in the ice; only it was not a search for oxygen, it was a search for less presence.

As Miles approached the tree entrance to our world he finally began reflecting; if he left the tree there might be no opportunity to return. Perhaps he should return to the original plan, visit Mimir, and see if there were other choices. If there were none he could return to where he now stood. But could he? His world had departed once, might it not do so again?

Another curiosity; not then nor later did Miles wonder at the return of our world. To enjoy reality, or connection with the tree, a world must be in the active mind of the Alfather. Our world had gradually slipped from the Alfather's mind and disappeared. After the Alfather hears stories of our world from one loved and favored by him then it reemerges. Did Miles bring our world back to the Alfather's awareness? Miles never asked or worried over this question.

Miles pondered his predicament carefully and decided to retrace his steps and talk with Mimir. He turned to do so and discovered the tree entrance, like a receding tide, had withdrawn and he was standing on the eastern margin of a mountain trail leading to the Joyce Kilmer Tree Sanctuary. The shoulder containing the entrance and tree path was gone; in its place was a lovely mountain view overlooking a pleasant valley. The view he had sought forty-two years earlier had been present all long; it had been hidden by tree magic.

Miles slowly mused his way down the trail to his car. On the way he passed several hikers and discovered he no longer carried the weight of Odin's presence. Good. He had long since lost or thrown away his keys, wallet, and cell phone. Fortunately he had hidden a car key in the left rear wheel well, and there was sixty dollars in cash in an envelope in the glove box. He had maps, and plotted a course for Evansville, Indiana. It was early Sunday afternoon on summer solstice; forty-two years may have passed, but on the home world there was no elapsed time and he was a vigorous thirty-six. At the time this counted little with him.

Miles got in the car and started home. He drove a mile, stopped, turned around and went back. He parked his car where it had been and walked to the foot of the great monarch where he had buried the curious seed so many years ago. He knelt and scooped way the recently disturbed earth; the seed was still there and unchanged. Miles put it in his pocket and returned to the car.

It was a three hundred eighty mile trip to Evansville and the first three hours of the journey Miles's thoughts were mostly on Newland and his family. Old age is frequently patient and valedictory, while youth looks and moves forward; during the second half of the journey the thirty-six year old Miles began considering things in the home world. He had forgotten his home address, but corporate headquarters was near 41 S about eight miles south of where HWY 64 intersects 41.

Security let him in and he got his address; by early evening he was pulling into his driveway. A vaguely familiar, beautiful young woman carrying a one year old baby girl came out to greet him. The good-natured one year old baby girl called him 'da da.' The beautiful young woman was Erin, and she clearly viewed him as 'husband.' There was no thought or mention of cancer, never mind metastatic cancer. The wonder of the weekend had been the first tottering steps of the infant, whom the mother called Caitlyn.

Miles was not ready for the embrace of strangers; pleading a cold, he slept in the guest room. Erin was surprised, but accepted things gracefully.

Early Monday morning an exuberant Matt bounced in; "We got the contract! Northwest Solar is on-board!!"

Miles stared at his friend for a long moment – and nearly forgot himself so far as to embrace Matt; he caught himself in time and settled for 'That's wonderful news!'

A month later Miles and Erin had Doctor and Mrs. Petersen over for dinner. In the course of a pleasant evening Miles told Doctor Petersen of a curious story where a Norwegian family held a curious artifact in trust for generations. Dr. Petersen had never heard of such an odd business.

It took awhile, but six months later Miles was fully 'back' and happy. Yet in many ways the norse and medieval mark was on him for life.

Miles's parents were both academics in a secular university, and liberal precepts had been taken in with his mother's milk. Abstract human rights and entitlements had come to seem artificial, contrived, and a bit silly – these things were off their pedestal, never to rise again.

Miles may have lost several treasured verities, but he appreciated his own world as never before. Hot showers, ibuprofen, books, television, and our roads never quite lost their shine. Credit cards seemed wonderful, electric lights a thing apart. Above all, the rule of law and the associated freedom it brought in its wake. In the norse world being ambushed by disgruntled neighbors was an ever present reality; in his own world he travelled with nothing on his mind but his hair.

Storms, especially at sea, are never quite the same after you have survived a number of rough ones in an open eighty foot boat.

Decks and screened in porches enjoyed a luster they never lost.

Summer solstice now and forevermore had overtones of the Althing (tenth week of summer), and Miles always wondered what his son Kjartan was up to.

It is curious, but Miles never wondered or speculated on the changes he found in his restored world; the world he left had Matt recently dead and Erin dying, while in the restored world both friend and wife enjoyed perfect health, and a beautiful daughter was on the scene. He accepted these things as he accepted and enjoyed a beautiful day – both were gifts to enjoy rather than puzzles to understand.

CHAPTER 57
Poppo's Day in Court

MICHAEL STUDIED THE GATHERING crowd with a sinking heart; it was already far beyond his worst fears. The audience room and antechamber were tightly packed and the crowd now filled the courtyard. Whatever was said would need to be relayed to the periphery, and would be.

The noteworthies of Moslem Mendero and its hinterland packed the front rows. Great.

Poppo, punctually on time, arrived in fresh monk garb and looking better than last time Michael had seen him. He appeared relaxed, dignified, and, well, very spiritual; the man radiated calm, strength, and authority. Michael realized he must vigilantly maintain the upperhand, keep Poppo firmly in his place.

'Well', thought Michael, 'let's get this over.' He nodded to the court officer, who immediately came to stiff attention and brought his oak staff of office down hard three times on the stone floor. These ringing blows brought a hushed silence over the audience chamber, which rapidly communicated itself to the antechamber and courtyard.

Then, in clear ringing tones; "Lord Michael, the eminent christian teacher and man of learning, Poppo of Salanti."

Poppo stepped forward; "On invitation, your lordship, I am come to hear whether or not you will join the christian community in worshipping the One True God."

Michael was seated at the head of the audience chamber; he sat straight and leaned forward slightly and spoke slowly and clearly.

"Thank you for the kind offer, Poppo, but I will not become a christian, not now, not ever. However Poppo, we norse admire a man of spirit and courage, and you have shown a large measure of both."

Michael now rose to his feet and walked to where Poppo stood; "I may not join you in worship, but I salute you and will join you in friendship."

Michael offered his hand, which Poppo shook.

"As a token of my regard I leave this small purse with you," and Michael offered a small leather wallet containing several gold pieces.

Instead of taking the purse Poppo shook his head slowly.

"The gift is both generous and kind, but as God's emissary I cannot accept; there is no price on his love or his invitation."

Michael had expected as much and was ready.

"I understand, Poppo. I will give the purse to Dorothy, who will distribute it amongst the poorest christians."

Michael had Dorothy nearby for this very purpose and was turning to give her the purse when a woman's voice rang out clearly, and with just a hint of desperation.

"If it please your lordship, start with me. I have born Poppo two children, a boy and a girl, and we have only rags and hungry bellies; Poppo is far more interested in God's work than in feeding and clothing his family."

Destiny laden immensities are frequently neither valued nor appreciated on the domestic front, and Poppo was yet another instance, but with the added embarrassment that he wasn't supposed to have a domestic front. Monkly vows of celibacy were public knowledge. Poppo stood there, perhaps just a bit pinker than when he walked in, and said nothing.

Michael opened the purse and handed Poppina two gold pieces. Then he had a shot of red hot inspiration.

"A friend stands by a friend, and I will stand by Poppo; are there any other debts he owes!?"

An old man worked his way forward through the crowd.

"May it please your lordship, Poppo owes me for the shoes he is wearing."

Poppo's pink tinge was now replaced with indignation; "Steven, these shoes are freely given tithe for the lord's work!"

The old shoemaker did not flinch; "So you say, Poppo, but I never understood it that way."

Michael paid the man, and then two others. After this was finished he turned to the crowd.

"I rule all of Mendero, not just the norse and christians. If there is a moslem holy man who finds himself cornered I will provide more hot iron bars. If the holy one be successful I will help him with his creditors. The offer is genuine, but think carefully before taking it up; I have found playing with fire tends to get you burned."

This was greeted with laughter and things were soon once again normal, only now everyone treasured normal.

CHAPTER 58
Matt McDougal's Memoirs
– Five Years Later

IT'S BEEN AWHILE; I'm five years older and God knows I don't feel any wiser. I have read my memoir up to the last entry. The last paragraph, about Erin dying with metastatic breast cancer; where did that come from?! That paragraph is truly, profoundly, baffling, but I will save it for later; first the easier stuff.

If what I have been through these past five years is the easy stuff one begins to see just how confusing my last paragraph has been!

The tone of my memoir was cautious optimism. The biggest problem shadowing the future was my proclivity to drop my trousers away from home; the problem was faced and day by day improving – nothing dramatic, just modest progress.

Two months after laying down my pen Ann runs off with her tennis coach! The good book urges us to get the beam out of your own eye before working on the mote in the brother's eye. I had a beam in my eye, I owned the fact and was struggling to remove it; I didn't see so much as a mote in Ann's eye.

So there I was, beavering away, and the 'brother' reaches into her eye, fetches out several beams, and hits me over the back of the head!

That was certainly the initial reaction; unbelieving, shocked, surprise. This was followed by a 'kicked in the stomach' feeling.

As I sit here pen in hand I am one year back with Ann. We have a working relationship that seems to be creeping towards I'm not quite sure what, but whatever it is I feel more like a husband. Warm fuzzy feelings? Trust? Not yet, but who knows? That we are back together (and back together for a whole year!) feels, what? Storybook? Unreal? Impossible? Something of all three, and the magician would be Erin Drake. I'm not sure how she did it, but understanding, tact, commitment to her friends figure prominently.

The fall of Ann was surprising in many ways. I had not realized how central to everything she had been. To give one example among many; after the separation I would have supposed my sex life would get back to something like college and football days. I know you can never really 'go back', but perhaps something like. In the event I couldn't have been more mistaken. For many months I wanted nothing to do with other women, and when eventually I crept back to the girls the excitement didn't amount to much. Why?

I thought about it quite a bit, and came up with two reasons. The first reason is well-known; there's something naughty and extra sweet about forbidden fruit. Of course there needs must be a wife to create this sugar. But beyond this a wife lifts the commitment spectre from other women – around other women there is no question of commitment and all this implies; the wife has it all locked up safe and sound. So, it's all light hearted fun and frolic, and naughty lighthearted fun and frolic at that! The wife folds up her tent and departs, and soon, far too soon, you are eating lentils and potatoes, as needed, for nourishment.

If these observations are true, there is a practical corollary that goes far towards repairing the damage; confine your attention to married women. Once again things are forbidden and juicy, once again the spectre of commitment is banished and things remain delightfully light. The trick is to be sensitive to developing fractures in the playmate's marriage; as early cracks appear one must decamp – immediately, if not sooner! Under these circumstances commitment and responsibility can arrive like an avalanche, and with pretty much the same result.

Ann's departure left huge voids and a thousand little gaps that would never have even occurred to me until we parted. The voids and gaps are probably the gas that drove this man's car back home.

I noticed in my earlier journal I was looking forward to throwing the football with my son Craig. Time has gently rocked this little dream to sleep; now I only hope and pray he grows up to like girls. The son and heir marches to a different drummer. But this has been little by little; no thunderclaps, no tennis coach equivalents.

Alice <u>does </u>like throwing footballs – it's not a bad consolation!

So, the domestic front has been something of a bucking bronco. Work, on the other hand, has been great – there is no other word. About five years ago, out of the blue, Miles gave me, free and clear, no conditions, fifteen percent of the corporation. My income and financial posture are now beyond anything I ever imagined. This is good, hell, it's beyond good! However, better yet the work itself is engrossing and fun. I'm a natural at sales and meeting people, and the 'daily grind' is so congenial I damn near skip to work!

Over the past five years Miles, always the best of friends and bosses, seems different. In years past we never socialized, whereas now seldom a week goes by without one or the other of us dropping by the house for a beer. My house is Miles home-away-from-home, and vice versa.

The Miles of recent years is sufficiently different from the earlier Miles that I have considered it something of a puzzle. Oddly, it seems to me I can pinpoint the change; it was five years ago and centers on a weekend he spent visiting the Joyce Kilmer forest. This must have been the secular equivalent of those spiritual retreats one is always reading about.

I went so far as to share this speculation with Miles. The trees, Miles told me, were very grand and created a cathedral-like mood and ambience; perhaps some of this rubbed off. Of course anything the least bit odd occurring around ages forty to fifty can be filed away as 'midlife crisis.' This is a transparent dodge; nothing is explained, but somehow appearances are preserved and the original puzzle mysteriously disappears.

I have toyed with a pilgrimage to the Joyce Kilmer forest. My life would certainly benefit from a bit of cathedral-like peace and dignity. But, when everything is said and done, it is just too fucking dull! Period.

Well, perhaps when I'm eighty; when there is nothing left but peace and quiet, then I'll officially get busy looking for them!

And so we arrive at that perplexing paragraph; Erin is reported as dying of breast cancer. It's my handwriting, and the ink matches the preceding paragraph. The paragraph leads nowhere, it dangles. I don't seem to be starting a novel, or dramatic story of some sort.

I have seriously entertained 'multiple personalities,' and just being crazy. However, being crazy, or one amongst many personalities, always have much company, and if you delete that paragraph what is left is normal. Also cuckooism and 'one amongst many' usually surface much earlier in life, and often the ancestors sport similar problems.

Last week I shared this burden with Miles. After showing the journal he looked very thoughtful and I briefly hoped he might enlighten me; of course he couldn't, but hope springs eternal and he <u>did</u> have a funny look on his face.

Miles said what I had already figured out; I'm not crazy and there is but a single Matt MacDougal. He advised forgetting the paragraph, cross it out.

Sometimes Miles can be quite funny and he went on to play up to my Joyce Kilmer idea. He said that while strolling amongst the ancient trees he learned the world was wider and stranger than our narrow interpretation allows. He smiled and told me that should I have a complete answer to my paragraph it would probably be of no use to me and could not be shared with others. 'Put it behind you and move on' was the way to handle the stray bit of oddness.

CHAPTER 59
After the Tennis Game

ERIN WAS FAST, AND arrived at the left boundary line with time to choose her shot. The ball was bouncing a little higher than expected so she moved back and a little further left, then delivered a solid backhand swing with a bit of topspin. Her return was fast and the ball had barely cleared the net when the topspin kicked in and brought the ball down on her opponents far forward left boundary line; tennis doesn't get better, only today, at least for her, good tennis was surfacing only now and then.

This match was a big one, college tennis Indiana state championship, and it was not going well. Her opponent, Amanda Michelson, was from Indiana University in Indianapolis and was the heavy favorite going into the match and a heavier favorite after the first set. The word was Amanda planned on going pro, and at the moment this was only too believable.

It was a thoughtful Erin Campbell-Drake that walked back to the baseline to serve. She knew exactly where this match was heading and her only chance, a thin one at that, was to change the game, roll the dice. If she 'stood tall', went toe to toe and played real tennis, she was forty minutes from driving back to Purdue in disgrace. Yes, it was time to lob, slice, and dice, to slow things down to a careful waiting game – and hope Amanda started making mistakes. If, and it was a big 'if', this should happen then opportunities might appear. If opportunity should knock, well, she was the granddaughter of Miles Drake. It was a proud thought, and it calmed and comforted her.

Erin was about to toss the ball for serve when she abruptly stopped and turned to look more closely. The bleachers were small and largely empty, afterall we are at a tennis match, not a football game, but in a lower central bleacher sat a well dressed elderly woman with a surprising and wonderfully erect posture; it was granny! Damn; Evansville was one hundred eighty miles south and west of Indy and grandma wasn't much of a traveler these days. This was a real honor.

In her day granny Erin had been a fine tennis player, a tennis player who never, never, ever had any use for slicing and paddycaking around. So much for spinning the dice and awaiting opportunity; noblesse oblige and all that.

Forty minutes later, after a game effort on Erin's part, Amanda Michelson was crowned the queen of Indiana college tennis.

After wiping the sweat from her brow Erin hurried over to give granny a hug and a hand. The two Erins drove in Erin's Toyota Corolla to a favorite restaurant. Eldon, who had driven granny up from Evansville in a company car, was instructed to meet them in two and a half to three hours.

The two buddies were soon comfortably settled, and after talking of this and that, grandma Erin brought the conversation to the reason she had driven all the way to Indy to see her granddaughter.

"Erin, do you remember this past summer when you came over to ask me about grandpa?"

"Was that when I told you about his visit to Reykjavic while I was an exchange student in Iceland?"

"Yes, we are discussing the same occasion. After you left I got to thinking; in fact, off and on I've given your question much careful thought for many months. I can't answer your question, but I want to share another equally puzzling item from early days of our marriage, around the time your mother was born."

Granddaughter Erin was surprised and pleased; "It is interesting you should bring the subject up. My professor of Old Norse, Unar Bjornson, sent me an email a few weeks ago. He has never forgotten his conversation with Grandpa. Remember? They chatted away in old norse and Granddad's Old Norse, in addition to being as fluent as a natively spoken language, was impossibly old Old Norse; every other word seemed to confirm or destroy some advanced view. Unar thought him an impossible come-to-life fossil.'

"Unar recorded much of the conversation and recently, about four months ago, several old documents have been discovered that confirm Granddad's 'interpretation' of Old Norse. Professor Bjornson is distraught at grandpa's death; on his view grandpa is flat out impossible, and now he's gone!"

Grandma looked pleased; "Erin, you are icing the cake; both of us agree there is a mystery to understand. I am unable to solve it, but I can make it deeper."

Erin loved talking about her grandpa; with a twinkle in her eye and a mischievous grin she interrupted; "Grandma, did I ever tell you about grandpa's duel with Robert Stanton?"

Granny sighed; her story could wait a few more minutes, but it <u>did</u> need to be told. Someone besides herself should be aware of it; she was getting on in years.

"No, Erin, I don't believe I have; is it a good tale?"

"Much better than good, granny.'

"I was sixteen and had been to my first renaissance festival; I was utterly charmed. In a corner of the fair Robert Stanton was demonstrating the quarter staff to the curious and arranging lessons for the interested. He was very good and made the quarter staff fascinating and nigh unto magical. I signed up for lessons. 'Genuine oak or hickory' quarter staves were fifty dollars, and an half-hour lesson was twenty dollars; when a number of us bought quarter staves and signed up for lessons Robert Stanton Esq. leaped forward in life.'

"Later, from the 'lessons', I learned my teacher was so-so as an instructor, and very much worshipped at his own altar.'

"One afternoon grandpa rode over and discovered me practicing. I remember what he said; 'No, no, Erin; you have it all wrong.' He then gave me the A, B, C's of quarter staves. I bought Granddad a staff and practiced with him. I dropped Stanton.'

"As I trained with grandpa I soon realized he knew exactly whereof he spoke, and that he was superb; far beyond the reach of myself or such as Stanton. A wicked idea occurred to me where I could make a few bucks and introduce Mr. Stanton to a more modest assessment of his own abilities.'

"I approached Mr. Stanton to arrange a quarter staff match where each of us put up a hundred dollars as a prize; this money held by a neutral third party.'

"On the day of the match I 'sprained' my shoulder and took grandpa along as my champion. In the event seventy-eight year old grandpa was an acceptable champion. Grandpa thought the injury real and didn't want me to forfeit my hundred dollars, so he agreed; but was hardly enthusiastic.'

"Away they went, with grandpa starting slowly. Soon a gleam appeared in his eye and he seemed twenty years younger. The quarter staff was coming at Stanton Esq. so many ways the man got dizzy. Robert Stanton was clearly overmatched and before long grandpa asked him to concede; the surly oaf replies 'Just keep waving your stick, gramps, and we'll see where this ends.'

Erin burst out laughing; "It ended two minutes later with fractures of both feet, several ribs, and a broken humerus; with truly christian restraint grandpa refrained from cracking his head. This all followed from a trick grandpa had never shown me; bending at the knees and using the staff as a spear to fracture bones in the foot. This makes the opponent slow way down and spend most of his time on his good foot. The good foot is carrying most of the weight most of the time and is a delightfully easy target for another foot fracture. In Robert Stanton's case grandpa fractured both feet with a quick one-two motion."

Granny was impressed; "Nice trick, Erin; were the rib and arm fractures strictly necessary?"

"Probably not, but grandpa was now viewing Robert as a 'rude bastard' and it seemed a good idea at the time.'

"As we walked to the car I inquired why grandpa had asked Robert to concede. He explained it was entirely a matter age. As a young man Robert would in ten minutes be in a much better relative condition. Older men must win soon, or not at all. So grandpa, much the better man, needed to win while he could. He had no trust whatsoever that Robert would spare him bruises should the chance arrive later in the duel.'

"That grandpa at seventy-eight should be such a master with the quarter staff struck me as not only unexpected but downright odd. I asked if he had been to a renaissance fair while in high school. He laughed and said he passed his second decade in the company of footballs and hadn't realized there was such a thing as a quarter staff.'

"So where had he picked up the art? Who taught him? Know what he said, granny?"

Granny smiled; "He always referred back to those norse stories he told you kids; especially you Erin, since you two were such buds and you enjoyed his stories so much."

"Exactly, grandma; he told me he had been trained by Yngvar. We both had a good laugh."

Grandma's eyes glistened and Erin almost thought she could see a tear; grandma had a faraway look.

"Erin, your story brings the man back to me; he was <u>so</u> fine, so magnificent. I wish you could have seen him pull a lost football game back from the precipice, and the standing roar and wild joy of twenty thousand people; <u>that</u> was exciting; that was a fairy tale. He was a wonderful man, an impossible dream come true, and I'm so, so lucky to have been his wife."

Grandma paused, and dabbed at her eyes. Erin decided to make a rescue.

"There are few things finer than four consecutive Rose Bowls, but I, lucky girl, have seen such a thing."

Grandma smiled through her tears; "Now, now, dear, you know there is nothing finer than four consecutive Rose Bowls."

Erin was firm; "There is; every ninety-one year old woman I have ever seen resembles a pretzel more than a real live woman. Recently, no kidding, I saw one with a back straight as an arrow; straight as an arrow!"

Grandma smiled; "Well, god knows I'm trying...'

"And succeeding', finished Erin. "If they ever have a granny competition at the state fair you'll clean up, carry off every blue ribbon on the table. A back as straight as yours is against nature; it's unheard of!"

Grandma couldn't hold it back anymore and burst out laughing, and Erin joined her. It was a very pink and ladylike laugh.

When they quieted down Grandma, looking very stern, said; "Young lady, I am here on business and you keep sidetracking me; I have important things to pass on."

"That's right, granny; I forgot and have interrupted shamelessly. The floor is yours."

"Erin, these memories were hard to recover and are not entirely certain; I may be reading and interpreting more into them than I experienced at the time. Things were puzzling, but the six month period involved really was more of a difficulty to cross, to survive, than a mystery to understand. Since then fifty-five years have gone by, and there have been many other difficult spots to work through. It was not easy, and perhaps I am attending to the wrong events; perhaps, but I think not."

"What happened?"; Erin was getting curious.

"Your mother was just starting to walk; I would have been thirty-four or thirty-five.'

"Miles had been away for the weekend, I forget specifically where he went or what he was doing. When he got home Sunday evening he treated me as though I were a stranger. He was, of course, courteous, but though he knew I was his wife that was about as far as his recognition went.'

"Over the next several months he came to know me again; it was a second courtship. Six months later we were once again deeply in love and had a strong bond – but the old Miles never returned; it was a good Miles, but a subtly different Miles Drake."

"Any specifics?"

"Well, he seldom, if ever referred to his football career, and his interest in the game was not even perfunctory; it was as though that had been another life, or happened to a different man.'

"He frequently would forget to shave or shower, and would be surprised when I'd remind him. Of course over the next several months he returned to his old habits. For quite awhile he would be surprised when I'd call him for lunch; he seemed to think two meals a day was the norm.

"How did he look when he showed up that Sunday evening?"

Granny's eyes grew wide; "Oh, I'd forgotten! His hair was unkempt and long and his clothes were old and very strange; I've seen something like them on movies of medieval or ancient times.

Erin was pale and excited; "Did he have any weapons?"

"No; yes! There was an odd looking knife in his belt. I never saw the knife or the clothes again; he must have gotten rid of them. The boots in particular were very different."

"What did he say? I mean the hair and the clothes would need explaining."

"Erin, he wasn't very interested in explaining himself. I did ask, and he dismissed it with saying he'd stopped at a store in Knoxville and bought primitive clothes, to be in character with his getting back to the land."

"Where had he passed the weekend?"

"Some forest, probably the Smokies; I don't remember."

"Did he talk any Old Norse?", Erin could barely contain herself.

"No', then Erin senior hesitated, and was momentarily confused; 'Erin, your questions are bringing things back. In the first few weeks he slept lightly and poorly. He would mutter in his sleep, and he wasn't speaking English, at least it didn't seem so, though with muttering it might be hard to be certain."

"Can you remember any words, any at all?"

Granny Erin thought for some time, then "Maybe Asgerd?"

Erin went white as a sheet; "Grandma, do you not remember Asgerd?"

"No, Erin; why would I?"

"Asgerd is a central woman in his norse stories; we grandkids loved her and know her well. She was wife to another central character, Ref Steinsson. They were very much in love and wonderfully mated, wonderfully matched."

Erin paused; "It is completely crazy, but is almost as though grandpa had a norse life that weekend. We are on a roll; let's figure out where granddad went. You pretty sure it was the Smokies?"

"No, not really; only a guess."

"Oh, boy', muttered Erin; 'this could be hard."

Nothing suggested itself to either woman and they sat in a companionable silence.

At length Erin, musing aloud; "Though he is ten years gone I still miss Uncle Matt. He was granddad's best friend and he'd be able to help us; if he were here he'd straighten things out in no time."

"He...', Erin stopped midsentence, her mouth open and her eyes big as saucers; 'He may have just solved the case!"

Erin senior didn't' know what to think; "How?"

"I was about ten. Aunt Ann had died two years earlier and mom would now and then drop off homemade bread and cinnamon rolls that Uncle Matt particularly liked. Late on Sunday afternoon mom and I drove over with the goodies and Uncle Matt had arrived just ahead of us and was unloading that old minivan he never would get rid of.

He was tired and a little subdued. I gave him a hand with the suitcase and asked where he'd been.'

"Apparently last week he had been reading a journal he used to keep and noticed he'd planned on visiting a certain spot in the Smokies.'

"I asked what made the spot so special and important and he told me it must be a magical spot since my grandpa had spent a weekend there and had come home forever changed; Uncle Matt felt it had been a good change.'

"I asked if he had felt or seen any magic. Apparently he had, and would not have missed the pilgrimage, despite the long drive; but the magic was not what he had expected. Apparently there were very old, very large trees and he was expecting something solemn and cathedral like.'

"It had started that way, then the sky, horizon to horizon, had gone ink black and there was jagged lightening. Amongst the huge trees it was so dark he almost wished he'd brought a flashlight.'

"This was quite ominous and frightening, but it was brief; a light rain, or rather mist, came, and the sunshine returned as quickly as it had left. Now the magic; it was as though the grove were in an unusually intense and beautiful rainbow. Uncle Matt found it intensely peaceful and magical; it seemed, in a quiet way, as though anything were possible.'

"Grandpa, who knew all the old norse stories and legends, would have said the grove was were bifrost touched middle-earth."

Grandma Erin, more from politeness than genuine curiosity, said; "What is bifrost?"

"It is the rainbow bridge joining Asgard, where the gods live, with middle-Earth, which is where man lives."

"How lovely; do you remember the name of the grove?"

"No, grandma; that was ten years ago and I had no particular reason to remember it. But…., I happen to have a personal computer.'

Erin went out to her car and returned with her computer. Five minutes later she looked up and said; "Grandma, does the Joyce Kilmer forest ring any bells?"

Grandma Erin thought a moment, then shook her head; "Sorry; it was too long ago."

Erin was very thoughtful. "I remembered as soon as I saw it; that is the grove Uncle Matt visited.'

"Something very unusual happened that long ago weekend, it happened at the Joyce Kilmer forest."

Granny was puzzled; "What sort of thing; maybe a vision?"

"No, grandma. Visions don't leave you speaking old norse, they seldom leave you with longer hair and old anachronistic clothes; they never, never leave you skilled with a quarter staff. This weekend was something else altogether. We now know as much as we ever will, which isn't much. But there is an equally puzzling aspect to the whole business."

"What would that be, Erin?"

The younger Erin thought a moment; "Grandma, we both know grandpa well. When he visited me in Reykjavic he didn't need to speak Old Norse with my professor. He spoke Old Norse intentionally, to put me exactly where I now am. The evidence and the mystery have been put right under my nose, where, with any sort of curiosity and gumption I had to notice, to wonder. Why? If I ever saw a dead end this is it. Why? Why?!"

CHAPTER 60
Nine Years Later

'WHAT WAS THAT NOISE?! Oh, the alarm.' Erin quickly reached over and turned it off. Ordinarily she allowed herself one 'snooze' interval as refereed by her alarm clock, but Gary had been up with some emergency case and had come in very late so she virtuously spared him the second wake up notice.

She launched the morning routine and by the time she got to brushing her teeth she was waking up. Anything on the schedule today? No, not really; but she needed to finish scouting the various job opportunities. Her MSR fellowship had nine months to run and it was high time to arrange her next step. 'What's next?' is always interesting, and is seldom without complications of some sort.

As Dr. Erin Campbell-Drake drove to the medical center sipping her coffee she considered the complication named Gary Seldon. What gave the matter urgency was the business of reviewing job opportunities; was she suiting herself alone, or was she accommodating Gary's plans and opportunities?

Which inevitably led to the more general question of accommodating partners. Her former boyfriend, Nick, had been a planet circling her star – Nick had been a little too accommodating, and she hadn't liked it. Over the last several months it seemed to Erin as though she was the circling planet, and it was getting old. Evidently the dance between men and women, never really easy, had become quite tricky; it was hard to get the balance exactly right. She knew she hadn't, but a perfect balance was for story books; 'good enough' was the stuff of life. Which left her exactly where with Gary? She suspected they'd be going each their own way, but for now she'd finish her lukewarm coffee and listen to a radio station she liked.

Erin enjoyed radiology, and musculoskeletal imaging in particular, so after arriving at the radiology department and her computer work station she was soon engrossed in the particulars of the day's work. Time flew by and Erin was surprised it was 11:30, thirty minutes till noon conference; this worked out nicely since she was starting her last case for the morning, the suffering right shoulder of a Miss Jeannie Smith.

Miss Smith was thirty-eight and there was no history of injury; Dr. Campbell-Drake felt she could dictate the report correctly without examining the images, but this procedure is frowned on and soon she was looking at the proton density coronal oblique images. The supraspinatus tendon was thickened and had increased signal and there was mild impingement where the coracoacromial ligament attached to the acromion.

She could dictate 'tendenopathy with mild impingement' now, and all would be copesthetic.

Erin stopped, and chuckled at herself. For the first time in months she thought of grandpa, and something he told her that stuck in her mind; 'words have a tendency to lull us into a yet sounder slumber.'

'Tendonopathy with mild impingement' satisfied her – and everyone else, too. But if she were alert and wakeful rather than 'lulled', what was the case?! The impingement was minimal and the tendon surprisingly thick and almost lobulated in appearance. In practice 'tendonopathy' meant 'abnormal and not torn'; that covers a huge variety of appearances: 'Tendonopathy' was a veneer on ignorance. What underlies the variation in appearance? Should Jeannie hike her shoulder off to acupuncture, physical therapy, or a subacromial steroid injection? Did the appearance of the tendon hold clues to these decisions?

These reflections were an obscure side-trail into a paper Erin intermittently thought of doing; or recommending to others, possibly Dr. Shields.

Then the phone rang. 'Dr. Campbell, this is Louise at the front desk. There's a lawyer here to see you, a Mister Donley. Want me to send him back?"

Lawyers give even the finest and most conscientious physicians a bad conscience; Dr. Campbell had a sinking feeling. There hadn't been any certified letters of late; still.

"Louise, what's his business?"

There was a brief conversation in the background which Erin sensed rather than heard; then Louise was back.

"He says he's from your grandfather's estate and this will only take a minute."

Whew, thank God! But grandpa was eleven or twelve years gone and all the grandkids were served with sensible trust funds; what on Earth could it be?

"Bring him back, Louise."

Jim Donley was a trim handsome man in his early forties. He had driven all the way from Evansville, which was at least three hours from Vanderbilt.

"Doctor Campbell, I'm Jim Donley with Dulin and Pearce. Your grandfather wanted us to give you something on your thirtieth birthday, which was yesterday."

Mr. Donley nodded to a bag he was holding; "I'm to give you three items, one by one, and see for myself that you thoughtfully examine and consider them."

Donley reached out a large loose leaf notebook filled with at least four hundred typed pages. He handed it to Erin.

Erin took the book, opened it, and scanned the first pages. It mentioned a Doctor Petersen and the Joyce Kilmer forest, amongst other things.

Erin turned to the middle of the book and saw names she knew well, names like Kjartan, Yngvar, and Asgerd. There was no Ref Steinsson; in his place she found the personal pronoun 'I'.

She paged to the end, which struck her as a shopping list: antibiotics, suture material, ibuprofen, narcotics, dynamite, matches, revolver, ammunition, and on it went. There was also a single page with a genealogy tree. Erin closed the book and put it to one side.

Donley handed her a very odd looking battered old axe that had a short, heavy, sharp blade extending beyond the end of the axe head. The handle was protected with a strong round hemispherical guard with a diameter of seven or eight inches. The axe was oiled and free of rust, but it had many nicks and divets; this axe was not just out of the box. Erin put the axe beside the notebook and looked up expectantly.

Jim Donley reached out a small leather bag and handed it to her. Erin opened the bag and removed a large furrowed brown seed.

Epilogue

IT WAS A BEAUTIFUL late fall afternoon as the long ship rowed into the cozy harbor below her home. There was a touch of back oar and the ship grounded gently. Several men jumped into the quiet surf and carried a strong line to shore; soon the ship was secured and men were busy unloading their gear.

Eventually Asgerd saw her grandsons, Njal and Svein, and hurried down to the shore to greet them. It had been a very long and dangerous voyage and Asgerd was relieved and happy they were back safe and sound.

Njal, Thora's eldest son, was short; at five foot six inches he wasn't much taller than his grandmother. But this was balanced by a very wide and powerful physique. Njal's boyish grin and merry dark blue eyes had conquered grandma's heart long, long ago. Now as a young man of twenty-four his quick mind, confident manner, and great ability marked him as a man to watch. He had led this long overdue exploratory probe far to the south.

Svein, Gyda's second son, was very different; he was lean, mildly stooped, and just under six feet. Svein was quieter and less aggressive than Njal, but he too was bright and capable. The two cousins had been fast friends from early boyhood, and Njal could no more go a Viking without

Svein than a man could take one of his arms and leave the other home.

Svein, his grandmother noted, was looking unusually good; he had a deep tan, and rowing thousands of miles had put some muscle on his bones. His chest in particular had filled out. Asgerd, somewhat to her surprise, thought the women might be noticing him now; good, it was about time!

THE OCCASION WAS LARGE, and both godi Kjartan and Uncle Gunnar were present. A voyage far south had been dear to the heart of Miles Drake, who had always intended to sail south. Unfortunately the years when he might have gone were filled with skraeling problems.

Now, much later, his grandson Njal had made the voyage, and succeeded brilliantly; their ship had much gold, and a large cargo of a new food, maize. They had traded furs for the maize, and the natives had shown them many tasty ways to prepare the maize.

They came by the gold in the usual Viking way i.e. without the owner's permission. But in truth, the circumstances were extenuating. The men of Newland had never seen streets and towns, so cities with large buildings, wide streets, and causeways were literally mind boggling. The civilization far to the south had many towns and several vast cities. They made a tourists stroll of one of the smaller cities and upon getting back to their ship realized they were missing Gilli.

Gilli was a sensible, reliable sort and his disappearance gave Njal a bad feeling. They scoured the city in heavily armed groups of four men.

Njal's group found the errant Gilli atop a vast mountainlike stone structure with a group of strangely dressed men just about to cut his heart out and eat him — all this to propitiate some god or other. This sort of thing removes the bonds of civilized restraint, and after killing the priests, the lads pillaged the temple and any rich looking building on the way back to the ship. The return to the ship was not a cakewalk; there was bitter fighting and four men were lost. However there was much gold.

In addition to gold and maize they picked up several slaves. On the return voyage Svein had made real progress in learning the southern language. The next voyage would be better. The general feeling was, and Kjartan and Gunnar agreed, that they should restrict themselves to trading with the more northern people of the far south, but below this free trading zone it was business as usual i.e. slaves and treasure.

There was only one problem, but it was big; the area of interest was way, way south. With favorable winds and currents it was over three months travelling time, and could easily go to four months. Clearly they needed a southern base, preferably with their maize trading partners.

Late in the evening Njal looked over to Asgerd; "Grandma, remember that dream you had of Grandpa's home? The wide, wide streets with buildings where you could see through the walls as though they weren't there; remember?"

Asgerd smiled; "Of course I remember."

"How wide were the streets?"

Asgerd thought a moment; "The streets weren't quite as wide as this hall is long. But, Njal, you are forgetting; these streets were inside a huge, huge building. The air was pleasant no matter what the weather outside might be. The streets had comfortable benches if you were tired or just wanted to sit; there were even small trees and beautiful plants. It was more like Asgard than a town. But the strange thing is that the smaller buildings with the invisible walls were like shopping stalls in a market place; you entered them to look at things and perhaps buy them. One of these market stalls had games, and it was here the Alfather visited your grandfather."

Kjartan hadn't heard the story for years, and sought clarification.

"Didn't the Alfather give dad a wish?"

"Yes, and your father wished for courage; luck, a gift for stories, and a gift for languages were thrown in free."

Now Gunnar was remembering, and curious; "As I recall, didn't Odin remove all memory of the visit? Dad never, not at the time or later, remembered the conversation or his wish?"

"That's right Gunnar; your father would have found the whole thing ridiculous, for children, so he never was in a position to judge or diminish the event; the visit and wish just were."

Godi Kjartan snorted at this; "Mom, dress it anyway you like, but Odin is a very dark and confusing bastard."

His mother thought this over; "This is true, son; but there is a greater truth."

Gunnar spoke for both of them; "What is the greater truth?"

Asgerd drew herself up, stood tall, and in a dignified, ringing tone; "The greater truth, sons, is that the Alfather is the wind under the wings of the eagle that was your father."

Both Kjartan and Gunnar loved it when Asgerd got high and exalted. In times past they would grab her and pitch her back and forth between them. Gunnar could still easily manage this feat, but fifty-two year old Kjartan, Kjartan of the iffy back, let the moment pass.

"Mom, do you know how things ended for dad? He walked away and we never saw him again; that is a hard thought in the wee still hours."

'Mom', coming off the mountain, said in a softer voice; "No, but in my bones I know he ended well."